"Deborah Running Bear's jc
that we must face - not run from - our deepest fears. By
doing so, we find the freedom we long for."

—Jean Snedegar
Reporter, producer,
BBC Radio and West Virginia Public Broadcasting

"This tale highlights one Native American's quest to discover where she came from and how to fit into today's society. She learns the power and necessity of forgiveness - of one's enemies and of oneself."

—JR LaPlante (*Tasunke Waste* - His Horse is Beautiful)
Cheyenne River Sioux Tribe, first secretary of
South Dakota Department of Tribal Relations, member
of first cohort of Native Nation Rebuilders, and first
director of tribal relations for five states, Avera Health

"Deborah Running Bear's search for wholeness is a remarkable story filled with layers of meaning. Just as the wounding of one affects us all, so does the healing of one. That's a story we need to hear."

—Patrick Dorn
Denver arts critic, playwright, and author

"An epic drama set within themes that make Dakota *Dakota*. A delicious read."

—Thomas A. Dempster
Former South Dakota State Senator
Author of *North of Twelfth Street: The
Changing Face of Sioux Falls Neighborhoods*

THE WOODEN INDIAN RESURRECTION

Trish Hermanson

Crouton Press / Lakewood, Colorado

ISBN paperback: 978-0-9989526-0-4
ISBN ebook: 978-0-9989526-1-1

Cover design by Anne Thompson of Ebookannie, ebookannie.com
Cover artwork from Shutterstock: 11707162, 468033503, 2510883
Fleuron design by Lauren Thompson of Nymphont, nymphont.com

Crouton Press, Lakewood, Colorado

To my husband, Duane,
who encouraged me to climb the mountain

CHAPTER 1

Dust to Dust

May 2000

Lifeless—that's what she must be to let a fly land on her nose and not flick it away. But what else was she supposed to do? As the mall's official wooden Indian, Deborah Running Bear shouldn't let even the fringe on her buckskin dress ruffle until the right moment.

Hoping no one would notice, she jutted her lower lip and aimed a puff of air at the critter.

It flitted up to a strand of white-streaked hair dangling between her eyes, then buzzed off.

Deborah maintained her rigid stance. Crowds were thin today, probably preferring the balmy spring weather outside. But she had to snag one more sale to make quota or she'd hear from her boss. Perhaps she could entice that family down the hall wandering toward her. From her periphery, she'd glimpsed the father, mother, and young boy scarf down sloppy buffalo burgers, the gamey scent wafting toward her. They'd lingered by the animatronic cowboy band playing its tinny version of "I Never Promised You a Rose Garden." Then they'd snapped photos of their blond preschooler riding the stuffed bucking bronco.

Finally their chatter moved closer to her kiosk. The boy pointed. "Hey, a wooden Indian."

His slender mother studied Deborah. "Looks so real you can hardly tell it's a mannequin. Let's get a picture."

The boy scampered toward Deborah.

She braced her knees.

He tumbled into her, but she held her pose.

The father stepped behind Deborah. The mother snuggled close in and reached out arm's length with her camera to snap a shot. "Smile nicer than this Injun." Deborah swallowed the insult. Anything for a sale. The shutter clicked.

Time to animate. Deborah lifted her arms and flicked her head, her braid twirling. The family screamed and jumped back. "Whaat? She's real." They broke into laughter.

Deborah made her voice deep, mysterious. "As subtle as a breeze, as powerful as bison—that's the Lakota. Know where we came from? Underground. We rose from limestone tunnels at Wind Cave to become the land's caretakers." She spread her fingers and gestured toward the jewelry case next to her. "The Lakota discovered gold in *Paha Sapa*, the Black Hills."

The boy gawked. "Real gold?"

A smile stretched Deborah's face, the joy of casting a spell. "Real gold. Crafted into rings, necklaces, watches, and earrings, with designs created here in South Dakota."

The mother focused on a necklace of rose and green leaves draped on a shimmering splash of gold. She gazed up at her husband and batted her thick eyelashes. "Would make a nice memento."

The man raised his chin and made a macho reach toward his pocket. "Sure. It'll remind us of this redskin."

Deborah flinched. "And matching earrings?"

His chin lifted higher. "Why not?"

Deborah reached for tiny boxes with cotton padding and winked at the boy. "You'll find cool buffalo souvenirs by the mall's entrance."

"He's got enough junk already," the mother said.

The boy's eyes dropped.

Deborah's heart sank. He ought to carry a memory home. She reached into her pocket, then grasped the boy's white hands in her brown ones and folded a treasure into them. "*Wopila tanka* for the privilege of meeting you."

He gaped at their clasped hands. "*Wo-pi-la?*"

"*Tanka.* It means thank you. May you soar on eagle's wings."

He unfolded his hands—a wooden medallion with a carving of an eagle. "Cool," he whispered.

"My father made that," Deborah said, "and it's my gift to you."

They moved on, but the boy turned back, his gaze lingering, his hand clutching the medallion.

Deborah waved. Introducing a slice of her Native American culture was the best part of this job. And what a potential audience with two million tourists rambling through Wall Drug each year on their way to Mount Rushmore.

The absurdity of all this didn't escape her as she stiffened into a statue again. She called others to soar as eagles, while she rotted away like a dead stump. And noble as she appeared in her Indian costume, was this simply an excuse to hide from her past?

More tourists drew near. White teenagers. Cocky. The type who might pull her braid. She'd try to blend into the background. Maybe they'd miss her.

She stared straight ahead. Didn't blink.

One of the guys pointed. "Not a bad bod on that old squaw."

Her jaw tensed, but she didn't move.

They sauntered past, their hands buried in frayed jeans pockets.

Deborah released her breath. Those teens were carefree like her friends in high school had been. That was the only time she'd attached herself to whites. They'd talked her into what sounded like an innocent prank, then split, leaving her lying flat on the ground, illuminated in the lights of a screaming police car. Her knee throbbed with the recollection. She took a step, loosening it.

Her stocky boss lumbered by in her cowgirl skirt. One of her boots stubbed Deborah's moccasin. The woman turned back and shook a pink feather duster. "See me up front." Her Dolly Parton hairdo quivered with each wave of the duster.

Deborah steadied herself. Something in Big Hair's staccato voice didn't sound right. Now what? Working the limp out of her gait, she approached the entrance.

Big Hair swished the pink duster across the top of a row of merchandise. "These buffalo bobbleheads are selling faster than our nickel coffee. Great idea to put the millennium year on the flank."

A compliment? Unheard of. Deborah picked up a figurine. Its shaggy head waggled, and she bobbled her head in response. "Glad I came up with that."

Big Hair glared. "All the big boss knows is that they're in my area. But even with the bobbles, profits are down."

"I've met *my* sales goals."

"Doesn't matter. You gotta move more merchandise if you wanna keep your job."

Deborah's mouth turned dry. "But my father. I help pay for his care."

"Come up with a new scheme by the morning. And before you leave today, clean off that jackalope." Big Hair aimed her feather duster high up the wall.

Deborah peered at the mounted jackrabbit with antelope antlers attached to it. Her bad knee already ached.

"While you're at it, dust the other animals, too."

She craned her neck toward the mounted heads of a deer, a bear, and a bison. A separate trip up a twelve-foot ladder for each. "But ladders—"

"You gonna do it?"

She bit down on her lip. "I'll dust them before we open tomorrow."

Big Hair jabbed the pink duster toward her. "And don't forget, you need a new plan."

Deborah turned away, her moccasins scuffing toward the parking lot. Her job on the line? That blindsided her.

After all, it was her ideas that fueled sales. But Big Hair never gave her credit.

In Deborah's history of jobs in the town of Wall, this was the best she'd found to showcase her storytelling skill. She *must* make this work. *Must* resist her reflex to cut and run when things got tough. And no way would she mention this to Dad or he'd worry. And lecture her even more than he usually did.

In the parking lot, she forced open the door of her beige VW Squareback wagon and let the hot air trapped inside escape. She dropped onto the cracked vinyl seat and turned over the ignition. The vehicle quivered, then died. She cranked it again. "Come on, Methuselah."

The car coughed, then found its breath.

"Atta boy."

She veered off Main Street onto a dirt road and bounced along. Less than a mile away, she let out a quiet "whoa" and steered Methuselah to a halt. She patted its haunch before she entered Trail's End Rest Home.

Nancy, the facility director, spotted her in the hallway and approached at a fast clip, waving an envelope. "Your father's check bounced."

"Again?"

"You gonna cover it?"

Deborah swallowed hard. "Somehow."

"Good. We can't do this dance every month." She shoved the envelope into Deborah's hand and sped off.

Deborah leaned against the cold, concrete hallway wall. Maybe she could work extra hours.

From the community room next to her, Will Running Bear's tenor voice spilled into the hallway. "Socrates said the unexamined life isn't worth living."

She often found Dad in that room, addressing fellow gray hairs while propped up by his cane on which he'd carved the face of a Native American.

"The philosopher's advice can save us from a meaning-less existence," he trumpeted.

When would he get off that high horse? Dad inhaled history like oxygen, then breathed it onto others, prodding them to emulate the lives of the great ones, as he called them. Inspiring? Yes. Practical? No.

"We'll meet again tomorrow to discuss that . . . "

Deborah squinted and mouthed the rest of his sentence: *It's never too late to become who you're meant to be.*

She peered into the open doorway. Seniors applauded and gave Dad shoulder pats as they ambulated away with walkers and wheelchairs.

Dad crumpled his notes and lobbed them into a trashcan across the room. "Score!" His lean frame pivoted with his walking stick, and he caught sight of Deborah. His face, a brown canyon of wrinkles, lit up. "If it isn't my favorite child."

She stepped forward into the glare of the fluorescent lights. "And your only child."

"Still my favorite." He eased into a plastic chair. "What's in the envelope?"

She buried it in her pocket. "Nothing."

"Got more carved eagles for you in my room."

"Thanks. Gave one to a boy today. He loved it. But I still have enough."

"Then let's get to our game." He motioned toward his hand-carved set of rosewood and maple chess pieces.

She'd been knee-high to a grasshopper when he'd whittled this set, the wood chips flying onto the floor and covering her bare feet. She flopped into a chair across from him and shook her head. "Need to get home and do some thinking."

"Thinking's always good." He cupped his hands on the gnarled top of his stick. "Anyway, the moccasin telegraph says you've been asked to speak at the hike up Crazy Horse Mountain."

She chuckled. "Gossip does travel. I couldn't make that climb. And talking to a crowd that size, I'd freeze like a Popsicle."

"What flavor? Tiramisu?"

"More like tapioca."

Dad scowled. "Get enough of that pap around here." He shifted in his chair. "You ought to consider this opportunity. Shouldn't let the past—"

"Why do you always dredge up the past?"

"I never do, unless I see you playing dodge ball with it."

"This has nothing to do with what happened."

His stare pierced like a bird of prey. "You know it does. You left high school, but high school never left you."

"Forget about it."

"Neither of us can. They wouldn't have come down hard on you if they weren't *my* enemies. And now, you make yourself your worst enemy by running from anything that scares you." He ran a hand across his jaw. "Anyway, you still get to speak at church sometimes, don't you?"

"No big deal. A few folks on folding chairs. We can't even find a pastor. Probably have to shut down."

"Bummer. You need a challenge big enough for who you are."

"Life is challenging enough." She worked herself upright. "I'm going home. I'm beat."

"You act like it."

She winced, but chose not to respond.

Dad raised himself from his chair. "Next time you visit, let's celebrate your birthday. The big five-oh." He extended both arms wide for an embrace.

Deborah returned a sideways hug. She limped out of the bright room and into the dim hallway. "Now to face *Ivar*." She tossed the name over her shoulder.

"You tell me to forget the past, then you name a rooster after the principal? Deborah, your shadow's gonna catch up with you one day."

"I'll dodge it. At all costs."

Will plopped back onto the plastic chair, releasing an *umph* as he landed. Why'd she leave so soon? And why wouldn't she consider that speaking opportunity?

His hand, etched with narrow blue veins, rubbed the carving of the Indian at the top of his cane. Deborah could have been anything. Done anything. But after her arrest, her confidence had evaporated like morning mist.

If only he'd done more to protect her.

CHAPTER 2

Crazy Horse

The sign ahead warned *Entering Badlands*. Right before it, Deborah steered Methuselah onto a dirt road and bumped past a weathered post with painted letters announcing *Tumbleweed Trailer Park*.

Ivar, her neighbor's rooster, paraded in front of her single-wide, daring her to cross the line he'd scratched in the dirt.

She stepped out and sidled beside her vehicle. "I knew you'd be waiting."

The bird screeched and attacked, his spurs tearing at her moccasins.

She kicked him away. "There's a reason they call you *fowl*."

She hurried to her rusty mailbox, straightened the lopsided wood post, and wrestled out a package. Book of the Month—the Kublai Khan biography. She pumped the package in the air like a victory salute. She couldn't wait to lose herself in its pages.

Before Ivar recovered and attacked again, she climbed the chipped concrete blocks leading into her trailer and let the aluminum door bang shut behind her.

Home. She could relax.

Her calico kitty jumped down from the bookshelf and rubbed itself against her ankles.

She scooped him into her hand and pressed his fur against her cheek. "Thanks for the lovin', buddy." Bobby was her newest cat, the replacement for Martin, who was the replacement for Jack.

His body vibrated with purrs that melted away the day's tension.

"Let's check the history forum." She settled into a creaky metal folding chair and scooted toward the card table, dropping Bobby onto it.

Her kitty attacked a frayed edge of the red vinyl top.

She powered up the PC her son Bill had passed on to her when he upgraded recently. She ought to be proud of Bill. But he'd shot an arrow into her heart when he left home after high school, embarrassed by her native ways.

She squinted at the computer monitor. "Where's that discussion group?"

Bobby jumped onto the keyboard and padded across it.

"No teasing now." She lifted him onto her lap with one hand and moused around with the other. "Here it is."

Halfway down the page, a posting blinked, alerting her to a private message.

She hovered the cursor over the line. Would she dare communicate directly with a stranger instead of playing it safe with public chats? No way. Who knew where that could go?

Bobby pawed at the mouse.

She snuggled the kitten. "Careful. Curiosity killed the cat."

But what did that post say?

Her finger trembled above the mouse.

Bobby meowed.

"Is it safe?"

He nuzzled her hand, pushing it back onto the mouse.

She laughed. "If you say so."

Click.

A message flashed onto her monitor:

> *Can't believe we finally found you.*
> *Elaine's in trouble—you've got to help!*
> *Meet at the fort on Wednesday.*
> *All for one.*
> *Haddy*

Her betrayers!

Dynamite exploded inside her. Deborah leaped to her feet, spilling Bobby onto the floor. "No!"

She paced the narrow living room.

Bobby scampered to a corner for safety.

"How did they find me?"

She'd been so careful when she set up her chat account. She'd chosen the pseudonym *Xanadu,* home of Kublai Khan. All she wanted was to talk with history buffs about the emperor who transformed his world. Her last post was a play on words: "We Khan chat."

That gave her away?

She dragged the folding chair to the bookcase, climbed onto the chair seat, and reached for her high school yearbook. Her hand traced across something. She pulled it out—a troll doll from Elaine, covered with years of dust. It tumbled to the floor.

Bobby pounced on it and pawed at the doll's long black hair.

Deborah stepped down from the chair and rested on it. Where was that photo?

She flipped through the annual. There—Elaine in her cheerleading outfit shaking pompoms along the edge of the basketball court. Deborah dressed the same, yelling into a megaphone the chant she wrote around the theme of Kublai Khan. Haddy screaming the cheer that spread like wildfire until the Arena rocked with the cry *We Khan take the world!*

We Khan. That was it. One step out of anonymity in a discussion group, and Haddy caught it.

Fear flooded over her. Years of shutting herself away like the contents in a hermetically sealed box, and still they found her.

"Blast it!"

She flipped to the senior photos, and the book fell open to the page with their portraits next to each other. Smiling faces, big Sixties hairdos shellacked into place. What an unlikely trio to become best friends: Haddy, a naive matzo ball. Elaine, a conniving Nordic bombshell. And herself, a shy Native American. But circumstances cemented them together with a binding loyalty oath.

"All for one, one for all," she whispered.

All for one until they *abandoned* her after she fell. She let out a huff. Where were they when she got tossed into jail? Thrown out of town.

And forced to leave Simon.

Pain simmered in her core, bubbled up, and boiled over into rage. She'd taken the rap. They'd suffered nothing. No way would she bury the hatchet. No way would she rescue Elaine as she did over and over in high school.

"Let them figure this out on their own."

She slapped the yearbook shut and hit the Logout button on the message board. "So there."

Fatigue wrapped over her with the weight of a buffalo hide. She scooped up Bobby and dropped into bed. She hadn't begun to hatch a plan to save her job. Too weary now. She'd work on it at breakfast.

Her foot slipped. She tumbled. The ground sped toward her. Gunshots. A blur of ragged noise. Of sweat. Of clawing through dirt. Warm blood running down her hand. A voice cackling like a rooster.

Deborah bolted upright, her forehead clammy. The same mash-up of nightmares that always haunted her.

She willed her heart to slow down.

Cock-a-doodle-doo. The rooster's crowing pierced the air again. Ivar's early morning call snapped her back from high school and from her principal's shrill crowing.

"Come on, body. Gotta climb a twelve-foot ladder today and dust a bunch of stuffed carcasses."

She ran her hand across her buckskin dress. She'd been so exhausted last night she hadn't bothered to change.

Wrinkled leather—all the better for authenticity. Still, a little tidying would be good. She rolled on deodorant, straightened her braid. Then she poured kibble and fresh water for Bobby, grabbed a bite of yesterday's Indian fry bread for herself, and let the aluminum door clang shut behind her.

At Wall Drug, Deborah found her boss in her cowgirl getup where she'd left her yesterday, arranging rows of bobbing bison heads.

"Ladder's in the back," Big Hair said without looking up.

Deborah trudged to the storage closet. Her knee had recovered overnight, but not her mind. That blasted chat message whirled inside her. What if Elaine and Haddy figured out where she lived? She didn't want a showdown.

She hefted the ladder toward the wall of mounted animals and spread the sides wide. They were three hundred miles away. They couldn't be a threat. Could they?

She grabbed the pink feather duster and took a step onto the ladder. But what if they showed up?

"Before you get lost in space, let's talk turkey."

Big Hair's shrill voice forced Deborah's thoughts back.

"I don't think your Indian storytelling thing is working. How're you going to make it more profitable?"

The job plan. She'd forgotten.

Deborah stepped off the ladder. "I don't know yet."

Big Hair braced an arm on her hip. "You don't?"

Deborah shook her head.

"If you don't have a plan, we can't keep paying you hourly. So, straight commission from now on. Ten percent of sales."

Deborah ran a quick calculation. "That's less than I make now."

Big Hair returned to straightening the bobbleheads. "Take it or leave it."

Fear foamed up inside Deborah. How would she pay bills? Help with Dad's care? Impossible. "I'll have to quit."

Big Hair's lips curved into a sly smile. "Saves me from laying you off, paying unemployment."

Deborah's fear morphed into rage. "Then buffalo chips on you!"

Her boss looked up, eyes as big as her hair. "Where did that anger come from?"

"From years of abuse here, you Saltine." Deborah raked the feather duster across the counter, sending the bobbleheads crashing to the floor.

She stomped to the parking lot, fell into her car, and slammed the door so hard the inside handle fell onto the floor. She forced the transmission into gear, bumped off the curb, and sputtered onto Main Street.

One of her fists gripped the steering wheel, the other clutched the pink feather duster. The feather duster? She'd left with it. No way would she return it now. She tossed it onto the dashboard. Its Pepto-Bismol hue reflected in the windshield like a sick reminder of the last five minutes of her job.

"That woman! Forcing me to move on." Deborah's eyes filled until the road blurred. She braked at the four-way stop and swiped at tears.

Move on to what? And where?

A herd of pronghorn flitted across the prairie beside her. A highway sign directed toward the Crazy Horse Memorial, ninety miles ahead.

The memorial. That's where she'd get her bearings. "Giddy-up, Methuselah."

She turned onto the interstate's gray ribbon cutting through tall grassland, then banged the steering wheel with her palm. "Why didn't I come up with a plan to keep my job?"

She had no answer.

The flat terrain gradually lifted into foothills, then mountains. Methuselah chugged in the climb.

"And why didn't I fight for my job?" Instead, she'd tucked tail and run.

Like always.

She passed stately conifers standing like sentries along the highway. Finally, she turned onto Avenue of the Chiefs and parked along the edge of the road.

She reattached the inside door handle and stepped into the crisp mountain air. Still as a sanctuary here. Even the breeze held its breath.

She lifted her face to the sky. From the top of the mountain, the partially-completed carving of a warrior on horseback leaped toward her—*Tasunke Witko,* Crazy Horse, the man who defeated George Armstrong Custer at the cavalry officer's last stand.

How long since she'd been here?

Too long. She'd avoided it. Whenever she visited, something gnawed at her deep into her marrow. That she'd let her people down. Let herself down, too.

One look at Crazy Horse, and she unraveled like rotten rope. The chief's head aimed forward with conviction. He'd known his way.

She'd lost hers.

He'd lived an open life.

She'd hid.

He'd faced his enemies.

She'd run.

Deborah extended her arm toward the horizon, imitating the image of her hero. She raised her head to the heavens. "*Wakantanka,* what should I do?"

She waited for the Great Spirit to answer.

A wind whipped through the pines, kicking up the fringe on her buckskin dress. Her heartbeat quickened.

But it wasn't her heart. A slow, steady drumbeat emanated from her core.

Boom . . . boom . . . boom.

Whispers filled her mind.

She'd heard this before. But not for years.

Chants, indecipherable, grew louder.

Her head spun. She struggled to keep her balance.

The drumbeat pulsed until she feared she would burst.

A memory crashed into her mind. Fleeing town. Running away. Driving through the dark of night with nothing but the sound of tires in her ears and the weight of troubles on her back.

The drumbeats ceased.

Now a deafening silence.

A thought drifted through her mind. Crazy Horse faced his traitors. She had to face hers.

What would she say?

Her lips tightened. Tell. Them. Off. A step toward living again. That would be wonderful.

When did Haddy say they should meet?

She searched her mind. Wednesday. That was *today*.

Why so soon?

Haddy would have a reason.

And the place?

Fort Robinson. They'd planned to party there after graduation, but instead, she'd fled town.

She jumped into her car and jerked the transmission into gear. "Make tracks, Methuselah!"

CHAPTER 3

Stowaway

When she reached home, Deborah called her son. She'd better tell Bill she'd be gone today in case Dad called him, wondering why she didn't visit. She didn't want to explain to either of them about seeing white friends. Dad was so adventurous, he'd want to join her. And all of Bill's life she'd warned him about the dangers of mixing with whites. A lot of good that had done. He'd changed his name from Running Bear to Rasmussen and married a Norwegian American named Britt. Now if that wasn't walking the white trail—

"Information technology. Bill here." He picked up her call.

"Hi, Bill. Wanted to tell you I'll be gone the rest of the day."

"Where to?"

She swallowed her anxiety. "To see some old friends."

"*Whaaat?* You told me you'd never go back."

"Never back to Sioux Falls. We're meeting at Fort Robinson. I won't venture any closer."

"You say I'm crazy for trying to assimilate." He spoke slowly. "Now you're trying?"

"No. I need to tell 'em off."

Bill chuckled. "You get vacation time?"

She gnawed on a knuckle. "I quit."

"Again?"

She pictured him raking his hand through his thick raven hair like he always did when exasperated. "Maybe you can flit from job to job, but I can't. I gotta get back to work."

Click.

Deborah hung up the receiver. So much for family support. But stewing about it wouldn't help. Time to hit the road. She wouldn't spend the night, so no need for extra clothes. But—her mind twirled over an idea—she'd pack some other things.

Deborah pulled a duffel from under the bed. She retrieved the troll doll that had fallen from the bookcase and grabbed her high school yearbook. She'd hurl these at Elaine and Haddy. A final act to say good riddance.

Her kitty jumped into the bag and cocked his head.

"You want to go road trippin'?" She nuzzled Bobby's soft nose. "Why not? I'd enjoy your cuddles, and you'll probably sleep the whole way."

He pawed at her face.

One more thing. Something she should have gotten rid of a long time ago. She dug deep in a clothes drawer and pulled out a boy's chunky class ring hanging on a gold chain. She ran her fingers over the raised letters: Class of 1968, Washington High School.

She slipped the chain around her neck. Her heart quickened as it had the first time she'd caught sight of the ring's owner.

"Simon," she whispered. The memory of his image seeped through her—his glorious crop of blond hair, his blue eyes matching the glimmering stone in his ring.

She shook her head to toss those feelings away. Dwelling on the past only ignited pain. Books were her closest companions now. She skimmed her hand across the row of biographies on the shelf. Books never hurt her.

She packed a bag of kibble and slung the duffel over her shoulder. Then she scooped up Bobby and hustled outside.

Ivar attacked from the scrub brush, his beak wide and his wings flapping.

Bobby hissed and swiped at the banty rooster, but Deborah held him tight. He would be no match for that demon bird. She kicked the fowl aside and dropped the duffel by her station wagon. Then she knocked on the door of the trailer next to hers, where a hand-painted sign with uneven letters read "Auto Mekanic On Call."

Hank, a Lakotan with a braid that trailed down his back, greeted her at the door. "What are you doin' here around high noon?"

"Going away for the day. You think Methuselah can make a four-hour trip?"

His face, as weathered as barn wood, cracked a smile. "It don't purr like that kitty of yours. But it should make it."

"Good, and *wopila tanka.*"

"You're welcome. *Anpetu was'te yuha.*"

She grinned. "You have a good day, too." She crawled into her wagon and set Bobby on the passenger seat, spreading out tuna morsels for him. "Settle in." She turned the key.

Methuselah hacked.

"Come on, fella."

The car quivered, then came to life.

Waving to Hank, she backed out, nicking her mailbox post back into its lopsided stance. She chugged down the dirt road and bumped onto the highway. "What am I doing, heading out to confront enemies? I must be as crazy as Crazy Horse."

She grinned. Yes, today she was as bold as the Indian chief, and that smacked of being right.

Deborah pulled into the Stop-N-Go and filled the tank. As she circled around the back of the wagon to go inside and pay, she glimpsed the old scar running across the wagon's cargo door. Some wounds never healed. But maybe her wounds would start healing from this trip.

Dad's nursing home was a block away. Should she go by? No. Too much to explain.

She paid inside and returned to Methuselah. "Take off, boy." The car rumbled into motion.

Bobby crawled onto her lap and snuggled in for a nap.

Ahead of her, *wambli,* a golden eagle, circled in the sky. A good sign. Of all winged creatures, the eagle flew highest and closest to the Great Spirit.

She followed Highway 240 into the Badlands, where red-striped rock spires punctured the azure sky. In the dry heat, her buckskin dress clung. Why hadn't she taken the time to change? She cranked down the window—Methuselah's air conditioning—and fanned her face. May as well let Elaine and Haddy see who she really was, a proud Native American.

Big Foot Trail led her to Bureau of Indian Affairs Highway 2. This was like time travel, covering routes from childhood.

Methuselah sounded winded. "Come on, baby."

She wasn't doing well either. Jittery as a prairie dog. Maybe tribal storytelling would calm her. She banged on the dashboard—the only way to turn on the radio—and tuned the dial to KILI, the voice of the Lakota Nation.

Bummer. No storytelling. And the last song in the world she wanted to hear: "I Am a Rock," *Simon & Garfunkel's* anthem about avoiding friendship. About being an island.

She'd tried being an island for years. A safe way to invest a life, but the only dividend was loneliness.

They crooned the worst line of all, that they never would have cried if they'd never loved.

She grasped the class ring hanging from the chain around her neck.

Simon. His irresistible smile flashed across her mind, and her eyes overflowed. She glanced in the rearview mirror and swiped at hot tears.

Her father grinned back at her in the mirror.

Dad?

She hit the brakes.

Bobby tumbled to the floor with a cry.

She scooped up her kitty, then spun toward the backseat.

Dad smiled. "Don't use that mirror much, huh?"

"What are you doing here?"

"Bill called, his boxers all in a bunch. Said you were going out of town, a trip to the fort. I thought maybe you're taking a *Wokahnigapi Oiglake?*"

She shook her head. "Not a journey of understanding. I'm on the warpath. To tell off Elaine and Haddy like I should have years ago. Then I'll ride into the sunset."

Dad's face darkened. "Should be interesting."

"So why are you here?"

"Nothing on my schedule today but canned pear topped with cottage cheese. So I broke out, hid behind the telephone pole by the gas station, and jumped in when you went inside to pay. Glad you finally spotted me. I'd pee my pants if we didn't stop soon."

She shook her head. "I've gone too far to take you back. What am I going to do with you at the fort?"

"Somebody's gotta take care of your kitten."

"As long as you don't say another word."

"I'll be as silent as a stone if you give this old man a bathroom break."

She couldn't help but laugh. "Get up here!"

He pushed open the back door. "I always say a life without risk—"

"Is no life at all," she finished, her eyes rolling.

He took the passenger seat and was true to his word to remain silent, until he asked about the neon pink feather duster on the dashboard.

"Big Hair and I parted ways."

"Then I'll make sure I rub some dirt into this memento," he said, grabbing the duster and flitting it around.

Bobby pawed at it.

"And when do I get to drive my old wagon?" he asked.

"After our rest stop. If you're careful."

Deborah passed a water tower marked with hand-painted letters spelling *PINE RIDGE* and pulled into a one-pump station. She phoned Trail's End Rest Home, explaining she'd return the escapee before day's end. Then she let Dad take the wheel. "But remember your age."

He pulled his shoulders back. "I'm a man in my prime."

"And what prime number is that?"

"The biggest one you can think of."

She smiled. Even though his body had withered, his humor had blossomed.

Dad turned the key. "Giddy-up, hoss."

He lumbered Methuselah out of the station, cutting such a tight turn he headed toward the ditch.

"Watch it!" Deborah yelled. She clutched Bobby to her chest.

Dad bounced the wagon back up. "Old beast is still a stallion. Like me."

The car coughed in response, and Deborah hid her grin.

Dad slowed as they passed through the town of Pine Ridge. They drove by rusty skeletons of cars edging the road and squatty houses thin on paint. Children scampered barefoot across scrub brush, and lean dogs moved in packs. A mound of trash overflowed a dumpster. The broken post of a fence teetered, dropping its barbed wire onto the ground.

Deborah's stomach knotted.

"What's wrong?" Dad asked.

She stroked her calico kitten so hard he arched his back. "This is where it all began. The reservation."

CHAPTER 4

Exodus

August 1967

Deborah scrunched in the passenger seat of her dad's new VW Squareback wagon and stroked her ivory cat so hard he arched his back. Why hadn't Dad bought a cool VW bus? Instead, he came home with this beige thing.

"It's a good deal," he'd said. "Should last so long, we'll eventually call it Methuselah."

Not funny. This square car was carrying her away from the only world she knew. Away from powwows with rhythmic drums and chanting, where elders captivated her with stories about the buffalo days.

"Moving into a city is a good thing," Dad had said. "We'll have things we've only dreamed of—electricity, a real stove, and indoor plumbing."

But attend a big high school? Her stomach constricted.

Behind her, Dad wedged their red vinyl card table and metal folding chairs into the back of the wagon. Brushing off his hands, he slid into the driver's seat and cast his gaze toward her. "We're ready."

All the pent-up pain inside uncoiled in a venomous attack. "I hate you!"

Franklin, her fluffy cat, startled.

Deborah held him tight.

"I understand," Dad whispered. He eased the car into first and headed away from their cinderblock home.

Deborah banged a fist on the dashboard. "Why leave when I have only a year left of school?"

Dad stared ahead at the bumpy dirt road. "Like I've explained, this job is a plum—teaching history and coaching the varsity basketball team at the state's biggest high school. A real career advancement. But more importantly, for you, this might be a stepping stone for a scholarship to—"

"I don't care about college!"

"I care. College changed my life. I couldn't have done it without the G.I. Bill. But I don't have the money for you. Besides, there's more at stake."

"Like what?"

"Our people." He paused. "I don't expect you'd understand yet."

Deborah rubbed Franklin's side until he growled. "I don't. All I know is we're leaving home, where my heart takes flight."

Sorrow darkened Dad's face like a cloud covering the moon. "You're good with words. Like your mother was. Princess, you can always come back here. But get an education first so you have options. What would you do on the reservation after high school anyway?"

"I don't know," she sputtered. But the limited options marched across her mind. Marriage? Babies? That was for grownups. Couldn't she stay being a kid?

Dad turned onto the highway.

In the sideview mirror, her life ebbed away.

Ahead on the eastern horizon, the rising sun dappled the sky with pinks and oranges, colors too bright for the pain in her chest. She turned the radio knob. Top-of-the-hour, and President Johnson rambled on about race riots.

Not a neutral subject once you stepped off the rez. Whites never treated her like she was human. Always staring. Or worse—leering.

From the corner of her eye, she caught Dad glancing her way. "Are you scared?"

She fiddled with a cuticle. "Yeah."

"Of what?"

"Of being different."

"Being Indian?"

"Uh huh."

He cleared his throat. "I'm scared, too."

"You are?"

"It's only three hundred miles, but we're leaving our people's land." He spoke so quietly she cocked her head to hear him over the rumble of the wagon's engine. "Only shadows of our heritage where we're going."

"Shadows?"

"Like the name of the town, Sioux Falls. Our people used to camp near The Falls there. Whites called us the Sioux, instead of the Lakota. And at Washington High, the school mascot is the Warriors."

"Are there any Indians?"

A smile flitted across his face. "There will be soon. You and me."

She threw her head back. "So you're *forcing* me to walk the white trail?"

"No, but this will help you learn to make it in the white world."

"Who cares?"

Dad didn't answer, and there was no use arguing. She settled into the monotony of watching white highway stripes streaking by.

She and Dad traded off driving every few hours while they sipped strawberry Kool-Aid from a thermos and munched on bologna wrapped into fry bread. Deborah fed her cat meat scraps, then Franklin settled into serious napping.

After they crossed the Missouri River, the wide-open ranch land turned into symmetrical rows of corn. On the radio, country western songs faded out, overtaken by rock 'n roll. *Simon & Garfunkel* sang about the pain of friendship, the safety of books.

She agreed with them. Friends were fickle. Books were safe. The library on the reservation was the size of a box of Cracker Jack, and she had devoured every book in it several times. She turned to Dad. "This high school have a library?"

His face lit up. "You bet it does. Double doors. Two stories high. A card catalogue deep enough to wear out your fingers."

She rested her head against the seat back. "That's how I'll survive. You told me once there's no friend as loyal as a book."

"Hemingway said that. But he needed companions, too."

"I don't need any."

Dad took one hand off the wheel and rested it on her shoulder. "Making friends doesn't come easy, but a life without risk is no life at all."

She winced. His little sayings drove her bonkers. But she'd always been safe as a fox in the den of his love. What else could she do but trust him now?

She peeked up at him. "I don't give an owl's hoot about making friends. But let me get lost in books, and I'll try to get a scholarship."

A smile filled his lean face. "Now you're living up to your name, Deborah. An ancient Hebrew woman brave enough to lead an army into battle."

She buried her hand in her cat's fur, and Franklin responded with a thrum of purrs. "Don't feel brave."

"Nor do I."

They rode in silence now, Franklin's body lifting with his slow, steady breathing.

"Dad, what I said about hating you?"

"You were just a little mercurial."

"Whatever that means."

Along I-90, signs for John Deere and International Harvester dealerships popped up. A billboard welcomed them into town.

Sioux Falls
The Heart of America

Deborah stiffened.

Dad exited the interstate and drove onto a four-lane avenue where more cars streaked by than Deborah had ever seen. Stone churches anchored street corners, their spires splitting the sky. She read their names. "Lutheran this, Lutheran that. They look like castles."

"Not exactly like our Quonset-hut church at home. But we'll get used to it."

"You mean we'll be Lutheran?"

"Not much choice," Dad said. "Even the cats here are Lutheran. Franklin will love the *lutefisk.*"

"The what?"

"A Norwegian delicacy. Basically, it's rotten fish."

She puckered her lips. "Cats eat that?"

"Actually, people do. But only for special occasions."

"Yuck!"

Dad turned onto Dakota Avenue and parked along the curb. He gestured toward a white clapboard house edged with a picket fence. "Here we are, within walking distance of school. Our new home."

"The whole house?"

His smile drooped. "Sorry, only the basement. Let's get our gear in. Remember? School starts tomorrow."

Her body turned stiff as road kill. "I'm petrified."

The next day, a wave of students surged by Deborah and Dad as they paused on their way into Washington High.

Deborah caught her footing and peered up at the drab, gray structure. Massive, rough-cut stones created a square fortress four stories high. A balustrade circled the roof. "Looks like a prison."

"Only if you see it that way," Dad said. "The first step is always the hardest, so imagine soaring on eagle's wings."

"When butterflies are batting around in my stomach?"

"I've got them, too. But don't forget—"

"I know. Everything I do reflects on our people. I *hate* being a walking billboard for Indians."

"It is what it is."

"But it wasn't that way on the rez." She tossed the words behind her as she climbed the granite stairs. She stopped to scan a stone engraving:

May the days spent here
be filled to overflowing
so high school shall ever remain
a happy memory.

Time would tell.

A bank of metal doors blocked her entry. She heaved against one, and it opened to reveal a sea of chattering students swirling every which way.

A blonde with a bouffant style pointed at Deborah. "*Squaw.*"

The red-haired guy next to her laughed. "For real."

Deborah touched her single black braid. She was a sparrow among flamingos.

Now where was her first class? She clutched her mimeographed schedule and hurried her saddle shoes across the gray tile. She came to an intersection. Which way?

Her heart thumped.

"Help you?"

The voice above startled her. She flicked up her eyes.

A lanky guy gazed down. His woodsy scent swathed her.

Her breath evaporated. He was tan—nearly as dark as she was—but with hair like a stack of hay.

He thrust his thumb at the white satin sash running across his chest. "I'm a student monitor. You lost?"

His eyes glistened like a blue river, and the current threatened to sweep her away. "No."

"Sorry I asked." He did a one-eighty.

"Wait. I don't know where Physical Education is?"

He turned back. "The gym? That-a-way."

He motioned down the hall. The blue stone facets in his chunky class ring gleamed like the cobalt of his eyes. "To the right. Down the stairs. You can't miss the smell." He gave a lopsided grin, then pulled his stare away.

"Thanks," Deborah whispered.

Head bent low, she scurried off. How'd she lose her focus? Let a white guy take her breath away? She'd vowed to be an island.

But just one peek? She spun around.

He was gazing at her.

Heat rose in her face, and she detected a glow creeping through his tan. She pivoted and zipped away.

CHAPTER 5

Broken Treaty

Will Running Bear threaded his way through the cacophony of students jammed in the school hallway. He'd gotten Deborah off. Now to receive final instructions from the principal and sign a contract. He didn't know why this job opened up at the end of summer. But when it did, he'd jumped on it. Anything to get Deborah into a school that might launch her into college.

Outside the administrative offices, a paunchy man in his twenties leaned against the wall with his arms folded across his orange paisley shirt.

"Hello," Will said.

The stranger's lips remained as taut as a bow ready to release an arrow.

So not everyone was friendly here.

Will passed by him and entered the offices.

In his rush, he nearly collided with a woman—a platinum blonde. "Excuse me, ma'am." He lowered his gaze with his apology, which put his vision right at her hips. A tight, lime-green dress showed off her curves. She would be the spitting image of Marilyn Monroe if she flaunted her stuff. Instead, she fumbled with a tattered piece of newsprint, stuffing it into her purse. She made a nervous hand motion for him to enter the principal's office.

Will smoothed his hair. He entered the room, which was large enough to bounce echoes. "Principal Ruud, Will Running Bear here, reporting for duty."

Ivar Ruud rocked back and forth in his wooden chair, chewing on a stogie like a dog working a bone. He hunched over papers Will recognized as his typed résumé. The principal glanced up, studying him. "Hmm. Forgot you're nothing but a twig of a man."

"I keep active."

"I'm an athlete, too."

That caught Will off guard. He tried not to focus on the principal's belly folding over his belt. "So, you like sports?"

"Yeah. I bowl every week with the police chief."

Will kept a smile from climbing his face. "Sounds fun."

Ruud riffled the papers. "You graduated *summa cum* something. What's that?"

Better not to brag. "A fancy way to say I did okay."

Ruud tossed the résumé across his desk. "And you coached your *Indians* to the top among small high schools."

Will winced at the way the principal emphasized the word *Indians*. "Yes, sir."

Ruud clasped his hands behind his head. "I've got one heck of a problem with my guys. A stain on my record. Our varsity landed in the cellar last year, even with Lyle Mykland's best coaching."

Will had heard. He figured Mykland had been sacked.

"And I've gotta squelch a scandal before it blots my reputation." The principal flicked cigar ashes onto the floor.

The platinum blonde sped in from the next room with a broom and dustpan, her spiked heels clicking. She swept up the ashes, then retreated.

"This summer," Ruud continued, "my Shop teacher took the Band director—a single woman—to his lake cabin for a little *fishing*. Got their lines tangled, if you know what I mean."

"I understand."

"I won't tolerate hanky-panky between public employees. So I told 'em to extend their fishing trip for the rest of their lives."

Will nodded. What did this have to do with his job?

"So let's get down to brass tacks. This morning Lyle came up with a plan so he won't have to mess with the j.v. anymore and can concentrate on the varsity."

Will's head jerked. "What?"

"You'll take the junior team."

"But—"

"And Lyle wants history classes, so he'll get 'em, instead of you."

"But—"

"No *buts* here. My decision is final, as always. You minored in shop?"

"Industrial arts."

"So you'll take the Shop class. Plus lunch monitor, Study Hall, seven-thirty a.m. Detention, and junior varsity." He sat back in his chair and blew a smoke ring. "Means a pay cut, of course."

The j.v.? Shop class? Babysitting students? A volcano rumbled inside Will.

But Deborah . . . .

Will forced a lid on his anger and managed a smile. "Sounds reasonable."

The principal let out a laugh like a rooster crowing. "Good." He pushed a piece of paper toward Will. "Put your *X* on the line, and you're in."

Will reached for the ballpoint. This was like signing a broken treaty.

"One more thing." The principal jabbed his stogie toward Will. "Make sure you don't interfere with Lyle. He's *developing* as a coach. I'm sure he'll pull the varsity together. And if you have any questions, ask my secretary, Mrs. Mykland, Lyle's mother." He shrugged his head toward the blonde in the next room.

She bent over an open file cabinet and trembled at the sound of her name.

"So Running Moose—"

"It's Running Bear."

"Whatever your animal is, here's your schedule and the curriculum for Shop." He shoved loose sheets across the desk.

Will retrieved them. "Thank you." He turned toward the door.

"By the way," the principal called after him, "your paperwork says you were in the war."

"Yes, sir. Ran troops and supplies back and forth to Europe."

The principal smirked. "Me and the police chief saw combat."

Will stiffened. "Glad to serve you fighting men."

Ruud broke into his crow again.

Will backed out of the room. He bumped into someone and turned around—the man in the orange paisley shirt. "Excuse me."

The man jutted his jaw forward. "You the new j.v. coach?"

"Yes."

"I'm Lyle Mykland, *varsity* coach. And history teacher. Enjoy your Shop class." He swaggered off.

"And a hearty welcome to you, too," Will muttered.

Now where was his classroom, and what in the world was he supposed to teach?

CHAPTER 6

Chicken Fat

Dressed in a baggy white t-shirt and shorts, Deborah struggled to keep up with exercise moves blaring from a scratchy 45 rpm record. A zealous man's voice sang a command to shed their chicken fat.

Huh?

Around her in the gym, thirty other seniors in the same white-on-white baggies followed the marching routine easily, their tennis shoes squeaking across the gym floor. They must have been doing this for years.

Stupid.

She imagined herself back home. There, she would be skipping through waving grass where pale pink prairie roses peaked out. Not sweating in a stinky gym.

She lost the beat.

"Pay attention, Running Bear!" P.E. teacher Lyle Mykland stared, his whistle hanging from his lower lip.

She struggled to pick up the rhythm.

Classmates laughed.

Mykland strutted in front, flipping his Paul McCartney mop-top side to side. His bulky, twenty-something body inflated his tight trousers and orange paisley shirt like a balloon about to pop.

He thought he was cool.

Instead, when he turned away, students rolled their eyes and mimicked his cocky saunter. Then when he turned back, they assumed dead seriousness.

The record yelled something about circling. Everyone rotated their arms.

The red-haired guy and the blonde Deborah had seen in the school lobby tossed flirts back and forth. When he gawked at her rising and falling stack, she lifted it higher.

Mykland scowled at the redhead. "Knock it off."

The voice from the record yelled something about the bicycle ride. Students hit the floor, lay on their backs, and raised their rears.

Four beats behind, Deborah scrambled to catch up.

Guys giggled at a plump brunette near Deborah. She panted as she pump, pump, pumped.

Everyone jumped up and ran in place slow motion. Deborah was mastering the command to run as slow as a tortoise when everyone switched into the frenzied pace of a hare. Her shoelace came loose, but she couldn't stop or she might get singled out again.

She peeked behind at the lanky guy with the thick outcrop of hair who'd helped her find the gym. Their glances collided, and he dropped his head and stared at his moving feet.

Had he been watching her?

Trip.

Her foot caught her shoelace, and she lost her balance.

The blond guy caught her fall, his arm supporting her.

The voice on the record yelled, "Dismissed!"

Students jostled by them on their way to the locker rooms.

"You okay?" the guy asked Deborah.

"Twisted my ankle."

He realized his arm circled her, and his tan face turned rosy. "Sorry."

Coach Mykland's whistle pierced the air. "Move it, Simon."

The boy loped toward the guys' lockers.

So his name was Simon.

Coach Mykland folded his arms over his belly. "Don't you know what a whistle means?"

"Yes, sir." She hobbled away.

Now where was the locker she'd been assigned to share? She surveyed the chaos of chattering girls changing clothes. There. With the blonde bombshell and the plump brunette.

"Excuse me." She stepped over the wooden bench and wriggled into the tight space.

The brunette struggled to pull a checked wool skirt up over her pear-shaped hips. Deborah turned her head away, trying not to view the half-dressed girl. How to change clothes privately? Maybe if she hunched over. She stripped off her white-on-whites and grabbed her plaid jumper from the locker. Her elbows ran into the girl with shoulder-length, flaxen hair. Great. Trapped between all this flesh.

"What a bunch of schmaltz," the brunette said. "Guys staring at us like we're today's cafeteria special."

The blonde laughed. "Let the guys drool." She lifted up her t-shirt to reveal an abundant rack, then slipped on a tight red blouse, miniskirt, pantyhose, and penny loafers.

Deborah peered down at her own body. She was nothing but a stick.

"Don't pay any attention to Elaine," the brunette whispered to Deborah. "She got all the good chromosomes. We got the crummy-zomes. By the way, my name's Haddy."

"I'm Deborah."

Elaine turned toward the full-length mirror and opened her cosmetics bag. "Hey, Haddy, walk with me to World Lit."

Haddy gasped. "You're asking *me* to walk with *you*? Sure!"

Deborah peeked in the mirror and straightened her braid. She didn't wear makeup. Didn't know how to.

She gathered her gym gear into her arms.

Haddy held out a paper bag. "Got an extra."

"Thanks."

"And to warn you, Rolly Tolly, the Lit teacher, can be real hairy."

"I love literature," Deborah blurted out, then regretted she'd shared that.

Elaine paused from applying bright red to her upper lip. "You *love* literature?"

Deborah nodded.

"You might be useful." Elaine turned back to the mirror and smacked her lips to spread the red. Then she fluffed her mane. "You walk with us, too, *Deb.*"

Deb? No one had ever called her that, but she couldn't imagine correcting this girl.

"Yeah, walk with us, *Deb,*" Haddy parroted.

"I don't know the way, so thanks."

The three stepped into the corridor. The slamming of maize-colored metal lockers created an ear-shattering din that made understanding anyone nearly impossible, yet the hallway buzzed with chatter.

Elaine and Haddy took a quick turn at a corner and headed up a flight of stairs.

Deborah hustled to follow, climbing marble steps that had taken so many treads they were concave.

At the top, Elaine cocked her head and raised an eyebrow at the red-haired boy who had ogled her in P.E.

He swaggered up.

She brushed him away.

The guy braced his hands on his hips and scowled.

"That's Erik," Haddy whispered to Deborah.

"Oh," Deborah said, not caring who he was. All she wanted was to find class and disappear.

"I don't have time for that Carrot Top," Elaine said, tossing a glance back at Erik as the three girls wound their way through the crush of students.

"So why do you flirt with Carrot Top?" Haddy asked.

"To see what he'll do." Elaine halted and gasped.

A slim man with broad shoulders approached, smoothing his honey-toned hair in place as he passed.

Elaine's mouth dropped open. "Who is *that?*"

"The new chorus director, Harley Hart," Haddy said.

"Chorus?" Deborah asked. "I signed up for that."

"Can we time-travel to his class?" Elaine asked.

"Sorry," Haddy said. "Have to wait 'til afternoon before we drool over that heartthrob."

Elaine's face clouded over. "First we have to face the impossible in Lit."

"What do you mean?" Deborah asked.

"You remember what Haddy said about Rolly Tolly being hairy?" Elaine said.

"Yeah?"

Elaine moved in close and lowered her voice. "If my GPA drops, I'm off the pep squad."

Haddy gasped. "But you're *head* cheerleader."

Elaine's lips pursed. "And if I get bounced, my father will throw a fit."

Haddy turned toward Deborah. "Elaine's father is the principal. When he throws a fit, it's a double-doozy."

"Oh," Deborah said. She didn't want to know about anyone's fits. All she wanted was to vanish from this chaos.

"But maybe you two can help." Elaine interrupted her thoughts.

"Us help?" Haddy asked.

Elaine punched a finger at her. "You're Little Miss Organizer."

Haddy beamed. "That's me."

Elaine turned to Deborah. "And you, New Girl, you said you love literature."

"Yeah."

She pulled on Deborah's braid. "I'm guessing you have some smarts under that hair. If Rolly Tolly assigns one of his group projects, we can work on it together."

Haddy's Mary Janes did a little dance. "That would be soooo fun."

Deborah's stomach twisted. A group project? Could she die first?

They reached the classroom. "Here, sit by me," Elaine said.

Haddy glowed at the invitation.

Deborah glanced around. No other seats available, so she slipped into a wooden desk by them.

Other girls gawked at the three, giggling and whispering. Was it her braid? Or was it something about Elaine?

The guy with the tangle of blond hair sat across the room. *Simon.* They caught each other's eye. She turned away, scolding herself to be a rock.

At the front of the room, the teacher gazed out of a massive window, his mustache twitching.

Deborah unfolded her class schedule. *World Literature: Roland Tollefson.*

Haddy whispered, "My pops told me Rolly Tolly tried to make it as a Broadway actor. But he couldn't get an audition."

Deborah could see why, unless he was auditioning for *weird.* His pencil-thin figure posed in front of the chalkboard, and he turned his head at a slight angle like he was waiting for a spotlight to hit him.

The class bell clanged. Students quieted.

Rolly Tolly rocked his feet on the worn wood floor. "WEL-come to your senior year. May this class be an IN-cubator before you launch into the world to become who knows what? Here in World LIT-er-A-ture, we will study the LIT-er-A-ture of the world."

"Brilliant," Erik muttered loud enough for students to hear, but soft enough so Rolly Tolly didn't. Giggles rippled through the room.

The teacher clapped his hands. "Attention, please. Your first assignment will acquaint me with your stage presence so I can evaluate your readiness for a role in the fall play. Many of you will par-TI-cipate in this drama."

Torture! Deborah slouched in her seat.

"I'll give you time in class to form groups of three," Rolly Tolly said.

Elaine winked at Deborah and Haddy.

Rolly Tolly gestured toward the chalkboard. "Pick a masterpiece from this list. Read it. Then in a five-minute presentation, show how its message still speaks to us today. Be VI-su-al. Be cre-A-tive. And be pre-PARED. Performances begin next Monday."

Haddy bounced in her seat. "This will be so much fun. Which book should we choose, Elaine?"

"Don't have a clue. You pick, Deb."

She speed-read the board. "Uh, *The Three Musketeers?*"

Elaine grinned. "Whatever you say. You two can come over to my house on Friday night, and we'll put it together."

Heat rushed to Deborah's face. What had she gotten into?

CHAPTER 7

Vandals

Will finally found the Shop classroom in the bowels of the building next to the boiler room. He shoved against a metal door. It creaked open.

Dark inside.

He ran his fingers along the wall until they bumped on the light switch. Still dim.

Grime flecked the garden-level windows. A central worktable displayed a haphazard history of spilled glue and stain. A vise hung precariously from one bolt.

He took a step. Something jabbed his shoe. A litter of nails.

Wooden stools lay sideways on the cement floor. Will turned one upright. Its uneven legs wobbled.

No lumber anywhere. No power tools.

He spread the loose pages of the curriculum onto the worktable. Nothing but simpleton projects. No budget.

Outrage flared inside him. This was obviously a left-over class. Why'd the principal hand history courses to Lyle Mykland? And why did Mykland get to coach varsity basketball when his players were bottom feeders last year?

He gripped the edge of the worktable and released a slow stream of air. Farewell to his dreams. And he'd better control his anger before it controlled him. At least he'd gotten Deborah into this school. That's what mattered most.

As for him? Somehow he'd have to procure equipment for this class. He wasn't going to babysit students and *talk* about tools, but never place them in their hands.

How much time until class? He checked the wall clock. Only enough to tidy up the place.

He found a broom in a closet and managed to sweep up nails before seven boys burst through the door like gunshot. They dropped onto stools, scraping the legs across the floor as they circled around the workbench. Then they slouched, their palms propping up their heads. No one met Will's eyes.

Will took a deep breath. "My name is Mr. Running Bear."

A tall redhead with freckles whispered, "Ooga-ooga." Snickers circulated the table.

Will ignored this. "Please answer when I say your name. Baruch Dimm?"

A round of chuckles.

A stubby boy turned crimson. "I go by *Barry* Dimm."

"*Very* Dimm," the redhead muttered.

More laughter.

Will glared at the redhead. "That's enough, Mr. . . . "

"Quisling. You can call me Erik."

"I will, Erik." Will turned back to the first boy whose name he'd called. "So your *sobriquet* is *Barry*."

"What?" The boy nudged his black plastic glasses up the bridge of his nose.

Will smiled. "Your nickname." He turned to his attendance sheet again. "Jordan Lundy?"

"Jord." The tiny voice came from a kid as skinny as a two-by-four.

"I'll remember that, too, Jord. Next, Simon Peterson the Second."

Someone whispered, "Haaaaay, Garfunkel."

A boy with blond, fuzzy hair like Art Garfunkel's responded with a polite "here."

Will finished running through the list. Now to determine what these city kids knew about tools. "Let's talk basics. What's the difference between a Phillips and a flat-head screwdriver?"

"We don't know nothin' about screwin'," Erik hollered. The guys roared.

Will braced his hips. "Look, you may have signed up for this class to pad your GPA, but you'll work as hard here as you do anywhere else."

Groans filled the air.

"What's Shop got to do with anything?" Erik said. "When I graduate, either the draft sucks me up, or I become a cop like my father. But if I get a basketball scholarship—"

"You're a basketball player?" Will interrupted.

"We all are," someone said.

"'cept for me." Barry slumped at his stool.

"Varsity?" Will asked.

"Yeah."

Will chuckled. So he'd have contact with varsity players after all—but not coach them. Maybe he could create a teachable moment here. "Listen, a scout won't notice you unless you impress him with your ability to overcome problems on the court. Industrial arts can teach you that."

"So, when I have a problem, I throw together some cheesy birdhouse?" Erik asked.

Students hooted.

"No!" Will shot back. "We *won't* build birdhouses in this class. We'll build *men*. Can you handle that?"

Erik shrugged.

"Sir?" Simon asked. "How will we, uh, build men?"

Will's pulse quickened. "By building minds. Martin Luther King, Jr. said, *Rarely do we find men who willingly engage in hard, solid thinking.* To learn to think as men"— his mind raced through options—"we'll build a replica of a Roman city."

"Huh?"

What had he said? He didn't have any materials. But he'd captured their attention and wasn't going to lose it. He lowered his voice. "Imagine it's 455 A.D. No basketball, but lots of action."

He grabbed the chalk, sketched an outline of the Italian Peninsula on the blackboard, and drew an *X*. "Here in Rome, the emperor is *murdered*." He paused for effect.

The guys leaned forward.

"The man presumed to be behind his death, Petronius Maximus, is proclaimed the new ruler." He tapped on his map. "Along comes Genseric, the Spear King—his *sobriquet*." He winked at Barry, who grinned. "The Spear King is commander of the Vandals, a tribe dominating the Mediterranean Sea. He's a pirate. You wouldn't want to run into him in a dark alley."

The boys slid to the edges of their stools.

"The Spear King says the emperor's murder voids his peace treaty with Rome. He attacks. His forces land on the coast and approach the capital. He's bent on looting. On blood. On taking slaves."

"Radical," Steve whispered.

Will tossed a piece of chalk in the air and caught it. "He nears *our* city. The one we're going to build. So how are you going to stop him?"

Simon's hand shot up. "Build up the walls?"

"How?"

"Concrete?" Wayne suggested.

"The Romans built the dome of the Pantheon with concrete. After eighteen hundred years, it's still the world's largest unreinforced concrete dome."

"Far out," Karl said.

"But we're talking about a scale model," Will said.

"I used to build airplanes out of balsa wood," Simon said.

"Light enough to fly, but not strong enough for our city. Other ideas? Come on. Practice hard, solid thinking."

Silence.

Barry pushed his glasses up. "What about sugar cubes?"

"Why sugar cubes?"

Barry placed his fingers close together. "They're small enough for a scale model."

"They're light enough to work with," Wayne added.

"We can stack 'em to build walls," Karl said.

Jord's hand lifted as slowly as a glacier moving. "This is probably stupid, but what about wooden stir sticks?"

"A splendid idea." Will's voice boomed.

Jord's face reddened, and a smile crept up his face.

"So where do we get these sugar cubes and stir sticks?" Will asked.

Erik waved a hand. "Leave it to us."

"Great! You come up with cubes and sticks, and we *men* will build that city."

The bell rang.

The boys huddled around Erik.

"Dig it," Erik whispered as they streamed out of the room.

Will exhaled. Dig it, indeed. He'd bought time until he figured out how to procure tools and materials. But where would they come up with sugar cubes and stir sticks? He hoped his trust in them wouldn't backfire.

That day at noon, Will wove between tables crammed with high-octane students. He glimpsed Deborah sitting with two girls. A good sign. But he'd stay clear. He didn't want his presence as lunch monitor to be awkward.

In his periphery, Will spotted a boy lobbing a sandwich across the room. He'd already ignored several minor infractions. This one, he couldn't let go.

He headed toward the offender. "That toss would be worth two points on the basketball court. But not in the lunchroom." He wrote out a ticket and handed it to him. "See you in detention."

The boy sneered.

Will forced a smile and moved on.

Lunch lady Elva Nyberg emerged from the Tribe Shack, a plastic tepee that reeked of stale coffee. She brushed past

Will. "They think my head is as thick as split pea soup?" she muttered.

Something was up. Will had better follow her.

Elva waddled over to her supervisor, Olly Olson, who stood like a sentry at the end of the line of meatloaf, mashed potatoes, and orange Jell-O. Elva adjusted her hairnet. "In my thirty-five years here, I've never seen this. Senior boys guzzling coffee and grabbing sugar cubes and stir sticks by the handful. I hate to mention the possibility"—she lowered her voice—"but are they doing something psychedelic?"

"Uff-da," Olly grunted. "I'll report it to the principal." He sped off.

Will masked his grin and moved back toward the student tables. Creative problem solving. That's what it was. He wouldn't say anything.

A bell resounded. Students shoved out of the room, avoiding him like he was poison.

Will sighed. What in the world possessed him to leave the reservation? He could have taught history and coached basketball there forever.

Except for Deborah. Colleges offered scholarships to kids from reputable schools. Not from the reservation.

This better work.

"Hope it's goin' well for ya." The voice from the doorway interrupted his musing.

A black man in gray-striped overalls sauntered toward him. "I'm the janitor."

Will held out his hand. "Will Running Bear's my name."

The man's mouth dropped—surprised to have a hand extended toward him—and his grin grew as wide as his Afro.

"What's your name?" Will asked.

"Folks call me Artie. Artie Brown."

"What would you *like* to be called?"

"Arthur. But Artie's fine."

"Then I shall call you Arthur."

Arthur grinned. "I came North 'cuz it's supposed to be the promised land. Even passed the test to drive a bus here." He scuffed a shoe against the olive-colored linoleum. "But no one hired me, so here I am, makin' the best of it."

"How?"

He smiled, revealing a set of teeth looking like they were rearranged during an unfortunate meeting. "I help my uncle with his church here, Jerusalem Baptis'."

"That's good of you."

Arthur traced a finger on a gray Formica tabletop. "But if you gonna make it in this town, you better go *Luthrun*. It's the *in* church."

"I don't care what denomination a church is. Just so people worship Almighty God."

Arthur shook his head. "Mmm hmm? Ain't the way folks here sees it. Anyways, I stopped by to ask if you needs anything. I shines shoes for the principal and for Coach Mykland. You being the j.v. coach, I'll shine yours, too."

A janitor shining shoes for staff? Belittling. "Thanks. I shine my own."

"Another thing. You might want to use the teachers' lounge."

"I don't smoke."

"It ain't just for smokin'." Arthur lowered his voice. "It's for gettin' along with the principal. *I* can't use the teachers' lounge, but *you* can. Don't know why, but the principal real soft with people like his secretary, Miz Mykland, and her son, Coach Mykland. They play the socializin' game better than anyone."

"Thanks for the tip, but I don't want to play *that* game."

"Okay." Arthur sauntered toward the doorway. "Thought I'd warn ya."

Warned? That was a strong word.

CHAPTER 8

Revelations

Deborah sat as straight as a Bic pen, not daring to touch the shiny dashboard for fear she might leave a smudge. "Like my pop's wheels?" Haddy asked as she turned onto Park Avenue.

"Never been in such a fancy car."

"A GTO," she said, her voice all dreamy.

Deborah shifted on the white bucket seat. "I don't mean to pry, but why does Elaine want us with her on this Lit project?"

"Simple. As Pops puts it, Elaine used up all her capital with others. That left only you, the New Girl, and me, the one who's never been in anybody's *in* crowd."

"What do you mean? With a car like this, you must be ri-"

She swallowed her words when she realized her brashness.

Haddy giggled in a nervous way. "Pops has this hot car, but everyone still sees him as the little Jew who lives in an apartment above our shop on Main Street. We don't even have the status to name the store after ourselves. People mangled Rabinowitz, so Pops planned to shorten it to Owitz. But then everyone would think we were Irish, so he shortened it to Witz Jewelers. Besides, even if we had money, we couldn't make it in this town."

"Why?"

"We're not Norwegian Lutherans."

"So why let Elaine use you in projects like this?"

Haddy's big brown eyes darted in Deborah's direction. "A bad friend is better than no friend at all."

"Oh. Sorry."

This conversation had gotten way too personal. But since she'd ventured this far, she'd ask something else. "Why is Elaine so . . . . "

"So *Elaine*? Imagine what it would be like to be the principal's daughter. Struggling to be successful when all you've got is blond hair and boobs. I mean, her locker combination must be thirty-six, twenty-four, thirty-six. And her father is always rigging the system for her. She's as clumsy as a Gentile in a synagogue, but she becomes head cheerleader? Go figure."

Deborah smothered a giggle.

"But we've got something Elaine needs if she's going to stay on the cheerleading squad." Haddy tapped her index finger against her temple. "Brains." She slowed the car.

Deborah looked up at a brick, two-story house with white columns. "Is that—"

"Elaine's mansion. Like little Tara on the prairie. I've only dreamed what it's like on the inside."

"How can a principal afford that?"

"He's probably mortgaged up to his bald spot."

Still focusing on the house, Haddy drifted toward the edge of the street.

"Watch it!"

Too late. Haddy skinned the curb. "Guess I circumcised that one. Anyway, welcome to Richville."

Deborah stepped out, making sure she didn't tread on the manicured grass. She followed the brick walkway curving toward the home's red double doors. She'd never seen a house like this before except on TV. "Who's gonna ring the bell?" she asked.

"I will." Haddy stabbed her plump finger at the bell. Its resonant chime called back.

Someone fiddled with the lock.

"I hope it's not the principal," Haddy whispered.

"Me, too," Deborah murmured. She hadn't met him yet, but hadn't heard one good thing about him.

One of the massive doors flung open.

Relief. It was Elaine.

"Hi Haddy, Deb," Elaine said.

That nickname again. Deborah must get up the courage to tell Elaine she didn't want to be called that.

Before she could, Elaine turned around, her golden hair bouncing on her shoulders. "I've got pizza and pop in my bedroom." She led them over the tiled entry, up a circular staircase, and down a wide hallway. "Here it is."

"Wow!" Haddy uttered.

Deborah's jaw dropped. This was like something from a Sears catalogue. One wall showcased an oversized white canopy bed with lime-green paisley linens. A lava lamp oozed orange goo through its purple capsule, creating moving shadows on the wall. The stereo's mammoth speakers amplified sounds about parsley, sage, rosemary, and thyme, while the smell of oregano and melted cheese wafted toward them.

Elaine handed them pink paper plates with white daisies. "Hope you like pepperoni."

"Sure," Haddy answered. She grabbed three slices.

Three pieces at once? Deborah couldn't imagine indulging like that. She reached for a single triangle and nibbled on the oozing cheese and soft crust. Not like the box pizzas she and Dad bought that tasted like cardboard.

In the middle of a bite, Haddy gasped and pointed. "Elaine, I've never seen such a huge collection."

Deborah followed Haddy's gaze to the dresser. Miniature plastic dolls with giant smiles and puffs of neon hair stared back. "What are they?"

"You grow up in a cave?" Elaine asked.

Deborah hesitated. "No. But never saw anything like that."

"They're troll dolls. Supposed to bring you luck."

"Oh." Who would want to collect those? But something else drew her attention. A book with orange and yellow splotches on its cover rested on a white wicker chair. She glanced at the girls. They were talking trolls, so she picked up the book and opened it.

"You like Rod McKuen?"

Elaine had caught her. Deborah snapped the book shut. "I didn't mean to snoop. Who is he?"

Haddy nearly choked on her pizza. "You don't know? He's America's pop poet. Writes about love and loneliness. All our teenage drama."

"Yeah, not like that junk Rolly Tolly gags us on," Elaine said. "Let me show you." She flipped the book open to a page marked with a bobby pin and read about drifting in life until someone found her.

Elaine hugged the book. "That's me. Waiting for Harley Hart to notice me."

Haddy scrunched her eyes. "A teacher? Why drool over forbidden fruit? With your looks, you could have any guy at school. Me? I'm ro-tic."

"What?" Elaine took a gulp of Coke.

"It's ro-MAN-tic without the man!"

Elaine cracked up, snorting soda through her nose.

This caught Haddy off guard, and she sprayed Coke from her mouth. "You made carbonated snot," she said.

Deborah hid her laugh in her hand. She'd never known girls so free with their emotions.

Elaine got control of herself and tossed a paisley pillow that glanced off Deborah's side. "What about you, New Girl? I bet you're quiet 'cause you left some good-looking Injun back on the rez."

Injun! Where could she hide?

Haddy threw a pillow that grazed Deborah's shoulder. "Yeah, 'fess up."

Confess to what? That she was as shy as a fawn. That she'd avoided boys all her life. Deborah lobbed a pillow back. "I didn't leave any guy behind."

Elaine smacked her on the head with another pillow. "That's good, 'cause the Coppertone King *likes* you."

"Who?"

"Simon," Haddy explained. "He lifeguarded last summer. Doesn't he look like some Norse god? He was eyeing you in P.E."

"And in Lit," Elaine said.

Deborah's face grew hot. She hurled a pillow back. "He was not."

Elaine laughed. "That goody-goody pastor's boy has the hots for you."

Pastor's boy? She didn't want to act interested, so she attacked both girls with pillows.

Haddy pitched one sideways, catching Deborah off guard. She flung it back before Elaine's landed on her cheek. The *thud* of pillows continued, mixed with laughter.

Deborah had never let loose like this. What if they got into trouble? She caught her breath. "Hey, we'd better cool it before your parents come knocking."

Elaine stopped mid-throw. "Parents?"

Haddy panted to catch her breath. "Yeah."

Elaine dropped cross-legged on the lime-green shag carpet. "My father's out at one of his stupid *education* meetings. And I don't have a mother."

Haddy gasped. "That's why we never see a Mrs. Principal around?"

"Yeah."

Haddy flumped onto the carpet. "I don't have a mother either."

This was too weird. Deborah sat down. "Me neither."

"You're kidding," Elaine said, glancing back and forth.

They shook their heads.

Elaine reached for a blond troll doll and smoothed its hair. "I'd give anything to know something about my mom."

"You don't know about her?" Haddy asked.

"No," Elaine said. "You both know about yours?"

"Sure."

Deborah dipped her head, not wanting to offer any more information.

She was safe for the moment because Elaine picked up a troll with curly brown hair and handed it to Haddy. "Tell me about your mother, and you can keep the doll."

Haddy smiled. "A Jewish troll. What a concept." Her fingers combed the doll's hair. "Mama was weak after the war."

"How come?" Elaine asked.

"She and Pops were in the Polish resistance, running from the Nazis. Lived off the land. Survived winters on the run."

"Awful." The words escaped Deb's lips before she realized it. "I mean, I'm sorry."

From her neckline Haddy pulled out a gold Star of David on a chain. "She named me Hadassah. It means *star*. I was her *Little Star*." She glided her hand over her gray herringbone slacks. "She taught me how to sew. Now every stitch I take, I remember her."

Haddy reached for her Coke, and her hand shook. "Her cough wouldn't go away. One day she died."

"Sad," Elaine murmured.

Haddy glanced up at Deborah. "What about your mother?"

Deborah dug her fingers into the shag carpet. Pain threatened to bubble up.

Elaine reached into her troll collection and picked out one with long black hair. She offered it to Deborah. "You're safe here."

Deborah's eyes dashed between Haddy and Elaine. She'd never talked about Mom with anyone, but something tugged at her heart. These girls carried the weight of loss like she did. Maybe they could share each other's loads.

She accepted the doll from Elaine. Her heart thumped. "A cheerleading accident."

Elaine startled. "What?"

Deborah reached for her purse, retrieved a yellowed newspaper clipping from her wallet, and unfolded it. The headline read:

Basketball Cheerleader Injured

"State beat the University." Her voice hovered at a whisper. "Everyone mobbed the floor. Mom got trampled. Dad saw it. He played on State's team.

"Mom lost consciousness for a while. Doctors said her brain had shifted. She couldn't finish school. They married. Had me. She was sweet, but simple."

She cleared the lump from her throat. "We were so poor in our cinderblock on the reservation. A wood stove. No electricity. Yet we were rich. Mom called me Princess." A smile climbed up her face. "Dad still calls me that sometimes. He used to play an old 45 record about not sitting under an apple tree with anybody else. He'd scoop Mom into his arms. They'd Lindy Hop, and he'd sing along."

The lump returned. "Then one day while dancing, mom died right in Dad's arms. He hasn't danced since."

Deborah lifted her gaze.

Elaine's face was red. "That's so sad for both of you. But at least you know something about your moms. I don't have jewelry. Or a newspaper clipping. Or a nickname. Don't even know my mother's name. My father *refuses* to talk about her. He's just *silent!*"

She stopped.

Somber voices on the stereo sang about "The Sound of Silence."

A tear tracked down Elaine's cheek. She hugged a pillow.

Haddy placed an arm around her. Elaine returned the hug. Deborah slipped toward them and wrapped her arms around both. Each clutched her troll doll.

"*Falsehood is a mask,*" Deborah whispered.

"What?" Haddy asked.

"From *The Three Musketeers*. We took our masks off. Faced each other. As we are."

Elaine wiped mascara from her cheeks. "Yeah, and it's pretty messy. Listen, what I shared, I don't want *anyone* at school to know. Understand?"

Deborah and Haddy nodded.

"So let's get this Lit report out of the way. Then we can play Twister. Haddy, what should we do?"

"How about a skit?"

Deborah stiffened. "You mean acting? I've never—"

"You can do it," Haddy told her.

"You've *got* to do it so I get a decent grade!" Elaine said.

Deborah would rather fall into the *Twilight Zone* than be in a skit. But she needed good grades to apply for a scholarship. She blinked slowly. "Okay. Then we need costumes."

Haddy shot a hand up like she was volunteering in class. "I can sew. And Rolly Tolly said we have to say something about how the book relates to our world. Can you write that, Deb?"

"Easy. What can you do, Elaine?"

"Nothing. That's why I brought you two in."

CHAPTER 9

Musketeers

Deborah squirmed at her tippy desk. She leaned toward Haddy and Elaine and whispered, "Hope we're not first." "I hope so, too," Haddy said. "But we'll pull it off. Right, Elaine?"

"Sure." Elaine flashed her Crest smile, but she drummed her fingers on her desk.

In front of the class, Rolly Tolly stood erect, his mustache twitching. "Now, who will be first?" He scanned the list in his hand. "Erik, Barry, and Simon."

The girls exchanged relieved glances.

Erik sauntered to the front. Barry and Simon followed and hid behind him.

What a strange group they were. Erik, the class clown. Simon, the shy guy. And Barry, the socially clumsy brainiac. Maybe Erik had pulled them together to make up for his lack of smarts.

Erik's freckled face flushed. He swung a gray plastic sword, accidentally whacking Barry on the shoulder. "*It was the best of times, it was the worst of times.* Like our senior year."

Classmates cracked up.

Erik motioned to Barry with his sword. The pudgy boy shuffled forward, his sword limp in his hand. He mumbled something about lacking *chutzpah*, then pushed his black glasses up the bridge of his nose. "The social unrest in *A Tale of Two Cities* is similar to the protests over the Vietnam War." His voice was a monotone.

Deborah's mind strayed. Her gaze fell on Simon, his face lowered. Was it really true what Haddy and Elaine said? That he liked her?

Erik nudged him. "Your turn, Garfunkel."

Simon stepped forward. "Dickens's story illustrates the expense of liberty. There is a cost, but if we believe something is wrong and we don't protest, the price is even higher."

He aimed his sword at his classmates, and the room hushed. "We must determine whether it's worth the sacrifice of lives from our generation for a war thousands of miles away. We must choose our actions so we'll be able to say, *It is a far, far better thing that I do, than I have ever done.*"

Suddenly Deborah understood what made Simon so appealing. Beyond those crystalline eyes and his crown of golden hair, it was his conviction. He was quiet, but he knew what he believed and was willing to share it.

"Ba-deep, ba-deep, ba-deep." Erik broke the stillness. "That's all, folks."

Students hooted.

Erik bumped elbows with guys along the way back to his desk. Barry rushed to his seat and slouched down. Simon rested easily in his chair, his long legs extending into the aisle.

Rolly Tolly waved his hands. "Now everyone, save your PAS- sion for your own presentation." He fumbled with his list. "Next, we will hear from"—his mustache twitched—"Elaine, Haddy, and Deborah."

Deborah's hands grew clammy. She followed Elaine and Haddy to the front. They turned their backs and donned purple felt hats, each with a single oversized orange feather. Then they flung red capes over their shoulders. When they turned around, Elaine and Haddy wore black felt beards. Deborah covered her eyes with a jeweled mask.

The class laughed and applauded.

A surge of electricity jolted through Deborah.

Elaine tossed her shoulder-length hair aside. "Alexandre Dumas wrote *Les Trois Mousquetaires,*" she simpered.

"The Three Musketeers for those of you who haven't taken French."

Classmates groaned.

Haddy took a step forward, tripping on her full-length cape. "This is a swashbuckling tale." She deepened her voice. "About three men whose loyalty to each other gives us a model of true friendship."

Now Deborah's turn. Her heart thumped so loud she feared the class heard it. Still hidden behind the mask, she moved toward the students. "The author writes—"

Her voice cracked.

She began again. "The author writes about searching for the real person behind a disguise. Good advice, because a person can hide behind a mask of confidence. Or shyness."

She slipped her mask away from one eye, and found herself staring at Simon.

He straightened at his desk.

"With attention"—Deborah unveiled both eyes—"we can find the true person behind the mask."

Simon's face reddened.

Deborah directed the girls into a half circle. They stacked their hands. "The Three Musketeers lived by this motto," Deborah said.

"All for one, one for all," the three chanted in unison.

Deborah and Haddy removed their hats with a flourish and took a deep bow. Elaine was supposed to do the same, but instead, she lifted one leg and bent it at the knee, revealing her pantyhose up to mid thigh. She winked and threw her hat into the rows of students.

Erik leaped high, caught the hat, and let out a howl.

Rolly Tolly raised his palms. "Calm down now. Good po-TEN-tial for the fall play here."

Deborah scurried to her desk and scrunched down. Even though more presentations followed, she didn't hear them. Her mind pirouetted with disbelief and pleasure.

She had faced a crowd, and she tingled from the memory of the applause.

And the memory of catching Simon's eye.

When the bell rang, students spilled out of the classroom. Deborah fell in step with Haddy and Elaine.

"Hey, uh, Deb?" A voice came from behind.

She turned.

Simon.

Her heart stalled.

He caught up, and his pine scent wafted over her.

"Um, it's cool what you said about discovering the real person behind a mask," he said.

Her feet moved automatically. "Thanks."

"You're welcome, *Ke-mo-sah-bee.*"

She gasped. *Ke-mo-sah-bee?* Did he see her as some Indian sidekick?

"How dare you."

She stomped off.

CHAPTER 10

Sniffing Glue

In Shop, Will Running Bear circled around the boys who hunched over the worktable. He stopped by Simon. "Glue the parapet on the north side of the city."

"Huh? Yeah," Simon answered, his voice a whisper.

What was wrong with him? The first week of school, Simon had been so alert. Now, his mind drifted like tumbleweed. Meanwhile, everyone else was mesmerized with work on their model of an ancient city.

"Mr. Running Bear," Barry said. "Our city is so secure, the Spear King could never destroy it like he did Rome."

"That pirate never did destroy Rome."

The boys' heads jerked up. "What?"

Will grinned. Nothing better than students ripe for a history lesson. "Rome hoped to appease the warlord, so it threw its gates open. And it worked. The Vandals plundered the gold and silver, but they didn't destroy the city. So, what's the moral of that story?"

"Don't count your empires before they hatch?" Erik said.

Will smiled. "Nice try."

"Make peace?" Simon asked.

"Right," Will said. "Make peace whenever you can. You won't get everything you want, but you won't lose everything either. The city survived, becoming an archetype in architecture, philosophy, law, and government. And the Vandals took their place in history, too. They bequeathed the word *vandal*, one who damages property. Something to avoid at all costs."

The classroom door whipped open. Principal Ruud marched in, his black suit so tight over his round body that he threatened to pop coat buttons. "What the Sam Hill?"

He grabbed a pile of sugar cubes and narrowed his eyes at Will. "Gotta talk to ya." He jerked a thumb over his shoulder. "Outside."

"Keep building up the wall," Will told the boys. He joined the principal in the hallway.

Ruud balled his fists. "Ollie says the boys are carrying off handfuls of sugar cubes from the cafeteria. I ignored it at first, but it's still going on. Must be overdosing. Then I smelled something down here. Are they taking *cycle-derelicts*?"

Will suppressed a laugh. "Not psychedelics. It's rubber cement. The boys collected sugar cubes for building materials."

"What the devil for?"

"Washingtonia."

"Huh?"

"That's what the boys call their Roman city. And Rome wasn't built in a day."

"Nor my reputation!" the principal exploded. "You'd better be on task by the end of this semester or it'll be your job."

Will's face turned cold.

"And another thing, I never see you in the teachers' lounge."

Will glimpsed Arthur, the janitor, mopping the floor at the end of the hallway. Will directed his attention back to the principal. "I don't smoke."

"It's *my* lounge. You be there."

Ruud stomped off, bumping into Arthur's pail, sloshing water onto his trousers. He glared at the janitor. "Clean up this mess."

"Yes, sir."

After the principal disappeared, Arthur turned toward Will and shrugged.

Arthur had warned him. Now everything might be lost because of Will's refusal to bow and scrape.

What had he told his students? Make peace whenever possible. That's what he'd do. He gave Arthur a quick nod, then turned back to his room. The door was ajar. The class probably heard everything. He strode in.

The boys busied themselves and said nothing.

His face grim, Will picked up a handful of sugar cubes. "Hope you guys didn't get high on caffeine while pilfering these." Then he smiled, and the guys burst out laughing.

Later in the day, seniors waved at Will in the hallway and called out, "Hey, history coach." He relished the moniker. Even Deborah slipped him an approving nod when she passed in the stairwell.

But when Will greeted Lyle Mykland, the actual history teacher and varsity coach, the man tossed an icy glare.

CHAPTER 11

Prisms

Deborah glanced across the field of wooden chess pieces. "Your move," Dad said from the other side of the card table in their apartment.

Panic hit her. "I don't know what to do." She flung her arms, nearly upsetting the board.

Franklin, her ivory fur ball, startled from her lap and landed on the orange shag carpet.

"You're wound up tighter than an eight-day clock," Dad said. "What's wrong, Deborah?

"Nothing. And you may as well call me *Deb*. Everyone else does."

"If you wish."

"And another thing. You stink like an ashtray. Did you take up smoking?"

"Heavens, no. I socialize in the teachers' lounge. Part of my job. You sure you're okay?"

From the edge of the chessboard, she pushed forward a white pawn. "I'm fine. But Simon is driving me crazy. He called me *Ke-mo-sah-bee*."

Dad sat back and chuckled. "Ah, that explains it."

"What?"

"Simon's been distracted in class lately. I'm guessing he's got his eye on you, Deborah—I mean Deb."

"You think he's interested . . ? That doesn't mean I care about him. And what he said is racist. I'm not some weird-talking sidekick of the Lone Ranger."

"Simon didn't mean that. *Ke-mo-sah-bee* can be translated as trusted friend."

She hadn't known that. "I'm not his trusted friend."

"Maybe he'd like you to be. Simon's awkward. Ignore his words. Listen to his heart."

"I'll ignore him."

Dad moved his black knight. "You're certainly opinion-ated about someone you intend to ignore."

This conversation was tipping sideways. "Let's cool it."

"Okay." He analyzed the chessboard. "Your rook is in trouble. See over there? Your castle. You don't want to lose your Xanadu."

She moved it. "What'd you call it?"

"Xanadu, the summer home of Kublai Khan. His castle."

"A castle, huh?" She glanced around their basement apartment. "Like this place?"

"You don't like our Xanadu?"

"Nothing like Elaine's."

Dad frowned. "I see. But the true beauty of a home is the happiness within. You're not happy with me?"

"Sure I am. It's . . . . " Her words stuck in her craw.

Dad left his folding chair and stood beside her, his arm touching her shoulder. "Let me guess. School?"

"Yeah. Even the building. One big cube. So weird."

"Not like our native ways, right? Not built around cir-cles like the sun, the moon, the sky."

"Everything's square."

Dad knelt and embraced her shoulder. "I know it's strange. But in this square place, doors may open for you."

She rested her head against his side, near his heart. "I don't know who I am anymore. I never imagined I could speak in front of a bunch of people. Then I did in World Lit. And liked it."

"I'm proud of you."

"But this year is so scary. Everyone's wondering what we'll do after we graduate."

"*Doing* comes from *being*."

"What do you mean?"

"Who we *are* is more important than what we *do*."

"So who are we?"

"We're God's kids, made to rest in his love. Like you're resting in mine."

"I still don't get it."

"Try this." He led her to the window and motioned toward a prism he'd hung when they'd moved in. He touched it, and the crystal tossed back a rainbow of color. "We're meant to refract the colors God shines through us."

"Can't be that simple."

"That simple. And that complex."

What did that mean? She chewed on the inside of her mouth.

"Something else bothering you? Is it friends?"

She gazed out of their tiny basement window toward the sinking sun. "Haddy and I are like planets sucked into Elaine's orbit. We spin around to keep her propped up. I don't know if I'd call them friends."

"Maybe they're doing the best they know. Give 'em time."

She blew out her breath and walked back to the chessboard. "So I protected my castle here, right?"

"Not exactly. It's a tough lesson. Even if you hide on the edge of the chessboard—or the edge of life—you can't avoid the action." He picked up his knight and knocked over her castle.

She tossed her head back. "No!"

Dad roared, but not a cry of victory. It was laughter filled with love.

Call me bored, Deb mumbled.

At the front of his classroom, Rolly Tolly's mustache wiggled. "I'll re-PEAT my question. *Call me Ishmael.* What does the name in this opening line of *Moby Dick* imply?"

Call me bored! Deb wanted to shout, but she stuffed her comment.

Rolly Tolly's lecture on symbolism was as murky as the water the white whale skimmed through.

She wasn't the only one drowning in analogies. One desk over, Haddy was comatose. On the other side, Elaine fidgeted. Strange for Elaine. Usually she broke up Rolly Tolly's lectures with wisecracking.

When the bell sounded, Elaine sped toward the door. Deb and Haddy hurried to catch up.

"What's wrong?" Deb asked Elaine.

Elaine huddled up to make sure no one around them heard her. "The S-A-Ts. I'm about to wet my pants over them."

Haddy's eyes grew big. "*So* embarrassing."

"I didn't mean it literally. I frazzle over tests. Like I have to prove I *know* something."

"That's the point of a test," Deb said.

"But I *don't* know anything. And if I botch these, I can't get into college. Then I'm in big trouble with my father."

Dad's encouragement to give friendship a chance came to mind. "We could study together."

Elaine squinted. "I *hate* studying."

Haddy's Mary Janes did their little dance. "Elaine, yesterday you told us you have to go to some old army fort with your father for the weekend. What if we join you and study?"

Elaine's mouth widened. "Perfect. And bring your swimsuits. In case we have time."

Haddy clapped her hands. "This will be so cool. The Three Musketeers working together again." She put one hand out, palm down. "All for one?"

Elaine placed hers on top of Haddy's. "One for all. Deb, you in?"

Deb stared at their stacked hands. A weekend with no escape from these girls? Scare-y. But she'd try.

She placed her hand on the pile. "One for all."

CHAPTER 12

Fort Robinson

That Saturday on the drive to the fort, Deb kept picturing Dad's face when she'd asked permission to go to Fort Robinson. He'd gone pale. She'd added, "We'll be chaperoned by the principal and his assistant."

Dad had rustled his open newspaper. "I'm not concerned about chaperoning. I'm concerned you'll learn a whole lot more *from* the fort than you bargained for."

"What do you mean?"

He stared at the paper. "I wouldn't know where to begin." Sadness filled his voice.

What had he meant? She might find out soon, because Fort Robinson State Park lay ahead.

The principal turned his black Cadillac into a parking spot. A skinny man in a crisp suit leaned against a turquoise Chevy and waved at the principal's car.

Ruud pointed his cigar. "An art dealer—all the way from New York City to see *me*," he cackled to Mrs. Mykland next to him.

The principal's assistant gave a tiny nod.

From the back seat, Deb scanned the horizon. Nothing unusual here. Only an open field edged with brick buildings. A sign indicated those were old officers' quarters. In the distance, a stone pyramid stood alone. Whatever she was supposed to learn from this fort, she didn't get it yet.

She pushed the car door open and stepped out.

A faint sound reached her ears.

Drumbeats?

She surveyed the field. Nobody around.

The hollow beat came again.

Were her ears ringing?

Now rhythmic chants joined the drums.

"You hear that?" she asked Haddy and Elaine.

"Huh?" Haddy said.

"Come on, girls." Elaine signaled them forward.

Deb hustled to catch up with them, the sounds surrounding her. She reached one of the red-brick buildings and stepped onto its wide porch with white columns. The drumbeats and chanting stopped.

Deb looked back at the field.

Nothing.

Weird.

The girls hauled their luggage up the worn oak stairs to the second floor.

Elaine threw open her bag and pulled out her swimsuit. "Let's go kayaking."

"What about studying?" Deb asked.

Elaine laughed. "And ruin a good time? Never." She turned her back, shimmied into a neon-pink bikini and shot out the door.

"A little fun won't hurt," Haddy said. She stuffed her body into a checked, one-piece suit.

Deb pulled out her solid brown tank. "I'm not going to let Elaine get away with no studying. Let's ask her questions at the river."

"Worth a try," Haddy said, forcing the straps over her shoulders.

Downstairs, they joined Elaine, who peeked from the entryway into a spacious living room. Mrs. Mykland crouched in a corner alone, cradling a drink with both hands. The thin man leaned against the mantel, stirring his drink.

The principal held up his highball. "I wanted to get out of town to keep this quiet—"

"Father," Elaine interrupted, "we're going to the river."

He shook a finger at her. "All right. But don't you forget that college test prep."

Elaine bolted. "Of course."

Haddy followed. "Come on, Deb."

"In a minute." She waited in the entryway.

"Keeping this quiet," the principal continued, "until the right time." He caught sight of Deb and stopped. "What now?"

His abrupt manner startled her. "Wanted to thank you for bringing us."

He waved her away. "Sure."

She took off. Whatever secret the principal held, he wasn't spilling it until the girls split.

When Deb and Haddy reached the river, they spotted Elaine ripping her double-bladed paddle through the river. Her blond hair flew behind. "Catch me if you can."

Deb and Haddy pushed their kayaks off the shore.

Haddy panted. "I hope I can do this." She wedged her chubby hips into a craft. It wobbled. *"Aaaa-aa-aaaa!"* she cried. The kayak steadied, and she paddled like a nervous duck.

"I'm right behind you," Deb called. With quick strokes, she passed Haddy and caught up with Elaine. "You're not getting out of studying. What is *pi r squared*?"

"Uh, cake are round?"

"No!" Haddy yelled from behind, chopping at the water. "Pi is an irrational number."

Elaine forged ahead. "Totally irrational."

Deb leaned forward, taking deep strokes. "It's one of the most important mathematical constants."

Elaine shot away again. "How can it be constant if it's irrational?"

Deb followed her. "Don't change the subject. Repeat after me: Three point one four—"

"Five six seven eight." Elaine splashed both girls in rhythm with her counting.

"Oh, Elaine," Haddy shouted. *"You're* the irrational number!"

"Who's irrational?" Elaine shoved their kayaks and tipped them over.

"I can't swim!" Haddy screamed.

"I'll get you." Deb lunged toward Haddy. No problem rescuing her. The water was waist deep, and they emerged with a layer of mud stuck to their rears.

From her kayak, Elaine burst into guffaws. "You got butt facials."

Haddy's lip quivered. "She thinks she's so cool."

Anger flared inside Deb. "Let's show her."

Deb marched over to Elaine and grabbed her paddle. "Your bikini isn't pink for long."

Haddy picked up goo with both hands. "Elaine, your bossing days are over."

Haddy smashed silt onto Elaine's head, and it oozed onto her shoulders. Then Deb tipped Elaine's kayak.

"*Eeeeeee!*" Elaine shrieked, plunging into the water. She emerged with two fistfuls of mud and flung it at them.

Deb and Haddy picked up handfuls of muck, smeared it across Elaine's bare stomach, arms, and thighs, and pushed her back into the river.

"That'll teach her," Haddy said.

"If she's willing to be taught."

Elaine attacked again, and mud flew until all three called *uncle* and sat in the river exhaling a mixture of wheezing and laughter.

Deb untangled her wet braid from its hair tie, raised her face, and let the warm shower water rinse the mud off her body. She hoped that river fight had changed the balance of power between the girls. From now on, she and Haddy might not be pawns running to the aid of Queen Elaine every time she got into trouble.

She had to admit it, though. She loved being Elaine's rescuer, like in that World Lit presentation. Maybe Elaine used them because she feared she couldn't do anything without them. But she must be good at something besides wisecracking.

Deb toweled herself, pulled on a slim black tee-shirt and shorts, and joined Haddy on the floor in the girls' bedroom.

"Have some grilled cheese on Wonder Bread?" Haddy asked, wiping one hand on her sloppy orange tee while reaching for a sandwich with the other.

"You always have an appetite," Elaine scolded. She lowered a pink baby doll pajama top over her head.

"What do you mean?" Haddy's voice carried an edge.

Elaine's head quivered. "Nothing, I guess."

Deb grinned. Score one for Haddy. She'd stood her ground. "So get over here, Elaine, and help us with these sandwiches."

Elaine joined them on the floor and touched Deb's wet tresses. "You've got great hair."

Deb drew back. "Me?"

"Yeah. With curls, you'd stun the guys."

"Can't imagine that. And I don't know how to do anything but braid my hair."

Elaine lit up like movie marquee lights. "Then it's make-over time. Haddy, plug in my curlers. While they warm up, paint Deb's nails." She unzipped her cosmetics bag and tossed Haddy a bottle of polish. "Hot tomato."

Haddy caught it. "I've got a red lipstick that'll match."

Deb winced. "I don't know about this."

Elaine lodged a hand at her waist. "You afraid you'll get whitewashed?"

Deb stiffened. "You saying that being Indian isn't good enough?"

Haddy grabbed Deb's hand and began painting her thumbnail. "Don't be prickly. You'll still be Indian, even when you get all glammy. I mean, look at me. Practically a cover girl and I'm still Jewish as a bagel."

Elaine smirked. "Not exactly ready for *Seventeen*. How about I tame your hair with Dippity Do?"

Haddy clapped, smudging red polish on her fingers. "Be stupid to turn you down. You do style better than anyone. Come on, Deb."

"Well, maybe I could learn a little."

"Great!" Elaine grabbed a tweezer. She tilted Deb's face toward hers. "Hold still, and I'll pluck that hedge above your eyes."

Hedge? Why couldn't Elaine lose the smart mouth? Still, Deb had never seen her so focused. So confident. She thinned their eyebrows, teased their hair, and applied foundation, shadow, eyeliner, and blush. Then she placed both girls in front of a standing oval mirror and set her hands on their shoulders. "What do you say?"

Haddy giggled and did her little dance. "We're groo-vy."

Deb faced her reflection. She lifted her bright nails and touched her rosy cheek. Gone was the prairie tomboy. Before her stood a young woman whose red-lipped smile widened. She gave a slight shake of her head, and her hair bounced across her shoulders. "I look great."

"Wait until Simon sees you," Elaine said.

Deb's face heated. "I don't care a bit about Simon."

"That boy likes you." Haddy's voice turned sing-songy.

What if he really did? Worse yet, what if he didn't? She had to divert this conversation away from Simon before they teased her anymore. "How about we play a game?"

"Hearts?" Elaine said. "Because you're gonna break that poor boy's heart by summertime."

"Am not!" Deb insisted. "And I don't know how to play hearts."

Elaine shot to the door. "Haddy, explain the rules while I grab something." She banged down the stairs toward the kitchen.

"Okay." Haddy grabbed a deck of cards from her suitcase. "Hearts count against you. You don't want to take any hearts, like you know whose."

"Stop it!" Deb said.

"A little edgy, aren't you?" Haddy said as she shuffled the deck.

By the time Haddy ran through the rules, Elaine had crept back into the room with one arm behind her.

Haddy looked up. "What are you hiding?"

Elaine unveiled a slender bottle. "A little surprise."

Alcohol. Deb's mouth dried. She'd seen the effects of liquor around her reservation home. Staggering men. Battered women. Trembling children. She didn't want anything to do with that bottle.

Haddy slapped the cards onto the floor. "Elaine Ruud, you naughty girl. How did you get that?"

"My father has half his sheets blowing in the wind downstairs. He didn't even notice me in the kitchen."

"So do we drink it straight?" Haddy asked.

Elaine smirked. "It'd burn." She unscrewed the lid and poured some into her Coke. "I add a little, and it makes me happy." She took a sip. "See? No harm."

"Okay," Haddy said. "Hit me."

Elaine poured a swig into Haddy's drink.

Haddy took a gulp. "Don't taste a thing."

"Deb?" Elaine asked.

She raised her palm. "Pass."

"Why?" both girls asked.

She'd sound preachy if she tried to explain. Maybe if she took a little, they'd get off her back. "Only a bit."

Elaine tipped some into Deb's pop.

She sipped it and didn't taste anything.

"Okay. On to our game. Deb, the only time you want to take hearts is if you win them all in one hand. Then everyone else gets penalized—called shooting the moon."

"Got it," Deb said.

They played until Deb successfully shot the moon. Not hard. She'd held back from drinking. But shortly after midnight, Haddy couldn't shuffle the deck without spraying cards, and Elaine couldn't tell a heart from a diamond.

Haddy stumbled toward her bed. "You shot the stars, Deb. Anyway, I'm seeing stars." She collapsed into bed and her mouth opened with a snore.

"I'm shot, too," Elaine said. She crawled into her bed, shivered, and blinked out.

Deb collected the cards and set the deck on Haddy's nightstand.

Haddy tossed and snorted, tugging at her orange tee-shirt. She was like a roly-poly puppy, willing to do anything to make others happy.

Deb pulled the sheet up.

She turned to Elaine's bed. At school, Elaine acted invincible. But now, with her pink pajama top framing her porcelain skin, she looked as fragile as a hatchling.

Deb covered her shoulders.

She slid into bed and turned to her side. What a perfect day, except for the booze. But even though she'd succumbed to their pressure to drink, she'd proved she didn't have to lose control. As for Elaine and Haddy, maybe a hangover would do them some good.

She cradled her head. She still didn't know what Dad meant when he said she'd learn more than she bargained for *from* the fort. But she'd experienced something *at* the fort she never wanted to lose. Friendship. She could nestle in the cocoon of these Three Musketeers forever.

Outside the open window, a choir of cicadas sang a hypnotic *chrrrr-rrrr, chrrrr-rrrr*. Rhythmic, like drumbeats. Was that what she'd heard earlier?

Laughter came from the dining room below. Then the clink of glasses and the sound of feet on the wooden steps leading to the bedrooms.

"This'll show that school board who's progressive, won't it, Karin?" the principal said.

"Yes, Ivar." Mrs. Mykland's tiny voice cheeped.

The art dealer chuckled. "It'll raise your social standing."

"To new heights," the principal crowed.

One door closed. Then another.

New heights?

Before she wrapped her mind around this, drowsiness overtook her.

Then came the drums. And chants.

CHAPTER 13

Legacy

Deb jolted awake. Light streamed through the open window. A breeze rattled the knob of the curtain string against the sill. Was that the noise that prompted her to dream about drumbeats and Indian chants?

Haddy turned over and rubbed her temples. "*Oooooh.* I have cramps in my brains."

Elaine lifted herself to her elbows and squinted. "It'll pass."

Haddy pulled her pillow over her head. "Hope I pass first."

They needed something to get them going. "I'll make coffee," Deb said.

"And if you find my father downstairs . . . . " Elaine's voice drifted off.

"Not a word," Deb said. She dressed in a brown tee-shirt and slacks and descended the stairs to the kitchen. No one around, but a piece of lavender stationery stood propped between the salt and pepper shakers. A feminine script, addressed to Elaine. Deb left it in place.

She tossed an extra scoop of coffee into the pot. It had finished perking when Haddy and Elaine appeared, dressed but disheveled, their skin ghostly. "You look like corpses," Deb said.

Elaine blinked slowly. "Only the smell of coffee got me up. Where's my father?"

Deb handed her the note. "I think Mrs. Mykland left this."

Elaine fingered it. "Actually, it's from Father. He doesn't always talk to me directly. Goes through Mrs. Mykland. The stupid woman turns his commands into fancy notes."

She paused to read it. "They're jeeping with the New York creep. When they get back, we head home."

Haddy lifted her face from a steaming mug of coffee. "Who wants to go to the gift shop? Pops would never forgive me if I didn't check out their jewelry for ideas for our store."

"I'll go," Elaine said.

Deb hesitated. She still didn't understand what Dad said she'd learn *from* this fort. "You go ahead. I want to check out the museum."

"Then be a spoilsport," Elaine said.

Deb flicked her wrist at her. "I will."

She left the officers' quarters and hustled across the field.

Something slowed her steps. Like she was tromping through snow banks instead of low grass. That sound again. Chants. Drumbeats.

Her legs wobbled. She searched around.

Nothing.

Once she stepped off the field, the sound ended.

Weird.

Ahead lay a white clapboard building that housed the fort's museum. In the entry, a woman behind an oak desk motioned her to an exhibit room.

The wood floors creaked as Deb threaded among glass cases holding displays. Signs identified a soldier's blue coat and Springfield rifle. Nothing unusual.

But what was this? A cream-colored Indian ghost-dance shirt. Turquoise-beaded moccasins. A red-beaded amulet. What did that have to with this fort?

She leaned in to study a sepia photograph. A line of troops stood stiff at attention on the parade ground. The caption identified Fort Robinson as one of the largest military installations on the Northern Plains. Another photo revealed tipis in the distance. A headline shouted *SURRENDER*. The photo's caption read, *With the surren-*

der of Crazy Horse and his followers in May, 1877, at the Red Cloud Agency, the Sioux War ended.

Crazy Horse? A Native hero. She'd never paid attention to what he'd done. And Dad never talked about him. Come to think of it, he rarely talked about their history. When he did, he chose his words carefully.

Too carefully.

Who was Crazy Horse?

Her eyes traveled outside the museum window to the stone pyramid. What was that anyway?

She stepped outside onto what must have been the old parade ground. Her foot touched the grass, and the faint chanting and drumbeats started again. The sound was similar to powwows she'd attended that echoed chants of warriors celebrating legendary hunts and victories over enemies. But this carried an eerie mix of victory and sorrow. Yet no one was around.

So strange.

She strode to the pyramid and lifted her head skyward to its peak. It rose twice her height, its sides covered with jagged stones larger than her hand and mortared into place. She shielded her eyes from the sun and read the plaque embedded into the cement:

Chief Crazy Horse
Oglala War-Chief
Of the Sioux Nation
Killed Near This Spot
Sept. 5, 1877
A Great Chief
Of Heroic Character
He Fought To The Last
To Hold His Native Land
For The Indian People

She touched the monument with one hand.

A slight tingling.

She pressed both hands onto the cold stones.

Something passed through her fingers, flowing up her arms.

Energy?

The drumbeats and chants grew louder, piercing the sky. Her body vibrated with their rhythm. Still, she clung to the pyramid as though mortared into it.

Beep beep.

She jumped back.

Beep beep. The principal's car horn.

The chanting and drumbeats ceased.

Her body stilled.

"Time to go," Mr. Ruud called.

Across the parade ground, Elaine and Haddy sped from the gift shop with sacks.

Deb jogged over and joined them. "You wouldn't believe what just happened."

"And you wouldn't believe the shopping you missed out on," Haddy said.

"But—"

"Come on," Elaine interrupted. "Let's get our stuff."

"I was at that pyramid." Deb tried to stop them, but Haddy and Elaine were gone.

She caught up, and the three scurried to their room.

"I heard these drums," she said.

"And I thought I drank too much last night." Haddy said.

"Move it," Elaine said. "When Father wants to leave, we leave."

They threw their clothes into bags and carried them to the principal's Caddy. They said a polite goodbye to the art dealer, while the principal pumped his hand and chuckled about "my little secret."

Clutching her purse and silent as usual, Mrs. Mykland climbed into the front seat next to the principal. The girls took the back.

Deb scrunched against the door and craned her neck to view the stone pyramid. What happened out there?

"Look what I found in the gift shop," Haddy broke in. "A bracelet made out of hematite, whatever that is."

Deb continued to stare at the parade ground. "Nice."

"Our studying for the S-A-Ts really helped," Elaine said loud enough so her father would hear.

"That's my girl," the principal called from the front. "We'll get you into college yet."

Elaine lowered her head. "We've *got* to plan another trip here," she whispered. "I had a blast."

Haddy clapped. "How about right after we graduate? Won't that be perfect, Deb? Earth to Deb. Come in."

"Huh? Sure. I was wondering why Crazy Horse got killed—"

"Wish I'd bought one of those bracelets," Elaine said.

Deb opened her mouth to say more about Crazy Horse, then gave up. She turned her head toward the back window. The stone pyramid and the army outpost grew smaller, then disappeared.

From outside their basement apartment, Deb peered into a window and caught sight of Dad with the *Argus Leader* covering his face. She turned the doorknob slowly and tiptoed in. "Notice anything?"

Dad lowered the paper.

She patted her bouffant 'do.

He bolted up. "And cosmetics, too. You look more like your mother all the time."

She gave a slight bow. "I know a compliment when I hear one."

He gave her a sideways hug. "It's great your friends help you with things like this. I can't."

Deb leaned into his embrace, then pulled back. "Wait. What's the deal with Crazy Horse?"

Dad's smile disappeared. "What did you learn?"

"I already knew there's a monument being carved of him in the Black Hills, but never paid any attention to it. How'd he get killed at Fort Robinson?"

Dad slumped at the card table that held his chess board. His face turned vacant, and his hand grazed a bishop. "I've tried to protect you. Didn't want you to hate whites."

Deb sat across from him. "What do you mean?"

"Hate sets us back." He took a deep breath. "This is what *Tunkasila* passed on to me. Grandfather said life was perfect in the buffalo days. Honor the land. Follow the bison."

He focused on the rosewood bishop in his hand, then picked up a white maple bishop and squared them off on the board. "Then another civilization arrived. Not a superior one, but more powerful. One that believed God ordained America to expand by any means. Even when it meant *stealing* land." He lifted the lighter-colored bishop and struck it against the rosewood one. The rosewood piece clattered off the board, landing on its side.

Dad moved the front row of maple pawns forward toward Deb, then advanced the front row of rosewood pawns to face the white ones. "But they couldn't move our warriors out, so the army forced a peace treaty on us."

He faced off two rooks, a rosewood and a white one. "The treaty created The Great Sioux Reserve, all of western South Dakota, including *Paha Sapa,* the Black Hills—the center of our spiritual world, where Heaven touches Earth." His eyes riveted Deb's. "Whites weren't supposed to enter."

"Then why don't we own the Hills now?" Her voice held a tension she didn't know she carried.

"Whites heard rumors of gold in the Black Hills." His voice slipped to a whisper.

Deb leaned closer to hear.

Dad held up a white knight on his horse. "That brought the army's hero, George Armstrong Custer, onto the scene."

He said the name with scorn she'd never heard in his voice.

"Custer took a thousand men in search of gold. When they found it, whites flooded our land." He advanced the white pawns across the board.

"What happened to liberty and justice for all?" Her voice surprised her with its panic.

Dad sat back and rubbed his forehead. "An inconvenient concept. The government offered us six million dollars for *Paha Sapa*. A pittance compared to the billion dollars worth of gold mined from those hills. But we refused to sell. Gold meant nothing to us. All we wanted was to steward the land our Creator gave us. What could the United States do? It couldn't defeat us. Couldn't buy our land. So the government *forced* all Native Americans to move onto reservations."

"Like Pine Ridge." Images of its poverty and desperation flashed through her mind.

Dad cleared some rosewood pieces off the board and left the maple knight on his horse at the front of the other white pieces.

"Camp Robinson was an outpost for one such agency to oversee natives. The official government policy for Indians who refused to move to a reservation? *Exterminate* them."

She gasped. "Like Hitler?"

He dipped his head. "Different methodology. Same results."

"Did Crazy Horse fight back?" Her question tumbled out.

"Did he ever. He gathered our people for one final battle. Custer intended to score a victory to get himself elected president—all he cared about." He held up a rosewood knight mounted on his horse. "But with the rallying cry of *ho-ka hey*—get 'em—Crazy Horse and his warriors killed that Long Hair and his Blue Coats." With the back of his hand Dad swept the row of white pawns and their knight from the board. "Custer's Last Stand."

"Victory!" Deb let out a cry.

Dad's sad stare pierced her. "But we'd lost our way of life. Whites had over-hunted the bison. We were starving."

She clutched the table. "What did we do?"

He lined up rosewood pawns with their knight in the lead. "No choice. Crazy Horse led nearly nine hundred of our people into Camp Robinson. The warriors, women, and children stretched out for two miles. Near the outpost, the natives began chanting, filling the White River Valley with their cries."

Chanting! The sound at the fort. Deb scrunched her eyes and pictured the valley filled with warriors. The rhythmic drumbeats and cries resonated in her head again. She stood. Her body quivered.

"Thousands of Indians already at the agency joined them, lining the route." Dad's voice rose. "What was supposed to be a surrender turned into a victory march."

The chanting and drumbeats filled Deb's body, coursing through her veins until she feared she'd burst.

Dad heaved a sigh, and the chants and drumbeats ceased.

Deb forced her eyes open. The room spun until she found her balance.

Dad stood by her. "Crazy Horse was too charismatic to keep around. The cavalry planned to ship him to prison, bound with a ball and chain. When Crazy Horse got wind of it, he drew a knife. A sentry bayoneted him." Dad reached down to the chess board, lifted a white pawn, and knocked over the rosewood knight with it. The knight tumbled to the floor, breaking off from his horse.

Deb picked up the pieces and clasped them in her palms.

Dad placed his hands over hers. "The Lakota were no longer free."

His grip tightened.

Something passed between them.

Something from his soul into hers.

"Do you understand, *Winyanyatapi?*" His voice held more of a plea than a question. "Do you understand, Princess?"

Her heart beat like a drum, throbbing so hard she feared it would explode. The pulse of legacy, the burden of responsibility, overwhelmed her.

She *must* get to college.

It had nothing to do with her.

It had everything to do with her people.

All those who came before.

Who didn't have this opportunity.

The legacy of Crazy Horse filled her. She couldn't let him down.

CHAPTER 14

Lounge War

Professionals? Will couldn't believe the war swirling amidst the smoke and stench of tobacco in the teachers' lounge. A cat fight like he'd never witnessed, and between two sisters.

To Will's right, Ronnette Sherwood, the obvious younger, stood and braced her hands on her curvy hips, right at Will's eye level. She faced her sibling. "It's simple. I need costumes for my swim program. Your Home Ec girls can whip 'em up."

To Will's left, Lena Sherwood faced her, crossing her arms at her ample middle, also at Will's eye level. She peered over thick glasses that curved up at the ends like bird wings threatening to carry her away. "No way. Not after you stole the beauty contest from me."

"Stole it nothing! "I won it fair and square." Ronnette shot back, leaning forward until the contents of her tight sweater threatened to tumble out in front of Will.

Will blinked twice.

"Fair?" Lena shot back. "I wore a boatneck, while your suit plunged down to your belly button. The judges salivated like you were a sirloin. Fitting, since it was the Miss Meatpacker Beauty Pageant. And now you want me to sew for you? Not a stitch."

Both women whipped their heads to Principal Ruud, begging for a referee.

Ruud cackled and sat back. "I'll let you *ladies* settle this."

Ronnette turned to Lena. "Go stew in *lutefisk*." She stomped out.

Lena headed the other direction down the hall. "Just because you're the cute one doesn't mean you always get your way."

Principal Ruud laughed until his double chins tripled. He flicked cigar ashes onto the floor and followed Lena. "If you're not helping with costumes, you must have spare time, and I need backup in the library."

Mrs. Mykland pulled a white hankie from her purse and scooped up the ashes. "Excuse me," she whispered, stepping by Will. She trailed after the principal.

Will rubbed his jaw. So this was socializing in the principal's lounge? Ridiculous.

But he'd come here to appease the principal. And to keep Deb in this school.

CHAPTER 15

Enchanted Forest

On Deb's walk home from school, the wind gusted and threatened to lift her skirt. She bent into the blast, holding the plaid pleats down while maneuvering books in her other arm.

"Wait up, Deb."

She turned back to Haddy's voice while red oak leaves scudded against her legs.

Haddy reached Deb and struggled to catch her breath. "Elaine's in trouble."

"Again?"

"She landed the part of the fairy queen in the Synchronettes show."

"She didn't show any swimming talent at the fort."

"Skinny Sherwood chose her."

"Who?"

"Ronnette Sherwood, the faculty advisor." Haddy peeked around to make sure students hustling by them didn't hear. "What choice did Ronnette have, Elaine being the principal's daughter? Anyway, the swimmers have to come up with their own costumes. You heard Fat Sherwood—Ronnette's sister—announce in Home Ec we aren't going to make them."

"How's that a problem?"

"Elaine couldn't sew a straight seam if her life depended on it. So I'll make her costumes. But she's unglued about her swim routine. You've got to help."

"I don't know anything about synchronized swimming."

"Don't need to. Follow the script and go over the moves. She'll get it."

"But I've gotta focus on my grades."

"What about our vow?" She placed one hand forward with her palm turned down. "All for one?"

"Why is Elaine always *the one*?"

Haddy's face filled with tenderness. "She doesn't have anybody else to help her. Not even a mom."

A pang edged Deb's heart. She knew that feeling. "Okay, as long as I don't have to attend rehearsals."

Haddy danced in place. "This'll be so fun! Call Elaine and tell her, okay?"

She sighed. "Sure."

At home, Deb fingered her troll doll with its pudgy cheeks and long black hair—Elaine's gift of friendship. Helping her would be one way to give back.

She found Elaine's phone number in the school's Buzz Book and dialed. "Elaine?"

"Yeah?"

"I'll go over your swim routine with you while we walk between classes. But nothing after school."

Elaine shrieked. "You're a lifesaver. But maybe come to one rehearsal?"

"Only one."

"A couple? There's a lot of scenes."

"Maybe. Gotta study now."

Deb hung up the phone. She fiddled with her troll doll. Its bulging eyes stared at her, and she bulged hers back. Was she nothing but a white girl's good luck charm?

Helping Elaine didn't go as planned. Rehearsals turned into more than a couple and stretched into evenings.

Often Deb got home long after Dad was in bed. She would settle in at the card table, and Franklin would curl around her books, purring. One night she nodded off, her cheek nestled against Franklin's ivory fur. Dad nudged them awake in the morning.

Although dazed with fatigue, she had to admit it— seeing a show come together was exciting. And without trying, she'd memorized the entire narrator's script of "Enchanted Forest."

But everything turned awkward when Simon joined the crew to run the show's audio. Deb avoided him. She didn't want another *Ke-mo-sah-bee* moment.

The night of the show, Deb and Dad found seats on the first row of bleachers facing the pool. Erik sprawled a few rows above, probably there to ogle Elaine. Across the pool, Mr. Brown helped Barry set up a microphone. On the other side, Simon sat on a folding chair by a boxy reel-to-reel tape player. He caught Deb's eye.

She turned away, pretending she hadn't seen him.

"Where's Haddy?" Dad asked.

"Helping with costumes." She checked her watch. "The show should start any time."

Just then Haddy emerged, searching the crowd. She scurried to Deb. "You've got to help! The narrator puked all over the elves. We hosed 'em off. But we need a narrator!"

"I can't—"

"You know that script forwards and back." She grabbed Deb's hand.

Deb stayed glued to her seat.

Dad grinned. "You can do it."

"Come on," Haddy said, yanking at her arm.

"I don't know," Deb said, pulled forward.

In the locker room, the narrator crouched on her knees, retching into a toilet. Miss Sherwood, the skinny one, sat on the gray linoleum in another stall, her legs splayed, her face chalk white. Elaine hovered over her, fanning her with a swimsuit.

"But-" Deb said.

"No buts." Haddy stripped Deb's shirt off and threaded her arms into the puffy sleeves of a white blouse.

A putrid smell hit Deb's nose. "This stinks."

"Be glad she hurled on only one arm. We wiped it off." Haddy pulled a black skirt over Deb's head and forced it down to her hips. She tied a white apron around her waist and pulled a red embroidered vest on her. Then she folded Deb's hair into a blond wig with braids and crowned it with an embroidered red cap. "There."

Deb faced her reflection in the mirror. "I look like a Scandinavian Barbie."

"A Norwegian storyteller," Haddy said.

"What if I blow it?"

Elaine wrapped an arm around her shoulder. Her lip trembled. "I *need* you to do this, or the program's dead and I'm dead."

Deb swallowed a lump of fear. "Okay."

She straightened the line of buttons on the vest, then hustled to the edge of the pool. She fumbled with the microphone. "Test?"

Screech. Her voice screamed.

She jerked away and searched the room for Mr. Brown.

A sea of faces stared back, waiting.

Mr. Brown waved from across the pool, his white teeth flashing against his black skin. He adjusted the sound system while Barry dimmed the house lights and aimed a spotlight on Deb.

Her hands went clammy.

"Go for it," a voice behind her whispered.

She glanced back.

Simon hunched over the tape player, his face a wide grin.

Her heart calmed.

Deb turned back to the mic and dared to open her mouth. "Long ago . . . . " Her voice quivered.

Barry ran a wide beam across the empty pool, and it danced on the water.

"In an enchanted forest . . . ." Her voice steadied. "Fairies lived, as gentle as the breeze on a summer's day." Simon clicked on the tape player. Airy tones of flutes and clarinets drifted across the room.

Swimmers tiptoed from the lockers, slipped into the pool, and positioned themselves in a wide oval.

Barry fumbled with the floodlight until he secured a blue plastic lens across it. The room took on a somber feel.

Deb lowered her voice. "Even in an isolated forest, winds of change may blow in."

Violins overtook the flutes, swirling up and down the scale. The swimming fairies entwined arms and moved in a circle.

Barry flipped the light to green. Swimmers moved in and out of poses as Deb told stories about dwarves, elves, and bewitching spells.

The climax approached. Deb forced more power into her voice. "Trees cast their dead leaves aside and dressed in a wardrobe of soft buds. The forest dwellers crowned a queen, the one who preserved them from dying." She gestured toward the pool's edge.

A yellow spotlight hit Elaine. She stood alone, dressed in a gold sequined suit and a sparkling crown.

The crowd gasped. So did Deb. This was Elaine's moment, and she relished it. Back arched, arms above her head, she lifted onto her toes and dove into the pool. She emerged in the circle of swimmers, who raised her aloft. Her face glowed. The music crescendoed, undergirded by trumpets and tympani.

Barry cut the spotlight.

Darkness.

A hush.

The houselights came up. The audience rose to its feet in applause. Erik wolf-whistled Elaine. She threw kisses all around.

Deb sought Dad's face in the crowd.

He pumped his arms in a wide clap.

"Way to go." A voice came from behind her. *Simon.* She turned to him.

He gave her a thumbs up.

She offered a slight nod before turning back to the pool. Elaine and the rest of the Synchronettes took their bows, then gathered around Deb. "You saved us!"

Haddy rushed to her. "I knew you'd do it!"

"I didn't think I could."

Elaine grabbed Deb by the wrist. "But you didn't know the narrator always gets dunked!" Other Synchronettes joined in, dragging her and pushing her into the deep end.

A swoosh of cold hit Deb, and her black skirt parachuted around her.

Deb swam to the pool's edge, where Elaine helped pull her out. Deb balled her fists. "Elaine Ruud." Then laughter rolled out of her. "That's the most fun I've ever had."

Elaine threw her arms around Deb, joined by other swim team members and Haddy. "We'll find something for you to change into," Elaine said.

They swept Deb away in a circle of love.

CHAPTER 16

Threat

Will's palms burned from his clapping at the edge of the pool. Deb performed! This might pull her out of her shyness.

"Mr. Running Bear?" A voice interrupted his euphoria. A man near him gripped a notepad and rested a pen behind his ear.

"Yes."

"I'm Lars Lundy."

Ah, the father of Jord, the least confident student he'd ever taught. Will offered his hand. "Jord's doing fine in class."

Lundy didn't shake Will's hand. "He doesn't believe in himself."

"All he needs is some success under his belt. Then he'll skyrocket."

"Unless he fizzles first."

A bizarre thing for a father to say.

"You gotta help him," Lundy said. "You mean the world to him."

Will ran his hand across his jaw. "I'm happy to."

From the corner of his eye, Will glimpsed Ivar Ruud swaggering toward them.

"Listen," Lundy said, "I'm a reporter for the *Argus*. I wanna interview you about that Roman village you're building. But I gotta bend the principal's ear first."

A newspaper article? That would be a huge boost for the boys. "I'll wait here."

Lundy waved a hand toward the principal. "Mr. Ruud, what do you have to say about your daughter's performance?"

Ruud lifted his chin. "Excellent, like her old man."

Will turned aside so they wouldn't see him struggling to hide his laugh.

"But I've got something more important to talk about," Ruud continued. "A secret to revolutionize our school's education."

Their school? Will leaned in a bit.

Lundy reached for the pen behind his ear and pushed his notepad open. "Tell me."

"Not yet. I'll reveal it in the spring."

"Give me a clue."

"All right. It'll be *monumental*. And don't quote me on this—" Ruud waggled a finger "—but it'll satisfy those school board morons. I'll leak more to you later." He hoisted up his trousers and swaggered off.

Will turned back toward the reporter.

"Wonder what he's up to." Lundy said. "Board's been on him to modernize. He sweat like a stuck pig at the last meeting. Anyway, his *secret* will add intrigue to this story. Now about your Shop project."

Will's pulse quickened. "Yes?"

Lundy checked his watch, then he slapped his notepad shut. "Sorry, I gotta get to the planning commission. Probably last 'til midnight. Then I'll be up before dawn, checking the police blotter. I'll try to catch you later."

Will released a weak puff of air. It looked like this opportunity was evaporating. "You're an important man."

Lundy laughed. "Like anyone notices. I make all the social climbers around here look good by giving 'em thirty-six-point headlines, while my name's buried in a ten-point byline. I don't want my boy to get overlooked like I am."

"I'll do whatever I can to help Jord."

Lundy aimed his pen at Will. "I'm counting on you." He forced his jacket zipper up and hurried toward the door.

Two women dressed like carbon copies of calico dowdiness blocked the way of the reporter. "Mr. Lundy," the older one said. "We're here to express a community concern."

"Another time, Miss Aasgard." He spewed out her name like a toxin and forced his way between them.

The women clutched their identical handbags and turned away. "Disrespectful."

Will shook his head. Strange man. And strange women. Not like anyone he and Deb knew from the reservation. But tonight, their move here had been worth it. In that swim show, Deb shone like a full moon on a cloudless night.

Something bothered him, though. The way Lundy said he was *counting* on Will to help Jord. Sounded like a threat.

CHAPTER 17

Romeo and Juliet

Reading about Mesopotamia was as dull as plain oatmeal, yet Deb had twenty more pages to get through tonight. Coach Mykland wouldn't make it any more exciting with another mind-numbing lecture tomorrow in World History.

With all the rehearsals for Synchronettes, this was the first time in weeks she'd been home before supper. She peered out the window of their basement apartment toward the driveway. Still no newspaper.

Across the room, Dad stooped over the card table he'd covered with newspapers. With a sock over one hand, he rubbed black polish on his shoes.

"How come you shine your shoes so often these days?" she asked.

"A matter of pride."

"Coach Mykland's shoes could blind a person."

Dad slowed his polishing. "Mine may not be as bright, but I polish them myself. That's all I'll say about that."

"Got it."

From the edge of her eye, Deb glimpsed the newsboy tossing a paper as he pedaled by. She raced out the door, retrieved it, and dashed back. She worked the rubber band off the bundle. "You think the swim program will be in here?"

Will crowded next to her. "Let's see. There it is." He pointed with his sock-covered hand.

Principal Hints at Education Change,
Comments Come after Swim Show

"What's that about?" Deb asked.

"Looks like Mr. Lundy highlighted something else."

"After all our work?" She bent over the paper and read:

Washington High School principal Ivar Ruud revealed last night he has a monumental surprise to revolutionize education . . . .

"Where's it talk about our swim show?" Deb asked.

Dad scanned ahead. "Buried down here."

Deb searched the column:

Ruud made his comments following the Washington High School Synchronettes swim show last night at the YWCA. In the production Enchanted Forest, Elaine Ruud carried the role of a fairy queen. Other participants included . . . .

Deb speed-read the cast list. There she was:

Deborah Running Bear, Narrator

She grinned. "Outta sight."

Dad set a hand on her shoulder. "I couldn't be more proud."

She giggled and moved away from him. "Watch the shoe polish."

"Oh, sorry." He removed the sock from his hand and gave her a sideways hug.

His embrace warmed her. "That show was a blast. And my grades didn't suffer."

"You counted coup."

"Huh?"

"You know, the Indian way of saying you accomplished something prestigious. And in this case, it's something you can add to a scholarship application. They look for those things."

"No kidding? What if I get a role in the class play? Would that be counting coup?"

"You bet."

She stared down at the orange shag carpet. "I wasn't sure I should try out."

"Why not?"

"You always talk about teamwork."

"Part of our culture."

"Then how do I know when to go for something for myself? Elaine's auditioning. If she gets a part, she'll want help with lines."

Dad lifted her chin. "It's a great accomplishment to succeed gracefully while still encouraging others. Then you aren't letting anyone down, including yourself."

He returned to polishing his shoes and did something she hadn't seen in years. Not since Mom died. He sang a line from the record her parents played about sitting under an apple tree with your true love. Dad's eyes flashed, and his stocking feet moved in a dance.

Dad's singing slipped to the back of her mind as she sat. What he'd said about not letting herself down? She hadn't thought about that. What if she and Elaine both got parts in the play? She could still help Elaine with lines.

Her heartbeat quickened. Was this legacy pulsing through her veins? Must be.

If it wasn't, would she make a fool of herself?

Deb's stomach roiled like she'd contracted the flu. But this wasn't a virus. This was show biz. Auditions!

One desk over, Elaine's face exuded a veneer of calm, but she drummed her ruby-red fingernails on her desk. She'd turned livid when her father upstaged her in the newspaper article. She was determined to get a part in the play.

"We live in a time of FAC-tions." Rolly Tolly's voice rang out, breaking Deb's thoughts. "Hawks and doves, those who sup-PORT the Vietnam War. Those who oppose it. Romeo and Juliet lived in hostile times, too. Theirs is a story of *star-cross'd lovers* bringing together two warring families. To portray this, I must find protagonists who exude CHEM-is-try. Who will read first?"

Deb inched her hand up.

Elaine flung hers into the air. "I will."

Erik's arm shot up. "Then I'm in."

Rolly Tolly smiled and held up scripts. "Come on up."

Deb's heart collapsed. Elaine might grab the role of Juliet before she had a chance. But Dad's admonition to offer encouragement came to mind, and she gave Elaine a nod.

Elaine wiggle-walked to the front. Erik followed with his swagger, his elbows jabbing guys along the way.

"Let's skip to something to show your mettle," Rolly Tolly said. "I've marked the BAL-cony scene. Elaine, start here." He tapped on the page. "Erik, jump in there."

The two took their places. Elaine flipped her blond hair off her shoulders and giggled. "Okay. Here goes. *O Romeo, Romeo! wherefore art thou Romeo?*"

She sounded like a wind-up toy.

Erik's face paled like all his blood had drained into his Ked's.

"He's goin' down," Simon whispered from his seat.

"You all right?" Rolly Tolly asked Erik.

He grabbed at his collar. "Need to catch my breath."

This was too funny. Deb couldn't be upset anymore.

"Then we'll continue," Rolly Tolly said.

Elaine opened her mouth to finish her lines, but Erik bolted in. "*Shall I hear more, or shall I speak at this?*"

"Cut!" Rolly Tolly said, waving his hands. "I shall speak at this. It's not your turn yet."

Erik's face turned as red as his hair. "Sorry."

The class snickered.

Rolly Tolly rubbed his eyes. "I know you two pretty well from class assignments. I have a general understanding of your po-TEN-tial. Who else wants to read?"

Deb jerked her arm into the air. Then a wave of terror rolled over her.

"Now I need a Romeo," Rolly Tolly said.

Across the room, Simon's hand flew up.

Electricity surged through Deb.

A group "*ooooo*" trickled through the room.

CHAPTER 18

Cold War

A chill ran through Will. Must be frostbite from the Cold War in this teachers' lounge. Through the haze of cigarette smoke, the two Sherwood sisters glared at each other from opposite sides of the room, their arms crossed.

Harley Hart smoothed his butterscotch hair into place and leaned toward Ronnette Sherwood. "Nice swim performance."

She flicked her fingers, her flamingo nails flashing. "In spite of not getting a *stitch* of help from Lena."

Lena lurched forward. Her eyes bugged through her thick lenses. "I wouldn't waste creativity on your cheap costumes."

Will anticipated the usual guffaw from Principal Ruud, but it didn't come. Instead, the principal bent across Will toward Roland Tollefson. "How'd the auditions go?"

Tollefson's mustache twitched. "I see POSS-i-bi-li-ty. Deborah and Simon are good."

Will's heart hammered.

The principal continued to lean over Will. "Be a feather in my cap if Elaine got the lead. She needs a boost to get into college."

Tollefson studied the ceiling.

The principal puffed on his cigar, releasing smoke on Will. "And Erik, the police chief's son, he's a Romeo if I ever met one. His father and I—"

"Go way back to the war." Tollefson finished his sentence.

"You understand?"

"Got it."

"Good."

An explosion threatened to burst out of Will. He wanted to call Ruud a bloviating autocrat without a shred of moral fiber. The principal wouldn't have a clue what that meant, but the eruption would cost Will his job.

He bit back his words.

Ruud cackled and crushed his cigar on the floor with his shoe. He stared at Will. "Your face is even redder than usual."

Will's stomach twisted.

The principal sauntered out.

"Excuse me," Mrs. Mykland whispered, cleaning up the stogie, then following Ruud.

Will studied the terrazzo tile, a confusion of orange-and-black colors.

No one said anything. Everyone else filed out, as quiet as though exiting a funeral parlor.

Will scratched at his jawline. What had he done? He'd hoped Deb's senior year would open doors for her. Now, when she'd dared to peek into one, it slammed in her face. What kind of a father was he, bringing her into this dysfunction?

Of course he didn't know for sure Deb would have landed the part of Juliet. But on a level playing field, she might have.

And she'd want to know why she didn't get it.

CHAPTER 19

Washingtonia

"**O**uch!" Deb screamed. Pain seared her hands, and she lost control of the meatloaf she was lifting out of the oven with hot pads. It plopped from the pan onto the gray linoleum.

From the living room, the apartment door opened. "I'm home," Dad called.

Great. Now to face him with not only one failure, but two.

Dad entered the kitchen. "How's supper coming?"

Deb splayed her stinging fingers. "Burned myself."

Dad gasped, and he pushed her hands under the faucet and ran cold water. "Hold them there while I rescue the meatloaf."

Water sprayed over her fingers. Heat lifted off them, but didn't remove the wrenching in her stomach.

Dad grabbed the potholders and a spatula and retrieved the loaf before Franklin pounced on it. "Supper's okay. But how're your hands?" He turned off the water and examined her fingers.

They throbbed. "Fine," she forced out.

"Maybe they're fine, but you're not. What's wrong?"

The volcano she'd held inside broke loose. "Rolly Tolly gave Erik and Elaine the roles of Romeo and Juliet. But Elaine stunk. And the only reason Erik tried out is to get to kiss her. Simon and I read. We were lots better. And then . . . ."

Sobs shook her.

"Then what?"

"Rolly Tolly appointed Simon and me understudies. We have to learn *all* the lines. We have to go to *all* the rehearsals. But we never play the parts. I don't know what happened. I heard the drums."

"What?"

"Like when you told me about Crazy Horse. Drums beat inside me, so I thought I should audition."

Dad pulled a handkerchief from his pocket and handed it to her.

She blew so hard her brains ached.

Sadness filled Dad's face. "Drums, huh. God's way of telling you to go for this?"

"Then why didn't I get the part?"

He placed an arm on her shoulder. "Some things we can't understand. But I'd say Mr. Tollefson handed you and Simon a huge compliment. He knew he could count on you."

Her eyes filled until the kitchen blurred. "This won't help me get a scholarship. I hate Elaine."

Several weeks later after school, Deb slumped at a table in the library, the only room in this prison where she could hide in a book and be alone. Clouds floated across the two-story arched windows, giving her the illusion she was back on the prairie, propped against a tree.

But only an illusion.

What was she doing here?

The chair next to her scraped across the floor, and Haddy flopped down. "Elaine's in trouble."

The last thing Deb wanted to hear.

"*Big* trouble," Haddy said loud enough that students lifted their heads from books and stared.

"No surprise," Deb whispered. "Elaine chokes if she isn't glued to her script at rehearsal."

"You've *got* to help her."

"Got to?" Her voice rose.

Students gawked.

She moved closer to Haddy. "It's hard enough to be nice when she gloats about getting the part. Now I'm supposed to help her?"

"Come on. We're her only friends. Remember our vow to stick together?"

Deb folded her arms. "I don't care about that stupid vow."

"Then you better have something to say to Elaine, 'cause here she comes."

Elaine strutted toward them, her mouth in a conniving grin. She eased into a chair beside them.

Deb straightened, but before she said anything, her attention shifted to the library entrance. Dad held one door open while Simon propped the other.

"Take her in easy, boys," Dad said.

The Shop guys wrangled in a bulky structure.

"It's their Roman city," Deb said. And I perfect way to avoid Elaine. "I wanna check it out."

She bolted up, but Elaine and Haddy followed. They gathered around as the boys set it on an empty table. It spread out about five-feet square on a piece of plywood.

Deb spotted a line of interconnected straws that ran through the model. "What's that?"

Simon slipped next to her. "The aqueduct system."

"Oh." She kept herself from looking at him.

"And that's the amphitheater," Erik said in a voice loud enough to attract more students. "The seats are made of stir sticks. Those colonnades and the parapet? Sugar cubes. Won't mention where we got 'em."

Deb chuckled. Everyone knew where they got 'em.

A magazine slapped on a table near them, and Coach Mykland marched over. "What's going on?"

Dad stepped forward. "Mr. Lundy is coming to get a photo of Washingtonia, our Roman village."

Mykland thrust his thumb at his chest. "I'm the history teacher."

Deb and other students shrank back, but Dad held his ground. "This project taught basic building skills—as well as history."

Mykland's face reddened. He stormed toward the door as Principal Ruud and Mr. Lundy entered. "Ruud, why'd that redskin get to make this?" Mykland asked.

Deb gasped.

Dad's face quivered.

The principal lowered his head toward Mykland. "Don't take this up now," he muttered.

Mykland cast darts at Dad, then stomped out.

Ruud moved Mr. Lundy forward. ""So this is what *my* progressive education produces."

Dad's eyes narrowed. Deb recognized the look. He was ticked, but he maintained a slight smile.

"Running Bear," the principal said, "you and your boys move along. Except Erik. He stays for the photo."

Erik beamed.

"But the whole class built this," Dad said.

The principal flicked his hand. "Doesn't matter."

Dad's lips drew into a tight line.

Lundy wrestled his camera out of its bag. "I want my son in there, too."

Jord backed off. "Let me outta here."

Dad stopped him. "Go for it, Jord. It's your work, too."

"If we have to include him," Ruud mumbled. He planted himself between Jord and Erik and braced his arms on the boys' shoulders. "Give us a front-page photo, Lundy."

Jord grimaced, Erik grinned, and the camera flash popped.

Dad herded the rest of his boys to the door. "You all did a tremendous job," he mumbled.

Why didn't Dad stand up for himself? Deb toed the scratched wood floor. It carried the scars of thousands of students who had passed through this school. Many had gone to college and moved into careers. Dad had said it was important to be here so a college might notice her.

That must be why he put up with this junk. If that was the case, she'd put up with it, too.

She walked back to Elaine, who doodled at a table. "I'll help you with your lines."

CHAPTER 20

Tragicomedy

In the hallway, Will's students dispersed, except for Simon and Barry. "Mr. Running Bear, what are we going to build next?" Simon asked.

"Ah, I'll announce that at our next class."

"Looking forward to it." Barry said.

The two boys headed down the hall.

What *would* they build?

Roland Tollefson approached, nearly running down Will. "What to DO? WHAT to do? I don't know how to build the *Romeo and Juliet* set. Or paint it. And I don't have anyone for costumes.

Will's pulse quickened. "My boys could build your set if we had tools."

"Steve's father from Widget Hardware might have store models you could use."

Will snapped his fingers. "And Ruud might kick in money for lumber since Elaine's got the lead."

"A SHOO-in."

"What about Valmar Dahl's Art students for painting? And Lena Sherwood's Home Ec girls for costumes?"

Tollefson shook his head. "Ruud has them on dou-ble-DU-ty already, Valmar with Band and Lena with library. All the faculty's spread thin doing things they don't like, not getting to do what they want."

"I know how the principal gets away with that. But what if I told Valmar and Lena they could run with their passions on this project?"

Tollefson's mustache twitched. "That could work."

The next day, Deb positioned herself on stage, a script in her hand. She surveyed the dim auditorium and visualized it packed. Rolly Tolly said the room seated seventeen hundred. She imagined delivering Juliet's lines to that crowd. *She* should be the one.

"Where'd you go, space cadet?" Elaine asked from her side, cracking her gum.

Behind them, Haddy sat cross-legged, hand-sewing faux jewels on a costume.

"Got lost for a minute." She focused back to the task at hand. "Elaine, you still sound flat. Don't forget, Juliet has feelings. Her mother wants to hitch her up with this other guy. But when Juliet meets Romeo, she can hardly breathe. So what does she want from her mother?"

"A glass slipper?"

Deb laughed. She couldn't resist Elaine's wacky humor, and the tension she'd been holding evaporated. "Wrong story. Juliet wants respect. R-E-S-P-E-C-T," she sang, riffing Aretha Franklin's hit song.

Haddy answered from behind with the *sock-it-to-me* refrain. She hustled to center stage, waving a strand of lace, and led the girls through the song.

At the end, the three collapsed in giggles and wrapped their arms around each other.

Haddy struggled to speak through her chortles. "I'm craffing."

"You're what?" Elaine asked.

"Laughing so hard I'm crying."

A spasm of delight overcame Deb. She still didn't understand why she hadn't gotten the role of Juliet. But right now, she didn't care. These friendships were priceless. "So you get what I'm talking about, Elaine? Juliet wants what any of us want. Respect."

Elaine tossed back her blond hair. "I get it."

The three helped each other up and danced arm-in-arm to the edge of the stage, singing along the way.

Deb glimpsed Simon and Barry in the wings where Barry arranged a pile of lumber. But Simon gaped, his slim hips swaying offbeat to their singing.

Her knees wobbled. He was watching her.

So what. She needed to focus on representing her people well by getting into college. Not fall for a white guy. She didn't care a hoot about him.

But why did he have to be so cute?

Several weeks later, Deb and her girlfriends hung their freshly sewn costumes on racks backstage.

Fat Sherwood held up a bejeweled gown. "*Haute couture*," she said, staring through thick lenses that magnified her eyes so they looked like brown bulges. "The best I've ever designed."

Valmar Dahl—all the students called him VD behind his back—approached from a side door, followed by Art class students laden with drop cloths and paint buckets. "Ready for us?" VD called to Dad, who hunkered down over a pile of tools with his Shop guys.

Dad lifted his head. "Ready for you to create the magic of perspective."

Dad had done it. Brought together Home Ec, Art, and Shop students to create costumes and set. He'd been at the school most evenings, working there while Deb prompted Elaine on blocking and lines. His face wore exhaustion, but he'd never looked happier.

A wheezing sound came from the back of the auditorium. Principal Ruud lumbered toward Dad, arms pumping. "Running Bear, what is going on? How come the Art class is here? And Home Ec?"

"We coordinated our curricula. This way students get hands-on experience and see the fruit of their labor. You'll be proud of it."

Ruud jabbed a finger at Dad. "Better be. I warned you, stay on task, or it's your job." He wheeled about. "Fruit of labor?" he muttered. "Coordinated curricula?" His voice trailed off as he plodded up the aisle.

Dad turned back to the crew on stage, who stared, waiting for his response to the principal. "No worries. We're on task." His usual smile was in place, but his mouth twitched slightly.

Once they had a break in activity, Deb stole over to him and lowered her voice. "What did Mr. Ruud mean about your job?"

"Just talk," he said, not meeting her eyes. He walked off.

That was odd. Dad never dismissed her questions.

Backstage on opening night, Deb held up her hands in front of Erik. "Stop!"

Too late. He'd snarfed down a giant bag of barbecue chips.

"Nerves," he said, his hands shaking.

"Nerves nothing," Simon said. "Pure stupidity. You smell like a barbecue pit. What happens when you kiss Elaine?"

Erik crumpled the empty bag. "I'm doomed."

"I'll look for mouthwash." Deb said.

The auditorium lights dimmed.

"Too late," Simon said. "It's showtime."

At the edge of the stage, Rolly Tolly rolled his arms in large circles, signaling for Simon and Barry to pull the curtains. They cranked them open, and lights onstage illuminated.

The audience gasped and broke into applause at its first sight of the town of Verona. In a courtyard, stairs climbed up to a balcony framed by an arched window. The cityscape, painted with gradations of shades and diminishing buildings, gave the impression of disappearing into the horizon.

Deb beamed at the crowd's response. Now it was up to the actors. Which could be challenging, because Elaine still stumbled over her lines.

In Elaine's first scene, she sounded like a robot. When it came time for stage hands to set up for the masquerade ball, Simon and Barry yanked the curtain shut. Deb sped out with a pillar and set a vase on it. Elaine scurried past, lifting the edge of her sapphire Elizabethan gown. Haddy trailed behind, still working Elaine's back zipper up.

"It's stuck," Haddy whispered.

"Then unstick it," Elaine said, a little too loudly.

Deb shushed her. "Remember, in this scene you meet Romeo. You play with each other's hands in an embarrassed kind of way."

Elaine scowled. "And I kiss Carrot Top. Wish I could fake it like we did in rehearsals."

Maybe Deb should warn her about the barbecue chips.

From the wings, Simon's arms flailed, and he mouthed *curtain.*

No time to warn Elaine.

With one more yank, Haddy forced Elaine's zipper up and fled toward the wings, bumping the vase on the pillar. It wobbled, and Deb pivoted stage right to steady it. But before she exited, the curtains flew open. She melted upstage out of the lights and froze, hoping her black slacks and top would camouflage her.

The scene opened. Elaine fumbled with her lines. Then she froze. She glanced at Deb. "Line?" she whispered.

Deb remained stiff and kept her mouth as tight as a ventriloquist. "*Saints do not move.*"

"*Saints do not move,*" Elaine repeated.

"*. . . though grant for prayers' sake.*" Deb whispered.

"*. . . though grant for prayers' sake.*" Elaine bowed her head as though she were in prayer.

An uncomfortable paused followed. Erik's turn. "*Then move not.*" he stammered.

His face blanched. He'd lost his place.

Elaine's jaw dropped.

"This must be it," Erik whispered. He dove toward Elaine and planted a wide kiss on her open mouth.

"Ewww!" Elaine rubbed her lips. "Barbecue!"

Erik held up his hands. "Sorry."

The audience roared.

Deb gasped. They weren't supposed to laugh. They were supposed to be inspired by this moment.

Elaine turned and began marching off stage. She forgot to lift her skirt and stumbled on the hemline.

Erik bolted to steady Elaine, but his foot caught hers and tripped her.

She landed face first.

Erik's arms thrashed about, and he hit the vase on the pillar, just missing Deb. It crashed to the floor, shards flying up into his face.

Rolly Tolly ran onto the stage, his arms waving. "Cut!"

Erik checked his face. "Don't think I'm cut."

The audience shrieked.

Rolly Tolly balled his hands."Cl-OSE the curtains."

"*Oy veh,*" Barry said as he and Simon jerked them shut.

"Everyone take a DEEP breath," Rolly Tolly screeched. He inhaled, then exhaled as his mustache jiggled. "Now that we are CALM, the show must go on." He stomped off.

Deb rushed offstage.

Simon and Barry whipped the curtain open so fast it flapped back and forth, its edge wrapping around Erik.

The audience howled.

From the wings, Haddy gripped Deb's hand until it hurt. "This can't get worse, can it?"

Deb gulped. "It could."

Elaine's face flushed with raw anger. From then on, when Erik struggled with his lines, she smirked. When he stood over her seemingly dead body, her anger turned to ridicule, and her chest rose and fell with snickers. When he drank poison and stooped to kiss her, she turned her head aside and said, "Don't you dare."

When Elaine revived from her sleeping potion, she reached for Erik's dagger to kill herself. "*O happy dagger!*" she said. "*This is thy sheath.*"

She struggled to unsnap the blade from its case.

Erik came alive. "I'll help."

"Don't bother," she said.

They wrestled with the blade until it sprang loose and clattered across the stage. Elaine crawled after it, poised the knife over her chest, and pronounced, "*There rest, and let me die.*" But she stabbed herself with the handle instead of the blade. She fell dead anyway, heaving with laughter.

The crowd went wild.

Deb winced. The tragedy had morphed into a comedy.

After the closing line, Rolly Tolly didn't signal for a curtain call.

Deb clutched her arms. A disaster.

Erik ripped off his velvet jacket. "Let me outta here."

Elaine shouted behind him. "That kiss was a garbage can!" She stomped toward the dressing room.

Haddy raised her palms. "I'll see what I can do." She took off after Elaine.

"At least it's over," Deb mumbled to no one.

"Yeah, they messed up royally."

She startled. Simon stood near her.

Cast members buzzed around, but the silence between them muffled everything.

"You did a great job prompting Elaine," Simon said. "You stood so still, you could have a future as a statue."

"Is that a compliment?"

"Uh, I didn't mean it as a put-down."

"No big deal."

She had to get out of here. Not let her heart toss her over a cliff. She spotted a backstage exit and headed for it. She'd skip the cast party.

CHAPTER 21

Monumental

Will stood among the milling crowd at the front of the auditorium. This play was destined to be a disaster the moment the principal forced Tollefson to make Elaine and Erik the leads.

Not a disaster for Will, though. By pulling teachers together, he'd created a camaraderie unheard of at this school. And the set his guys built? As good as a college production. They wouldn't have been able to do it without the money the principal provided. He ought to thank Ruud again.

Will searched around for him. Lyle Mykland was by the principal, dumping on him, as usual.

Will wrangled his way through the throng, but stayed back enough to give Ruud and Mykland space to talk. He couldn't help but hear Mykland.

"How come that Injun got to do this?"

Will winced.

The principal continued smiling and waving at the audience like a campaigning politician. "Don't go into your rant here. I have my crowd to greet." Ruud brushed him away.

Mykland spotted Will. He pushed against Will's shoulder as he passed, knocking him aside.

Will recovered his balance and drew near the principal. "Mr. Ruud."

"Not now. The press is coming."

Lars Lundy approached at a fast clip. He broke away from two tight-lipped women, the same ones who had stalked Lundy at the Synchronettes's performance. "I don't have time to discuss your community concerns," Lundy tossed back to them.

"The nerve," the older one said. She clutched her purse, and the younger one copied her. They stomped off.

Lundy pulled out his notepad. "Mr. Ruud, what do you have to say about this performance?"

The principal placed an arm around the reporter's shoulder. "The acting was a little off, but my idea of integrating curriculums worked good."

Will tensed. The principal taking credit for his idea? He forced a smile.

Ruud continued. "Gives the students hands-up experience."

Lundy's pen stopped. "You mean *hands-on?*"

"Sure. They get to see the meat of their labors."

Lundy's brow furrowed. "The fruit of their labors?"

"Yeah."

Will swallowed a laugh. This was too ludicrous to be maddening.

"Anyhow," Ruud continued, "don't forget my secret I hinted about. Remember? *Monumental.* Come springtime, you'll see what progressive education is."

"No more clues?"

Ruud cackled. "It's *massive.* The school board will love it. And they'll love me."

Will turned away, shaking his head. No reason to thank Ruud. He was thanking himself enough.

CHAPTER 22

Mrs. Robinson

Beep beep! At the sound of the horn, Deb brushed the curtain aside from her basement window. She squinted through ice crystals at the falling snow, then gasped. "You won't believe it. Elaine's got a new car. A red convertible."

Dad lowered his newspaper and joined her at the window. "A Mustang, no less."

Deb laughed. "Look at Elaine putting the top up and down. And Haddy waving from the backseat. Crazy girls. Must be twenty degrees out."

"That car's a beauty."

"An early Christmas present from her father."

"Oh." Dad's voice quavered. "Deb, I can't—"

"I know. I'll get a book for Christmas."

"You want something else?"

She threw on her wool coat and tossed Dad a smile. "Never. What would Christmas be without curling up with a classic novel?"

He clasped his hands. "Thanks for understanding."

She planted a kiss on his cheek. "No problem. I'm off to the movies. Love you."

Deb caught his slight wave as she pulled the door shut. She clutched her coat tighter against the wind and dashed to the curb, the snow stinging her face. She pulled open the passenger door and brushed off flakes that drifted onto the black bucket seat. "This car is incredible, Elaine."

Haddy called from the back. "Some wheels, huh?"

"For sure," Deb said. "Thanks for picking me up at my Xanadu."

"Your what?" Elaine asked.

"A palace of Kublai Khan. A little joke between Dad and me. Anyway, tell me about your car."

"First Father brought home a horrid black T-bird. I broke down and told him it was square. He didn't know what I meant, but he took the car back and drove this baby home." She caressed the steering wheel. "That's love."

"I guess," Deb said. She didn't want to burst Elaine's bubble about what love was. The love of listening. Of caring. Maybe she and Dad didn't live in a mansion. Or drive a hot car. But their home was a palace because they had each other. She'd choose that over Elaine's flimsy relationship with her father any day.

Deb glided her hand across the wood-grained dash. But this was way cool.

From the back seat, Haddy clapped. "Elaine, we ought to take this pony to our Fort Robinson getaway after we graduate. I'll wear my shades and look ga-roovy."

"Only five months 'til then," Deb said.

"And I found the perfect movie for us seniors," Haddy said. She handed a torn newspaper page to Deb, pointing to an ad. "It's about this guy."

A young man with dark hair and a rumpled jacket stood alone with his hands in his pockets. Deb read:

The Graduate.
This is Benjamin.
He's a Little Worried
About His Future.
Music by Simon and Garfunkel

"He's worried about *his* future," Deb said. "What about *ours?*"

Elaine flicked her fingers. "I don't think about it."

"Maybe *you* don't," Haddy said, "but the guys do. Live in fear they'll get called up after they graduate." Her voice dropped so low Deb struggled to hear it over the Mustang's rumble. "Could wind up in Vietnam. Erik. Jord. Barry. Simon."

Simon?

"Get shipped home in body bags."

Deb's throat constricted. Simon embodied the best of their generation with all its dreams for a better world. What if one day she unfolded the *Argus* and faced a black-and-white photo of Simon in uniform, smiling proudly, with the headline screaming:

Another Hometown Boy Killed in Action

And dying for what? Nobody understood this war.

"Don't be gross talking about body bags." Elaine's voice rose. "So which theater are we going to?"

"The Egyptian," Haddy said. "Eight o'clock."

"Good. We've got time to cruise downtown so I can show off my wheels."

Elaine veered onto Phillips Avenue and *beeped* at cars cruising by. When some guys pointed at her Mustang, she lifted her chin.

Deb's mind swirled like the snow around them. Maybe Elaine could shut out thoughts about the war as easily as switching off the TV, but she couldn't. Not when boys she knew might end up there.

Especially Simon.

She wiped fog off the passenger window with her knit glove. In the wind, twinkling Christmas lights swung on street lamps. Fresh snow powdered the walks. Shoppers laden with bulky sacks hurried between Shriver's and Fantle's. Some stopped to throw change into a bucket next to a Salvation Army bell ringer who moved his wrist rhythmically up and down. All was calm, all was bright. Maybe she should push thoughts of war out of her head.

They covered the cruising loop three times before Elaine snagged a parking spot on Tenth Street. Then they crunched through snow and joined a swarm of students in a lobby saturated with the scent of popcorn and hot butter. In the theater, they searched for three seats together.

"Rescue me." Elaine's said. "There's Carrot Top. Don't make me sit by barbecue breath."

"Nothing else available," Haddy said.

Deb spotted the seats. One row ahead of Erik, Barry, and Simon.

Elaine pushed her way into the row. Then Haddy.

Deb avoided looking at Simon as she threaded around people's knees, then allowed herself one peek.

Simon caught her glance and straightened.

She spun her head toward the front and scrunched down.

"You been *Simonized* again?" Haddy whispered.

"Don't give me grief," Deb said.

Elaine cracked up. "One of these days you'll admit the guy likes you—and you like him."

"He does not. And I do not," Deb said.

"*Su-r-r-e*," Haddy and Elaine said simultaneously.

The theater darkened, and the curtain cranked open. That was a relief. Elaine and Haddy wouldn't bug her anymore. Haunting music about silence, visions, and restlessness crackled through the theater speakers. A guy named Ben returned home from his college graduation. His hazel eyes riveted Deb. Innocence. Wonder. Hope.

Ben's parents presented him with a red convertible as a graduation present. Elaine laughed. "I got mine *before* I graduated," she said loud enough for those around to hear.

Deb turned back to the movie. All hope drained out of Ben's face as he squandered the summer in an affair with Mrs. Robinson, a middle-aged woman.

Deb's body grew hot. Her skin tingled. "I can't believe we're watching this."

"Not as boring as World Lit," Elaine shot back.

Haddy shushed them.

Ben's parents set him up with Mrs. Robinson's daughter, a brunette beauty named Elaine. To sabotage the date, Ben took Elaine Robinson to a strip joint. As a topless dancer gyrated on the big screen, the sound of crunching popcorn ceased throughout the theater. Haddy's mouth gaped, a corn kernel on her lower lip. Deb's hands turned clammy.

Ben fell in love with Elaine Robinson and ended his affair with her mother. But in jealousy, the older woman told her daughter that Ben had raped her.

Deb's insides roiled. How could anyone be so deceptive? Elaine Robinson moved ahead with her parents' scheme for her to marry another man. Then Ben crashed the wedding, and she broke away and ran off with him.

With no warning, the theater lights came up, blinding Deb.

"That was some flick," Haddy said.

Elaine checked her makeup in her compact mirror. "Come on, girls. Let's go show off my car." She moved toward the aisle.

"But . . . . " Deb began.

Erik called out loud enough for everyone to hear. "Burgers at the Barrel."

Chatter rose, and students streamed toward the exit like nothing had happened.

Deb couldn't move. Images from the film bombarded her. Ben in bed with an older woman? Slimy! The strip tease? Awful! Ben making a scene at Elaine Robinson's wedding, and the two of them running off? Horrible? Or good?

Haddy stepped around Deb's knees. "Come on."

"But the movie?"

Haddy turned back. "We'll discuss it tomorrow."

"Huh?"

"At Luther League." Haddy gestured toward the balcony. "Pastor Pete and his wife always attend the hot movies."

Deb glanced up. Simon's father, the only middle-aged man in town with wire-rimmed glasses and a goatee, leaned forward in the front row with his wife. They sat ahead of the make-out section, where couples untangled limbs and straightened clothes.

"It'll be a steamy discussion," Haddy said.

CHAPTER 23

Filthy

Will peered over the top of his Sunday *Argus*. "You need the car tonight?"

Slumped at the card table, Deb glanced up, then returned to her textbook. "Elaine's getting Haddy and me."

Will let his gaze linger on Deb. She was unusually quiet today. Said nothing on the way to church this morning. The same at lunch—mute as a stone. Whatever was on her mind, she didn't want to discuss it. He'd let it go for now. Maybe pry a little later. "I'm heading over to the *Argus* to see Mr. Lundy."

Deb didn't look up. "Okay."

Will pulled on his mackinaw and wool cap. He leaned over and kissed the top of Deb's head. "See you later."

"Yeah," she said.

He headed out to his Squareback wagon, cranked it, and brushed snow off the windshield. Then he waited in the driver's seat for the car to thaw, his breath fogging the inside of the windshield. Something had haunted him since the last time he talked with Mr. Lundy. The reporter had aimed his pen at Will. Said he was *counting* on Will to pull Lundy's son out of his funk.

Not reasonable. The best teacher in the world couldn't guarantee to turn around a student. Especially when the student was stuck in the mire of self-doubt.

Meanwhile, Lundy coiled like a snake ready to strike anyone who crossed him. It was best to tread carefully. Will didn't want any bad publicity to ruin Deb's quest for a scholarship.

Will lumbered the wagon in and out of ruts of snow, slid through an icy corner, and eased to the curb. He stepped out, the cold biting his nose, and pulled open the door to the *Argus*.

"Thank you for your politeness." A crackly voice from behind stopped him.

An ancient woman, as thin as a rail even in her wool coat, bustled past him into the office. A copy of herself, but half a century younger, followed her.

The women who stalked Lundy at community events.

They clutched matching handbags, wore matching sturdy pumps, and unwrapped matching herringbone scarves from their heads.

Lundy peered up from pecking at his typewriter. "Running Bear. What are you doing here with the Ladies' Decency League?"

"Got the door for them."

"Have you met Sigfrid Aasgard? And her great-niece Sylvia?" Lundy said their names like they were a disease.

Will tipped his hat at them as he removed it. The Aasgards were gossip fodder in the teachers' lounge. Sigfrid, an old maid. Sylvia, on the way to claiming that title.

Lundy rolled his chair back from his wood desk. "I was about to wrap up tomorrow's paper. No man should be forced to work on a Sunday, but I am."

"Mr. Lundy." Sigrid's voice bristled. "As president of the Ladies' Decency League, it is my civic duty to monitor cultural events to ensure nothing occurs that is not on the up-and-up. I am here to report something."

Lundy reached for his notepad. "Do tell."

"That filthy movie about an affair between a dissolute young man and a married woman."

"You mean *The Graduate?*"

Will's ears perked up. The movie Deb attended?

Sigfrid clutched her handbag with her black gloves and sniffed. "That's the one."

Sylvia copied the clutch and the sniff.

Lundy cocked his head. "You saw the movie?"

Sigfrid pressed her hand to her heart. "I would *never*. My niece, who is president-in-training for the Decency League, forced herself to go."

A slight smile quivered on Sylvia's lips, then vanished.

"I certainly can't attend all these—what do they call them—*happenings*," Sigfrid said. "But the town ought to know the movie is filthy, filthy, filthy." She punctuated each word with a tap of her finger on Lundy's notebook. "And you may quote me. But make sure you spell my name correctly. It's double *A*, not double *S*, then *G-A-R-D*, like a guard, which is what I am for this community." She sniffed and stood stiff as a sentry.

Will swallowed a snicker.

Lundy scribbled in his notepad. "What is your Decency League planning to do?"

Sigfrid winced. "There's nothing we can do about this *smut*."

Lundy put a hand on each of the women's shoulders and moved them to the exit. "Sad you can't, but thanks for your vigilance."

He closed the door behind them, ripped his notes out of the pad, and tossed them into the trash. "Like I told you, Running Bear, people always demanding stuff from me. I'm sick of it. And I don't want my son ending up like this."

"That's why I came."

Lundy spun around. "What?"

Will gripped his cap tighter and lowered his voice. "To tell you Jord is doing better." It wasn't true, but Lundy was desperate. "All your son needs is encouragement. I know you can give that."

Lundy glared. "Encouragement? Who gives me any?" He threw on his coat and thrust open the door.

A blast of cold swept in.

Will stopped him. "Wait. Don't you recognize the power you hold?"

"Darn right I do. I can make people. Or break 'em."

"I'm not talking about your job. I'm talking about your role as Jord's fa—"

"I'm tired of people telling me what they want. Maybe one of these days I'll *break* someone." He pointed his index finger at Will. "I don't want my son turning out a flunky. Hear me?"

Will's insides twisted. "I hear you."

CHAPTER 24

Luther League

Deb, Elaine, and Haddy scurried out of the frigid air and entered the front room of the church. "Let's check our makeup," Elaine said, turning toward the bathroom.

"You go ahead," Deb said. "I'll wait here in the lobby."

"It's not a lobby," Elaine said. "It's a *narthex*."

"I didn't know it had a religious name."

Haddy patted Deb on the shoulder. "Just church talk."

They bounced off to the restroom.

Deb folded her arms. How was she supposed to know this was a *narthex*? Even though she and Dad had attended since the fall, Oslo Lutheran was as confusing as a jumble of alphabet soup letters. A *nave*, a *chancel*, and now a *narthex*? They sounded like body parts of a grasshopper.

Then the liturgy—what she called the lethargy. Confusing. More than once, she'd sat when she should have stood. She'd sung *ah-men* when she was supposed to say it.

This was nothing like the church she and Dad attended on the rez, a circle of folding chairs in a Quonset hut. In balmy weather, they'd rested outside under a cottonwood, its rustling leaves lifting prayers to the Great Spirit.

But this? Nothing but pipe-organ stiffness. Except for one area—the basement where Luther League met. There, her spirit rose up to meet *Wakantanka*. And when Haddy and Elaine emerged from the restroom, that's where they headed.

On the stairway down they passed by three-foot-tall paintings of daisies on lime-green walls. In the basement, girls gathered at tables where orange candles dripped wax onto plastic purple tablecloths. Guys gathered around a record player and argued whether "Lucy in the Sky with Diamonds" was about LSD.

Rumor was that Pastor Peterson put up a fight with the church council to turn this fellowship hall into The Rap Shop. Stuffy Lutherans still muttered on Sunday mornings about the *hippie joint* downstairs. But the pastor's strategy had worked. This was *the* happening place in town, a magnet for youths of all faiths, or no faith at all. Which is why Jews like Haddy and Barry showed up. And someone like Erik, who didn't believe in anyone but himself.

It wasn't paint and candles that made this place popular, though. It was Pastor Pete. He was way cool, like his son.

Deb sighed. She had to admit it. She was *Simonized*. She glanced over at him, alone in a corner now, his head bent over his guitar as he tuned it.

"Come on, girls," Elaine said. "Let's grab a spot with the seniors."

Deb followed Elaine and Haddy to the tables, where Simon's mother, Mrs. Pete, and others from the Lutheran Women's Missionary League poured Cokes into paper cups and distributed boxes of pizza as fast as their hands and feet could fly.

Simon settled in across from them with the guys.

Deb avoided looking up, instead fiddling with orange candle wax.

"I'll divvy up the pizza," Karl said, tossing triangles from boxes onto their plates. When he finished, he stared at his plate. "I got nothing but plain." He grabbed a supreme from Erik.

"Hey!" Erik protested. "Don't be an Indian giver!"

Heat coursed through Deb.

Simon rose and leaned over Erik. "That's racist. And totally wrong. It's whites who stole from the Indians."

Erik scowled. "What got into you, Garfunkel? All I wanted was olives and peppers."

"So have one of mine." Simon slapped a piece face-down onto Erik's plate.

Deb glanced at Simon. She mouthed *thank you,* then turned away.

"We told you he likes you," Elaine whispered.

"Don't be a butt-in-skee," Deb said.

Haddy laughed. "You're living by De Nile River."

"Huh?" Deb said.

"*De-nial?*"

Deb elbowed her, then concentrated on her pizza.

After students finished everything but the crusts, they dragged their folding chairs across the linoleum and formed a circle.

Simon strapped his guitar onto his lean torso and picked a minor chord that hung in the air like frost on the windowpanes. When everyone quieted, his soft tenor voice sang about darkness, neon gods, cobblestones— "The Sound of Silence"—and others joined him.

Deb swooned under his spell. He was *marvelous.*

When the song ended, Simon dropped his lanky frame back into his chair. A hush filled the room.

Pastor Pete stroked his goatee. "Probably all of you saw the movie *The Graduate* last night."

Slight nods all around.

Haddy leaned over and whispered to Deb. "Told you we'd talk sex."

The minister caught Haddy's comment. "We *could* talk sex."

Erik broke in. "Or about a strip joint."

Students sputtered with nervous laughter.

Pastor Pete adjusted his wire rims. "That, too. But what *is* the sound of silence?"

No one answered.

The pastor cleared his throat. "Okay, why was Ben so unhappy? He had a degree and money and a cool sports car."

"He knew what he *didn't* want," Erik said, "like I know I don't want to be a cop like my old man."

Jord hung his head. "At least you have a clue of *something* you can do."

"But Ben saw his life as a waste," Barry said.

Haddy wiggled in her seat. "I got an idea. Ben's parents were so busy with the neon gods—materialism—they didn't pay attention to what was going on with their son."

"Did Ben know himself?" Pastor Pete asked.

"Not really," Deb said. "He was like the fish in his aquarium, swimming in circles." She sat back, her face burning that she'd offered a comment.

Simon leaned forward. "He was trapped by his parents' expectations." He glanced at his father. Pastor Pete didn't catch his look, and Simon slumped in his seat.

"What about Elaine Robinson?" Pastor Pete asked. "What was she like?"

"She was like gorgeous," Erik said. He gaped at Elaine.

Elaine giggled and bobbed her head about.

"But what was she *like*?" Pastor Pete asked again.

Deb flexed her fingers. This conversation was too good for her to stay on the sidelines. "She was drifting, willing to marry the guy her parents wanted because she couldn't face up to who she cared about."

"What does any of this matter?" Erik said. "We guys will probably end up being compost in some Vietnam swamp."

The pastor's lips tightened. "Ah, yes, the war. You may not be able to avoid the draft, but you can avoid the *drift*—avoid having no purpose in your life. When Ben crashed Elaine Robinson's wedding, Mrs. Robinson yelled something at her daughter. What was it?"

"That it was too late," Haddy said.

"What did Elaine Robinson answer?"

"It wasn't too late for her," Deb said.

"Right." Pastor Pete pounded his fist into his palm. "Elaine Robinson could still live fully. Embrace love completely. God gives second chances," Pastor Pete said. "When he does, grab 'em."

He surveyed the room. "Think about it, especially you seniors. As you step out into the world, who will you become? Ben's parents—caught up in materialism? Or Elaine Robinson and Ben—drifters? Or Mrs. Robinson—a manipulator?"

Pastor Pete's words echoed in the silence of Deb's mind. Who would she become?

Deb struggled to cut her chicken-fried steak. The card table in their apartment shook from her sawing across the beige melamine plate. She should have checked the meat in the pan earlier, but her mind was as jumbled as a jigsaw puzzle still in the box.

Jumbled around thoughts of Simon. He'd stood up for her at Luther League. Her stomach turned cartwheels.

"You okay?" Dad said from the other side of the table.

"Huh? Yeah."

She was half-aware of Franklin, his soft body threading between her legs, but she paid no attention. Her mind had turned back to the discussion at Luther League about *The Graduate*. The movie wasn't about sex, but about living beyond the status quo. And not using others, like Mrs. Robinson did.

"Picked up some chatter in Shop." Dad interrupted her thoughts. "Something about a strip scene in *The Graduate*."

Deb's knife clattered onto her plate. She raked her fork through her mashed potatoes and lifted a bite big enough to fill her mouth.

"You saw that, didn't you?"

Her heart thumped. She moved the food to one side of her mouth and mumbled, "Yeah."

"What's it about?"

She swallowed. The lump stuck in her throat. "That it's never too late." Her words came out mushy.

The lines between Dad's eyes deepened. "Never too late for what?"

She swallowed again, forcing the potatoes down. "To become who you're meant to be."

He sat back. "Really? I like that."

She gulped down half her milk.

"And the strip scene?"

She coughed. "A minor deal." She concentrated on cutting another bite of steak.

"So anything to process?"

She shook her head.

"You're okay with the movie?"

"Sure." Would he ask more about the strip scene?

Dad placed a bite of meat into his mouth and chewed and chewed. He scrunched up his face. "This chicken is definitely not as tender as my heart is for you."

Deb giggled and pointed her fork at him. "Aw, Dad."

CHAPTER 25

Handoff

W ill pounded two chalk erasers together over the trash can, releasing a cloud of white dust that left him coughing.

The classroom door burst open, followed by the clamor of anger. "Don't ever grab the ball from me again."

"Foul Out King."

"Would've scored if you hadn't tripped me."

"You missed the tip by a mile."

Will slammed down the erasers. "I will not be a referee in my classroom. Sit down!"

The guys scraped their stools across the concrete and up to the worktable. They dropped their books to the floor with a thud. Frustration filled their faces.

Will flung his arms wide. "Guys, performance is one percent inspiration and ninety-nine percent perspiration."

"We ain't working hard enough?" Erik yelled. "*JE*-sus—"

"Jesus Christ was a great warrior," Will broke in. "Especially compared to *some* Warriors I know. I suggest you use his name only when you're speaking directly to him or talking reverently about him. And regarding your basketball performance, I'm *not* your coach. So get out your hammers and work on your toolboxes."

He flopped into his swivel chair and turned away, staring at the blank chalkboard. He couldn't blame the boys for being agitated. His junior varsity squad was doing great, beating Yankton and Huron by ten points each. But Lyle Mykland's varsity squad had fallen 66 to 29 against Yankton, then 71 to 26 against Huron. Will had heard the guys sneering about *Loser Lyle* in the cafeteria.

During games at the Sioux Arena, empty bleachers echoed the hollow bounce of the basketball. At school, pep rallies were so tepid—students passing around *Mad* magazines and tossing paper airplanes—the principal cancelled future ones.

But Will could do nothing.

He crumpled a piece of paper into a ball and gripped it. Behind him, the hammering sounded like the guys were punishing their toolboxes.

"Mr. Running Bear?" Barry asked above the din. "Who said performance is ninety-nine percent perspiration?"

Will continued staring at nothing. "Thomas Edison. And actually, he was talking about genius."

"How come you're always quoting famous people?" Simon asked.

Will squeezed the paper ball tighter. If only he didn't have to siphon out history in sips so he didn't rile up Lyle Mykland. "I've learned from the great ones. Not like my grandfather did, though. He met the queen in London and the pope in Rome. He climbed to the top of the Eiffel Tower in Paris when it first opened."

The hammering ceased. "What?"

Will swiveled his chair around and viewed their sloppy hammering. "I'll give you a little background, not a history lesson, while you use medium sandpaper to clean up those gouges."

The boys grabbed some sheets and rubbed the paper back and forth across the wood.

Will stuffed the paper ball into his pocket. He folded a sheet of medium and demonstrated. "Go with the grain. If you don't, you get into trouble. Now back to the story. The government rounded up my people and dumped them onto Pine Ridge Reservation. Then along came this showman, William Cody."

Barry lifted his head. "Buffalo Bill?"

"The greatest celebrity on earth at the time."

"As big as the Beatles?" Erik asked.

"Bigger," Will said. "He produced the Wild West show with horses and bison, cowboys and Indians. Traveled to

England and Europe. And where did he get Natives? Pine Ridge. He treated them well. Taught them how to read and write, including my grandfather and father. When I came along, my dad had such good memories of Cody, he named me after him." Will pressed his fist to his heart. "William Cody Running Bear. A name like that inspires you. Like the name of our school."

"Huh?" Simon asked.

Will was on a roll and couldn't stop. "Washington was one of the greatest military leaders the world has ever known. If it weren't for him, we'd all be English."

"Like the Beatles," Erik said, and they all laughed.

The classroom door whipped open. Principal Ruud glared at Will, then jerked his head toward the hall. "Gotta talk to ya."

"Switch to fine-grade," Will told the boys. "It'll bring out the shine." He strode to the hallway. What was so important the principal would interrupt a class?

Ruud glanced up and down the empty corridor. "Been getting pressure from the police chief—I mean the booster club."

"Yes?"

"Chief Quisling bought new uniforms for the varsity this year, so he thinks he owns them. Anyhow, this could get me into big trouble, you being Indian. But I'm making you varsity coach."

Will's heart stopped.

"Not a promotion. Just this season. And you better come through. The police chief's counting on a state championship, especially with his son on the team. He wants Erik to shine."

"What about the junior varsity?"

"Lyle will take 'em." The principal turned and disappeared down the hall.

The varsity? Will breathed slowly, forcing his pulse down. This was the opportunity to extend what his guys were learning in Shop onto the basketball court. Lessons that mattered, like discipline. Teamwork.

He turned back to the classroom. The door was open. The boys must have heard.

He strode in, grabbed the paper ball out of his pocket, and lobbed it into the wastebasket. "Call me the varsity coach."

The boys whooped and hollered. Erik strutted as if he'd made it happen, and class turned into a celebration.

Will crunched through the snow toward the school bus where the varsity and j.v. teams milled around. Maybe he shouldn't have gone against the grain, but he hadn't been able to stop himself. He'd asked Barry to be the varsity team manager. Even told him he could suit up for games.

"Yes, sir," Barry had said, standing taller than usual for his pudgy frame.

Erik wouldn't like that. He loved to bully Barry. And if Erik didn't like it, his father, the booster-club—of-one, wouldn't either.

Then Will had asked Arthur Brown to be his assistant. The custodian had grasped Will's brown hand with his black one. "If color don't matter, I'm in."

Principal Ruud, always status conscious, wouldn't like Will promoting a black janitor. Nor would Lyle Mykland, freshly demoted from the varsity coaching job.

But Will couldn't pass by these opportunities to elevate those who deserved it. And if this created trouble, so be it.

Just so it didn't touch Deb.

Will reached the school bus. Lyle Mykland leaned against the side, his arms folded across his paunch. Hoping to melt the ice between them a little, Will offered his hand. "Hello, Coach Mykland."

Mykand didn't reciprocate. "See if you do any better with those loser seniors."

Will opened his mouth to answer.

"Ah'm comin'." A voice from the distance interrupted him. Arthur's lean figure appeared, running high speed across the parking lot. He slid to a stop, tossing up a spray of snow on everyone. "Now ah'm here."

Guys burst into laughter and brushed snow off themselves. Arthur stood out like a psychedelic poster. He spread his arms wide to display his red Nehru jacket with pink buttons. A pink shirt collar and sleeves peeked out from the jacket. Maroon bell-bottoms completed his look. He smiled at Will. "This suit okay?"

Will glanced at the rest of the guys in their black jackets and skinny striped ties. "Can you add a tie?"

"Brought one just in case." From his pocket he pulled a wide, pink paisley tie.

Will forced back a chuckle. "Put it on, and let's roll."

Arthur threw the tie around his neck and began dragging athletic bags into the luggage compartment.

Will stopped him. "No, Arthur. The boys stow their own gear."

"No kiddin'?"

"Definitely."

Mykland unlatched himself from the side of the bus. "Some assistant." He boarded, taking up two seats in the front with his outstretched legs.

The guys stowed their bags and jostled each other as they piled on board. Finally, Will and Arthur climbed the steps.

Students yelled, "Hey, Artie."

Will held up his hands. "You will call my new assistant by his proper name, Mr. Brown."

"Hey, Mr. Brown!" everyone yelled.

"He's a janitor," Mykland muttered.

Arthur grinned and waved, then began working his way to the back of the bus.

"No, Mr. Brown." Will stopped him. "Up here." He gestured toward the driver's seat.

Arthur's eyes grew wide. "I's the driver?"

Will held out the keys. "We're putting your license to good use, and I'll sit with the team."

Arthur's smile wrapped across his face. "Mmm hmm. Look out world, here I come." He slipped into his seat, turned over the engine, and ground it into first.

Erik stood and waved his hands like a conductor. "Onward, Sioux Falls, you're the best of all." The guys joined in, hope filling their voices.

All their hope drained away. The Kernels crushed the Warriors 59-25.

Will shuffled off the basketball court, searching the bleachers. Thorvald Quisling, the one-man booster club, glared with his arms crossed over his green police chief's shirt.

Will smiled and waved.

Quisling remained stone-faced. Thankfully, he didn't return another gesture.

On the ride home, the bus was as quiet as a graveyard. It didn't help that the junior varsity squeaked by with a 38-36 win. Mykland sauntered down the aisle past Will. "Look who's the winner now."

The following Monday at practice, Erik elbowed Simon, Karl tripped Jord, and Steve shoved Wayne until a shouting match turned into a brawl. Will broke it up and sent the boys home early.

He slumped on the bottom bleacher, his eyes tracing the pattern in the gym floor. What if he didn't turn these guys around?

Footsteps approached. "Coach?"

Barry. His voice held its usual curiosity.

"I don't mean to *kibitz*, but I've got an idea."

Barry couldn't even dribble a ball. Still, Will should pretend to listen. He lifted his head.

Barry hunched on his knees. "We need something to unite the guys. Like you talked about the Roman army coming together?"

"Yeah?"

Barry's hands danced with enthusiasm as he laid out his idea.

"That's crazy, Barry."

The boy's eyes dropped.

"It's so crazy, it might work. Let's give it a try."

CHAPTER 26

Be There!

Before sixth period, Deb, Haddy, and Elaine huddled in the hallway planning a shopping date when Deb spotted Dad approaching at a fast clip.

"I need your help," he said, breathing hard. "I've talked the principal into reinstating pep rallies. Meet me in the auditorium after school. We'll need costumes, so I'm bringing in Home Ec." He turned to Elaine. "They'll be assisting your cheerleaders."

"Home Ec working with cheerleaders?" Elaine asked. "But the Sherwood sisters are cat fighting."

Will grinned. "Not anymore." He hurried off.

Deb shrugged. "Whatever he's up to, I hope I can stay in the background."

After school, Deb pushed open the door to the auditorium and entered with Haddy and Elaine. She glanced at the stage. Dad had worked his magic again, gathering staff like he did for the *Romeo and Juliet* production. Rolly Tolly's mustache twitched and his arms folded in a dramatic pose. VD Dahl squinted, a narrow paint brush behind his ear. And Mr. Brown pushed up his janitor's shirtsleeves like he was ready to get to work.

But most amazing was the Sherwood sisters, Fat and Skinny, standing together. How did Dad bring together what the students called the feuding females?

The only student there was Barry, scuffing a shoe against the floor. When he saw Deb, Haddy, and Elaine, his face lit up.

Dad was talking fast, his arms waving. "Steve's father offered scrap lumber from his hardware store."

Rolly Tolly stepped forward. "Any help you need with STAGE-ing, I'll do it."

VD joined him. "My students will paint whatever props you create in Shop. And I'll put together a pep band."

"Ronnette and I are in," Fat Sherwood said. "Time to mend fallen hems between us, what with the team needing our help. And I can talk the Needle 'n Thread into donating fabric. Our sewing machines will be humming." She smiled at Haddy.

Haddy clasped her hands. "More costumes."

Skinny Sherwood waggled a finger at Deb. "And *you* can help. My girls can move their hips, but we need new cheers from their lips. You'll write 'em."

"Me?"

Barry opened his arms to explain. "Cheers around a different theme for every game. It'll be far out."

"Far out, indeed," Dad said.

Deb stared at Dad. "You forcing me—?"

"My idea to bring you in," Skinny Sherwood interrupted. "We need you."

Elaine squealed. "This'll be so fun."

Deb turned cold. What if she failed?

Deb gripped her hands as she sat in the front row of the school auditorium, waiting for the pep rally to begin. "This better not flop."

"Anything will be better than those *poop* rallies we had before," Haddy said from the seat next to her. "And even if it's a bust, we got out of class early."

Maybe so, but Deb didn't want to look like an idiot. What if students panned it?

She glanced around the auditorium. Principal Ruud sat stiff, his jaw shifting back and forth. Coach Mykland slouched next to Mr. Ruud, wearing his usual sneer. If this rally failed, they'd look for someone to blame. The principal might be on Dad's case more than ever.

From the back of the auditorium, the double doors heaved open. VD high-stepped the pep band in to the beat of the school song. Instead of their usual blue uniforms, the band wore orange three-cornered hats, billowing white shirts, orange slacks gathered below the knee, and white stockings. Musicians swung left to right, their brass instruments reflecting on the walls of the auditorium.

Haddy jumped up and began to clap to the beat. "Our costumes look great!"

Students pointed and gawked. A few rose to their feet, their wooden seats snapping shut behind them. With only a dribble of enthusiasm they sang *fight, fight, fight for Sioux Falls High*.

Deb's heart sank. This wasn't working.

The stage curtain yanked open, and Elaine and her cheerleaders marched in dressed as Continental soldiers. They kept time with their orange and black pompoms.

Students laughed and clapped.

Deb's pulse picked up. Now they were getting into it.

The varsity team rushed onstage, wearing orange Continental jackets and tricorn hats.

Students hooted and cheered, and a flush of relief ran through Deb.

Principal Ruud stood in front, waving his hands around, trying to get control of the crowd. Still seated next to him, Mykland maintained his smirk.

No way could they control this crowd.

Dad jogged onto the stage wearing an orange coat and tipping his three-cornered hat as he reached the microphone. "Today we'll honor our school's namesake for his brilliance in winning battles." He nodded to Elaine. "Give us a cheer."

Elaine and the other cheerleaders danced forward and yelled, "Give me an S."

"S," the students called back tentatively.

"Give me a T."

"T," They yelled back.

"Give me an R."

"R." Their heads turned, wondering what they were spelling.

On and on they cried out until they yelled, "Strategy, strategy, stra-te-gy!"

The house shook.

Deb grinned. They'd captured them. Now to galvanize them to attend tonight's game.

"Next, the Strategy Stomp," Elaine hollered.

The pep band broke into "Louie Louie."

The cheerleaders moved into complex dance moves, but the pep band drowned out their words.

Students fidgeted. Some sat down.

Deb's hands went sweaty. How could they save this?

Elaine signaled to Deb. "Get up here," she screamed.

Deb shook her head. "I can't."

Haddy pushed Deb forward. "Go!"

Deb stumbled up the steps.

Simon detached the microphone from its stand and handed it to her, his hand brushing against hers. "We need you," he yelled over the pep band.

She took the mic and fell into the beat of the song. "Strategy, strategy, who-o-o, we're gonna win, yi-yi-yi-yi-yi!"

Students picked up the words, and cheerleaders led them in a foot stomp so raucous it could collapse the balcony.

Deb scanned the screaming audience. Coach Mykland still slunk in his seat, his arms crossed, but Principal Ruud's face glowed as he watched his daughter leading the cheer. He was even trying to clap in rhythm.

When the song ended, Simon grinned at her, his head nodding approval.

Dad motioned to Mr. Brown to enter the stage from the wings.

Mr. Brown had plopped an orange hat over a white wig, and tight curls of his Afro peeked out, making the black of his skin darker and the gleam of his teeth whiter. Dressed in his red Nehru jacket and pink paisley tie, he pushed a plywood cannon.

Guffaws filled the room with his appearance.

Snare drums rolled. Erik lit a fireworks sprinkler and held it to the cannon's mouth. Then a bass drum boomed. With a slingshot, Karl flung a beach ball through the cannon. It bounded into the audience, where students flipped it around.

Dad came to Deb's side. "Thanks for helping."

She beamed and handed him the mic.

Dad raised one palm until students quieted, then placed the mic to his mouth. "Tonight we meet Belle Fourche."

"Boo," students cried.

"We'll surprise the Broncos, as General Washington surprised the world when he beat the British. Come with your voices. Come with your cowbells. Come with your stomping feet." He stamped one foot and jabbed the air with his index finger. "Be there!"

The pep band struck up the fight song. Students followed Will's example. They stomped, chopped the air with a finger, and chanted, "Be there!"

Deb's pulse hammered. Standing in the front row of bleachers in the Arena, she still couldn't believe she'd hopped on stage that afternoon. But the cheerleaders and the team had needed her. Tonight, even if all the lights here cut out, the place would be electrified with students stomping feet, the pep band and cheerleaders in Continental dress, and Mr. Brown in a white wig, shooting beach balls from the cannon into the stands.

Deb nudged Haddy next to her. "We've got 'em."

Haddy pointed to the lockers. "And here comes the team."

The Warriors surged onto the court wearing three-cornered hats and orange Continental coats over their warmups.

The Broncos' coach pulled a referee aside and cupped his hands up to the ref's ear to speak over the clang of cowbells. But by the time the ref turned back around, the Warriors had stripped down to their silky white shirts and trunks trimmed with orange and black.

Elaine started the "Louie Louie" stomp, and the cheerleaders ran through their dance routine. She threw her megaphone to Deb. "They can't hear me. Come on."

Deb hesitated, then moved alongside the cheerleaders. Power surged through her. She'd never been so alive, so much a part of something. She filed up and down the bleacher line, drawing each section into one cheer, then another.

CHAPTER 27

Clobbered

After the final buzzer sounded, Will and the guys escaped to the dressing room. Clobbered by fifteen points.

Erik slammed his high tops against a metal locker, sending a shock wave through the room. "Ran all over us."

"And why?" Will asked.

No one answered.

"Come on. Think!" Will said.

The heaving of the boys' lungs slowed.

Simon raked his fingers through his damp hair. "The Broncos got into position for every shot."

"We didn't," Jord mumbled.

Will smashed his fist into his palm so hard it stung. "Don't you remember what I told you about the Roman army? *Organized*. If we'd been like them, we'd have won. So are you ready to become the Team Machine of the Dakotas?"

Simon stepped forward. "Ready."

Teammates massed around him. "Ready."

"Then let's do it! No game until after Christmas, but I expect to see you in the gym every day but Sunday and the holidays." He shook a finger at them and shouted. "Be there!"

"Be there!" everyone yelled back.

All but Erik. At the edge of the group, he crossed his arms.

Will aimed his eyes at him. "If you're going to be on this team . . . ."

Erik met his teammates' stares. "I'll be there," he muttered.

"All right!" Will turned toward the door. Energy sizzled through him. This could be the beginning.

He strode out of the room right into Lyle Mykland's chest.

"Watch what you're doing," Mykland said.

Will reached out to pat Mykland's shoulder. "Good game, Lyle. Your guys pulled it off."

Mykland pushed Will's arm away. "Call me *Coach* Mykland. And you still have the losers." He strode off.

Will's eyes trailed after him. "Not for long."

During Christmas break, Will drilled the varsity guys on the fundamentals until they could have performed them in their sleep.

But they still moved like a train whose cars were disconnected. Was it Erik's temper? When Will named Simon the starting center, Erik fumed. Then when the guys voted Simon to be team captain, Erik stomped off.

During a five-on-five scrimmage that had just ended, Erik screamed at his teammates for no reason. Will shook his head and turned to Arthur. "I don't know what to do. The tighter I coach Erik, the angrier he gets. Then all the guys pick up his vibes like stomach flu."

"Mmm hmm," Arthur said. "Maybe he needs lighter reins."

"What do you mean?"

"I trained horses back in Memphis. Had this powerful Arabian with an attitude big as his stride. When I held his reins tight, he fought me. But when I loosened 'em a bit, he flew. He knew I was still in control, but that I respected him."

Will rubbed his jaw. "You may be onto something, Arthur. Call in the guys."

Arthur blew his whistle. "Y'all come in."

The boys huddled up, catching their breaths and wiping their faces with their tees.

Will palmed the ball. "Black squad, take center court while I give orange squad instructions."

He waited until black squad left. "Simon, you tip to Erik, because Erik's so tall he can grab it."

Erik straightened. A smile spread across his face.

"You'll be ready, right, Erik?"

"Of course."

"You decide who to move the ball to."

He lifted his chin. "Will do."

"Then you race to the basket, where you wait for the ball. All of you, move it back and forth until someone is open. Everyone is absolutely crucial to get the ball to the net. Got it?"

"Got it."

He clapped his hands. "Let's do it!"

The guys moved to center court. Simon tipped to Erik, who passed to Karl, who advanced it to Steve. He moved it to Wayne, who flipped it back to Simon, who found Erik open. He angled it off the glass and into the basket. Erik let out a "yes!" and Simon high-fived him.

Will gave Arthur a knowing nod.

Arthur grinned. "Now that stallion's runnin' with you."

But it wasn't enough.

Against Vermillion next Friday, at the end of the fourth quarter, Jord missed a free throw that would have tied the score. Another loss.

Now, as the team waited in the locker room before facing Worthington, Will's thoughts dashed around. What had he gotten into? Coordinating pep rallies. Fending off the police chief. A team without a single win.

Yet what mattered was Deb. She was a rose opening for the first time. No, not a rose. More like a sunflower with its wild yellow petals stretching toward the sky. She was as surprised as he was with her ability to lead cheers before the student body.

But if the team didn't come through, the principal might toss Will. Then Deb, his sunflower, would wilt, dropping petals on a prairie path leading back to the reservation. Back to a dead-end life.

He needed a win.

Will pulled the boys into a huddle. He signaled to Simon. "Words from our captain?"

Simon's face glowed. "We're a unit." He placed one arm around Jord's shoulder and the other around Erik's.

Erik followed suit and put an arm around Simon, then turned to Barry on his other side. He stared down at the guy he'd called *dim*. "Whatever," he said, and dangled his arm across Barry's shoulder.

Barry smiled and did the same. The team locked together in unity.

Simon flashed a smile. "Tonight's our night, guys. Be as bold as Leif Erikson!"

"Bold!" they echoed. They jammed horned Viking helmets on their heads and raced out onto the floor. Arthur followed, pushing their Viking longship. Winds of confidence had filled the pep rally earlier today when the team highlighted the Norwegian explorer. Now, that confidence coursed through the Arena.

But when the ref tossed the opening ball, Simon missed it. A Trojan grabbed it and dashed down the court for an easy two. The tribe moved like mush. By the half, the Trojans held a five-point lead.

In the third period, Simon and Erik finally picked up their rhythm. Their momentum spread like flames in a forest, and the Warriors wore out the Trojans. When the final horn sounded, the tribe had squeaked by 60-58.

Fans converged onto the court. Deb sprinted over to Will. Her eyes sparkled, and she enveloped him in a huge hug. Then she threw one arm into the air and yelled, "Be bold!" over and over, nearly pulling Will to the ground.

Will blinked back tears. Even sweeter than this victory was seeing Deb so alive. But he needed some place to be alone. He forced himself away and headed to the locker room.

When he entered, the crowd's roar muffled. A slight rustle came from somewhere, and Will scanned the room. Lyle Mykland slouched in a corner. His junior varsity had lost by four buckets, their first defeat of the season.

Will touched Mykland's shoulder. "Sorry about the loss."

Mykland turned. His face red, he shrugged off Will's hand. "Your days are numbered." He stomped off.

CHAPTER 28

We Khan

A week later, Deb stood with fans in the Arena, waiting for the final buzzer. The pep squad had decided that because she led cheers, she should join them in wearing a uniform. She displayed the orange sweater and black skirt with pride.

"Five, four, three, two, one," everyone counted. Pandemonium. Then Deb's megaphone cut through the noise and united everyone in a chant. "We Khan take the world!" The junior varsity had stumbled by fifteen, but the varsity had smoked the Heelan Crusaders by twelve points.

Five months ago, if anyone had told Deb she'd be leading the school in cheers, she would have turned and run. After all, she had been the rez girl, as quiet as a field mouse. Not anymore. Here she was, hollering the silly cheer she'd taught the student body at the pep rally earlier today that highlighted emperor Kublai Khan.

So strange being in the spotlight. Students she didn't know called out her name in the school hallways. "Great cheers, Deb." Heat rose in her face every time, but she made sure she smiled back. Succeed gracefully—that's what Dad said.

She didn't mind everyone knowing she was the varsity coach's daughter. He was the coolest teacher in the building.

The coolest man in town, for that matter. He'd brought the whole community together. Today at the pep rally, Haddy's father set up a table with basketball charms and pins for sale in the school lobby. Erik's father blasted his police siren in the school parking lot before sauntering into the auditorium in his puke-green pants with a black stripe. And Simon's father, Pastor Pete, showed up, laughing and gesturing the sign of the cross as if he were giving a blessing.

Dad always appeared confident at school. But at home, he'd get lost in thought at the supper table. Then he'd spot her studying him and paste on a smile. "It'll be okay."

Beyond okay tonight. Simon, drenched in sweat and a smile, winked at her as he jogged off the court.

Deb jumped up and down and led the crowd in the chant. "We Khan take the world!"

Anything seemed possible.

Deb couldn't stop grinning from the edge of the auditorium stage. At this pep rally, the student body was as energized as the giant plywood cutout of a light bulb the basketball team carried onstage. And for good reason. The Warriors had won every game in the past weeks, launching them through the sectionals and into the state championship. Now, one more win, and they'd be in the finals.

Barry gestured to the plywood cutout glowing with real bulbs. He aimed his mouth into the mic. "My name is Barry Dimm, but no way am I a *dim* bulb."

The crowd howled. The nerd was coming on strong.

Simon joined Barry at the mic. "Thomas Edison tried six thousand materials before he found the right one to turn on the power."

That was Deb's cue to lead the audience in her new chant to *turn on the power*. But Simon stayed at the mic and thrust his index finger at the audience. "Edison teaches us that where there's a will, there is a way."

Students jumped to their feet. "Where there's a Will, there is a way," they hollered. They chopped their index fingers toward Dad at the edge of the stage.

He stiffened and took a step back.

Cheerleaders picked up the chant and shook their poms. Deb joined them. "Where there's a Will, there is a way."

Dad waved his arms to get the crowd to stop.

They didn't.

"Where there's a Will, there is a way. Where there's a Will, there is a way."

Why didn't Dad soak up the attention?

She followed his glance as he searched through the auditorium. Principal Ruud and Coach Mykland sat next to each other, cross-armed and crimson.

CHAPTER 29

Culturally Acceptable

That night, the Warriors turned on the power, defeating the Brookings Bobcats 82-66. Afterward, the varsity snapped towels at each other in the locker room.

"Guys." Will raised his voice to get their attention. "You've earned your place in the finals."

"Right on!" They danced around.

"You've pushed hard, so you've got to rest like Chief Crazy Horse's warriors before they fought Custer. Custer's men rode into battle exhausted, and they were creamed. So you have a nine p.m. curfew until game time. Break it, and you're benched. Got it?"

"Got it!" everyone yelled, lifting their arms.

Will strode away with shouts of victory echoing in his ears. He hoped his rule wasn't too severe.

The following Monday, Will locked his hands behind his back and paced in front of his Shop guys. "I don't know. Every other historic figure we've spotlighted for a rally was—how can I say this—culturally acceptable."

"But *you* gave us the idea of Crazy Horse," Erik said. "Now you're saying you're not proud of him?"

"Of course I am. But focusing on an Indian? It's like drawing attention to myself. Like that cheer last week—*Where there's a Will.* Too much."

"But we are the Warriors," Simon said.

"Seems logical," Barry added.

Will brushed at his jawline. "People aren't always logical."

"It'll be fine," Erik said.

On Friday morning before school, Will and his Shop boys struggled to set up a tepee on the stage even while the Art class applied the last touches of paint to its sides.

"Hold it," Will yelled.

Too late. It collapsed in a heap. A can of orange paint tipped over, and Art students chased after the spill with rags before it oozed off the stage.

Will let out a huff. "Brace it with a two-by-four."

For the umpteenth time, he reminded himself these rallies were worth it.

Arthur rushed up with panic on his face. "Coach, gotta talk to ya."

"Not now. Need to check with the cheerleaders. I don't want students picking up on the wrong cheer like they did last week." Will jumped down from the stage.

"But—"

"Not now, Arthur." He raised his voice more than he wished. "Catch me after the rally."

CHAPTER 30

Ho-ka Hey

The auditorium vibrated with rhythmic clapping as students stood and waited. In front of the closed curtain, Deb called out to the cheerleaders at her elbow so they would hear her. "The moment the band appears, we harness this energy."

From the back of the auditorium, the doors flew open. Band members marched down the center aisle showing off fringed, tan slacks and shirts and headbands with feathers. Deb and the cheerleaders ran to center stage in Indian dresses. Mr. Brown yanked the curtain open, and the varsity team spilled out of a tepee, lines of orange paint decorating their faces and bare chests. They carried bows and arrows. Students cheered.

Jordy approached the lectern. He held a bow and arrow at his side and quivered like a trapped rabbit.

Mr. Lundy jumped up from the audience and flashed a photo of his son.

Deb cringed. Jordy was rattled enough without imagining his bare chest on the cover of tomorrow's newspaper.

Jordy buried his head in his notes. "Chief Crazy Horse," he mumbled, "defeated General Custer."

"Tell 'em. Jordy," Simon hollered.

A flash of confidence straightened Jordy's skinny body. He crumpled his notes. "We can defeat Rapid City." He glued his lips to the mic and raised his bow. "We are the Warriors!"

"Warriors!" the throng repeated.

"We fight with Crazy Horse's cry: Get 'em! *Ho-ka hey!*"

Deb and the cheerleaders moved forward, intending to lead a chant of *get 'em.* Instead, the student body roared into a repetition of *ho-ka hey.*

Deb beamed. She'd taught this phrase to Jordy, but hadn't intended for it to be a cheer. Maybe this was better.

The team joined in the chant. They stormed the aisles, beating their chests and shouting war whoops, then exiting through the auditorium doors.

Deb jumped up and down and hugged the cheerleaders. They truly were Warriors.

CHAPTER 31

Stolen Reins

Ho-ka hey? Where did that come from? Will had stayed in the back of the auditorium for this rally. He didn't want attention drawn to him like at the last event. But the repetition of that Indian phrase had thrown the spotlight on him again. Where did the cheerleaders learn it?

From Deb?

Had to be.

That was a mistake.

As students crowded around him and cheered *ho-ka hey,* he held up his palms and backed toward the doors.

This rally's focus on being warriors was an error. Without his permission, the guys had added war paint and war whoops, an insult to Native Americans. But they didn't understand that.

He surveyed the audience. Lyle Mykland's face was icy. No surprise there. His j.v. guys had ended the season at the bottom of the pack. And Principal Ruud didn't look happy, even though Will was taking the team to the state finals. Only a win would satisfy that man.

Will exited the doors and maneuvered to get out of the tangle of students who gathered around like he was a rock star.

"Coach?"

The weight of an arm on his shoulder slowed him. He turned.

Arthur stood before him, bare chested, made up with orange war paint and a feathered headband running through his Afro. Even though his getup was ridiculous, his face held unutterable sadness.

Will moved him out of the pack of students. "Yeah, Arthur?"

"Been tryin' to tell ya. Your stallion done steal the reins."

Will called Erik aside in the locker room before the game. "Need a word with you."

Erik pranced over and pounded on his bare chest streaked with orange paint. "With the ball, I do it all."

"Mr. Brown says he drove to the Barrel for a burger last night."

Erik stiffened. "Yeah?"

"Says he got there about eleven, and you were leaving."

Erik scuffed a hightop. "I, uh, got hungry."

A volcano rose up in Will, but he shoved it down. "You broke curfew the night before—"

"No big deal. I didn't get drunk or nothin'."

"Defying your coach is no big deal? Letting down your team is no big deal?"

Erik raised his chin. "It was no big deal."

Sorrow washed over Will. If he let Erik play, he'd communicate that doing the expedient thing was more important than doing the right thing. "You'll warm the bench."

"No!" Erik screamed.

"Yes," Will whispered.

Erik stomped off.

Will huddled up the rest of the guys. "As we planned, starters are Simon, Karl, Wayne, and Steve. Completing the lineup will be"—Will searched around the tribe—"Jord."

Jord's face turned as white as a turnip.

Guys gasped.

"Why, Coach?" Simon asked.

"No time to explain. Let's go."

Will jogged out of the locker room with his boys. The Arena rocked from the beat of the pulsing pep band dressed in Indian garb. Fans wearing headbands with feathers stomped their feet and chanted *ho-ka hey*. But all this was muffled by the sound of Will's pounding heart.

He was vaguely aware of the team taking a lap around the court with their chests bare, then throwing on their silky white shirts and running through their warmup.

He didn't remember calling the team around him, but they gathered.

Erik stared at him, his mouth tight.

Will shook his head.

Erik stomped to the end of the bench and flopped down.

Will turned to the others. Their eyes held fear. How could he imbue his team with hope that they could take the Cobblers without Erik? "Men." His voice quavered. "We're a unit. That's how we practiced. That's how we play it. Tonight we're digging deeper into ourselves than ever before. So let's get 'em!"

They clasped their hands together. "Get 'em." They mouthed the words without energy.

At the referee's whistle, Simon tipped the ball toward Jord, but he missed it. Rapid City bounded down the court for a quick bucket. The Cobblers continued to flash by them. By halftime, the tribe was down by ten.

When the team assembled in the locker room, Erik stayed off to the side, his face twisted with embarrassment that his jersey was still fresh. The rest of the guys slumped on the bench, gasping for breath and wiping their faces with their shirts.

What could Will say? He paced, studying the chipped concrete floor. Peace gradually filled him, and he raised his head. His heart swelled with feelings that would make his boys blush if he expressed them. Affection. Pride. Love.

He kept his voice low. "Don't forget, guys, we never *work* basketball. We *play* basketball."

They lifted their heads. Their breathing slowed.

He made eye contact with each of them.

Tightness in their faces dissolved.

"We do this for fun. We love the rough of the ball on our palms. The squeak of the shoes on the court. Even love the taste of sweat."

They chuckled.

"So go out there and have some fun. You're the comeback kids, remember? Keep moving the ball down the court, and we'll show 'em how games are won in the second half."

They grinned, and an energized tribe emerged from the lockers, moving with the lightness of a Saturday pickup game.

But a chorus of chanting met them. "We want Erik. We want Erik."

Will searched the stands. Erik's father stood, his arms folded over his green uniform shirt. Principal Ruud flanked him, his face a scowl.

Had Will punished Erik enough? If he put Erik in now, the boy would easily bring the skill they needed.

Erik sulked like he was playing to the crowd.

Will bit his lip. He couldn't. He shook his head at Erik, then turned back to his team. A smile filled his face. "Play *our* game, boys."

They huddled and clasped hands. "Get 'em," they yelled.

Setup by setup, the Warriors found their footing and gradually narrowed the gap between the scores. Near the end of the fourth period, Steve passed to Wayne, who banked it off the glass into the hoop from the far corner. The tribe moved one point ahead.

Rapid City advanced the ball down the boards slowly, eating up the clock. With five seconds left, they swished a basket to take a one-point lead.

Simon captured the ball and searched down the court.

Jord was free, jumping up and down like he had ants in his shorts.

Simon rocketed the ball to him. Jord grabbed it and dribbled once.

He was open.

An easy shot.

He fired.

Silence filled the Arena.

The ball drifted up as though in slow motion.

It hit the rim. Rolled around twice. Then fell off the side with a deafening *thunk.*

The buzzer sounded.

The Warriors had lost by one point.

Erik stomped off.

Fans booed Will and mobbed him on the floor, jostling him until he nearly fell.

Lars Lundy bolted up to Will and grabbed his collar. "Why'd you put Jord under that pressure?"

Will placed a hand on Lundy's shoulder. "None of us can prepare for everything."

He trudged toward the lockers alone, booing pounding in his ears. He scanned the bleachers. The police chief's glare propelled a hand grenade into Will's soul.

CHAPTER 32

Lost

Deb clenched her fists as she waited for Dad to arrive home from the game. The doorknob turned, and he entered. But not with his usual ramrod posture. Slouched.

She raced forward and buried her head in his chest. "We lost."

He folded his arms around her, and his breath brushed her face. "We didn't lose. Just didn't win this one."

She pulled herself away. "Why didn't you play Erik? Everyone's saying we would have slaughtered 'em if you had."

"That's between him and me. Now why aren't you out with your friends?"

"I didn't want you to be alone."

He held her shoulders. "Kind of you. But I bet you'd like to get a burger." He offered his keys. "My car's square, I know, but it'll get you there."

She wiped her eyes. "You sure you're okay?"

"Go."

"Thanks." She planted a kiss on his cheek and left.

A gust of cold wind hit Will as Deb slammed the door behind her. Still in his coat and gloves, he fell into a folding chair. So the whole town blamed him.

Ruud had demanded he capture the state championship. He hadn't.

Erik's father and Lyle Mykland thirsted for blood. They might talk the principal into anything. Even sacking him.

He'd lay low and hope he could make it through spring.

CHAPTER 33

The Real Romeo and Juliet

Deb's head flopped forward at her desk like a wilted daffodil. Was there air in this classroom? Around her, students sprawled and fanned themselves with blue-lined sheets of notebook paper.

"Mr. Tollefson, can we open some windows?" Simon asked.

The teacher turned from the chalkboard. "They swell in the winter. Re-FUSE to budge when spring comes. But you can try."

The guys extricated themselves from their desks and shoved at the windows until they forced them open. A breeze drifted in.

Students sucked air into their lungs. Deb tapped her Bic pen and stared out the windows at the budding trees. Rolly Tolly scrawled something on the blackboard, but she paid no attention.

"A bad case of *senioritis* going around," Rolly Tolly said, his mustache twitching. "But I can't set you free until I rip sixty more pages off the daily calendar. So we're revisiting something I was SORE-ly disappointed in." He motioned toward the board.

In large letters—*Romeo and Juliet*.

Erik sat straight. "That nightmare?"

"For once, I agree with Carrot Top," Elaine said.

Deb squelched her laugh.

"We didn't get to experience the beauty in this story of star-crossed lovers," Rolly Tolly said. "Today, I call on the two who didn't get to live those scenes. The UN-der-studies."

Deb's breath left her.

A chorus of *"oooooooos"* filled the room.

Deb glanced at the wall clock. Ten minutes until class ended. No escaping. She peeked at Simon at the other side of the room. His face was as red as a ripe tomato. Did hers look the same?

Rolly Tolly spread his arms wide. "Romeo and Juliet, step forward."

Deb's legs turned wobbly, but she made it to the front. She and Simon accepted scripts and planted themselves on opposite sides of the room.

"First, the context," Rolly Tolly said. "Romeo sees the en-TI-cing, innocent Juliet dancing at the ball."

Another ensemble of *"oooooos"* rippled through the room.

Deb buried her head in her script.

"Romeo is overcome," Rolly Tolly said, placing a hand on his heart. "He says, *O, she doth teach the torches to burn bright!* Simon, repeat that."

Simon mumbled the line.

Rolly Tolly glared. "NO. Look at her. Pick it up in Act One, Scene Five."

"Tell her, man," Erik whispered loud enough for everyone to hear. "You've been burnin' with it all year."

Snickers flowed around the rows of desks.

Deb dug her head deeper into the script.

Simon fumbled with his pages. *"O, she doth teach the torches to burn bright!"* His voice was as bland as unbuttered potatoes.

He stopped.

Deb glanced up. Why did he stop? It wasn't her turn to read.

He lowered his book and locked his eyes onto Deb's.

She couldn't turn hers away.

"Did my heart love till now?" His voice dropped to a breathless whisper. *"Forswear it, sight. For I ne'er saw true beauty till this night."*

Deb's pulse sped.

"Great PAS-sion." Rolly Tolly's voice filled with excitement. "Now Romeo, walk toward Juliet and raise your palm. Start down the page with *If I profane*."

Simon moved forward. He raised his palm and let the book fall to the floor. Sweat beaded on his brow. His mouth opened.

"If I profane with my unworthiest hand
This holy shrine, the gentle sin is this:
My lips, two blushing pilgrims, ready stand
To smooth that rough touch with a tender kiss."

Deb's brain froze. She'd dreamed of a time like this with Simon. But in public? Her voice quavered. "S*aints have hands that pilgrims' hands do touch."*

She raised her palm. It trembled. She placed it against Simon's. Her breath caught. His hand stilled the tremors in hers. The joining of her slender hand with Simon's large one stunned her. Warmth flowed through him, up her arm. *"And palm to palm is holy palmers kiss."* Her voice cracked.

Simon's mouth quivered. *"Have not saints lips, and holy palmers too?"*

The heat from his hand traveled to her heart and quickened its pulsing. *"Ay, pilgrim, lips that they must use in pray'r."*

Simon pressed his palm deeper into Deb's. *"O, then, dear saint, let lips do what hands do!"*

He inched closer and leaned down so their faces were inches apart. His pine scent rolled over her. His liquid eyes called her into their swirling waters.

Deb struggled to find her voice. *"Saints do not move-"*

"Then move not," Simon interrupted, *"while my prayer's effect I take."* His lips parted. They poised above her.

Their breaths mixed as one. A holy exchange.

Simon's lips edged closer.

Their naked palms pressed together, hotter every second. Their pulses beat as one. Their lips lingered an inch apart.

Rolly Tolly's arm flashed between them. "Cut! Didn't you hear me say *cut*?"

Deb and Simon jolted back.

The bell sounded.

"Ah, we'll revisit *Moby Dick* tomorrow," Rolly Tolly said. "PLEN-ty of water there to douse any flames."

Snickering students filed by Deb and Simon on their way out.

Elaine and Haddy dragged Deb to the hallway. "Come on, swoon loon," Haddy said.

Deb's lips radiated.

Shoulder to shoulder, Elaine and Haddy moved Deb down the hall.

Up ahead, guys surrounded Simon.

Simon turned back to Deb, his face pleading, but the guys swept him away.

Throughout the day in the classes they shared, Simon stole glances at her.

Her mouth was in a permanent curve upward.

Would something happen at school tomorrow?

CHAPTER 34

Tryst

The next morning, dressed in her baggy white t-shirt and shorts for P.E., Deb jogged around the outside of the school. Her mind was still a jumble from what happened yesterday. Something holy, like with Romeo and Juliet. A transfer of trust. A union of spirits. A bond that couldn't be broken through time and trouble. Her breath heaved from excitement more than from running.

"Pick up the pace." Coach Mykland's voice bellowed from where he lolled on the school lawn.

Let him holler. She floated in a happy daze.

Footsteps sounded from behind. As her left arm swung back in the rhythm of her run, something wedged between her thumb and fingers. Then Simon loped next to her for a moment, his eyes forward, his face a sheen of sweat. He sprinted past, his slender hips a blur.

She squeezed her hand. A slip of paper. Her heart raced faster than her feet. She unfolded the note: *Madam, I am here. What is your will?*

A line from *Romeo and Juliet*.

What was her will? That she longed for the touch of Simon's hand again. The nearness of his breath.

But Simon hadn't voiced his will. He should play his hand before she revealed her heart.

She stuffed the note into her shorts pocket. When she, Elaine, and Haddy squeezed together around their gym locker she didn't say a word.

"What's up?" Elaine asked. "Your face is so bright we could get sunburned."

"Recovering from yesterday."

"May you never recover," Haddy said.

In second period World Lit, Rolly Tolly assigned an essay on water imagery in *Moby Dick* and gave students time to work in class.

Water imagery? Who cared? She touched Simon's note in her skirt pocket. Maybe she could write back with a line from *Romeo and Juliet*. Rolly Tolly would be suspicious if she borrowed a classroom copy. She waved her hand. "Mr. Tollefson, can I go to the library for a reference book?"

Rolly Tolly's mustache twitched. "I always welcome i-NI-tia-tive."

Haddy's and Elaine's foreheads scrunched.

Deb mouthed to them, "No big deal." She scooped up her books and brushed past Simon, who bent over his spiral notebook.

At the library, Deb sifted through the card catalogue for *Romeo and Juliet*. She copied down the Dewey Decimal number and headed to the shelf. She skimmed her hand along the spines. *Gone!*

Her body turned cold. She hurried to Fat Sherwood at the front desk, who slouched over a book. "Miss Sherwood, I can't find *Romeo and Juliet*."

Fat Sherwood lowered *Valley of the Dolls* and peered up at Deb through lenses that distorted her eyes. "Couples like that are in short supply." She tightened her bun. "But if you're looking for the book"—she reached toward a stack—"Simon returned it before school."

Deb's face warmed at the mention of his name. "Thanks."

Fat Sherwood stamped the inside flap and handed it to her.

Deb excused herself to a heavy oak table and sat alone. She flipped through. In his note, Simon asked what her will was. She'd answer with a question. And this one was perfect. She copied it onto a sheet of lined notebook paper and creased it, then returned the book.

The librarian's brow furrowed. "Didn't need it long."

Deb blinked fast. "Guess not."

She returned to World Lit.

"Find anything on WA-ter imagery?" Rolly Tolly asked.

"No."

"A shame."

As she passed by Simon's desk, Deb dropped her note. From her seat, she glanced up to watch him open it. How would he answer her question? *What man art thou?*

He unfolded and refolded it three times.

When the bell rang, Deb walked with Haddy and Elaine to Home Ec but didn't absorb a word of their chatter. Simon would be in Shop now. He'd probably ask for a library pass. Make an excuse about studying the history of tools or something.

Fat Sherwood arrived at Home Ec from her library duties and called the class to order with a clap of her hands. "Ladies, today we will discuss the latest fashion trends."

Deb zoned out until she heard her name and something about toothpicks. She jerked to attention. "I don't have any toothpicks."

Girls around her snickered.

Fat Sherwood's glared. "I was saying the miniskirt is passé, which is fine because it only looked good on people with toothpick legs like you."

Deb slid down in her chair.

"Earth to Deb," Haddy whispered. "Come in for a landing."

After class, the three girls walked toward their lockers. "You're so gone," Elaine said, "you might walk into a wall."

"Am not," Deb said. She turned sideways and smacked into a post.

Haddy and Elaine doubled over in laughter.

Deb shook the stars out of her eyes enough to spot something pressed into the air vent of her locker—a folded note. She grabbed it before her girlfriends saw it and shielded herself to read: *Call me but love.*

"I'm skipping lunch," she said. "Not hungry."

"Gotta be a *Simon Says* game going on," Haddy said.

Deb took off down the hall without answering.

When she entered the library, Fat Sherwood lifted her head from her book, *Couples*. A grin covered her face. She handed Deb *Romeo and Juliet*. "Popular book today."

Deb's face flushed. "Guess so." She moved to a pillar and leaned against it. How should she respond to Simon's message to call him *love*? Her hand trembled as she riffled through the pages. Here was something. *If thou dost love, pronounce it faithfully.* She transferred it to a note.

On the way to Homeroom, she sneaked her message onto Simon's stack of books in his arm and kept moving, but peeked back to watch him.

He tugged the note open, stiffened, then took off, vaulting the steps two at a time until a hall monitor yelled, "Slow down!"

He never showed up for Homeroom.

On Deb's way into World History, Simon slipped her a message.

While Coach Mykland cleaned the board, she read: *Lady, by yonder blessed moon I swear.*

Her palms moistened.

Coach Mykland asked for a volunteer to return magazines to the library. Deb shot up her hand. "I'll do it!"

He smirked. "A Running Bear running an errand for me? Love it."

She winced, but grabbed his stack of magazines.

"While you're there," he said, "pick up the latest *Sports Illustrated* for me."

"Sure," she called back.

At the librarian's front desk, she plunked Mykland's magazines onto the return pile.

Fat Sherwood smiled, set down *Peyton Place*, and handed Deb *Romeo and Juliet*. "You might ponder the scene I marked. Extremely romantic." She blinked rapidly.

"Yes, ma'am." Deb disappeared behind the stack of biographies. She opened to the librarian's cloth paisley bookmark and read the context. This was *hot*. Would she dare send this to Simon? Her lips opened as she took a slow breath in, and her eyelids closed as she released it.

She would.

She copied the text and returned the book. "Thank you."

Fat Sherwood smiled. "Glad to be helpful."

When Deb entered World History, Coach Mykland glared. "Well?"

"Huh?"

"*Sports Illustrated*?"

Her jaw dropped. "I forgot."

He crossed his arms. "Knew I couldn't trust a Running Bear."

She ignored his tone and took her seat.

On the way into Art, Deb sneaked her note to Simon.

He tumbled into his seat and opened it.

How would he respond to her bold question? *O Romeo, Romeo! wherefore art thou Romeo?*

Blood drained from his face.

At the front of the room, VD tidied his combover. "This is the chic of Cubism," he said, displaying a print of a woman whose oversized eyeball had shifted toward her nostril.

Simon raised his hand. "Mr. Dahl, I think I'm gonna barf."

VD squinted. "You're white as a clean canvas. Go see the school nurse."

"Thank you." Simon stumbled toward the door.

VD lectured on and on about "abstraction" and "avant-garde."

Deb drummed her fingers on the desk. Simon had been gone too long. Maybe he *was* sick.

The door burst open and Simon dashed in, his face flushed. He fell into his chair.

VD cocked his head. "Looks like you got a blood transfusion."

"Sort of."

On the way out of class, Simon slipped a folded note to Deb. He rushed off to Study Hall.

She buried the note in her palm and headed to Chorus. Elaine and Haddy caught up. "You think we're thick as bricks?" Haddy asked.

Deb said nothing.

"So ignore us," Elaine said. "I'm gonna get my daily dose of *Hart* throbbing in Chorus."

Haddy laughed. "What good is it to rev your heart over a teacher five years older than you? That's ancient."

"He's the only man in this school worth looking at," Elaine said.

Deb held back a snicker. Little did she know.

The girls took their places among the altos. Mr. Hart smoothed his honey-hair into place and lifted his baton. "We'll open with *The Impossible Dream*. Altos, let's nail down that section about loving in a chaste way."

The heat of Simon's note burned in Deb's hand as she sang.

Finally, the altos got a break. Elaine continued her ogle-fest of Heartthrob's tight torso. Haddy rolled her eyes back in boredom.

Deb opened her sweaty palm and unfolded the note. *"Library after school. R & J together?"*

Elaine nudged her. "You okay? You're as pale as us white people."

Deb squeezed the note. "Fine." Although she was about to burst.

"Fantle's got in new capris," Haddy said. "Wanna check 'em out after school?"

"Right on!" Elaine said.

Deb smiled. "I have some research."

Haddy nodded slowly. "Lovesick."

When class let out, Deb hightailed it to her locker. She was so flustered, she couldn't remember the lock combination. She messed with it until she landed on the numbers, then dumped her books. She rushed to the lavatory, combed her fingers through her hair, and freshened her cranberry lipstick. Then she hustled to the library.

At the entrance, she paused and took two deep breaths, then pushed against the door. No sign of Simon.

Fat Sherwood signaled her over. The librarian handed her the copy of *Romeo and Juliet*. "Looks like something inside for you." Her voice was all sing-songy.

The corner of a sheet of notebook paper stuck out of one edge. Deb unfolded it. *I take thee at thy word. North side, by the windows.*

How did Simon know this was her favorite area? Had he watched her stealing away there to hide in a book?

She passed by the card catalogue, wound around the periodicals, and threaded through bookshelves.

She was on the north side now. Her sanctuary. But today she was as rattled as a pane of glass in a storm. The two-story arched windows flooded the area with light, and as her vision adjusted, she recognized Simon's lanky frame in silhouette, facing the windows.

He turned toward her.

She took a step forward and caught his details. He was as grand as when she spotted him on that first awkward day of school. Blond hair moving to its own rhythm. Liquid eyes to drown in. Deb's heart leaped as it had then. But this time, she didn't hold back in responding. She allowed her whole being to soar.

"I didn't know whether you'd come," Simon whispered.

She moved next to him. Her body vibrated at his closeness. "*I take thee at thy word.*"

He pursed his lips. "I've never been so scared in my life."

"Me neither."

"Then we're on the same page."

She lifted the copy of *Romeo and Juliet*. "Which page?"

"I don't know, Deb. All I know is that we've been *star-crossed,* like Romeo and Juliet, all year. My fault. I've been such a klutz."

She opened the book. "We could take our lines from here."

"As long as we skip the tragic part."

She grinned. "So where do we start?"

His paused. "Pick up in the scene from class?"

Her mouth turned dry. "Okay."

He glanced around. "We're safe. Sherwood's not in the forest."

She giggled.

Simon took a deep breath, then siphoned it out. "I don't remember my lines." He fumbled to find the page and cleared his throat. He raised a trembling palm. "*If I profane with my unworthiest hand this holy shrine, the gentle fine is this.*" He lowered the book. "*My lips, two blushing pilgrims, ready stand to smooth that rough touch with a tender kiss.*"

Simon's presence overwhelmed Deb. He was a magnet, drawing her to him. His pine cologne wafted over her. Tingles filled her. She raised her palm and placed it against his. "*Saints have hands that pilgrims' hands do touch.*" The heat of Simon's hand ignited a fire. She whispered, "*And palm to palm is holy palmers' kiss.*"

He drew his face toward her.

Their breaths mingled.

Her eyelids closed. Her mouth opened, quivering.

His lips met hers, a kiss as luscious as a fresh-picked strawberry.

His arms slid around her waist.

Electricity.

She placed her hand on his shoulder.

His kiss deepened, their mouths one.

The room spun.

Nearby, someone coughed.

Deb's lips broke from Simon's.

Fat Sherwood stood before them. She clasped her hands, and her eyes danced through her thick lenses. "Time for the library to close. Try the courtyard scene somewhere else. It's my favorite."

CHAPTER 35

Wildfire

The next day in Chorus, Deb counted off the seconds until the hands on the wall clock hit three-thirty. The bell clanged. She bolted from her seat.

"Wanna go shopping?" Elaine asked.

"Uh, not today."

"More library research?" Haddy asked.

Deb's face burned. "Yeah."

She headed out of the room.

"She's twitterpated." Haddy's voice drifted from behind.

When Deb and Simon shared a kiss yesterday, they'd agreed to meet again in the library after school. But he'd avoided her all day. What was going on?

Deb reached the library and headed to the north side. Simon stood under the arched windows, his face lost in silhouette.

She moved toward him, and her eyes adjusted to the light. His mouth was a tight line. What was wrong?

He ran his hand through his thatch of hair. "I, uh. We probably shouldn't go over more *Romeo and Juliet lines,*" he whispered.

"You don't want to meet?" Deb turned to leave.

"Wait." His hand touched her arm and stopped her.

Numbness filled her. She sat.

He joined her, but kept a distance. "Deb, this guy-girl thing is new to me. I want to be with you, and I know all we've done is kiss, but I don't know what to do about this"—he shoved his hands into his pockets—"wildfire inside me."

She released the breath she'd held unconsciously. "It's burning in me, too."

"Really? I guess that's good. We're on the same page. But I don't know how to control myself. I don't want to do anything we'd regret."

She traced the outline of graffiti on the wooden table, a heart with an arrow through it that a couple had left behind. This guy-girl stuff was new to her, too. She'd never had a boyfriend. Never trusted guys. With all their bravado, they'd always been impossible to read, so she'd avoided them. Never opened her heart even a crack. But Simon was as transparent as a spring stream. She didn't want to lose whatever might be between them. "This is new territory for me, too. Can we somehow be careful?"

"Yeah. So maybe, no kissing? But still greet each other with a palm-to-palm?"

She lifted her shaking hand toward him.

He raised his, burying her hand in his massive one. "Thanks. And we better not rely on Billy Shakespeare anymore. Have to create our own script."

"That could be better, since we don't want a tragedy."

He reached into his pocket. "So here's my first offering." He placed two Hershey's KISSES on the table.

Deb grinned. "But no food's allowed in here."

"No one will see us," he said. He unwrapped one kiss and offered it to her.

She opened her mouth.

He popped it in, his finger brushing her lip.

She tingled from the touch and savored the chocolate. It was sweet, but not as tasty as yesterday's kiss.

She unwrapped the other KISS and placed it into Simon's mouth, touching his lip.

Simon slowly closed his eyes. "Delicious."

Delight ran through her. This guy was so appealing.

The wooden floor creaked near them. Footsteps.

Simon moved the chocolate into his cheek. "Sherwood's in the forest." He grabbed the candy wrappers and shoved them into his pocket.

Fat Sherwood came around a corner and smiled. "Checking if you need anything." She smoothed her bun and passed by.

"Looking for secondhand romance," Simon whispered.

Deb smothered her laugh.

From then on, the librarian passed by them once each afternoon, announcing closing time. After a few days, Simon asked, "Miss Sherwood, you want a chocolate?"

She smiled and accepted it. "Haven't had a kiss for a long time." She sashayed away.

One day when Deb entered the library, Fat Sherwood had loosened her hair, letting it fall onto her shoulders. Rolly Tolly hovered around her desk, the top button of his shirt open. "Haven't found a SA-tis-fy-ing STO-ry," he said, gazing at the librarian.

Fat Sherwood dropped her glasses on her desk and stumbled to a remote book stack with Rolly Tolly following like a lost puppy.

Love was in the air.

Deb giggled as she watched them disappear, then joined Simon on the north side. When he offered her a chair, his scent floated over her. "I like your cologne. What is it?"

"L'air du Lutheran."

She clamped her hand over her mouth to squelch her laughter. "So what's L'Air du Lutheran?"

"A mix of love and loyalty. And a little aimlessness, too."

"I definitely pick up the first ingredients. But aimlessness? Not a hint."

He shrugged. "I'm nothing but a drifter."

"But you've got your basketball scholarship. How can you say you're drifting?"

"Can't imagine being a pastor, like everyone expects. I don't want to settle in this town, Soo-er Falls."

She giggled.

"I wanna join the Peace Corps." He paused. "What about you? Wanna see the world?"

"If there's good company."

Simon squeezed her hand. "I could promise that."

A shiver traveled up her spine.

Deb fiddled with the fried-chicken leg on her plate.

"Don't like my cooking?" Dad interrupted her daydreams.

"Huh? No, it's fine." She picked up the greasy drumstick and nibbled.

She'd had no appetite for weeks, ever since she and Simon started meeting after school. Hadn't said a word about Simon to Dad. Didn't know how to bring this up.

Dad set his fork aside. "Guess you're not hungry again. Your turn to wash or mine?"

"Yours," Deb said.

He ran water in the sink. "A lot of homework these days?"

She carried their beige melamine plates toward the counter. "Not much."

"But you stay after school every day."

The plates escaped her hands and clattered to the linoleum.

Dad bent over and retrieved the plates before Franklin moved in to explore. "No damage done." He washed and rinsed the flatware and handed it to her. "Must be some attraction in the library to keep you after school, huh?"

Her face grew hot. "A good attraction."

"I've seen you walking with that attraction in the hallway."

She clutched the dish towel. "Dad, Simon is the most amazing guy. He's . . . . "

"Indescribable?"

"Yeah, and . . . . "

"Incredible?"

"Yeah."

A smile edged Dad's lips. "Reminds me of when I first cast eyes on your mom. Exciting times."

She exhaled her pent-up breath. Dad was cool about this.

Then he cleared his throat. "But are Simon's parents okay with it?"

"What do you mean?"

"How can I say this delicately? You're not a blue-eyed blonde."

"What?"

"People get leery about interracial mixing."

"Mixing? We're just friends. And Simon's parents are totally progressive. Aren't you?"

"Of course. I mean, I think I am. Simon is sturdy as an oak. Couldn't think of a better guy."

Deb leaned against the counter. "You're the one who wanted me to go to this *white* school. Make friends, and Simon's one of them. I should hear back from State anytime about that scholarship. And if I get it, Simon and I will be there together. Haddy and Elaine and Barry are applying. Even Erik—if he can get his act together."

Dad chuckled. "That *would* be a miracle." He slid the plates into the dish drainer, then checked his watch. "I'm happy for you. Really. I'm just being a dad with my questions. And I don't want to spoil the celebration, but do you mind if we catch the news? I want to hear what Kennedy's saying. You remember he'll be here soon?"

Deb grinned. Dad was okay about Simon and ready to move on. "Can't wait to see Kennedy."

She finished wiping dishes while Dad tuned their TV, adjusting the rabbit ears until the snow and black lines converged into a picture. Then she plopped down in a folding chair next to Dad's.

He draped his arm around her shoulder and gave a gentle squeeze.

Walter Cronkite flitted between his notes and the camera, waiting for his cue.

"Unusual for Cronkite to be flustered," Dad said.

The anchor cleared his voice. "Good evening. Dr. Martin Luther King, the apostle of nonviolence in the civil rights movement, has been shot to death in Memphis, Tennessee."

Deb gasped.

Dad startled and gripped her arm.

"Dr. King is remembered for telling people, and I quote, "Everybody can be great because anybody can serve," Cronkite said.

He cut to reports of riots breaking out around the country, then to Bobby Kennedy on the presidential campaign trail. Kennedy spoke from the flatbed of a truck, pleading for calm. When a commercial came on, Dad reached for the TV knob. "I can't listen anymore."

A rap came at their door.

Deb opened it.

Mr. Brown stood there, his face drawn.

"Arthur," Dad said as he rose. "Come in."

Mr. Brown removed his cap and collapsed in a chair. His eyes overflowed onto his brown cheeks. "Killed in my hometown. Now who gonna fight for justice?"

"Maybe Bobby Kennedy," Dad said.

"Someone need to. I'm tired of race bein' an excuse to keep us from hittin' our stride."

"Nobody's stopping us here, Arthur."

He lifted his head. "Don't you be so sure."

Deb leaned forward in her bleacher seat, mesmerized by the speech.

"The *vahst* majority of Americans seek to *undastand* one *anotha* in their *suffaring*," Senator Robert F. Kennedy said.

Deb sat back. With his jabbing finger and his Boston accent, Bobby Kennedy may as well have been from another planet. And here he was in their town, campaigning for President.

Bitterness and polarization could end, he said. Justice would prevail.

Deb's heart soared with his vision. Maybe he'd bring sanity to the craziness around the country with the race riots and anti-war protests.

When he finished, she turned to Dad. "I've got to get closer."

She wiggled her way through the crowd surrounding him. He brushed his hair off his forehead, reached into the sea of arms stretching toward him, and gripped her hand. "Thank you for *cahming*," he said as he met her eyes. Then aides whisked him away.

She found Dad near the doors of the Arena, and they joined the mass moving toward cars in the parking lot.

"I can't believe it!" she said. "He thanked me for *cahming*."

Dad chuckled. "One speech, and you're a fan?"

"If I were old enough, I'd vote for him. He's got a vision for the future. *My* future."

A mass of bodies ahead slowed their steps. "There's the Injun who lost the state tourney," a gruff voice said.

Deb stiffened and searched the throng. Erik's father marched forward, his hands gripping his gun belt. His wide-brimmed police chief's hat cast a shadow across his face.

Dad held his arm in front of Deb to stop her. "Hello, Chief Quisling. Haven't seen you since the tournament."

"Would've been a *championship* if you'd got your roster right."

The crowd tightened. The heat of bodies smothered Deb.

Dad's cheek twitched. "Played those who were eligible, according to team rules."

"Your rules!" Erik's father yelled.

Dad aimed his eyes at Quisling's. "My rules. As coach."

Sweat rose on Deb's palms. She ran them over her pant leg.

Dad raised his chin and lowered his voice. "Now my daughter and I will proceed to our car."

He gripped her shoulder.

Deb's heart pounded.

They stepped around the police chief. His stale coffee breath gagged her.

"Keep moving," Dad whispered.

They reached their station wagon. He opened Deb's door and pushed her in. "Lock it," he said.

She punched the knob down, her fingers trembling.

Dad climbed in on his side and locked his door. He started the engine and surveyed the parking lot.

"What was that about?" Deb whispered.

"Only chatter, I hope. I thought blaming me for that loss was over. But frustration can be an excuse for racism."

"But we're not black."

His head jerked toward her. "We're not white either."

CHAPTER 36

Invitations

Deb craned her neck, scanning the mass of students in the cafeteria after school. No sign of the guys. Next to her, Elaine crossed her arms. "So, we're waiting."

Haddy chewed a fingernail. "If this is what I think it is, Elaine, why would you say *yes* to Erik when you've avoided him all year?"

"I don't despise Carrot Top if he's useful," Elaine said.

Deb caught sight of the boys. "Here they come."

Simon wore his usual welcoming smile. Erik's face matched his red hair, and Barry's was a shade of vomit.

Erik cleared his throat. "Elaine, can I talk to you—alone?"

"By the Tribe Shack." Elaine swivel-hipped away to the coffee shop.

Erik followed like a robot.

Deb swallowed her chuckle. Two down.

Simon nudged Barry.

Barry straightened his glasses. "I'm so *fertummelt.*"

Haddy clutched her hands. "I get confused, too."

Barry's eyes widened. "You understood that?"

"My father talks Yiddish all the time."

"Wow! I forgot you're *kosher.*"

"Isn't that why you're asking me?"

"No, it's because I dig you. Oh, I can't believe I said that. And I was going to do this in private—not that I'm trying to get private with you."

Simon gestured across the room. "Maybe you'll want to finish over there."

"Yeah, by that column," Barry said. "That'll be romantic." He pulled at his hair and marched off, not waiting for Haddy. "I can't believe I said that."

Haddy gave a slight wave to Deb, then followed Barry.

"Four down. Two to go," Deb said.

"Yeah."

"So, are you going to invite me?"

He lifted his face and smiled his knock-out grin. "Get down on my knees if I have to."

Deb crossed her arms. "You're asking me to prom, not proposing. Besides, here come the others."

"Then we'll say goodbye." He raised his palm.

She raised hers and pressed it against his, absorbing his warmth.

"See you tomorrow," Simon said.

"Tomorrow. And by the way, the answer is *yes.*"

Simon winked, then fell into step with Erik, who was still the color of a carrot, and Barry, who was a faded puce.

"'Bye," the girls said in unison.

"Let's go to the bathroom," Elaine whispered.

They ambled into the lavatory without saying a word, closed the door, and shrieked.

After the echoes of their cries died down, Deb leaned against the cool tile wall. Her heart pounded with the thrill of going to a dance with Simon. Then anxiety crested over her. "Never been to a formal."

Haddy clutched her pudgy hands. "Me neither."

Elaine propped her leg over a sink and pulled out her nail polish. She dabbed pink lacquer onto a pantyhose snag on her thigh. "Have no fear, Musketeers. Let's go shopping."

In Elaine's upstairs bedroom, Deb covered her face with both hands, and a lilac-scented spray hit her hair.

"You're shellacked," Elaine said.

Deb pushed her eyes open. In the mirror, she studied her dark hair, lifted into an elegant fold with strands escaping along her high cheekbones. She blinked, her iridescent green eye shadow shimmering. "Elaine, you're a pro."

Elaine's face appeared in the mirror, her blond tresses drawn into a crown with curls trickling down. "It's my thing."

Haddy peeked into the mirror. Her short brown hair, teased into a saucy 'do, framed her face. "Call us the Fab Three."

A voice boomed from downstairs.

Elaine cracked her bedroom door open. "What?"

"The guys are here," Principal Ruud yelled.

The girls squealed.

"Not ready," Elaine called to her father.

Deb shimmied into her ruby-red gown. Then she helped Haddy struggle into her indigo dress while Elaine pulled up her hot pink number. They slipped into heels they'd spray painted to match their gowns.

"Now the perfect lipstick," Elaine said, extending her arm toward Deb. She filled in Deb's lips with a sizzling red.

Deb faced the mirror. "So bright?"

"Paint it on now so the boy can take it off later," Elaine said.

"So wicked," Haddy said, staring at Deb.

"Get off it," Deb said, but she shivered as she attached a thin gold chain around her neck. What about the agreement she and Simon had made not to go beyond holding hands? Was tonight different?

Time would tell.

She pulled on elbow-length white gloves and grabbed her white-beaded clutch bag. Then she followed her girlfriends to the stairway overlooking the foyer.

Below, all three of their fathers gathered on one side of the entry, clinging to Instamatics. Dad gasped when he saw Deb.

She gave him a grin.

On the other side of the foyer, Erik stood out like a Popsicle gone wild. His neon-pink shirt clashed with his carrot-top hair and contrasted with his cranberry Nehru jacket.

Next to him, Barry smoothed the navy fabric of his double-breasted jacket.

Deb found Simon. She lost her breath. He could be a male model in *Seventeen*—slender, relaxed in a white jacket with matching trousers and shoes. He straightened his white bow tie that stood out against his ruby shirt. And he'd actually tamed his tangle of hair.

He caught her stare, and his mouth opened.

Electricity.

Elaine cleared her throat, commanding everyone's attention. She hopped onto the bannister and glided down, her blond curls bouncing.

Erik jumped forward and received her in his arms.

Everyone laughed.

Haddy took careful steps down the stairs, but near the bottom, her two-inch heel turned, and she tripped.

Barry steadied her. "Sorry. Didn't mean to grab you," he said.

Haddy regained her balance. "Glad you did."

Now Deb's turn—her moment. Her hands jittered, but she took a slow breath and remembered how lovely she had appeared in the mirror. She lifted her chin, knowing the red of her gown picked up her rich pigment and played against the raven black of her hair. She descended the stairs, the folds of her dress swirling.

Dad strode forward to meet her, but Simon moved ahead, his woodland scent swirling around her.

Dad moved aside.

Simon handed her a corsage of white roses. "I'll pin it on." His hands brushed against her silky bodice.

She quivered at his touch.

Simon fumbled with the pearl-tipped pins. "Don't know how to do this."

Dad cleared his throat. "You have to bend the pins a little."

"Thanks, Coach." Simon secured the corsage.

"It's lovely," Deb said.

Haddy's father waved his arms. "Time to capture Kodak moments."

Deb smoothed her dress and smiled for the flashing bulbs. This must be how royalty felt.

Principal Ruud dropped the keys to Elaine's Mustang into Erik's hand. "Don't gun it."

"Yes, sir."

Haddy's father jabbed his finger at Barry. "Take good care of my daughter. And you know what I mean."

Barry clutched the knot of his tie. "I do."

Then Simon took Deb's arm and led her to the door. "We're ready."

Deb paused, kissed Dad on the cheek, and whispered, "You always have a place in my heart."

Dad's eyes welled up.

The couples strolled to Elaine's red convertible.

Elaine giggled. "It'll be tight for you four in the back."

Deb gulped. Four in the back?

"Barry and I will have to get in first," Simon said, "and you'll have to, uh, sit on our laps."

Deb snickered.

The guys climbed in, and each offered a hand. Haddy stepped in and collapsed onto Barry's lap, taffeta flying around her.

Awkward. Deb would attempt a more graceful entrance. She took Simon's hand and settled onto his lap. Close.

"No place for my arms unless I put them around your waist," Simon murmured.

His arms encircled her.

Her breath left her.

"Guess I'll do that, too," Barry said. "And by the way, Haddy, you look *farputst.*"

Haddy gasped. "Barry, I didn't know you were such a romantic."

"I am? I didn't know either."

Simon smothered a laugh and tilted his face toward Deb. "I don't know what Yiddish Boy is saying, but you look great."

"You too." She could stay here forever.

Erik turned the key, and the Mustang revved into a throaty roar. KISD radio came on with *The Rolling Stones* grinding through "(I Can't Get No)Satisfaction." The convertible sprang forward, and a miracle occurred—hairspray held the girls' 'dos in place.

Minnehaha Country Club welcomed them with a banner of a rocket and the words "Blasting Off." Deb scanned the room.

Rolly Tolly ladled a drink from the punch bowl for Fat Sherwood. In his tux, he looked like a black pencil, and in her Barbie-doll-pink gown, she resembled a fat eraser. She'd shed her thick glasses and squinted until she recognized Simon and Deb. "Hi there."

Deb waved back.

Simon chuckled. "Some chaperones they'll be."

Elaine gasped and pulled Deb and Haddy away from the guys. "Look who's over there."

Deb followed Elaine's gaze. Heartthrob stood sideways in his baby-blue tux that accented his golden hair.

Elaine raised her chest. "I didn't know he was coming."

Heartthrob slipped his arm around a woman whose back was toward them.

"He's not alone," Deb said.

Elaine tensed. "Who is it?"

Dressed in a sleek gown that matched Heartthrob's blue suit, the woman turned.

"Skinny Sherwood," Deb and Haddy said at the same time.

"I could throw up," Elaine said.

Deb steadied her. "Been trying to tell you. You're nothing but a kid to him."

The clang of electric guitars and drumbeats interrupted them. Onstage, the *Gemini 6* band, dressed in black suits with skinny black ties, broke into *The Beach Boys'* "Do You Wanna Dance?"

Erik stepped up to Elaine. "You wanna?"

Elaine brushed away tears. "Sure."

Simon offered Deb his hand. "Dance?"

She clasped his hand, absorbing its warmth. "Definitely."

They headed out into a sea of bodies taking fast steps. Simon jerked around like a bouncing marionette.

"Catechism didn't teach you to dance?" she teased.

"This is most certainly true," he yelled over the music, repeating a phrase from the Lutheran teaching.

"So move to the beat. Then the *wacipi* flows through you."

"The what?"

"The dance. We're made to move in rhythm."

He grinned. "Then we'll have to *wacipi* more."

"I can handle that."

Deb caught sight of Barry and Haddy standing on the sidelines, his hands buried in his pockets, hers clutched in front of her. "You think Barry will get up the nerve?" she asked Simon.

"Don't know."

Barry didn't during the first song. He and Haddy looked like they were waiting to get cavities filled.

The band transitioned into "(Just Like) Romeo and Juliet." Simon gave Deb a grin. "Our song."

Barry flexed his fingers. Then, without warning, he grabbed Haddy's hand and led her out. Their feet flew across the floor as fast as their mouths moved.

Deb laughed. "I'm glad the boy came through."

The band switched to "You've Lost that Lovin' Feelin'," and Simon's arm enfolded Deb in a slow shuffle.

Heavenly.

Elaine and Erik moved like stick figures, their heads erect, staring past each other. Worse yet, Elaine gawked at Heartthrob dancing body-to-body with Skinny Sherwood.

Deb lifted her head to Simon's. "Wish we could do something for Elaine and Erik."

"Can't lose what you never had. Let's never lose our lovin' feeling."

"Never." She buried her head into Simon's chest.

He relaxed into the beat, leading her smoothly. Their bodies melted into one.

When the set ended, Elaine signaled to Deb and Haddy. "Let's use the powder room."

The three girls joined others flocking toward the girls' restroom. Inside, they powdered cheeks, refreshed lipstick, and checked that bra straps weren't showing.

"Gotta pee," Elaine said. "Help me hold up my dress." She plopped onto the pot while Haddy and Deb held up layers of taffeta.

Deb's mind swirled. She'd never been so close to Simon before. It was crazy exciting.

"I didn't know Barry and I have so much in common." Haddy bubbled over.

Deb barely caught her words. The tingling running through her must be magic.

"He wants to get a business degree, like I do," Haddy continued, then paused and sniffed her underarm. "Did I pit out my dress?"

"Huh?" Deb said.

Elaine peered at Haddy's armpit. She pulled a few squares of toilet paper off the roll. "Dab it."

Haddy blotted her underarm. "You look like you're in a trance, Deb."

"Yeah, a happy one," she said.

"Must be nice to care about somebody," Elaine mumbled.

Haddy paused from blotting her armpit. "Give me the straight skinny here, Elaine. You feel *nothing* for Erik?"

Elaine flushed the toilet and pulled up her pantyhose. "Nothing for the Carrot."

"At least be nice to him," Deb said. "He's done you no harm."

"I'll be polite, if that's what you mean."

Haddy shrugged her head toward the door. "We'd better get out there or they'll think we've fallen in."

Back on the dance floor, students ponied to *Gemini 6's* signature song, "Two Faced Girls." Haddy and Barry joined the crowd in a furious gallop. So did Deb and Simon. But Elaine and Erik's pony was a dead horse.

When students flopped to the floor to do the alligator, Heartthrob and Skinny Sherwood jumped right in. Elaine stomped off, her eyes rimmed with tears.

Simon still moved like a sack of potatoes when they fast danced, but slow dancing was indescribable. With their bodies separated only by his suit and her dress, Deb wondered whether she'd collapse from a fever. But his steady hand on her bare back held her up.

They said little. They didn't need to.

After the last dance, Simon turned to the others. "Something I want to show all of you."

CHAPTER 37

The Question

Deb squished in the backseat of the Mustang on Simon's lap. His fingers played with hers, and she let her head rest on his chest. So comfortable. So right. "Where are we going?" she asked.

"A surprise," Simon said.

From the front passenger seat, Elaine groaned. "Better be good. I've had enough excitement tonight."

"Take the road to the right," Simon said.

"Out of town?" Erik asked.

"Yeah."

Erik made a quick right.

"Whoa!" Deb called out, her body flying off Simon's lap.

"Gotcha," Simon said, circling her waist tighter.

She clasped his hands and held on for the ride.

"Now pull over, Erik," Simon said.

Erik eased the Mustang to the edge of a country lane, and they all climbed out.

No other cars around. No street lamps. Silence.

Through the moonlight, Deb took in the landscape. "Nothing but a dirt path through those bushes."

"But wait till you see what's beyond here," Simon said.

"I'm not going into a weed patch with this dress," Elaine said. "I'll stay in the car."

"Then I'll stay," Erik said.

Haddy turned to Barry. "We could walk the path along the road."

"Sure," he answered.

Deb peered into the underbrush. What did Simon have in mind? She searched his eyes.

They danced.

"I'm game," she said.

He grinned and took her hand, pushing back branches and leading her through a narrow cut in the bushes. Ahead came the muffled sound of moving water. When they emerged from the thicket, they entered a grassy plain.

"Let's go barefoot," Simon said. He kicked off his white dress shoes and socks and rolled up his white trouser legs.

Deb cupped her mouth. "I'll have to take off my panty-hose. Turn around."

He gulped. "Okay." He turned his back and shoved his hands into his pockets.

She steadied herself with one hand on his shoulder as she peeled off her hose, then stuffed them into a shoe. "Ready."

He turned around. "Is it hot in here, or is it me?"

She giggled. "Must be you."

He grabbed her hand and moved toward the sound of the water. "Come on."

"Where are we going?"

"It'll be worth it."

He picked up the pace, even as clouds obscured the moon and left them jogging in the dark. Spring grass tickled Deb's toes. Her breath came in pants.

Soon a roar filled the air. They stopped at a knoll of smooth rock. "I can't see anything," Deb said over the deafening sound.

Simon squeezed her hand. "Wait."

Clouds skidded away from the moon, and the outline of cliffs came into view, framing a cascade of water.

She gasped.

Simon gestured. "The Falls of the Big Sioux River," he called over the rumble of the churning water.

She gasped, then lifted the edge of her dress and scampered ahead, her feet skimming the smooth rocks. She skidded to a halt at the edge. Tumbling water spewed and bubbled around her. She shivered with the pleasure of mist falling on her shoulders.

Simon caught up.

"Incredible!" she yelled over the thunder of The Falls. The water's music swelled around her like a full orchestra. "Why don't people come here?"

"It's all hidden behind that briar patch. The only ones who come are looking for a place to make out."

She spun her head toward him. "So that's why—"

He waved his hands. "No. I've never brought a girl here before."

"But you brought me."

"Because it's my favorite place."

"For what?"

"To wash all my cares away." He lifted his head, letting the cool mist cover his face. "Somebody ought to turn this whole place into a decent park."

"You could do it."

"I'd like to." He licked foam from his lips. *"But he that hath the steerage of my course direct my sail!"*

Deb laughed. "So it's back to Shakespeare? Does your mind fear *some consequence, yet hanging in the stars?"*

Simon shook his head. "It's the end of our senior year. Everything's ahead of us. Nothing can spoil *our* future."

Our future? What did he mean by that? Her head spun. She needed to get away from these tumbling falls before she got dizzy. She lifted her skirt, skipped off the rock knoll, and lay onto the grass, staring at the clouds drifting by the moon. This was calmer. A place to get centered. Her breathing slowed.

Simon dropped down beside her. "Whatever I do in life, I want to make a difference."

"You will."

He propped his head up with one elbow and turned to her. "What about you?"

She undid the tie holding her hair, and it relaxed onto her shoulders. "What about me *what?"*

"What do you want in life?"

Her heart sped. She wanted this guy who was inches away. But she wouldn't come out and say it. She turned sideways toward him and combed her fingers through her hair. "I want a cat."

He shifted his weight to one arm. "Besides a cat."

"Maybe two cats."

"You're playing with me." His breath mixed with hers, and he took her hand as gently as though he were picking up a kitten.

Heat washed over her.

"Would you like to change the world with me?"

What did he mean? "Simon."

Her thoughts jumbled. She couldn't find words.

Her lips tingled, and she leaned forward and placed a light kiss on his mouth. Then she drew back. What had she done? She jumped up and rushed across the rocks to the edge of The Falls.

"Deb." His voice came from behind.

He caught up.

She turned to him.

The wind lifted her hair.

He pulled her toward him, kissing her hard as mist sprayed over them.

She opened her mouth wide and received his kiss. Her arms wrapped around his neck.

Time stopped.

When the kiss ended, she lay her head against his chest, his arms circling her.

"Oh, Deb," he whispered. "I'm not good with words like you." He pulled his class ring off his finger. "But will you wear this?"

Her heart stopped. "Go steady? I'd be honored."

"I mean more than that. Sounds crazy, I know. But will you keep this until I give you one for our wedding?"

She caught her breath. What did he say?

He slipped the band onto her finger.

It was huge. Heavy. "You're asking me—"

"Yes."

She twirled the ring around. "There's a feather engraved on the side."

He touched her hand. "We are the Warriors."

"We are. I accept your ring, Simon Peterson. But it's too big. What if I wear it on this?" She touched the gold chain around her neck.

"Close to your heart."

"Where you'll always be."

He unclasped the chain and helped her secure the ring on it. His breath tickled her neck as he fastened it.

"Garfunkel." Erik's voice came from the distance. "Where'd you go?"

Simon pulled Deb against his chest. His breaths came in pants. "We must never be *star-crossed*. Never let anything separate us. Promise?"

"Never," Deb said, her breath shallow.

"We're ready to go," Erik called.

Simon took her hand. "Come on."

They sprinted back to where they'd dropped their shoes.

"We're coming," Simon shouted.

They slipped on their shoes, and Deb straightened her gown. She squeezed her pantyhose in her palm.

He grasped her shoulders. "Better make sure the town's Decency League doesn't catch you."

Behind her, The Falls rumbled. In front of her, Simon's eyes begged her to jump into his waters. "We've nothing to be ashamed of," she said, tipping her head back.

His lips pressed against hers. Long. Hard.

She'd hold onto Simon's taste forever.

The scent of Folgers drifted from the kitchen, but Deb turned over in her bed for a few more winks. Then her hand brushed against the ring on the chain around her neck.

Was this a dream? She clutched the bulky band, and a smile stretched her face.

This was real. She was Simon's girl.

How many glorious hours had she worn this gold circle? She lifted one eyelid and focused on her clock radio. Noon—a half day since she'd promised herself to Simon Peterson.

Promised forever.

She exhaled a contented sigh. She couldn't wait to show this ring to Dad.

But how much should she tell him?

Maybe not everything.

She threw on her fuzzy black robe and strolled barefoot to the kitchen doorway.

Dad sat at the table, staring at nothing.

She leaned against the door frame. "Coffee smells good."

He startled and turned. "Deb! Thought you might like a cup."

She slid into the chair next to him.

Franklin jumped onto her lap and arched his back.

She caressed the cat's ivory fur, and Franklin produced a thrum of purrs.

Dad reached for the coffee pot and began pouring into an empty mug on the table. "Have a good time?"

She pulled the ring out from under her robe and twirled it between her fingers. "Fabulous."

His mouth dropped open. "Wow." He kept pouring, and coffee overflowed the mug. "Oops." He grabbed a towel. "Guess your cup runneth over, huh?"

She laughed.

He gave her a sideways hug. "Brings back memories of when your mom and I started going steady."

Going steady—that was enough.

Dad's face tensed, and he eased into his chair. "But what about race? Not a problem?"

"Dad, we already talked about that."

"But going steady is different from—how'd you put it?—just friends."

"So is it okay with you that I'm going steady with a white?"

He fiddled with his cup. "Simon is tops. I don't have any problem with him. But race goes beyond a person's color. There's culture. And stereotypes."

She crossed her arms. "So what are you saying?"

He sat back. "I guess that anything interracial is difficult."

"How would *you* know?"

"Through working and living around whites."

"I've done okay with that this year."

"You have, Deb. And I only want to protect you. So let's leave it there. I don't want to spoil your excitement."

She uncrossed her arms. "Apology accepted."

Silence hung in the air.

Dad cleared his throat. "I have some news, too." He pushed a thick envelope across the table.

She glanced at the return address. South Dakota State University—a response to her scholarship application?

Her eyes darted to Dad's.

"I didn't open it."

She grabbed the envelope and ripped it.

Dad read over her shoulder. "*We are pleased to announce your receiving a Citizenship Scholarship to cover your academic expenses . . .*"

"I got it!" Deb screamed, launching from her chair into a dance.

Dad joined in the dance, clasping her hands. "I knew you could. What else does it say?"

She gripped the sheet of paper. " *. . . based not only on academic success and extracurricular activities, but because of—and dependent on—good citizenship.*"

"Means you gotta keep your nose clean," Dad said.

"I'm good at that." She sat again and took a sip of coffee. Its warmth filled her, and she absorbed this news. All the craziness of this year—leaving their home on the rez, entering a strange school, going out for extracurriculars—had paid off.

"Before you're done counting coup," Dad said, "Principal Ruud called this morning. Wants me at a meeting in a little while. Don't know why. But he mentioned something else."

"What?"

"I told you the faculty voted on which senior should give the graduation address?"

She sneered. "Everyone knows it's rigged so Elaine gets it."

Dad folded his hands. "Guess Ruud didn't twist enough arms."

She set down her cup.

He pointed at her. "Deborah Running Bear."

Her hand flew to her mouth. "You're kidding."

"You're the one."

"I can't believe it. Simon gives me his ring, I get a scholarship, and I'm picked to give the graduation speech?"

"Your cup runneth over."

"Like a waterfall. I gotta call Haddy. And Elaine—she's probably relieved to death she doesn't have to give that speech. But her father must be fuming." She caught her breath. "Is that why you got called to his office?"

Dad's mouth tightened, and he checked his watch. "I don't know. But it's time to find out."

CHAPTER 38

Michael Angelo

Deb's question plagued Will as he bolted up the granite steps leading into the high school. The principal would be fuming that the faculty chose Deb to give the graduation speech instead of Elaine. Was that why he called Will into his office on a Saturday?

Will pulled a double door open and jogged down the hall. The last thing he needed was to be late. He hustled into the office and skidded to a stop before he ran into the backs of three men.

Will took his place next to Lars Lundy, who looked at him cooly.

Abram Rabinowitz stood next to Lundy, wringing his hands. He glanced at Will, seeking an explanation of why he'd been called in.

Will gave a slight shrug.

Next to Abram stood Harley Hart, his hair coiffed into place and his white pants pressed crisp as always. But the pearly smile of the chorus director was absent. He must not know what was up either.

In front of the four men, Principal Ruud sprawled in his chair with his feet on the desk. "Glad you found time in your schedule to show up, Running Bear."

Will checked the wall clock. He wasn't late, but he wouldn't push it. "Time got away from me."

The principal took a drag on his cigar and blew smoke in their direction. "Time is on my side now that my little secret is ready. That cockamamie school board won't ride me anymore about my education not being progressive."

Will exhaled. So this wasn't about Deb.

Lundy pulled his pen from behind his ear. "You're finally going to reveal your surprise?"

"You bet." The principal dropped his feet to the floor and leaned forward, his wooden chair squeaking. "And your job, Lundy, is to give this a front page spread when I unveil it at the Syttende Mai celebration."

Lundy scratched on his notepad. "Norwegian Constitution Day always brings out the masses."

"Exactly." The principal thrust his stogie at Rabinowitz. "I want you to create some commemorative trinket to sell."

The jeweler rubbed his hands. "That could carry me through spring season."

Ruud turned to Hart. "I need your chorus to sing something about fulfilling dreams."

The director's smile returned. "I've got the perfect song."

"Good. Running Bear, you're the history jock. Write me some lines to deliver about how this statue of *David* will inspire students to reach their dreams."

Will's mouth dropped. "Statue of *David*?"

Hart ran his hands awkwardly at his groin. "Mr. Ruud, have you seen it?"

He shook his head. "The art dealer assured me it's fantastic. The idiot who ordered it wouldn't pay because a big toe is missing. So I got it for ninety percent off. Still, I had to mortgage my house up to its shingles. It came in on a train from New York, all crated up. A full-sized copy of a statue carved by an Eye-talian, Michael Angelo. Sounds like he runs a pizza parlor." The principal crowed.

Rabinowitz's face blanched, and he raised his palms near his waist. "But—"

"This'll establish my standing in town in a *monumental* way. Get it?" He pulled himself up from his chair and latched his thumbs into his belt loops. "So all of you, make this memorable." The principal waved a hand. "Now get out of here so I can have my Saturday."

Will hesitated. He should warn the principal a nude statue might not be well received. "Mr. Ruud—"

"I don't want to hear anymore."

Hart grabbed Will by the sleeve and pulled him away. "He wouldn't listen to reason if it ran over him with a truck," he whispered.

Lundy clicked his pen shut. "Ruud's right about one thing. It's going to be memorable."

CHAPTER 39

Birthday Bash

"Happy birthday to you," the Musketeers sang to each other as they stood in Elaine's bedroom. Deb raised her troll doll that Elaine gave her at the beginning of the school year, its long black hair flowing. She lifted her Coke with her other hand. "To my friends as we all turn eighteen this week."

Haddy raised her bottle and her troll doll with its short brown hair. "And here's to all of us for getting accepted into State. And to Deb for her scholarship."

Elaine held up her bottle and her doll with long blonde hair. "And to Deb for getting picked to give the graduation speech. Then I don't have to."

"I'm nervous about it," Deb said, "but excited. And here's to all of us for going to prom." She twirled Simon's ring on the chain around her neck.

"I wouldn't be surprised if you two eventually become mister and missus," Haddy said.

"Well, maybe."

Elaine and Haddy squealed.

"Tell all," Elaine said.

Deb's face turned hot. She shouldn't have said anything. She and Simon were keeping their engagement a secret. Their parents might hit the roof if they knew. "That's all I'll say. But it's obvious Barry's got a thing for you, Haddy."

She did a little dance. "I hope so, 'cause I've got a thing for him."

Elaine flopped onto her bed. "I'm happy for you two. But there's not a guy at school who moves me like Heartthrob."

Deb sat on the edge of the bed. "Give up fantasyland, Elaine. He's old enough he probably takes Geritol."

"But it's like I have this hole in me that nobody—no real guy anyway—can fill."

"It's your mother loss," Haddy said. "I read about it in *Seventeen.* An article about how we try to fill the holes in our lives."

Elaine brushed away tears. "I hate this time of year. Girls at the dime store buying Mother's Day cards."

"And the Lutheran women throwing a mother-daughter tea," Deb said. "That's like salt in a wound."

Elaine leaned back against a pillow. "Sometimes I fantasize what it would be like to hang out with my mom and comb each other's hair."

"Or serve breakfast in bed to my mom," Haddy said. "What a dream."

Deb's mind twirled with an idea. "We're celebrating everything else tonight. Why not turn this into a *Motherless* Day party? Do all the things we wish we could do with our moms."

"Let's," Elaine and Haddy said in unison.

They stayed up until the sun rose, combing each other's hair while they planned a getaway to Fort Robinson after graduation. Then they headed down to the kitchen where they made pancakes with apple slices and cinnamon sprinkles and served each other breakfast in Elaine's oversized canopy bed.

After her last bite, Elaine set her dishes on the night stand. "I am so loved." She pulled up a cover and settled in at the edge of the bed.

Haddy yawned. "So am I." She curled into a ball in the middle of the bed.

On the other side, Deb hugged her pillow and played with Simon's ring. She had the best girlfriends in the world. And, she had Simon.

Nothing could spoil this.

CHAPTER 40

David Unveiled

"Try some," Will said, offering Deb a bite of *lutefisk*. Don't you think she'll like it, Simon?"

Standing next to Deb, Simon shook his head. "Nah, you gotta be Norwegian to dig it."

A crowd surged around them, wandering among booths at the *Syttende Mai* celebration.

"What is it anyway?" Deb asked.

"Fish soaked in lye," Will said.

Deb took a bite. Her face screwed up, and she gagged. "Tastes like plain gelatin drowned in butter."

Will and Simon roared.

"So I did my duty," Deb said, then turned to Simon. "Now let's go see friends."

Hand-in-hand, they disappeared into the throng.

A smile came over Will's face. Deb and friends, one of the great results of living here this year.

Near Will, accordions struck up an *oom pah pah* beat. Members of the Sons and Daughters of Norway, dressed in embroidered black-and-red costumes, twirled to folk dances. Across the way in the Herring Toss Contest, men aimed dead fish toward a bucket of water. In the Miss Meatpacker Beauty Pageant, young women in one-piece swimsuits posed while judges analyzed their curves.

What a relief Deb wasn't in that.

Will checked his watch. Only a few minutes until the unveiling of the statue of *David*. To the public, Ruud had revealed only that the bronze was a Biblical character. How would the town respond when the tarp fell away and a towering nude stood before them?

Their shock might be as big as the carving. The pedestal was taller than a man, and the statue, now wrapped in a tarp, rose the height of another three men. Arthur stood guard at the base, clutching rope lines and shooing away anyone who tried to peek.

One good thing about this event was Ruud was so riveted by the fanfare, he hadn't complained about the faculty voting for Deb to give the commencement address instead of Elaine.

Will spotted Lyle Mykland a few feet away. The junior varsity coach's icy glare pierced the distance between them.

Will would give friendliness a chance again. "Hello, Coach."

Lyle crossed his arms and turned his head.

So much for friendliness. If only Mykland would let this basketball season go, they could work together toward the next one.

"Running Bear. Over here." The voice came from Will's left.

"Abram," Will said, moving toward him. "Got your goods?"

Abram Rabinowitz stood behind a table draped with a blue cloth. "As soon as Ruud unveils his statue, I'll offer my commemorative jewelry. The principal didn't want to review it. Hope he doesn't think it's risqué."

"We tried to warn him about the statue."

Will caught sight of Lars Lundy. A rabid look covered his face, like he was ready to bite anyone who came close. But Will would make the effort again to sooth the troubled reporter. He strode up to him. "How's it going?"

"The principal leaned on me for twenty minutes, preening about how *advanced* his education is. I'm sick of people demanding I promote them. Sick of this job."

He jammed his face close to Will's. "If you'd helped my boy more this year, he might not end up in a dead-end job like mine."

Will opened his mouth to answer, but Sigfrid Aasgard bustled up, followed by her niece, Sylvia. They clutched matching handbags, wore matching sturdy pumps, and balanced matching pillbox hats over their tight curls.

"Well, well." Lundy feigned friendliness. "If it isn't the president of the Ladies' Decency League and her president-in-training."

Sigfrid sniffed. "I'm suspicious about this statue." The rail-of-a-woman tapped her white-gloved hand on Lundy's notepad. "Might be Communists or hippies infiltrating. And you can quote me. But make sure you spell my name right. It's double *A*, not double *S*, then *G-A-R-D*, like a guard, which is—"

"What you are to this community," Lundy interrupted. "You've told me that umpteen times, Miss *Assssgard*," he said.

Her hand shot to her lips. "I never . . . . " She and Sylvia marched off.

"Time for my surprise." Principal Ruud's voice squawked over the P.A. system.

Will joined the crowd circling the statue.

Ruud introduced Mayor Blatherborg, who welcomed everyone with too much enthusiasm. It was an election year, after all. Then Harley Hart tapped his white baton on a music stand and blew into a pitch pipe. The chorus hummed the note, then broke into "Climb Ev'ry Mountain."

Will searched the tiered stands of the chorus. There she was. Deb sang about fording streams, following rainbows. When she caught Will's eye, she winked.

His heart burst with pride. Deb took risks this year, and it had paid off with friends, recognition from teachers, and a scholarship. She was ready to launch into the world.

The ensemble soared into the final measures about searching to find your dreams. They held the last note until Harley Hart swished his baton to signal the cutoff.

Will blinked away moisture and clapped until his hands hurt.

Deb and the other chorus members melted back into the crowd as the applause died.

Ruud positioned himself next to the statue's pedestal. He stood as upright as his rotund figure allowed and checked to his side to make sure KELO-TV had a clear shot of him. He raised the note cards Will had prepared. "Education is about vision." He paused. "And vision is what made me who I am today."

Will cringed. A digression already. Would Ruud turn this into a self-glorification monologue?

"The vision of my great love of students and my ability to respond to the future." He rambled on for ten minutes.

Groans leaked from the audience.

Ruud returned to his notes, shuffling to the last card. "This statue captures the essence of someone daring to conquer a giant of a problem, to risk himself for the greater good of others." He lifted his head. "Like me."

Will's stomach twisted.

Ruud stuffed the cards in his coat pocket. "Anyhow, have you guessed who I'm talking about?" He gestured toward the figure. "I give you the statue of *David*."

Arthur wrestled with the tarp until it fell, revealing the buck-naked man.

A gasp followed, large enough to suck the air out of the sky.

Will caught his breath, too. The gray-green bronze was more magnificent than he remembered from pictures of the original. Eyes steely. Nostrils flared. Muscles taut. Masculinity with not an ounce of bashfulness.

How was the crowd responding? He glanced around.

Sigfrid Aasgard had fainted dead away, her feet flying up, the garters of her hose exposed. Sylvia Aasgard bent over Sigfrid and fanned her with her hat.

Erik and Barry gaped at the nude.

"You Jews are built," Erik said.

Barry gulped. "Not like that."

Students heard that and began snickering, then laughing.

The mayor glared at the principal. "Idiot," he muttered and stomped off.

Ruud, who'd been staring at the crowd, finally glanced skyward at the statue. His jowls dropped onto the knot of his tie.

What about Deb? How was she reacting? There she was, next to Simon. They were smirking, but keeping control. That was good. Wouldn't want the principal to see Deb react negatively.

Guffaws cut through the crowd. Valmar Dahl dodged around, his arms waving and his combover flying. "It's a masterpiece."

Lifted from the ground after fainting, Sigfrid straightened her hat and thrust her white-gloved finger at the statue's posterior. "I'm going to get to the bottom of this."

Lars Lundy laughed. "You already are at the bottom of this."

Sigfried brushed by Will and collided into Abram Rabinowitz, who held up miniatures of the nude statue for sale.

"What are these?" she demanded.

"Girls' charms and boys' lapel pins," Abram said.

She grabbed one. "I'll see what the Ladies' Decency League says about this."

Abram worked to pry it out of her fingers. "Only if you pay for it."

She gripped the miniature nude. "Not a penny for pornography."

Police Chief Thorvald Quisling stepped in. "I'll take that." He seized it, then startled when he saw he was clutching David's groin.

Sigfrid stomped off, but her niece, Sylvia, pushed dollar bills into Rabinowitz's hand and grabbed a nude. She stuffed it into her purse, a smile climbing up her face.

Lundy scribbled in his notepad. "Time for payback. Nobody's gonna look good in this story." He slapped his notebook shut and zipped away.

Payback? Nobody look good? What did that mean for Will?

The next day, the bell of a bicycle and the *thunk* of a newspaper on the sidewalk drifted into the apartment. Will sprinted out and unfolded the paper as he stepped back in. An oversized photo of the statue of *David* emphasized the guy's gear. A headline screamed:

David Revealed Without a Thread

He scanned the article.

Lundy portrayed the principal as a buffoon, which wasn't difficult. He quoted Ruud: "I didn't remember from Sunday school David was naked."

Then Lundy committed spelling errors that appeared to be purposeful. He listed Sigfrid's last name as Assguard and said she was from the Ladies'Decency Lag, not League. Finally, he quoted Police Chief Quisling. "My men will step up patrols in the park to ensure youngsters don't gawk at the guy's jewels."

Will exhaled and flopped into a folding chair. Lundy hadn't fired any volleys his way. That was good. Ruud might use any excuse to block Deb from giving the graduation address.

An arm circled Will's neck.

Deb peered over his shoulder at the front page. "Wow."

"Graphic photo, huh? But I'm relieved."

"Why?"

"I was concerned Mr. Lundy might take a swipe at me." He set the paper down. "Deb, we've got to be straight arrows until you've graduated. Then you'll be off to college with your scholarship."

Her brow furrowed. "Are you paranoid?"

"No, but cautious."

She scooped up Franklin and hugged him. "I'll be as cautious as a cat."

"But don't be as curious."

CHAPTER 41

Senior Prank

"**R**eally should go," Deb whispered into the phone whose cord she'd stretched into the apartment kitchen so she could get some privacy.

"Don't you want to dream together about all the good times we'll have at State?" Simon asked.

"Of course. But my nerves are fried until I practice my speech more."

"So, see you tomorrow?" Simon asked, a flirt in his voice.

She giggled. "Wouldn't miss it. Bye." She wrangled the cord back into the living room and hurried to her bedroom. She'd gladly gab all night with Simon, but only after she'd nailed this talk.

She stood before her mirror and jabbed the air with her finger like Bobby Kennedy did. "Do we have a foundation? Do we have integrity?" She brushed a lock of hair from her face, like the senator did.

When she pushed her hair aside, she realized how much she'd changed during this school year. Gone was the girl with a single braid, clutching her books and staring down at the floor.

Before her stood a young woman dressed in a red and white pin-striped shirt and red shorts that complimented her slim figure. She smiled at her reflection. She liked herself. Had the best girlfriends. The best guy a girl could have. And the honor of speaking before the whole town.

Only a few changes to make on the speech now. She moved to the typewriter in the living room.

Dad sat at the card table, slipping a pile of papers into a manila folder. "Jim-dandy tests. The guys wrote an essay about the difference between being great and being famous."

"What does that have to do with Shop?"

"Everything. We live in a fame-driven world. But real living is learning to take the tools you're given and use them to serve others. That's greatness."

Deb smiled. Dad never got off his soap boxes, always calling others to a higher plane. That was one reason she loved him.

The phone rang and she reached for it. Must be Simon again, and warmth filled her in anticipation of hearing his voice. "Hi there."

"I need your help."

It was Elaine, and her voice sounded strained.

"With what?"

"Haddy's here, too. We need your father's car."

Odd. Elaine would die if she were seen in Dad's boxy wagon. "What about your Mustang?"

"Too small. Gotta do something for my father."

Double odd. Elaine kept her distance from her father. "I'll ask." Deb called from the kitchen. "Can I use the wagon tonight?"

"I'm staying in. Watching "The Ed Sullivan Show" while I turn a piece of burl wood into a walking stick." He opened his case of whittling tools. "You'll take good care of the car?"

"Of course."

When Deb pulled up at the house, Elaine and Haddy rushed to her from the front yard. Elaine's mascara had slid onto her cheeks. "What's wrong?" Deb asked.

Elaine motioned to a straight ladder lying on the lawn. "My father needs it. Won't fit in my Mustang."

"Where is he?"

Elaine's lip trembled. "One of his stupid *education* meetings."

Deb wasn't about to ask why the principal needed a ladder at an education meeting. "Let's load it." She unlatched the cargo hold while Elaine and Haddy each grabbed a rung at opposite ends.

"Hurry." Desperation edged Elaine's voice.

"I'm going as fast as my little legs will carry me," Haddy answered.

They rested the ladder across the top of the front seat. Deb slid behind the wheel, Elaine took the passenger's side, and Haddy wedged into the back.

Deb turned over the engine. "Where's your father's meeting?"

Elaine fingered her white cardigan. "We're not going there."

"Then where are we going?"

"The statue," Elaine said.

"What?"

"A little prank."

Deb shifted the wagon back into park. "Elaine Ruud, a minute ago you were fighting back tears. Now you're talking about a joke. Are you schizo?"

"I *need* you to take me to the statue. Then you can stay in the car if you want."

"You're not planning on doing any damage, are you?"

"No, silly. I'm only going to tie my cardigan around David's middle like he's wearing a diaper."

Haddy burst out laughing. "Hilarious."

Deb smothered her snicker. "Funny, but I don't want anything to do with it."

Haddy leaned forward. "It's nothing. And nobody will know we did it."

"So drive, Deb," Elaine said.

"But—"

"Please?"

Please? Elaine had never said *please* before. What was going on? And how did Elaine's being upset with her father have anything to do with committing a prank?

"Please?" Elaine repeated, her lip quivering.

Deb chewed on her lip. She couldn't refuse a hurting friend. And Haddy said this was harmless. Still, she'd stay on the sidelines.

She headed to the statue.

"The Three Musketeers ride again," Haddy cheered. "All for one."

Deb shook her head. Always the same one.

Within minutes, they reached the edge of the park. The last rays of sun outlined David's naked body. He rose before them, a silent giant perched on his pedestal.

"Kinda spooky here," Haddy said in a quiet tone. "Police chief has extra patrols out so no one will hang around. Maybe we shouldn't have come."

"Haddy's right," Deb said.

Elaine pushed her door open. "The sooner we get this done, the faster we leave. Help me with the ladder."

"You are impossible," Deb said. She unlatched the cargo door, and Elaine and Haddy tugged at the ladder.

Deb stood aside and folded her arms. "Be careful you don't hit something."

Her friends maneuvered the ladder out, then swung it at an angle, banging the cargo door.

Haddy gasped. "Sorry."

Deb winced. Even in the dim light, the gash and scraped paint stood out. Her heart sank.

Elaine groaned under the ladder's weight. She turned toward Deb. "Help us."

"Only so you don't cause any more damage." Deb reached her arms under the middle of the ladder and moved with them to the base of the statue.

"Now lift it in place," Elaine said.

They hoisted it, and it clanged against the marble pedestal.

Elaine pulled off the white cardigan over her blouse and knotted it around her waist. She threw her bag over her shoulder and climbed, her footsteps reverberating on the rungs.

At the top, she boosted herself onto the pedestal with an *umph* and straightened up. She wrapped one arm around David's knee for support. "Too tall. Can't reach his middle."

Deb squinted up at her. "So you've had your fun. Let's get out of here."

"Not until I do this. But I don't know how."

Deb clamped her hands at her waist. "I'm only telling you so you get this over with. You can climb up the stump that's behind David's leg. Use the notches for footholds."

"Perfect." Elaine edged up the notches and reached the top of the bronze stump. Her breath came in spurts. She leaned against David's hamstrings, the side of her face resting onto his flank. "Gives a new meaning to dancing cheek to cheek."

Haddy cracked up, and Deb stifled her own outburst.

A noise came in the distance.

Haddy clutched Deb's arm. "What was that?"

"Nothing but a dog," Elaine called down. "Don't be so skittish." She untied her cardigan from her waist and flung a sleeve about David's middle, trying to catch it as it came around. Her reach fell short. "Can't get it."

Haddy clenched her fists. "You can do it."

Elaine tossed the sleeve again, but missed. She burst into tears and beat her fist against David's rear end. "Why won't he pay attention to me?"

"Who?" Haddy asked.

"My father!" Elaine yelled.

Her father? Deb caught her breath. Was that what this was about? All year, Elaine had sought her father's attention, but he always turned the spotlight back on himself.

Deb's heart ached. "Elaine, this isn't the best way—"

"I won't leave now. One of you get up here and help me."

Haddy turned to Deb. "I'm too short."

Deb backed off. "No way."

"Come on," Elaine said, sniffling. "For a friend?"

"You get down right now or I'll drive off and leave you."

"You know you won't."

Elaine was right. Deb wouldn't leave a friend stranded. Even a dumb one. Besides, this was nothing but a silly prank, wasn't it? "All right."

Deb shimmied up the ladder and stood on the pedestal.

"Move to his front," Elaine said.

With her back against David, Deb worked her way around the statue's side, clutching his massive cold hand for support. When she reached his front, she turned toward him and looked up. David's stuff! Way more graphic than those drawings in Biology. "You wouldn't believe the view."

"Like I'll ever see anything like that up close," Haddy said.

"Stop ogling and grab a sleeve when I throw it," Elaine said.

"Okay."

Elaine tossed a sleeve around David's middle.

Deb stretched toward it. She touched it, but it slipped away. She swayed and grabbed David's leg to regain her balance. "Try again."

Elaine grunted with her next toss.

Deb lifted onto her toes and reached. The fabric brushed against her fingers. She teetered, but grasped it and steadied herself. "Got it."

Haddy let out a whoop.

"Quiet down there," Deb said.

"Sorry, but this is the most exciting thing I've ever done."

Deb pulled the body of the sweater to the front of David's middle. "Grab the sleeve when I throw it back." She groaned with her toss.

Elaine flung her arm out. "Got it."

Sweat stung Deb's eyes. She mopped her head against her arm. "You'll have to stretch the sleeves super-long to tie them."

A pause.

"Done," Elaine said.

Haddy clapped down below.

"Not so loud," Deb whispered.

"But it's funny. You gave him a loincloth."

"Perfect." Elaine chuckled. "His butt is still exposed."

A car turned at the edge of the park.

"Freeze!" Haddy called. She hit the ground.

Deb smashed herself between David's legs, her head resting against his groin. "You okay?" she whispered to Elaine.

"Yeah. A good place to freeze, hugging the biggest buns in the world."

Deb squelched her giggles.

The sound of the car receded.

"Let's get out of here," Deb said.

"One more thing. Gotta cover this guy's you-know-what. Reach your hand under his crotch and hold this for me."

"What?"

"Do it."

Anything to get this over with. The sun had dipped below the horizon, leaving the statue a naked silhouette in the moonlight. Any move Deb made now was in the dark. She leaned against David, held onto his wrist, and reached between his legs. Her fingers grabbed something round. Plastic. A lid? "Elaine, what are you doing?"

"You'll see."

A spraying sound, and a mist ran across Deb's hand. An acrid smell.

Paint!

Another spray, and Elaine screamed, "There!"

Below them, headlights traced the ground.

"Car's coming!" Haddy yelled.

A siren pierced the night.

Something clanged onto the top of the pedestal, then landed on the ground with a *thunk*.

Elaine scampered down the ladder. "Split!" she called.

The ladder teetered away from the statue. It clattered to the ground.

"Wait!" Deb cried.

The sound of Haddy's and Elaine's footsteps receded.

They left her.

A car door flew open.

Deb's heart pounded so loud she was sure it echoed. She squished between David's legs.

A beam of light pierced through the dark and blinded Deb. She wobbled, but caught herself and gripped onto David's leg with both arms.

The flash hit her again. She lifted a hand to shield her eyes.

Her balance shifted.

Her weight moved backwards.

Her foot slipped.

She twisted to grab the top of the pedestal.

It flew past her.

The ground hurtled toward her.

Thump!

CHAPTER 42

The Fall

Throbs of pain overwhelmed Deb. She opened an eye. Everything hazy. She blinked. Her vision slowly moved into focus.

Two rays of light illuminated a green pant leg with a black stripe.

The man jostled her shoulder. "You okay?"

She recognized the voice—deep, gruff. Erik's father, the police chief. He bent over, his face close enough that his stale coffee breath choked her.

Pain surged over her. "My knee."

Chief Quisling aimed his light on her leg. "Tarnation. Blood." He flashed his beam over her and stopped at her fingers. "What's that?"

She lifted her hand. A plastic lid. A spray of orange paint coated her fingers.

The chief straightened. "Huh."

His flashlight beam darted across the ground, then stopped. He bent down and shook something that rattled.

His light shot up at the statue. "Girl's sweater, huh?"

He circled around to David's exposed rump and snorted. "Choice."

His light flashed back across the ground and blinded her. "You over eighteen?"

"Yes, sir."

"Then your goose is cooked. And looks like you did this on your own."

"But . . . ." She couldn't string words together.

"I'll book you and let you sweat until your uppity father gets you out. Come on."

She struggled up. Her head spun as she limped to the police car. "Dumb as a hunyuk," Quisling muttered ahead of her.

At the station, the police chief led Deb to a cell where she flopped onto a stiff cot. She extended her leg. Smears of blood soiled her capris.

The chief flashed a Polaroid camera in her face. The jail door clanged shut.

From the other room, the phone rang. "No worries, Ivar," Quisling said. "Open and shut case."

The chief appeared at the cell door. "How come you had a ladder with the name Ruud on it?"

"It's the principal's—"

"Ruud says someone stole it. He's been home with his daughter all evening."

Deb's heart stopped. She opened her mouth to explain.

"You've been read your rights." He flicked the light switch.

Darkness.

She fell into a nightmare of falling, falling.

A voice punctured the dark. "Where is she?"

Dad.

"Caught her red-handed," Quisling chuckled. "Or, in this case, orange-handed."

"She'd never—"

"Deputy radioed he'd seen a car, but he was pulled away on another case. So I checked."

The light switched on.

Deb threw her hand up to her eyes to block the glare.

Keys jingled.

"Princess." Dad's arms wrapped around her.

"I scraped your car."

"Never mind that." Dad spotted her swollen knee. He spun to the chief. "Where's an ice pack?"

The chief lifted his palms. "Too busy booking her."

"If you have a grudge"—Dad's voice rose—"take it up with me."

The chief folded his arms. "Doin' my job, which is more than you did, *Coach.*"

"I do my job as a coach *and* as a father."

The chief stepped forward. "What are you sayin'?"

Dad opened his mouth, then paused. "Nothing."

The chief thrust his thumb sideways at Deb and grinned, revealing nicotine-stained teeth. "You got a *vandal* for a daughter."

Dad's face quivered. "Let's get out of here." He placed his arms under her and lifted.

She reached around his neck and held on as he carried her into the night. At the curb, Deb recognized his car. "How'd it—"

"A deputy brought it in."

Dad carried her past the cargo hold. He caught sight of the scar left by the ladder, and his body tightened. He wrestled with the passenger door, then set her on the seat as gently as though she were a flower. "We've got to get your knee examined."

"I don't want to go anywhere."

Dad slid in and gripped the wheel. "Guess you've taken enough jostling around. I'll check it at home, and we won't go out unless it's worse than it looks."

Her tears hadn't fallen so freely since Mom died.

The phone rang from the living room.

Deb stirred in her bed. Aches pulsed through her.

The ringing stopped.

"Yeah?"

Dad's voice, but not cordial as he usually was. He must have picked up the phone.

"Be right there."

The receiver smacked onto the phone cradle.

The apartment door banged shut.

Dad was ticked. He hadn't been that way last night. She'd tried to explain what happened, but he'd shushed her and said they'd talk about it in the morning.

What time was it? She peered at her clock radio. Five o'clock, but sunny. She must have slept all day.

She turned. Her leg screamed. A cold pack covered her knee. Dad must have been changing it.

She pulled herself up and took a step. More like a hobble. She shuffled to the living room, then grabbed ahold of the walking stick Dad had whittled on last night, the head of a Native American on top.

The *Argus* lay wadded up on the table.

She unfolded it. On the front page, a photo of the statue, four columns wide, jumped out at her. *David* glared at her, his front midsection covered with Elaine's white cardigan. Below the photo, the banner headline screamed:

David No Longer Running Bare

Deb gasped. Running Bare—a play on their last name. Dad's conflict with Mr. Lundy? Could this be the reporter's way of getting even?

Her eyes jumped to another photo on the bottom of the page. A mugshot. Of her with a terrified stare.

She fell into a folding chair and scanned the story:

Ever since the statue of David *arrived, the community has been concerned that morals might slip among youth. However, the massive nude was partially clothed last night with a 'loincloth' covering his private parts.*

She turned the page. Another photo—the rump side of David.

Sprayed with orange paint onto one cheek of the statue's exposed derriere was IVAR. The other cheek was sprayed with BUTT OUT.

Deb's mouth dropped.

Orange and black are Washington High School's colors. The statue was donated by the school's principal, Ivar Ruud.

Police Chief Thorvald Quisling said he found Deborah Running Bear, 18, at the scene with orange paint sprayed on one hand and a knee injury from an apparent fall. She is a Washington senior and the daughter of William Running Bear, the school's varsity basketball coach. The coach's car was parked near the statue, Quisling said.

Deb's hands shook.

A ladder with the name Ruud on it lay on the ground near the statue. The principal reported its theft from his home.

Her stomach twisted.

"We're investigating whether the delinquent climbed the statue and tied the sweater before she fell to the ground," Quisling said.

Delinquent!

Sigfrid Aasgard from the Ladies' Decency League said she had warned that 'the graphic nature of the statue could create a spiraling down of community morals led by a troublemaker.'

Troublemaker!

Deborah Running Bear was treated for her knee injury.

Some treatment.

She was booked and released pending charges being filed.

Charges?

Principal Ruud called this 'an outrageous act of vandalism that should be prosecuted to the highest level.'

The rest of the article blurred in a field of tears.

CHAPTER 43

Principal's Office

Will bolted down the high school hallway. As if it weren't enough Deb blew it, now he'd been called to the principal's office. He knocked on the closed door.

"Get. In. Here!" Ruud's voice boomed.

Will slipped in and closed the door. The room was as dark as a cave.

A cigarette lighter struck, its flame igniting a red-orange ember.

Will gradually recognized the outline of the principal facing the wall, rocking on his heels, and fingering the cigar.

"Looks like we have a little problem here," Ruud said. "What your daughter did was an embarrassment to our entire community."

Will cleared his throat. "She didn't act alone."

Ruud spun around and jabbed his cigar at Will. "*Your* car. *Your* daughter. No one else there."

"What about the ladder?"

"Stolen."

"Deborah couldn't carry a ladder on her own. She couldn't tie a sweater around the statue on her own. The police will figure that out."

The principal's head turned slowly toward the other side of the room.

Will's eyes gradually adjusted to the darkness. The police chief leaned against the wall. He tipped the brim of his hat. "She must be mighty strong. And I left the evidence in place so the whole community could see what she done."

Will's fingernails dug into his palms.

Ruud waved his stogie. "We've come up with a solution to the problem."

"What problem?" Will asked.

"The problem of what to do with you."

"So now it's about me?"

"It always has been. We can't have a basketball coach scandalizing our school with his name on the front page of the *Argus*." He lifted the paper from his desk.

"That's not my name."

"*Running Bare?* Close enough. All your big talk about heroes. Then appointing a janitor as assistant coach."

"Arthur is my assistant."

The principal waved his hand. "And Indian gibberish and a war dance at a pep rally? It's gone too far. But the booster club came up with a solution."

The police chief raised his chin. "If you resign, your daughter won't be charged. Otherwise, I press charges for vandalism and theft."

"I have a contract."

"Which warns about moral turpitude, whatever that is," Ruud said. He took a drag on his cigar and blew out a plume that smelled as bad as this whole affair. "As for that citizenship scholarship? State got wind of this."

"How?"

Ruud adjusted a Venetian blind. A shaft of light fell onto his desk.

The principal's chair swiveled around. Coach Lyle Mykland smirked at Will. "Let's say a little bird told 'em."

Will bit his lip so hard he tasted blood.

The principal hooked his thumbs into his trousers pockets. "And there's something else."

CHAPTER 44

Exiled

Deb stared at her dazed face in the newspaper mug-shot. How could she be so stupid? The phone rang, jolting her thoughts.

Maybe it was Elaine. She'd left her hanging on the statue.

Deb wouldn't talk to her.

The phone rang again.

Or Haddy. She'd ditched, too.

A third ring.

Or Simon. What would he think? She had to explain that the vandalism wasn't her idea.

She grabbed the receiver, then pulled her hand away.

She'd gone along with the crime. She'd violated all the principles of right and wrong she and Simon had held dear. No way to explain that.

Deb plugged her ears and let the phone ring until it stopped.

Now only the sound of her pounding heart.

The door to the apartment flew open. Dad. His face red. His eyes glaring. "Talk about losing focus."

Her stomach knotted. "I blew it."

"More than you know, young lady. Did you forget who you are? Forget what's at stake for our people? What were you thinking?"

"I wasn't."

Dad paced. His breath came in gasps. "All you worked for this year. For nothing."

She sobbed. "I don't know what to do."

He ran his hand over his jaw. "In this case, you won't have to decide.

"What do you mean?" His face carried a sadness she hadn't seen since Mom died. "We need to talk."

Deb gripped a sheet of paper under the folds of her orange graduation gown and fell into place in the line of seniors. Directly ahead of her stood Haddy. Behind was Elaine, both in gowns.

What she was about to do hurt from the tassel of her orange mortarboard down to her heels.

She slipped the sheet of paper to Elaine and said nothing.

Elaine palmed the sheet.

Haddy glimpsed the handoff. "What was that?"

"Nothing," Deb said.

Haddy didn't press her. Deb's expression must have communicated that if anyone said anything, she'd blow up.

Around her, girls giggled with excitement about the ceremony. Guys whooped.

She, Elaine, and Haddy stood stiff as robots.

Deb searched in the line ahead for Simon. If only she had the words to explain. To try to make it right.

Simon turned toward her. His eyes—always so beckoning before—held something she'd never seen. Was it anger? Embarrassment? Contempt?

She glanced away and swallowed her heart.

Strains from the student orchestra reached her. Students snapped to attention and moved forward to the tempo set by violins. But there was no pomp in this circumstance for her.

Ahead, next to the line of students stood Mr. Brown dressed in his red Nehru jacket with pink buttons. "Y'all keep movin' till you hit your seats."

Deb came up even with him.

He leaned in. "You gonna make it," he whispered.

Tears blurred her vision.

Her swollen knee ached with every step. But she was going to get through this ceremony if it killed her. She'd earned that diploma. She longed to grasp it in her hand.

She reached her folding chair and dropped into it.

Pastor Pete—Simon's father—moved to the lectern.

He'd welcomed her at Luther League when she was the new kid in town. He'd encouraged her comments during rap sessions. Now, he bowed his head. "Almighty God, grant these graduates the wisdom to always do what is right."

He said a quick "amen" and glanced her way, his face ashen.

Had he written her off?

The chorus was next on the program. Deb dragged herself, stiff-legged, up the risers and took her place among the altos. She turned and faced the packed room. Everything spun, but she steadied herself.

Heartthrob moved his conductor's baton through the air. Deb mouthed lyrics about envisioning impossible dreams, reaching stars, righting wrongs. She'd loved these words—a call to a life of high purpose. After all, she and Simon had planned to make the world a better place.

Instead, she was the community thug.

A blanket of shame smothered her.

The song ended.

Deb limped back to her seat. She forced herself to look forward. The faculty sat on stage. Coach Mykland assumed his usual slump and sneer, but this time he crossed his arms in a triumphant air.

Loser Lyle. She hated him.

She glanced at the faculty. Roland Tollefson. Rolly Tolly's classroom dramatic readings had helped her shed her shyness. She'd miss his twitchy mustache.

Lena Sherwood. Fat Sherwood had given Deb and Simon space between stacks of library books for their relationship to grow.

Ronnette Sherwood. Skinny Sherwood had trusted Deb's creativity, pushing her into writing pep squad cheers.

Valmar Dahl. VD's pep band had backed up Deb when she led cheers at all-school assemblies.

Deb's insides ached. Only days ago, she'd wanted to etch the faces of these teachers into her memory forever.

Then she let them down.

All she wanted was to forget them now.

At the end of the row of teachers sat Dad, his head erect, his face placid. She knew better. Behind that facade boiled a volcano of anger.

Principal Ruud—that banty rooster—strutted to the speaker's stand. A smile spread across his face. "Prior to handing out diplomas, I have the privilege of welcoming our student speaker. There's been a change to the program."

Pages rustled as the audience flipped to the section where Deborah Running Bear was listed as student speaker. Mutters reached her from the audience. "The girl who got arrested?"

"Juvenile delinquent."

"Should be in a detention center."

The voices taunted Deb. She wanted to clamp her hands over her ears, but that would draw even more attention.

"Proudly representing her classmates tonight," the principal continued, "will be my daughter, Miss Elaine Ruud."

Haddy gasped.

Deb stared at her shoes, black heels that pinched.

Elaine rose. She bumped around Deb's knees, her hand gripping the speech Deb wrote. She reached the lectern and turned toward the crowd.

Even from this distance, Elaine's pallor broadcast her fear.

Deb's jaw tightened. Let Elaine cook in her own juices. For once, she wasn't rescuing her.

Elaine pressed her palms into the edge of the lectern. "Principal Ruud, faculty, and fellow classmates." Her voice quivered. "We live in troubled times. With the war in Vietnam and with riots in the streets, we graduates face an uncertain future." Elaine's voice dropped to a whisper. Deb clenched her fists. Elaine was faltering. Let her sink.

Elaine's shaking hand tucked a loose lock of blond hair into her mortarboard. "Now that we are graduating, we are often asked what we are going to do. No matter which direction we take, a more important question is who we will become."

She paused too long.

A murmur rippled through the audience.

Elaine's mouth trembled. "Do we have a foundation? If we don't, we will drift."

Deb mouthed the next words with Elaine. "Do we have integrity?" *She* didn't.

Elaine glanced at her father.

The principal's lower lip protruded.

"If we don't have integrity, we will someday carry a burden of regrets."

Let Elaine shoulder those burdens for the rest of her life.

Elaine gaped at the text. She opened her mouth, but nothing came. She swiped at tears. "A burden of regrets," she repeated. A sob burst from her. She raced from the stage and out of the room.

The auditorium was soundless.

Slow clapping broke the silence. Dad. He sat straight, a slight smile lifting his lips. He continued his solo clapping.

Leave it to him. He was saving the show.

Students and the audience picked up his cue and began applauding over their murmurs.

Principal Ruud returned to the lectern, his face crimson. "I will now hand out diplomas. My assistant, Mrs. Mykland . . . "

He turned to his left, the spot where Mrs. Mykland should be sitting.

But she wasn't. That was odd.

The principal mopped his brow and turned to his right. "Lyle, you help."

Coach Mykland swaggered up to the principal.

Ruud pasted on his public face. He worked his way through the roster, announcing a name, handing a diploma, and shaking hands.

In the line, Deb drew near him. She wished she could spit on him.

He glanced at her, didn't say her name, and thrust the diploma at her. He didn't shake her hand.

The diploma landed like a brick in her palm.

She limped from the podium. No way was she going back to her seat to wait for the benediction. She veered toward a side exit, hit the crash bar, and hobbled into sheets of rain pelting the concrete at a slant. She found Dad's car and crawled inside, greeted by her shivering cat.

She tossed her mortarboard into the backseat. It bounced off the folding table and thumped against a stack of Piggly Wiggly boxes filled with melamine dishes, clothes, and books.

She scooped up Franklin and hugged him.

With every crack of lightning he stiffened.

She stilled him. Stilled herself.

A moving figure outside the wagon caught Deb's attention.

Dad swung the driver's door open. He hit the seat and pulled the door shut. "Left after the *amen*." He started the wagon and backed it in a wide arc. The car lights panned across the stone walls of Washington High. They drove by Oslo Lutheran Church, then the Sioux Arena.

Deb's pent-up feelings broke loose like the cloudburst around them. "It's all my fault."

"Not true. It was revenge toward me. If it hadn't been your prank, they would have found another reason to fire me. Still, it was worth it."

"How could this be worth it?" Her voice cracked.

"Because the glory of God is in man fully alive."

"I don't have a clue what you're saying."

"Saint Irenaeus said we're happiest when we're doing what God designed us to do." He took a deep breath. "Teaching young men to be heroes this year—I've never been more alive."

"But look what happened to me?"

"What happened? You glowed at the Synchronettes program and when you led cheers. Then the graduation speech you wrote? That was a *wow,* even with Elaine's clumsy delivery."

"This wasn't worth it for me."

Dad reached over and squeezed her shoulder. "I hope some day justice rolls like a river, flooding over all these wrongs."

He turned west onto Interstate 90.

A fresh downpour pinged the car roof, hammering Deb's mind. She stroked Franklin's back, and he hunched in response. "What'll we do back in Indian territory?"

"I'll get a job. Save until I can send you to State."

Deb sniffed. "Like I'd want to be there. Around backstabbers."

"It'll take time to heal the wound with Elaine and Haddy. But you still have Simon."

His ring! She touched it on the chain around her neck—cold as an ice cube. She should have returned it, but she'd been too ashamed to talk to him. "That's over."

"What?"

"For a while, I imagined myself white. Didn't realize I'd become an apple—red on the outside, white on the inside. I'll never trust crackers again. Hope this rain washes away all memory of them. And don't try to convince me otherwise."

Dad said nothing.

The wipers slapped against the windshield. The wagon rolled over interstate seams with a wearisome beat. Finally, the rain slowed to a tedious sprinkle.

They remained silent for what seemed like hours. Then, Dad cleared his throat. "Mind if I turn on the radio? Primary results should be in."

"Sure." She'd forgotten all about the presidential primary. Didn't care about it now.

A news report crackled into the car. "South Dakota has gone for Robert Kennedy."

"I'll be," Dad said. "If he carries California, he might take the nomination."

Deb recalled the sturdy grip of Kennedy's hand at the Arena rally. He'd thanked her for coming. That was a moment worth remembering.

The report continued. "We are breaking to California for a news bulletin now."

A pause. Static.

"It has been confirmed. Robert Kennedy has been shot in the head at point-blank range."

Deb gasped. She grabbed the volume control and cranked it up.

"The senator had been declared the California primary winner. We don't have his victory speech, but we're going now to a clip of a previous speech."

Deb gnawed on the inside of her mouth, waiting to hear the man whose oratory had moved her.

His voice came on, his Massachusetts's accent punching out the words. "Each time a man stands up for an ideal, or acts to improve the lot of others, or strikes out against injustice, he sends forth a tiny ripple of hope."

Dad steered the car to the side of the road and coasted it to a stop under the beam of a highway lamp. The speech ended, and Dad moved his arm in slow motion toward the radio and clicked it off. "I can't stand to hear more."

"You think he'll live?"

"Point-blank range? No. First, Martin Luther King. Now, Bobby Kennedy. Ripples of hope. Gone."

Deb's stomach roiled. Hope. Gone. What a fool she had been to be idealistic. To believe things could change. Maybe Simon still believed. She didn't.

Dad eased the car back onto the interstate.

Deb fiddled with her nails, painted bright red for the commencement ceremony. She balled her hands, forcing her blood-red nails to disappear.

A tear slid down her cheek and onto her graduation gown, darkening the silky orange.

She squeezed her eyes shut.

CHAPTER 45

Showdown

May 2000

Sunlight danced on Deborah's eyelids. Judging by the long shadows of telephone poles along the road, it must be late afternoon.

She glanced down. No orange graduation gown, but a buckskin dress. A teardrop had left one dark spot.

She un-balled her fists. No red-tipped smooth fingers. Instead, rough cuticles. Dry skin.

A playful paw swiped at her. Not Franklin, her ivory cat, but Bobby, her tiny calico kitty.

Their wagon, Methuselah, didn't canter with the spirit of a stallion. It wheezed like a broken-down horse.

Next to her, Dad gripped the steering wheel, but he wasn't the strong-backed man she'd once leaned on. He stooped with age.

"You've been quiet since we left Pine Ridge." His voice carried the rasp of an old man. "Never noticed when we entered Nebraska. Thinking back to the past?"

"As though it happened yesterday."

His lips narrowed. "Been thinking about it, too. The land of regrets is a heck of a place to visit. But maybe this trip will be healing."

She fingered the fringe on her sleeve. "Telling 'em off—will that heal anger? Or shame?"

"You're about to find out." He lifted his head a notch toward the road. Ahead, a white sign with green lettering read *Fort Robinson State Park*.

Her showdown with Elaine and Haddy.

Dad drove through the entry and reined in Methuselah at the curb.

Deborah pulled herself out of the car and clutched her kitty. His purrs calmed her speeding heart. She scanned the horizon—the grassy cavalry parade ground, the row of red-brick officers' quarters, the white clapboard post headquarters, the stone pyramid. "All the same."

Dad maneuvered from the driver's seat and hobbled toward her with his walking stick. "American history. Smack dab in front of us."

"My history, too. Only one weekend of my senior year, but the beginning of the end."

"What do you mean?"

"When I began to *go white.* An intoxication."

Dad startled. "You got drunk here?"

"Drunk with the desire to fit in. I didn't see I was running around with backstabbers."

"We don't know the whole story."

Deborah raised her chin. "I know enough. I intend to tell them off. That'll be the first step toward reclaiming myself."

"While you plan your attack on the cavalry, I'll take a stroll with Bobby. Got to work the hitch out of my giddy-up."

She handed him the kitty. "I'm going to visit the pyramid. But once I confront Elaine and Haddy, we're leaving. Pronto."

Dad shuffled off. "I hear you."

Deborah stepped onto the parade ground to cross over to the pyramid. A slight vibration hummed in her core.

She took another step.

The vibration grew stronger, pulsing into the rhythmic beat of drums. Then chants.

The same sensation when she visited here in high school. And when she visited Crazy Horse Mountain in the Black Hills this morning, where *Wakantaka,* the Great Spirit, told her to come.

Another message?

With each step, the beat grew stronger. She reached the pyramid that towered twice her height. The death site of Crazy Horse. Whites promised sanctuary here for the chief and his people. Instead, they killed him.

White traitors. Like Haddy and Elaine.

At this site she'd begun to comprehend her responsibility to represent herself well as a Native American. She'd let Crazy Horse down. Let her people down.

She placed both palms onto the pyramid and lowered her head. "I won't let you down again," she whispered. "You faced your enemies. I'll face mine."

The drumbeats and chants quieted.

She straightened herself and toed the ground with her moccasin. Haddy's chat message from yesterday ran through her mind:

Can't believe we finally found you!
Elaine's in trouble—you've got to help!
Meet at the fort on Wednesday.
All for one.
Haddy

She wouldn't help. It was time to them off.

Beep beep! A car horn broke her thoughts. A Mustang with its top down pulled in next to Methuselah. The contrast was too great—a sprightly red convertible next to an ancient beige wagon.

A woman extricated herself from the passenger side. Stuffed in orange pants, the pear-shaped woman waved a wide arc toward Deborah with a floppy straw hat.

Another woman glided out of the driver's seat with the grace of a gazelle. Her lavender cropped pants and tight knit shirt showed off her hourglass figure. She turned toward Deborah and planted her high-heeled sandals as though she were posing for a magazine spread.

Deborah turned around to see if they might be looking at someone else. No one there. She turned back to them.

The pear-shaped woman did a little dance, her salt-and-pepper curls shaking. "It *is* you!"

Haddy!

The hourglass woman slid her sunglasses down her nose.

Elaine!

What should she do?

Before Deborah could decide, Haddy scurried her stout legs across the field and clutched her with a bearhug that nearly toppled her.

Deborah steadied herself and held her arms wide, not returning the embrace.

Haddy pulled back. "I *knew* you'd come." She glowed with the eagerness of a puppy as she had in high school, but she was chubbier than before. She clasped her pudgy hands. "The Three Musketeers together again. All for one."

Not this one.

Elaine strode across the parade ground as though it were a model's runway. Her sunglasses swung easily at her side. She stopped a yard away, raised her chin, and tossed back her honey-toned hair. "Look at you. You've gone Indian, Deb."

Deb? No one had called her that since high school. Her palms dampened. She blotted them on her buckskin dress, then straightened her braid. "I didn't *go* Indian. I am Native American."

Elaine licked the edges of her carefully painted lips. "You've changed."

A fury burst out of Deborah. "You bet I have. I refuse to be manipulated by you anymore, you double-crosser. It's because of *you* my mugshot got plastered in the *Argus*. And because of *you* I didn't get to give the student graduation speech—*my* speech, which *you* so conveniently delivered. And because of *you*, my dad lost his job and we were forced out of town. And because of *you* I lost my scholarship."

Elaine's mouth fell open. The color drained from her perfect complexion.

Waves of grief crashed over Deborah. Her body quivered, and she shook a finger at Elaine. "*You* abandoned me when I was hanging on that statue. *You* let me fall. I don't care what kind of trouble you're in now."

Deborah turned to Haddy. "As for *you,* you inflated matzo ball, I'll never trust you again."

Haddy's lips trembled.

"I wouldn't help either of you if you crawled on your bellies to me."

She shot them one more glare to make sure her words had landed. Then she spun on a moccasin and strode off.

Her breaths came in gasps. *Victory!* Now to get out of here. She reached Methuselah. Where was Dad?

She glanced around.

He ambled toward her with his cane in one hand and a paper bag in the other. Her kitty's head poked out of his shirt pocket. "Cool car keeping company with Methuselah."

"Let's get out of here."

"Gotta eat our burgers first."

"What?"

"Saw you were having a powwow, so I bought some for all of us. Always better to have food in your stomach when you're smoking a peace pipe."

Deborah crossed her arms. "I'm not cutting a treaty."

Dad pulled Bobby from his pocket and slipped him to Deborah, then handed her a burger. "We can't leave. I checked us all into that brick building over there."

The same place she'd stayed with Haddy and Elaine before? "No way."

He strode onto the parade ground. "Then sleep in the car. I'm going over to eat with them. Sort of like the first Thanksgiving." He grinned and turned away.

"*Arrgh!*" She stomped to the side of the wagon, jerked the door open, and let Bobby tumble onto the seat. She flumped down after him and yanked the door shut so hard the inside latch pulled off in her hand.

How dare Dad put her in this position. She couldn't just leave him there. Or could she? Her hand reached toward the ignition, then fell back.

She peered through the bug-spattered windshield and couldn't believe it. Dad edged across the field with his walking stick. "It's me," he called to Elaine and Haddy.

The women squinted. "Coach Running Bear?" they said in unison.

"An older version."

They hurried over. Elaine hugged him, and Haddy pranced her dance like she always did when she was excited.

Deborah leaned out the window. "Dad, you get in this car right now."

He waved his hand back at her and kept talking to Haddy and Elaine.

Disgusting. He'd make her wait. Deborah unwrapped her burger.

Her kitty let out a mournful *meow* and pawed at her hand.

"Not now, Bobby. I'm trying to see what's happening."

Across the field, they talked and chewed on burgers. Then Dad sauntered back across the parade ground to her and rested his arm on the window sill. "Too much excitement for one day. I'm going to bed. But you ought to listen to them. You haven't walked a mile in their moccasins."

He reached for his bag from the backseat and hobbled toward the officers' quarters.

Now what should she do?

Haddy and Elaine approached.

Deborah scrunched low behind the steering wheel, as if to hide, which was ridiculous. They could see her.

They stopped at the Mustang and pulled their bags out of the trunk.

Elaine made no eye contact and turned toward the brick building.

Haddy slipped up to Methuselah's window. "You deserve to be angry. But you don't know the whole story. I didn't either until Elaine came back into town."

The chubby woman put her short legs in motion to catch up with Elaine.

What did she mean?

Bobby let out a plaintive cry and climbed onto her lap.

"Don't ask for anything now, fella. Gotta think."

She should feel triumphant. Exuberant. She'd confronted the past. Told off Elaine and Haddy. But she was as hollow as the wooden Indian she'd portrayed at her crummy, demeaning job.

Loneliness crested over her.

She cupped her hands under Bobby, hoping for some kitty comfort.

A warm liquid oozed into her palms and spilled onto her lap.

Cat pee!

"Bobby, I should have known better than to ignore you." She rubbed his face against hers, and his rough tongue kissed her. "You need water, too."

She gazed at the brick house. "I guess that's our destiny."

CHAPTER 46

Destiny

Deborah unlatched the car door from the outside. She found Haddy and Elaine sitting on Adirondack chairs on the porch. Across from them, Dad seesawed in a rocker.

She avoided eye contact with the women and spoke to Dad. "You were going to bed?"

"A dad always waits up for his daughter."

Even when she was nearly fifty? How ridiculous that must look to Elaine and Haddy. "I came to get water for Bobby."

"I'll get some." Dad reached for the kitty, then ambled off.

Poor planning. Now she was stuck with Elaine and Haddy.

Stillness hung in the air like a wound-down clock until Haddy cleared her throat. "What happened to your dress?"

"Cat pee."

"Got something to change into?" she asked.

"No. I didn't intend to stay."

"That's got to feel awful," Elaine said. "You can borrow something." Her voice didn't carry the bravado with which she'd greeted Deborah on the parade ground. "Follow me."

She didn't want to follow that woman anywhere. But she didn't want to sleep in a cat-stained dress. She walked behind Elaine into the house. Everything was military-simple, just as it had been when they stayed there during their senior year.

In a bedroom upstairs, Elaine fished through her bag and placed black pants and a ruby-red top on the bed. "This brings out your color, like your prom dress did."

Prom? *Simon.* Deborah's hand fumbled to the chain around her neck, hidden under her buckskin dress.

Elaine left the room.

As Deborah slipped into the outfit, exhaustion overcame her. All she wanted was to find another bedroom, pull the covers over her head, and get out of there in the morning with Dad. But to close off this painful chapter of her life, she must get Simon's ring back to him. Maybe Haddy and Elaine knew where he was and could return it.

She spot-cleaned her buckskin dress, then walked back to the porch.

"You look good," Elaine said from an Adirondack. She cradled a full goblet of red wine.

"Thanks. For letting me borrow it."

Haddy was squeezed into another chair. "Your dad turned in." She directed her goblet toward the kitty lapping at a saucer of water on the floor. "His name is Bobby?"

"After Bobby Kennedy."

Haddy's face fell. "What a senior year we had. First, Martin Luther King. Then Bobby Kennedy. When he was killed, something inside me died."

The emotions of those deaths swept over Deborah. "Me, too. Dad and I were on the highway when it came on the radio. The last of my heroes—gone."

Elaine took a swig of wine. "When you drove out of town, my hero left."

"You mean my dad?" Deborah asked.

"I mean you, Deb." Elaine offered her a goblet.

What did she mean by that? Deborah reached toward the glass before she realized what she was doing. She hadn't intended to enter into conversation. And she bristled to hear the nickname Elaine dubbed her in high school. "I go by Deborah."

"I'm sorry. Deborah."

Deborah did a double take. She'd never heard *I'm sorry* pass through Elaine's lips.

"There's something I wish you'd known a long time ago." Elaine downed her wine and poured another.

Deborah sat. Curiosity wouldn't allow her to leave.

"The night of the prank, my father claimed he had an *education meeting*." Sarcasm filled her words. "I always wondered why he left for these unscheduled meetings, so I followed. He drove to a motel at the edge of town. Then Karin Mykland arrived. You remember her? My father's secretary."

Who could forget that blond bombshell who acted as scared as a cornered rabbit?

Elaine's manicured fingers traced the edge of her goblet. "Mrs. Mykland went into the room my father checked into. I waited a few minutes, then burst in and found them in their underwear."

Deborah gripped her goblet stem until her palm hurt.

Elaine gulped down half her drink. "Mrs. Mykland screamed at father, *Are you going to tell her?* He was stone silent, so Mrs. Mykland stared at me and said, *I'm your mother.*"

Elaine's mother? Deborah hadn't suspected.

A tear trickled down Elaine's cheek. "Mrs. Mykland split. Father said he never told me because he didn't want an *illegitimate* child to *interfere* with his career."

Deborah leaned forward. "So when Mrs. Mykland passed messages from your father to you, your *mother* was writing to you."

"And always on lavender stationery. I've loved that color ever since." Her gaze fell on her lavender pants. "But as soon as I found her, I lost her. She left town."

Deborah gasped with another realization. "Then Lyle Mykland, Mrs. Mykland's son, is your—"

"Brother. Another spawn of my father. How sick is that?"

"Why didn't your father marry Mrs. Mykland?" Deborah asked.

"Marry a slut? Not good for his career. Although he was plenty happy to sleep with her."

"But Mrs. Mykland went by *missus.*" Haddy said.

"Easier to say you're divorced than admit you've produced a couple of bastards. She raised Lyle as her own, but Father was moving to Sioux Falls for his big promotion as principal when she had me. He decided a child would enhance his standing. So I was nothing but a *career asset.*" Elaine reached toward the wine jug, her hand shaking.

Haddy put an arm out to stop her. "That's enough."

Elaine pushed Haddy's hand away. "Never enough to forget the past." She poured a tall one. "When Lyle threatened to expose my father, Father gave him whatever he wanted, like the coaching job."

Haddy turned to Deborah. "And the police chief, Quisling, had all the dirt on the principal. That's why the principal bowed and scraped to him."

"I was so angry with my father," Elaine said. "The best way to get back at him was to vandalize his prize, the statue. Then you got caught. I was going to 'fess up to the police. But Father threatened to disown me if I did."

A hush hung in the air. "I should have stood by you." Elaine lowered her voice. "I've regretted it ever since."

"I got sucked into Elaine's plan like you did," Haddy said. "The principal knew if I went to the police, Elaine would be implicated. So he threatened me he'd turn the town against Pop's business." She clutched her thick hands. "So I didn't say anything. But Pops sensed something was wrong. He convinced the school board to fire the principal. And Loser Lyle coached one more disastrous year before he disappeared."

So justice had rolled like a river over Ruud. But what about her? And Dad? When would justice roll for them? Anger rose inside Deb. She stood, her breath coming in shallow puffs. "This doesn't justify your abandoning me. I took all the rap. You took none."

Elaine and Haddy reached toward her.

She pushed their hands aside and aimed her words with the force of bullets fired in slow, steady succession. "You ruined my life."

She scooped up Bobby and whipped open the screen door into the house.

"Deb, wait."

The screen door slammed shut behind her.

Where to go? She didn't have the strength to climb the stairs and find a spare bedroom. She stumbled through the dark until she crashed into a sofa and collapsed onto it.

The ground slammed into her. Pain seared through her knee. The jail door clanged shut. The newspaper paraded her mugshot. She limped through the graduation ceremony. Sheets of rain fell as she dashed to the car to get out of town. Rain clung to her face. And scratchiness, like sandpaper.

Deborah pushed her eyes open and brushed at her cheek.

Not sandpaper, but a rough tongue.

Bobby.

She reached through the dark and found her kitty. "What would I do without you to chase nightmares away?"

He ran his tongue across her cheek again.

A shuffling from the next room startled her. She lifted onto one elbow and squinted toward the kitchen. A faint light in the room. She recognized the hunched figure shuffling with a cane. "Dad?"

He turned toward the living room. "You out there?"

"Yeah."

"Didn't hear you come in. Was making cocoa while I waited up for you. Want a cup?

"Why not?"

She carried Bobby into the kitchen, and he pounced on a shadow. She dropped into a wooden chair at the table, fiddled with a small vase of wilted daisies, then rubbed her knee.

"You hurting?" Dad asked.

"A little."

"Besides your knee?"

Her face tightened. Dad always saw right through her. "Yeah."

He poured cocoa packets into two mugs, then gazed at her. "Nice outfit."

Deborah skimmed a hand across the soft ruby top. "Elaine's. She said the color looks good on me." She loosened her braid and let her hair fall.

"Your hair looks good down, too."

She sneered. "You trying to *white-i-fy* me?"

"No, just hoping someday you're free to be—"

"Who I'm meant to be." She finished his line with a sing-song voice. "Still hammering away on that?"

"I never quit. What matters most is not what color we are, but what colors we reflect, like a prism."

She smiled. "I remember you saying that when I was a kid. All the colors from a crystal danced around the room like magic."

The tea kettle whistled.

Dad filled the cups and shuffled toward her. "Told you then, and I'll say it again—we're meant to be like children resting in the arms of our heavenly Father."

"I haven't rested in God's arms for a long time. Or yours, either." She circled his lean waist with an arm. "Elaine and Haddy told me the whole story."

He hugged her shoulder. "Explains a lot, doesn't it?"

"But changes nothing. They still ruined my life."

"How?"

"Haddy and I were only accessories in the vandalism. Elaine should have taken the rap."

"So play that forward. What if Elaine had?"

Deborah fiddled with her hair. "Elaine wouldn't have given my graduation speech. Nor would I. But you wouldn't have been fired—"

"Don't kid yourself." Dad's voice hardened. "Lyle Mykland was looking for any excuse to get rid of me. I'd been successful with the team. He hadn't. And Quisling was hell-bent on revenge after I didn't play his son."

"But I lost my scholarship."

He eased into a chair. "A scholarship based on good citizenship, as I recall. Whose fault you lost it?"

She cupped her drink with both hands. Its warmth seeped into her, melting something frozen a long time ago. "Mine."

"And I eventually got together the money for you to go to college, but you wouldn't."

"I didn't trust whites anymore."

He shook his head slowly. "Not trust whites? Or was it that you didn't trust yourself?"

"I was so full of shame for going along with the vandalism. I couldn't face Simon. All our idealism about how we'd make the world a better place?" She opened her hand.

Dad reached across the table and plucked one of the limp daisies from the vase. He set it in her outstretched hand as tenderly as though it were perfect. "Idealism—the beauty of the Sixties. And its downfall. None of us lived up to our standards. Eventually we had to face who we really were."

She clasped the daisy. "But when do *I* get justice?"

"What would that look like?"

"For the town to know I didn't vandalize the statue. For my reputation to be restored."

"No one cares about your reputation but you." His voice lowered. "Everyone's worried about their own. And you want justice? What we all need is mercy. Lots of it. From others. And from ourselves."

"You bring up mercy like it's easy to dish out. I don't know how to forgive Elaine and Haddy."

He sat back. "Starts by forgiving yourself."

Deborah squeezed her eyes shut, but a trickle of tears oozed out.

Dad worked her clenched fist open and laced his fingers with hers. "You broke your standards. You ought to forgive Haddy and Elaine for breaking theirs."

"I can't forget what they did to me."

"Of course you can't." His voice dropped to a whisper. "But you can choose how you *remember* the times, Deb."

She startled to hear him use her high school nickname.

Bobby *meowed* and jumped onto her lap.

She slid her hand through his fur.

"Deb," Dad repeated. "Soften up a little, like your kitty. Your senior year ended horribly. But before, remember how wonderful it was?"

He unlaced his hand from hers and rose.

She mopped at her tears. "Why didn't you talk to me like this before?"

He chuckled. "Like I never tried? Every year, your notions hardened like growth rings on a tree. It took seeing Elaine and Haddy face-to-face to bore a hole through those lies."

He moved toward the door with his walking stick.

As he pulled up next to her, she squeezed his hand.

He paused. "You'd better get some sleep. Still have to face what brought you Musketeers together."

She glanced up. "Elaine's trouble?"

"Exactly." He shuffled off.

CHAPTER 47

Peace Pipe

Dad's thoughts ricocheted in Deborah's head for the rest of the night as she tossed on the living room couch. He was right. She would never forget Elaine and Haddy's betrayal. But she could choose to remember their good times. She needed to forgive herself, and forgive them. Then maybe she could move on.

She pushed herself to a sitting position. She was determined to make peace.

But how?

On the arm of the sofa, Bobby lay limp, lost in cat dreams.

She slipped on her moccasins and strode outside. The earliest birds announced the first traces of dawn.

Her foot touched the grass, and the earth pulsed beneath her, as it had when she entered the parade ground yesterday. She took another step. The pulse turned into a slow, steady drumbeat. Then a wailing filled her head—the cries of warriors.

Her heart leaped. God had something to say.

She arrived at the stone pyramid, placed both hands on the cold rocks, and bowed her head. "Spirit, how do I make peace?"

Leaves on a cottonwood rustled—prayers flying upward.

The chants and drumbeats vibrated through her. Then, the pulse dropped to a whisper. *Love your enemies.*

She pulled her hands off the pyramid and clenched her fists. It was hard enough to forgive them. But love them? How?

No answer.

She returned to the officers' quarters, where Bobby greeted her at the screen door with his "I'm hungry" meow. She scooped him up and carried him to the kitchen. Only yesterday, when Dad approached Elaine and Haddy, he'd brought them burgers. What if she met them with food this morning?

Worth a try.

After she sprinkled some kibble for Bobby into a saucer, she searched the kitchen. Milk, flour, yeast, sugar, salt, and oil. Indian fry bread ingredients.

Deborah got the coffee brewing and assembled ingredients. She didn't know what she'd say, but at least she'd present a peace offering.

She'd finished frying a batch of bread when a voice startled her.

"I'm hungry enough to eat my knuckles."

Deborah glanced back. Haddy.

Elaine peeked out behind her. "Can we come in?"

Deborah gulped and pointed to the cupboard. "Grab some mugs."

A *tap-tap* came from the hallway.

Dad appeared in the door, his cane one step ahead of him. "Don't mind me. I'm on my way to a hot date with the museum curator."

Deborah's insides flipped. A date?"

"Met Katharine yesterday. Or was it Kathleen? Don't remember. She's not that old, if you count in dog years. And she was thrilled to meet a real Indian, like I'm some freak show. Think I'll break into a war dance for her." He cupped his hand to his mouth and let out a few *whoops* while his feet shuffled.

The women burst out laughing, breaking the awkwardness among them.

He waved at the door. "So I'll say *toodle-oo,* an old Indian farewell."

Haddy set the cups on the table. "Your dad is amazing."

Elaine pulled out a wooden chair. "I'd have given anything to have a father like him, Deborah."

"You can call me *Deb*."

Elaine gave a cautious smile back.

Deb brought a plate of fry bread to the table and sat. She took a bigger drink of coffee than she intended, and it burned all the way down. "A little nervous here. I've spent years hating you two. Believing you'd thrown me away, but I guess I threw you away. That was the beginning of throwing my life away."

She drew in a long breath. "So let's talk about the vandalism."

Elaine stiffened.

Deb handed her a piece of fry bread, and Elaine accepted it. Each took a bite. "The night of the vandalism, with what you'd learned about your father's affair, you were too upset to think. Still, your prank was irresponsible."

Elaine lowered her head. "Been haunted by it for years."

Deb gripped her cup, its heat penetrating her palms. "But I was stupid to go along with you. What I did is *my* responsibility."

Elaine lifted her eyes. Her face flushed. "What I did to you was terrible."

Deb trembled from Elaine's admission. No other words came to her, so she turned to Haddy and offered her a piece of bread. "You were so naive, you fell right into that prank."

Haddy accepted the bread and stuffed it into her mouth. "Dumb, dumber, and dumbest."

"Another thing," Deb said, "yesterday I called you an inflated matzo ball. That was cruel." She rested a hand on the table with her palm up. "I'm sorry."

Haddy clasped Deb's hand. "Aw Deb, call me anything you want. Just call me."

Elaine added her palm to the stack of hands. "Like the old days," she whispered.

Deb squeezed their hands, and they squeezed back. Relief flowed through Deb that she'd gotten these words out. But she wasn't done. She stared at Elaine. "You're in trouble?"

Elaine shivered. "And the clock is ticking. Picture the scariest thing in the world for me."

Deb sat back and studied Elaine. Such a contrast. On the surface, beauty and brashness. But under the bravado, a porcelain doll convinced she was a ditz. At school, the one thing that scared her spitless was . . .

Deb sat straight. "To face an audience without clowning around?"

"Bingo."

Haddy leaned forward. "And what she has to do is like a ghost from senior year past."

Elaine slumped. "Wouldn't have to if Father hadn't croaked."

Deb quivered. Principal Ruud was dead? "I'm sorry."

"He dug his grave, one cigar at a time."

Haddy reached for another piece of fry bread. "After Elaine's father donated the *David* statue, the Ladies' Decency League threw a stink. Then Alfreda Fernberg from the Beautification Committee planted Norwegian maples around it. They grew into such a forest you couldn't see the naked guy without hacking through with a chainsaw. In the meantime, the Decency League died off except for Sylvia Aasgard. Remember that stiff lip?"

"Yeah."

"Sylvia experienced a conversion of sorts." Haddy talked between bites of bread. "She traveled to Paris to get her masters in art history. Focused on Rodin's nudes—the only way she was going to see a guy's gear. When she returned, she declared *David* wasn't smut after all."

"What does this have to do with Elaine's speech?" Deb asked.

"The Beautification Committee got a bug in its buns," Haddy continued, "to move *David* so he'd have three-hundred-sixty-degree viewing. Part of a big renovation at Falls Park."

Park renovation? Simon's dream. Was he involved? Deb yearned to ask but didn't want to reveal her curiosity.

"You remember when we visited the park after prom?" Haddy asked.

"Uh huh." Electricity shot through her with the memory of Simon's kiss. His proposal.

"Nothing but a weed patch then, but it's totally landscaped now, ready for *David* to be unveiled again in all his buff beauty."

"And because my father's not around," Elaine said, "*I* have to give the dedication speech. I'm horrified. Petrified."

"Stupified," Haddy added.

"The last time I faced a crowd was when I gave your graduation speech," Elaine said.

Pain seared through Deb with the memory. Giving that speech would have been the pinnacle of her senior year. But she'd lost the privilege. "A great speech," she murmured.

"But I ruined it," Elaine said. "And now, I get to make a fool of myself again in front of the whole town."

"When do you give it?" Deb asked.

"Friday night."

"You mean tomorrow?"

Elaine gave a slight nod.

"And you're ready?"

She jerked her head sideways. "Hoped I'd drink myself to death first. When that didn't work, I called Haddy."

Haddy opened her arms wide. "Not a peep for years, then she calls from Minneapolis, a blubbering mess. I told her to get to Sioux Falls and I'd search for you. I'd hunted a thousand times before."

"Really?" The warmth of happiness spread through Deb.

"I figured since your dad was into history, you might be, too," Haddy said. "So I checked chat sites. Saw the post *We Khan chat*. Remembered the high school cheer you wrote, *We Khan take the world*. And you signed out *Xanadu*, what you called your apartment. Had to be you."

"You were always clever."

She tapped on her temple. "This matzo ball has starch."

Elaine gripped Deb's shoulder. "You've always come to my rescue, Deb. So you've got to write this speech for me. And go back to Sioux Falls for moral support."

"What?" Deb pushed Elaine's hand away and stood. "Face the town that exiled me? That would rip open a wound that never heals."

She paced the narrow kitchen, pressed her palms on the counter, and scanned the field outside the window. Ahead rose the stone pyramid marking Crazy's Horse's death site. This morning she'd sought God there. Asked how to make peace. God's response: love your enemies.

Did she have to go to Sioux Falls? No way! She had to find a compromise. She spun toward Elaine and thrust an index finger. "I'll write your speech, but I'll *never* go back."

Elaine rose and hugged her. "Fantastic. Then I won't have to get pickled and deliver something like the Gettysburg Address."

Haddy clapped her hands. "Musketeers to the rescue again."

"Not exactly. As soon as I write this speech, I leave. I don't want to get sucked into some friendship vortex that swirls me to Sioux Falls." Deb sat at the table. "So let's finish this fry bread, and I'll work on your speech."

"Wait," Haddy said. She bustled from the room, reappeared with her oversized purse, and dug down to the bottom. She pulled out a package of pink-and-white striped candles. "I brought these in case we marked our fiftieth birthdays together. Just around the corner, and pretty special to celebrate together like when we turned eighteen."

"But only one candle each," Elaine said, "or we'll burn up the place."

"You got it." Haddy inserted a candle into each of three pieces of bread and lit them.

The three interlocked arms.

Haddy led in singing happy birthday.

Deb's voice cracked with the opening notes. She couldn't deny it. They shared a history that lit a flame of happy memories.

At the end of the song, they blew out the candles, and the mountain of fry bread dwindled as they chitchatted. But no one shared about life since graduation. Like each feared revealing something.

Deb wouldn't dare share a shred of her meaningless life.

CHAPTER 48

Who Did You Become?

After breakfast, Deb leaned over the laptop she borrowed from Haddy and worked on the speech. In her periphery, Elaine tapped her red-tipped fingers on the table. Like always, she was a bundle of nerves. But suddenly, she chuckled. Then cupped her hand to her mouth to suppress a laugh.

"What's going on?"

Elaine waved a hand. "Thinking."

"She gets lost in thought because it's foreign territory," Haddy said from the sink.

"Hush," Elaine said. "I was planning what we can do when you finish the speech."

"Like practice it?" Deb said.

"Of course." A grin wrapped across Elaine's face. She picked up Bobby and cuddled him, her body rocking slightly. "If all else fails," she whispered.

"What?" Deb asked.

"Nothing," Elaine said. She hummed into the kitty's ear.

Deb turned back to the laptop. It wasn't hard stitching together this speech. Just a knock-off from the homily she'd delivered recently at her church about the historic David. When she finished, Haddy made copies at the administration building, then the three munched on roast beef sandwiches from the general store as they looked it over. "Now let's work on delivery," Deb said.

Elaine tossed her copy onto the table. "I'd rather you coach me on the way to Sioux Falls."

"I said I wasn't going."

"But I want you there," Elaine said.

"Never."

"Give it up, Elaine," Haddy said. "Sometimes, where there's a will, there's a won't."

"So I'm finding Dad now and heading out of town," Deb said.

"But this is our first time together in decades," Elaine said. "Why not commit some fun today?"

"It'll be like our first trip to the fort," Haddy said. "Deb, you have to stay."

Fun was more tempting than driving home and hunting for a job. And it would be easier to get Dad on the road in the morning instead of forcing him away from his curator date. "Okay. For old times' sake."

Haddy did her little dance and patted her hands. "Musketeers ride again."

The rest of the afternoon was a blur of girl time Deb had never imagined. On the internet, Haddy found "Chicken Fat," the exercise routine they were forced to do in P.E. She led them through it until they collapsed on the floor in giggles. Elaine lent Deb a canary-yellow bikini, and she giggled with embarrassment as they kayaked down the White River. But Haddy called out, "Lookin' good, girl."

Deb pulled her shoulders back. She *was* looking good.

Then Elaine offered to give makeovers, like in high school. "I've got a makeup sampler kit along," she said. "I'll teach you tricks so you're all glammy for the ceremony tomorrow night."

"Wait a minute," Deb said, raising a palm. "I'm not going, Remember."

"Oh, yeah."

Deb had painted her toenails scarlet and was applying blush when Dad sauntered into the kitchen carrying a grocery bag. "A beauty pageant?" he asked.

Deb grinned. "Girl fun. Join us for supper?"

"Katharine wants to show me the sunset over the river."

"So *she* wants to show you the sunset, or *you* want to show her?" Haddy teased.

"You'll make this red man blush. Anyway, I picked up groceries. You can build Indian tacos with your leftover fry bread."

Deb took the bag. "Thanks."

"Gotta get to playing at the river."

"Dad!"

"Chess, that is." He reached for his boxed chess set from the counter and ambled toward the door, tipping an imaginary hat.

Elaine followed him. "I'll see you out in case I miss you in the morning."

They disappeared through the doorway.

Haddy helped Deb unload lettuce, tomato, and grated cheese. "Your dad knows how to stay young at heart."

"But old in the head. Year after year, he spews out the same pablum about taking risks, being great, and becoming who you're meant to be. Sometimes grinds on me like a whetstone."

Elaine returned, a smirk on her face. "Just dishing out a little love advice."

"You'd be the one to give it," Haddy said.

The three devoured open-face Indian tacos, then Haddy cooked a pot of popcorn on a burner "to top it off." Elaine grabbed a bottle of chablis and three goblets. Then the three headed upstairs, where Elaine pulled out a silky red pajama set for Deb to borrow.

"Look at me." Haddy turned around to show off an orange t-shirt and black sweats. "Our school colors. And I have the perfect entertainment for tonight." She pulled open her laptop.

Deb's heart sank. Their last night together. She still hadn't gotten up the nerve to ask about Simon. How could she steer the conversation into the past? She pulled her yearbook from her duffel. "Let's look at this first."

"Great idea," Elaine said as she slipped into lavender PJs. "I don't know what's happened to anybody."

Haddy's face beamed. "I'm a root-bound tree of knowledge. And I tell all."

Deb eased onto the floor, her kitty beside her, and flipped to the gallery of senior photos in her yearbook. If she played it cool when they turned to Simon's picture, she might learn something about him. "Look at these black-and-white photos. All the girls in white blouses. Guys in suits and ties."

Elaine joined her on the floor and poured chablis for all.

Haddy plopped down next to them and reached for the book. "Let me tell you about one guy in particular."

Deb's heart sped. *Simon?*

Haddy tapped on the photo of Barry and turned to Deb. "That prom date you set up for Barry and me? Yiddish Boy and I found out we were like lox and bagels. He popped the question the moment we graduated from State, and I said *you betcha.*"

"Marvelous," Deb said.

Elaine leaned forward. "Whatever happened to Carrot Top?"

"Ah, *your* prom date," Haddy said. She thumbed forward in the book.

Deb's heart sank. She'd skipped over the page with Simon's photo.

"Here he is," Haddy said. "Erik and Simon's draft numbers came up at the same time."

Vietnam?

"They were in the same platoon," Haddy said. "Simon made it through okay."

Then he's alive?

"But Erik?" Elaine asked, her voice low.

"Bucked authority, like always. He wandered off in the jungle. Stepped on a land mine. That was it."

"Awful," Deb said.

"Erik's father never recovered," Haddy said. "Became more of a bully as police chief than ever. My pops rallied a citizen's petition and got him fired. Pops hated how the chief treated you and your dad after the vandalism."

Deb caught her breath. So someone had stood up for them.

Elaine sat back and fiddled with a fingernail. "Carrot Top was nice to me."

"You finally admit it?" Haddy said.

"I guess."

An uncomfortable stillness filled the room. If Deb was going to ask about the lost love of her life, this was the time. "What about Simon?" Her voice was a whisper.

"I wondered when you'd ask." Haddy riffled through the yearbook and stopped.

There he was. Deb had studied Simon's senior picture a thousand times, but her throat still constricted. The photo was black and white, but she pictured Simon's liquid eyes. She imagined his golden hair moving with its own rhythm.

Deb had memorized every yearbook photo of him. The shot with other guys gathered around the Roman village they'd built. Moving sets in the *Romeo and Juliet* production. Palming a basketball before he flung it toward the net.

And placing his palm against hers when they met secretly in a secluded spot in the library. Then his lips—

"Simon's still in Sioux Falls," Haddy said.

Deb lost her breath. "He is?"

Haddy nodded, but offered no more.

Deb bit her lip and forced back a tumble of questions. Who did he marry? What if *they'd* married? "Will you see him tomorrow?"

"He spearheaded the whole park renovation. He'll be on stage with Elaine."

The room whirled. Deb caught her balance with one hand on the wooden floor. She could change her plans. Go back. See Simon's face that had brimmed with idealism. Hear his voice that called her to a life of purpose.

But what would she say? He'd catch any attempt to hide behind small talk. She'd end up telling him what a meaningless life she'd lived. And she'd have to meet his wife.

She couldn't face him.

Deb moved her hands to her neck. She lifted the chain holding Simon's ring and pulled it over her head. She held it out. The cobalt-blue stone caught the light.

Elaine gasped. "You still wear it?"

"Only to travel here." Deb couldn't force her voice above a whisper. "I never talked to Simon after the arrest. Too ashamed."

She moved the ring toward Elaine's hand. "You give it back, okay?"

Elaine opened her hand, and Deb released it.

Deb had imagined that when she relinquished Simon's ring, she'd finally break free from him. Instead, hollowness filled her.

"Want me to tell him anything?" Elaine asked.

Tell him what? That he was the most complete man she'd ever known? That she'd turned away from everything they hoped for and believed in? That she became nothing but deadwood?

Deb squeezed back tears. "No."

Elaine dropped the ring into her suitcase. "Awfully serious in here. Uh, Haddy, you brought something to show us?"

"Yeah." Haddy pulled her laptop onto her legs, slid in a DVD, and positioned the monitor between them.

Whatever Haddy brought, Deb hoped it took their attention from her and got her mind off Simon.

The opening strains of "Sounds of Silence" floated toward them. A fresh-faced Dustin Hoffman appeared on the monitor.

"*The Graduate?*" Elaine asked.

"The backdrop of our senior year," Haddy said.

And a good diversion. "Haven't seen it for decades," Deb said.

They watched Dustin Hoffman's character of Benjamin drift into the nylon-stockinged temptation of the cougar, Mrs. Robinson.

Elaine fanned herself. "Hot in here."

"At our age," Haddy said, "must be the flashes."

The movie continued with occasional giggles and "oohs" from the three. But when Benjamin took Mrs. Robinson's daughter to a strip joint, Haddy slammed her laptop shut. "I never let my kids watch this. Can't believe our fathers let us."

Elaine smirked. "They didn't know."

"Remember when we talked through the sliminess of the movie at Luther League?" Deb asked.

"Yeah," Haddy said. "Pastor Pete asked us which movie character we'd become. And here we are years later. So, who did we become?"

Elaine took a sip of wine. "You want to go there?"

Deb shook her head.

"Come on," Haddy said. "Let's share like we used to." She dug in her suitcase, pulling out the troll doll with short brown hair that Elaine gave her during their senior year. "Sounds silly, but I brought this mascot of our sisterhood. It's what I always held onto when we talked. So pretend you have your dolls, and let's spill all our emotions like we used to."

Elaine laughed. "Don't have to pretend." She reached into her suitcase and displayed her troll with its long flaxen hair. "Brought mine, too."

Deb had packed her troll doll with the plan to throw it at them, an act of good riddance. She rustled in her duffel and retrieved her doll with its long black hair. "These meant a lot to us."

"I'll go first," Haddy said, struggling to cross her stout legs. "Not much to say, really. Guess that's what you get when you marry someone with the last name of Dimm.

Barry's a good man, but we've done nothing but eat, work, and procreate four kids." She dipped her head toward Deb. "Our oldest is *Deborah*."

A tingle of joy flowed through Deb.

"Right out of college, Barry and I started working full time for Pops at Witz Jewelers. Took ownership when he died of a heart attack."

"I'm sorry," Deb said.

"Miss him every day." Haddy said. "Barry and I kept the name Witz Jewelers. Dimm-Witz wouldn't have been cool."

Elaine and Deb giggled.

"Turned every dime we made back into the store. Like Pops used to say, *Jesus saves, but Moses invests.* I raised our kids at work, then married 'em off. Now they're producing grands, and I'm the cook and chauffeur for another generation."

Haddy fingered her troll doll's hair. "So, we're fine. But I've done nothing. And ask me which character I became in *The Graduate?* I'm Dustin Hoffman's parents. Take care of business. Back up other people's acts. Like in high school, I made costumes to dress up all you stars in *your* grand performances."

Haddy buried her hands in the popcorn bowl, pulled out a fistful, and shoved it into her mouth.

The only sound in the room was her chewing.

Deb hadn't expected this emptiness from Haddy. What could she say?

Before she formed her thoughts, Elaine placed a hand on Haddy's shoulder. "You were the real cheerleader in high school, lifting up everyone. And as for the life you've lived? I would *die* to be surrounded by people who love me."

"Maybe you're restless because you've never asked what *you'd* like to do," Deb said.

"Didn't know I could." Haddy's face widened. "So watch out world. This goose-on-the-loose could be dangerous. But that's enough about me. Your turn to dish, Elaine."

Deb exhaled. At least she didn't have to share—yet.

Elaine gripped her wine goblet. "I was so angry with my Father, I got into that red convertible from him and drove it until I ran out of gas in the Twin Cities."

"What did you do?" Deb asked.

"Modeled."

Haddy clasped her hands. "Glamorous!"

Elaine took a slug of wine. "Not like you're thinking. I learned faster than a Minneapolis-minute that the less I wore, the more men liked me."

Deb leaned forward. "Elaine, you didn't-"

"I did whatever I had to," she yelled. "Not proud of it. Finally saved enough to go to cosmetology school. So don't tell me all dumbs are blond."

"Girl," Haddy said, "you got your twords wisted."

"I also twisted up three marriages. But never had kids."

"Thank God for that," Haddy said.

"So you want to know *who* I became?" Her voice lowered to a whisper. "I'm Mrs. Robinson. Used anybody and everybody."

Deb ached for Elaine. "What did you want?"

Elaine blinked back tears. "To be loved. That's all." Her words turned raspy. "I spent years angry with Father, who was always busy building his *monumental* career."

"Monumental—like the *David* statue," Deb whispered.

"So I manipulated everyone, including you two. Hoped your brains would help me be someone so my father would notice me."

Haddy placed a hand on Elaine's. "You were using me, but I *loved* every minute of it. It made my dull life exciting. So I was using you right back."

Deb placed her hand over theirs. "I knew you were using me, too, but I was willing to put up with it because you reached out when I was new at school."

An awkward stillness slipped its arms around them.

Deb looked beyond the walls of the room. "I guess Mrs. Robinson was in all of us. Maybe still is."

She lowered her gaze. This conversation had revealed way more than she'd expected. Now, her turn. She didn't want to divulge anything. She might suggest the night was late—

"What about you?" Haddy's soft voice coaxed her.

Deb pulled her hand away. She glanced around, searching for an escape.

She found none.

CHAPTER 49

Wounded Knee

Deb's vision spun. She crouched, wrapping her arms over her head. Her heartbeat turned into hammering gunfire.

A swish of softness brushed across her cheek. Fur.

Bobby!

She pulled her kitten to her chest.

A slight pressure on her shoulder jolted her. She lifted her head to see Haddy's hand resting there.

"You okay?" Haddy asked.

How could she explain the pain so great she couldn't allow her senses to go there or she'd be swallowed by them? "It hits me sometimes."

"What?" Elaine asked.

Where to begin? She locked onto one scene—the rain-soaked trip when she and Dad fled Sioux Falls.

"We didn't know where we were going, other than back to Indian country. We holed up in a Motel 6. Ate canned beans. When Rapid City High School found out Dad was available, they offered him their basketball squad. It would have been sweet revenge to make mincemeat out of Washington High. But Martin Luther King's words echoed in Dad's ears—that all he wanted was to do God's will."

Deb forced her breathing to slow. "Dad started a shop program at the reservation school. Stayed until he retired. What a gift he bestowed on a generation of boys. Skills to build their lives on."

"But why didn't you go to State?" Haddy asked.

"Shame. I'd lost my scholarship. Didn't know who I was. I'd gone white for a year, then got kicked out. Now back at the rez, I didn't fit in. Then I met Glen Clear Creek."

"A man," Haddy said, leaning forward.

What would she dare tell them about Glen?

What would she not tell them?

"He was a man of character, of principle. He revived that idealism that energized me when I was a teen, that we could make a better world. He reminded me—" She stopped herself. She had almost let it slip that she was attracted to Glen because he reminded her of Simon.

"Glen was a gentle man," she continued, "even though he'd been forced into a boarding school when he was a kid. Part of the government's integration program."

"Integration of Native Americans?" Elaine asked.

"To de-Indianize 'em. Cut their hair. Don't let 'em speak Lakota. After graduation, Glen enlisted. He returned from Nam a decorated hero for saving five white buddies. But once out, he was the wrong color again. We lived on the rez—"

"You were living together?" Elaine asked.

"We were *married*," Deb said. "Racism was rampant. I couldn't shop outside the rez without getting hassled, or worse."

More images flooded her mind. Men pawing at her in the grocery store. Calling her *squaw*. She rubbed her forehead, trying to remove the memories. "Glen got fed up with hearing *doksha*."

"What?" Elaine asked.

"A word that resonated like a broken promise. *Dokshsa—after a while* you can get a better job. *After a while* you can live in a nicer house. *After a while* you'll be safe. But *after a while* never came.

"Anger welled up in Glen. He called in AIM—the American Indian Movement—to change things. AIM brought in two hundred Natives with guns. We barricaded the town of Wounded Knee and declared it the Independent Oglala Nation."

"I watched the news reports," Haddy said. "Women with braids. Men wearing face paint and headbands and carrying guns."

"Natives from as far away as Canada joined us," Deb said. "Then the government surrounded us with armed troops and APCs."

Elaine's brow furrowed.

"Like tanks," Deb explained. "But they didn't dare roll in. Three hundred Indians were massacred at that site less than a century before in the last battle between whites and Natives. A repeat would have been a PR disaster for the Feds."

"How did you survive?" Elaine asked.

Scenes crashed into Deb's mind, each a knife slicing open a wound. "We heard gunfire all night. The FBI cut off our electricity and water. Tried to starve us out. We limited our food to half a meal a day. I made pancakes out of calf feed."

"Awful," Haddy said.

Deb reached for her throat. "I got this cough. Pneumonia. One night a plane dropped something. A cloud of white rose up through the light of the flares. We feared we'd been gassed. But *friendlies* had flown in sacks of flour that burst when they hit the ground. Glen and I rushed out, dodging gunfire. I tried to drag a sack. Then, I heard my name."

Deb caught herself. She hadn't meant to reveal she'd heard someone calling to her from the distance. Someone lanky, like Simon, his arms reaching out. "I must have been delirious.

"Glen and I hauled the flour back into this little church where we slept on the floor.

"We finally had food. I hunched there, shaking from fever, laughing and crying, Glen holding me. *We're gonna make it,* he said. Then a bullet pierced the plasterboard, whizzed past my face, and tore through his head."

Elaine and Haddy gasped.

"I cradled Glen's head." She rubbed her thumb against her fingers and felt his blood again, first warm, then cold. "I told Glen how proud his son would be of him."

"His son?" Haddy asked.

She touched her belly. "I had a bun in the oven."

Haddy clasped her hands.

"But what happened?" Elaine asked.

"In the morning, AIM and the Feds declared a ceasefire long enough for us to bury Glen. We dug his grave at the site of the 1890 massacre. Glen had been our inspiration for seventy-one days. But when he died, our hope died, too. And the last flicker of idealism in me was snuffed out.

"The Feds would press charges against anyone they caught. So that night, we prayed and slipped away. I was so sick, I stumbled along, trying to make it through the line of soldiers surrounding us. We followed the hoot of an owl in the moonlight. He led us through."

"A miracle," Haddy said.

"The Feds hunted us, so I changed my name back to Running Bear. I took jobs in the town of Wall." She paused. She wouldn't tell them she'd most recently portrayed a wooden Indian. So demeaning. "The town was a safe place to lie low from my Indian past and"—she shifted her eyes between them—"from my white past. And a safe place to raise Glen William."

"Named after your husband and your father," Haddy said.

"Bill never understood what a warrior his father was. When he grew up, he chose to live as a white. Changed his name to Rasmussen. Married a blue-eyed blond."

She could tell more. That she'd coaxed Bill through a learning disability until he thrived in school. That he considered her a loser. But what good would it do to rant?

She raised her chin. "I don't regret Wounded Knee. Our culture had been nearly obliterated. Then, because of Glen, we took a stand—our last stand—and regained our pride." She lowered her head. "But what a price."

Deb kneaded her calico kitten's fur. "So who did I become from *The Graduate*?"

Elaine held up a palm. "You don't have to—"

"I became what I condemned. Stagnant. Drifting. Like Dustin Hoffman's character. Not during Wounded Knee. But since then, I've been nothing."

"Don't be so hard on yourself," Haddy said. "You raised a child on your own."

Deb sneered. "If that's what you call it. I was angry with whites, AIM, myself. Anger's not the way to raise a child. Bill turned out great. But our relationship is prickly."

The room grew too quiet. Vulnerability crashed over Deb. She'd never shared like this. But Haddy and Elaine had taken off their masks, too. She wasn't alone in her nakedness.

"In *The Graduate*," Deb whispered, "Mrs. Robinson told her daughter it was too late to change. Her daughter answered, *Not for me*. What do you think? Is it too late?"

Silence hung heavy.

Deb stood. "I don't know either. I'm going to bed."

Elaine joined her. "Me too."

Haddy worked to uncross her legs. "Me three."

In the bathroom, they lined up by the sink. They cleaned off foundation and set their makeup-stained washcloths aside without a word. They peered into the mirror.

Their unadorned, fifty-year-old faces stared back.

"Where did those eighteen-year-olds go?" Deb asked.

The curtains danced at the open window. A light breeze filtered through the bedroom. Haddy and Elaine had long since fallen asleep in their separate beds, but Deb couldn't. She turned onto her side, spooning her kitty.

Shame flooded her from what she'd shared. Sure, she'd stood up for Natives at Wounded Knee. But since then, nothing but hiding. No wonder her son wasn't proud of her. No wonder Dad railed on her.

Speaking of Dad, where was he? She hadn't heard him come in from his date.

She slipped out of bed, holding Bobby in one palm, and headed into the hallway. A light shone downstairs.

She found Dad in the kitchen, hunched over the table with his chess pieces spread out on newsprint. "What are you up to?"

He startled. "Cleaning these before I put them away. Want some hot chocolate?"

"Sure." Deb dropped Bobby onto the table. He tiptoed on silent paws around the chess pieces, sniffing them.

Deb poured a cocoa packet into a mug. "I told Haddy and Elaine my story. Made me realize I've been nothing but deadwood for years."

"Only takes a little oil to bring back the shine to old wood," Dad said.

Another platitude. She poured hot water into her cup and stirred it.

Dad picked up his walking stick with its carving of a Native American at the top and rotated it. "Burl is what a tree produces when it's under stress. See this grain with all these beautiful twists and turns? Trouble creates that. Same as what life's twists and turns do to us."

She slumped. "Didn't create any beauty in me."

He riveted his ebony eyes on hers. "Life didn't shut you down. You did that to yourself."

"Dad." Her voice rose. "I forgave Haddy and Elaine. And forgave myself. You saying there's more I have to do?"

He propped his stick, resting his hands on top. "Take a risk."

"Wasn't it a risk coming here?"

"Only half the job." He massaged his oil cloth across his stick, and the dull brown turned a burnt umber. "What would it take to finish the task?"

She banged her cup onto the counter. "I'm *not* going back to Sioux Falls. I'm going to bed now, and we'll leave for home in the morning."

She reached to pick up her kitty, but he'd gone into his playful mode, pawing at chess pieces, knocking down a rook and a queen. "Now how am I supposed to get any sleep with a restless cat?"

"Leave Bobby with me," Dad said. "I'll slip him into your bedroom when he settles down."

"Thanks." She turned away.

"And you ought to reconsider. It's better to face your past before it smacks you in the face."

"I won't let it."

CHAPTER 50

The Chase

Deb's shoulder lurched. *Another bad dream?* No. Someone jostling her. She rolled onto her side.

"Deb."

She forced her eyes open.

Haddy's orange t-shirt came into focus. "They're gone."

Deb sat up. "Who's gone?"

"Elaine. Your father. And Elaine's car."

"What?" Deb glanced toward Elaine's bed. Rumpled and empty. She rushed to the window. Elaine's red Mustang nowhere to be seen.

"Dad?" She rushed to the bedroom next door.

His bed was neatly made. His bag gone.

She bolted downstairs. The kitchen table was clear except for a vase of freshly-picked white daisies.

Deb clenched her fists. "The old coot. That's what he meant when he talked about the past smacking me in the face. He's trying to force me to Sioux Falls."

Behind her, Haddy's breaths came in gasps as she descended the stairs. "What was Elaine thinking?"

"More like *scheming.* But I'm not falling for this one. Let 'em go. We'll find you a bus to Sioux Falls, and my dad can book his way back when he's done with this escapade."

"What's this?" Haddy pointed to a heart-shaped piece of lavender stationery sticking out from under the vase of daisies.

Lavender? Elaine's favorite color. Deb slid it out from the vase. Dad's angular handwriting:

Princess,

Don't stay wilted. Life's an adventure. Take the risk.

Love, Dad

P.S. I have Bobby

"Bobby?" Deb dropped the note. "Dad knew I'd chase after him if he took my kitty."

Haddy picked up the stationery. "There's an arrow pointing to the back."

Deb grabbed it. Elaine's curvy handwriting:

P.P.S. As for Simon's ring, give it to him yourself. It's with the hot dress in the living room.

Hugs, Elaine

Deb spun around. A full-length scarlet gown lay over the back of the sofa. At the neckline rested Simon's ring. Next to it, sparkly earrings. Coordinating heels sat on the floor.

Was Elaine trying to re-enact prom?

How dare she.

Haddy joined her. "This explains why Elaine told me to pack something snazzy."

Deb glanced down at her red silk pajamas. "And I'm gonna have to wear that dress because I don't have anything else."

Haddy gestured next to the dress. "Look what else Elaine left. Her makeup kit. She planned all this."

"Methuselah will take longer than Elaine's Mustang, if he can make it at all."

"Then we should leave by nine."

Deb checked the wall clock—quarter to nine. "We've got to get out of here."

"But we haven't had breakfast."

Deb grabbed Simon's ring and dashed toward the stairs. She tossed words back. "Eat in the car. We'll dress along the way."

"Exciting." Haddy's voice bubbled. "Like the chase scene in *The Graduate*."

Upstairs, Deb looped the chain with Simon's ring around her neck, slipped into her moccasins, and grabbed her duffel. Haddy plopped an oversized straw hat over her curls and reached for her bag. They scooped up the gown and accessories. Within minutes, they hustled into the beige VW Squareback, Deb in the red pajama set and Haddy in black sweats and her orange tee.

Haddy positioned a cereal box, a carton of milk, and a bowl on her lap before she pulled on her seat belt.

Deb cranked the engine. "Giddy-up!"

The wagon wheezed.

"Come on, Methuselah." Deb glared at the tachometer. "Prove that you're not ready for the glue factory." She turned the key again.

The car coughed as though it were clearing phlegm from its lungs, then started.

Deb shoved the stick into first, and Methuselah jerked forward.

Haddy grabbed the pink feather duster off the seat and waved it out the window. "Hi ho, Silver. Away!"

Deb winced, but chose to ignore the reference to the Lone Ranger and his sidekick, Tonto.

Haddy turned the radio knob. Nothing.

Deb pounded on the dash, and Willy Nelson's "On the Road Again" blared out of the dusty speakers.

"Cool," Haddy said. "And speaking of cool, where's the AC?"

"Keep your window propped."

They pushed north, crossing from Nebraska into South Dakota. As they bumped along, Haddy poured a bowl of corn flakes and milk. She fed bites to Deb and herself with one plastic spoon, some dribbling onto Deb's PJs.

Haddy punched Elaine's number into her cell. She paused, then snapped it shut. "Incommunicado. But we'll catch her at the dedication, and what a night it'll be. Champagne and dancing and . . . "

Deb blanked out Haddy's babbling. She was so mad at Dad she could wring his wrinkled neck—after she got Bobby back. But she'd change into that scarlet dress before they arrived. She didn't want to be searching for Dad in milk-soaked pajamas.

Why did Elaine want her there anyway? Elaine must know Deb was angry enough to rip that woman's bottle-blond hair out.

By the time they neared Mitchell, the gas needle had dropped dangerously low. Haddy lit up. "Let's stop at the Corn Palace."

"Never. It exploits Natives."

"There's probably a station across the street."

"All right. I'll gas while you gawk." Deb pulled off the interstate, crossed Norway Avenue, and followed signs leading to the Corn Palace.

"There it is." Haddy pointed. "And there's your gas station."

Deb pulled up to a pump, prayed Methuselah would start again, and turned off the ignition.

She got out and studied the square building across the street, its purple and yellow Russian-style domes and Moorish minarets piercing the blue sky. "Bizarre."

"But look at the walls," Haddy said. "*A-maizing.*"

Deb grimaced. "Very punny. Go grab us sandwiches. We'll change in the restroom and eat on the road."

Haddy disappeared, and Deb lifted the pump into place. "Drink up, fella." While Methuselah guzzled, Deb studied the murals covering the walls of the Corn Palace. It must have taken thousands of ears of corn—shades of red, orange, black, yellow, blue, brown, and white—stapled into place to create these tapestries that created a timeline of South Dakota's history. Truly works of art. First, they depicted Natives hunting bison with bows and arrows. That was good. Next, the railroad crisscrossing the grasslands. Then white settlers streaming in. Progress? Maybe to some, but not her. It portrayed the loss of her civilization. What was she doing here anyway?

Haddy bustled back, and they carried their dresses, shoes, and makeup around the side of the station to the restroom. It featured a one-holer, a dripping faucet, and a cracked mirror.

"Not that it matters," Deb said, "but I may as well put on makeup and do my hair in case I run into anyone." Like Simon.

The bathroom door rattled.

"Out in a minute," Haddy called, her voice lilting.

They applied makeup. Deb swept her hair back and let it fall onto her shoulders.

Louder bangs on the restroom door.

"Out soon," Haddy called as cheery as a morning bird.

Deb stripped off the red PJs and shimmied into the scarlet dress.

"Wow," Haddy said. "Side slits practically up to your armpits."

"At least the neck doesn't drop to my belly button." She hid Simon's ring under the neckline.

"Honey, you're an hourglass. Better than being a pear like me. Now help me into my dress."

Deb lifted the chartreuse gown over Haddy's head and helped her step into matching heels.

The bathroom door rattled like a mob threatening to break in.

Haddy pulled back the latch to find a line of women with crossed arms, crossed legs, and glares.

"Sorry." Haddy lowered her voice. "Bad case of the trots."

They snickered their way to the wagon.

Methuselah's engine turned over, Deb gave him spurs, and he lurched forward.

"Now let's see if I can eat this turkey and rye without my dress becoming mustard's last stand," Haddy said.

An hour and a half later, they reached Sioux Falls. As they drew near Tenth Street, Deb's body tingled with fear. How did she get into this?

"Look at all these boutiques." Haddy motioned. "Everything's changed, except there's still Witz Jewelers for all your sparkly needs. And one block down is the old high school building." She checked her watch. "We've got time. Let's stop."

Deb shook her head. "Too many memories to face at once."

"The school doesn't meet there anymore. It's an arts and science center now. Town fathers like Simon raised money to renovate it."

Simon did it? "We could stop for a minute."

Deb reined in Methuselah at the curb, climbed out in her snug dress, and read the sign—Washington Pavilion. The square edifice, like an ancient four-story fortress, rose before her. A balustrade edging the roof completed its medieval appearance. But the building wasn't as foreboding as when she was a student. Lit by the afternoon sun, the massive quartzite stones radiated a pink glow.

She caught sight of the engraved cornerstone, the one that grabbed her attention on her first day of school:

May the days spent here
be filled to overflowing
so high school shall ever remain
a happy memory.

That hadn't happened.

Haddy pulled her forward. "You won't recognize the auditorium."

Their high heels clicked up the granite steps, and they pushed the bank of green doors open. Haddy pulled Deb around other visitors, across the polished terrazzo tile, and entered the auditorium. Gone were the creaky wooden folding seats that popped like gunshots when students snapped them shut. Now, plush plum theater seats filled the silent great hall to three levels. On the walls, rose quartzite stone sections towered from floor to ceiling, framed by wainscoted wood panels.

Deb craned her neck. "Incredible."

She climbed the stairs to the stage, and a memory rolled over her. She raised one hand as though she were holding a microphone and called into it. "We Khan take the world!"

In her mind, the seats in the old auditorium filled and students jumped to their feet, echoing her words. Joy swelled inside her, the pleasure of capturing an audience. On this wide stage she'd discovered her gift to move crowds.

But she'd buried that.

Haddy hurried her away. "You've got to see the old library. A visual arts center now, as chic as a New York gallery."

They entered, and Deb's breath escaped her. Her head tilted up to the arched, two-story windows that framed the area where she and Simon had hid behind bookshelves for trysts. Simon had shared he wanted to get out of this town, where his father's legacy as a Lutheran pastor dominated. Why did he stay?

Haddy pulled Deb away. "More to see."

They moved to a far corner on the second floor. "Here's the only area they didn't refurbish," Haddy said. "Rolly Tolly's old classroom."

Deb stepped onto the scarred oak floor where Roland Tollefson once presided as the school's lit teacher and drama director. She placed a hand on a wooden desk. Tippy— and probably still encrusted with gum underneath. The same dusty, gray slate board covered the front wall. Here, at the front of the class, she and Simon had pressed their palms together when they acted the roles of Romeo and Juliet.

This was too much to remember. "Let's get out of here."

CHAPTER 51

Falls Park

Haddy chatted nonstop on the short drive to Falls Park, but her words didn't register. Deb shouldn't have allowed herself to visit Washington High, where the school unleashed specters of *regret* and *loss*. Instead, she should dwell on what she'd had in life—a good man in Glen, and their son, Bill.

She circled the vast parking lot twice before finding a spot. Now to get her kitty, pass off Simon's ring, and leave.

She stepped out in her scarlet dress. All the senses of her first visit here after prom coursed over her. The cool breeze lifting her hair. The smooth rocks on her bare feet as she scampered across them in her ruby dress. The taste of foam floating up from The Falls. And the taste of Simon's lips. The warmth of his hand when he slid his class ring onto her finger, telling her to keep it until he replaced it with a wedding band.

Haddy touched Deb's arm. "I'll look for Barry by the speakers' stand." She sauntered off, then turned back. "By the way, you're absolutely vampy."

Deb sneered. "Not that it matters." Yet she trembled that she looked good. The best in years. What if she ran into Simon?

She glanced to her left. The statue of *David*—that naked guy who'd gotten her into trouble—stared back. He rose the height of three men, the patina on his taut muscles glistening. *David* glared at her, his brow furrowed as though he were thinking, *You again? The one who climbed up on me and tied a sweater around my groin?*

"I'm the one," she whispered.

She turned away and wandered at the fringe of the park, avoiding the crowd strolling across acres of open land. No tangle of trees around here anymore. Instead, manicured grass flowed up to the smooth boulders edging the cliffs of The Falls. Just how Simon had envisioned it.

She entered a scene that verified she was back in Lutheran territory. The Sons of Norway had set up Syttende Mai activities, as they did at the first unveiling of the statue. What a mash-up: the celebration of Norwegian Constitution Day at the dedication of the statue of an Israelite on the river banks where the Sioux once camped. A sloshing together of cultures. Good? Or bad? Maybe not bad unless one culture eclipsed the others, as it had.

"Deb?"

Dad's voice.

He ambled toward her with his cane. "Look at you."

She braced a fist at her waist. "You ran off."

"Couldn't resist an offer to drive Elaine's Mustang."

"You *drove* it?"

He toed the ground. "A hundred miles, or so."

"And you stole my kitty."

"Borrowed him. To get you here."

"So give me Bobby."

"Can't. He's at the Holiday Inn." Dad lowered his voice. "Sneaked him in, but he's so cute I'm sure they won't mind."

"Give me your room key. I'll get Bobby and go."

He pushed his hand into his pants pocket and came out with a lint ball. "Guess I left it in the room."

Deb groaned. "Incorrigible."

"A five-syllable word delivered in anger? Impressive."

She swiped at tears that threatened to ruin her makeup.

Dad placed an arm around her shoulder. "You may as well let this scene play out."

"I can't."

"Yes, you can. And before you get more teary, turn around. You won't believe who you'll see."

Her heart stopped. Simon?

It wasn't. Deb studied the profile of a lean, African-American man. He looked like her dad's basketball assistant and the high school's custodian, yet he wore a black suit and hadn't aged.

She took a step toward him. "Mr. Brown?"

He looked her way. "That's my name." The man spoke with precise diction. "But people call me Artie. Are you looking for my father?" He motioned to a man in a suit with salted hair near him.

Deb squinted. "Arthur?"

"Yeah?" His mouth dropped open and he hustled up. "Deb? Never imagined seeing ya again."

"Nor did I."

"You met my son Artie? He's the new basketball coach at Washington. A good one, too, like your daddy."

"Deb?"

She turned toward a woman's voice. Before her stood a slender older woman dressed to kill in a forest-green wrap with a plunging neckline.

"Don't recognize me? You students used to call me *Fat Sherwood*."

Deb gasped. "Miss Sherwood?"

"Not any more. Roland and I have been *mister* and *missus* for a long time." She placed her arm around the waist of a balding man with a gray mustache.

"Rolly Tolly? I mean, Mr. Tollefson?"

He laughed, and his mustache twitched. "Re-SPEC-fully yours."

A gangly middle-aged man with a camera strapped around his neck and a notepad in one hand moved up to her. "Hey, Deb."

"Jordy?"

"Right on."

She couldn't help but be excited, seeing these people from her past. "You were the star of our pep rally where you delivered the *ho-ka hey* cry."

"Get 'em!" He laughed. "It's great you and Coach came back. Mind if I get a statement for the paper, seeing as you have a history with the *David* statue."

Her stomach clenched. "Rather not. You'll get good quotes from my speech. I mean Elaine's speech."

He grinned. "The old gang together."

Haddy scurried up. "And look who I found." She held the arm of a short, stocky man with graying hair.

"I don't—"

He straightened his plastic-framed glasses. "You look *farputst.*"

"Barry!" She embraced him.

"Didn't know whether I'd get out of the store in time for the ceremony. Worked all night making little naked *David* charms and lapel pins." He pulled a couple out of his pocket. "For sale right after the ceremony."

Haddy kissed his cheek. "You are the brightest Dimm ever!"

"I saved front row seats for all of us," Barry said. "All but Elaine. She'll be on stage with Simon, since they're bigwigs."

The front row? What if Simon spotted her? She glanced at the chairs. Still far enough away to be a safe distance. But close enough to get a good look at him. That's all she wanted. Then, she'd slip Simon's ring to Dad or Haddy and make an excuse to wait in the parking lot for Dad.

Haddy took Deb's arm and moved her toward the seats. "Elaine is so relieved we made it. She would have drunk herself to death if you weren't here to give moral support."

Moral support? She was mad enough at Elaine to tell her off in public. But what good would that do? Elaine would go into a tizzy and ruin the delivery of Deb's speech. She didn't want it compromised like Elaine ruined Deb's graduation speech.

Deb took a chair with Haddy on one side and Dad on the other. She peeked at the speaker's dais. Elaine sat there, her legs crossed above the knee. She was drop-dead gorgeous in a turquoise gown hugging her hips. She chatted up a man with buttery-blond hair and a model's torso.

Deb turned to Haddy. "Who's by Elaine?"

Haddy giggled. "You don't recognize Mr. Heartthrob—Harley Hart, the town's middle-aged Ken doll? He was married to Ronnette Sherwood, the cheerleading coach, until she died of cancer. Looks like Elaine's moved right in to enjoy his landscape."

Another man in a navy sport coat and pressed khaki pants stood on the platform with his back turned. He leaned toward others who were already seated, greeting them. A woman in a shiny black sheath followed close behind, her hand caressing his back.

The man straightened slightly.

Deb caught a glimpse of the back of his head, a mound of blond.

Her body tensed. Simon!

The woman in the slinky black dress must be his wife.

CHAPTER 52

Simon

She should bolt to the parking lot. But she longed to see Simon's face first. His back to her, he continued shaking hands, probably thanking everyone for their part in the park renovation. So like him—gracious, self-effacing.

He turned, and a flash of white at his neckline caught her eye.

A clerical collar? Simon followed in his father's footsteps? Just what he didn't want.

"A pastor?"

"The Reverend Peterson." The words floated off Haddy's lips.

"Why didn't you tell me?"

"You never asked."

Deb peeked back at the platform. She hadn't seen Simon's face yet, and now she could. The edging of gray at his temples lent a touch of authority. Even with the clerical collar, he didn't look standoffish. His boyish grin was a welcome mat to his heart. And those blue eyes? Still a river, drawing her to jump in.

Flee!

Her feet wouldn't budge.

Simon moved to the center of the stage. He rested one hand on the lectern and drifted the other to his pocket. "I'm pleased to see all of you tonight."

If she left now, he'd spot her.

Simon scanned the audience.

She hunched down.

His gaze stopped at her. His hand jerked out of his pocket and gripped the edge of the stand. His mouth opened, then closed. "Thrilled," he mumbled, "to see some I haven't seen in a long time.

Deb's heart pounded.

Simon stared at the lectern. When he finally raised his head, he thanked the Beautification Committee for the park renovation. "We'll hear from our keynote speaker after the sun sets and we illuminate The Falls and the statue. Until then, the *Gemini 6* will take us into a blast from the past."

To Simon's left, a group of middle-aged men grabbed their instruments and split the air with a frenzied version of "Breaking Up Is Hard to Do."

Elaine clattered down the steps and bounced toward the seats. "Come on. It's the same band we had at prom." She paused before Deb. "Hated to trick you into coming, but I *wanted* you here." She flitted off. Their friends followed, except Haddy, who caught Deb's eye. She cocked her head to her right, then sauntered away.

Deb followed the direction of Haddy's signal.

Simon. Alone. His hands buried in his pockets. "Got a minute?" he asked.

"I'll be leaving soon."

He moved a step closer. "Then I guess you have a minute."

His voice hadn't changed—smooth, beckoning. Eager.

He took another step, hands fidgeting. "Gorgeous dress."

Heat rose in her face. "It's Elaine's."

"Looks great. On you."

What should she say? Maybe pleasantries. "Congratulations on the park renovation, Pastor."

He chuckled. "I prefer to be called Simon, Deb."

Deb. Tingles vibrated through her at the sound of her name from his lips. She studied her scarlet toenails rimming her stilettos. "Don't want to keep you long." She reached to lift the chain from around her neck. Her hands shook. "There's something—"

"I saw you at Wounded Knee."

Her hands dropped. "You were there?"

"They let clergy in. We brought in food and medicine, but couldn't get past the tanks. The night of the food drop, I slipped through the barricade. Recognized you in the moonlight."

"I was delirious. Thought you were a vision."

His eyes lit. "Then you *did* see me." As quickly, his face darkened. "I watched you on the news the next day. At the burial. I'm sorry about your husband."

Glen. She should be thinking about him, not Simon. But she wasn't. And now the truth she'd known all along, but struggled to keep buried, finally surfaced. She'd loved Glen's character and his cause. But she'd never loved *him*. Never loved him as she did Simon. "Glen was a good man." Her voice quavered. "And what a price he paid. We paid. I raised our son, Glen William, on my own."

"William, huh? After your father. Walk with me, and I'll tell you about *my* dad."

She shook her head. "I shouldn't." What she should do was hand him his ring and get out of here before his wife showed up. It would kill her to meet that slinky black dress.

He turned and strode off, his words trailing behind. "I want to show you the park."

"But—"

"Come on." He signaled with his long arm.

She followed, teetering in her heels. What was she doing?

He slowed until she caught up. She finally allowed herself to study him. He wasn't a lanky boy anymore. His broad shoulders filled his sport coat, tapering to a narrow waist.

"After you and Coach were forced out of town, Dad delivered a slew of sermons on integrity. He glared at the principal until Ruud got so mad he stomped out and joined the Methodists."

She clapped her hand to her mouth, first in humor, then relief. Simon's father hadn't rejected her because of the statue fiasco after all.

"Dad never slowed down until a heart attack took him, probably from too much *lutefisk*."

"I'm sorry. And your mother?"

"She passed shortly after Dad. Found it hard to live without someone she'd been close to. I know how that is."

What did he mean?

"Enough about the past," he continued. "I want you to see The Falls from the observation deck."

She eyed the wooden tower near them, high enough that she couldn't imagine climbing the steps. "I have this bad knee."

"We can take the elevator."

"I don't do well with heights."

"I'll stay close."

He touched her elbow.

Her heart fluttered with excitement—and fear.

They rode the elevator in silence. When the door opened, a panorama of the Big Sioux River stretched before her. The water twisted toward the chute of the tumbling Falls. As if pulled by a magnet, Deb rushed to the railing. Below her, the crowd appeared as small as ants. "Spectacular!"

He leaned against the rail. "This renovation is the only project I've enjoyed in years."

"What about your church work?"

"I liked pastoring."

"What do you mean *liked?*"

He straightened. "The clergy has a hierarchy. The local congregation. Then conferences, synods, assemblies—all paper pushing. God knows how long it's been since I've counseled someone."

"I can't imagine you tolerating meetings."

He shoved a hand into a pocket. "That's all church is anymore."

"Simon, you should see my little church. Spirit of the Hills, we call ourselves. So small, we can't find a pastor. But our hearts beat in rhythm."

"Someone's got to sit on committees."

"Is that what *you* want?"

He didn't answer.

Below them, the band shifted from its fast set into a sultry version of "Do You Want to Dance?"

Simon glanced her way. "You want to dance?"

She raised a hand in protest. "Oh, no. You should join your wife."

"Wife? I don't have a wife."

Deb's heart stopped. "You're not—"

"Never been. People kid me I should have become a monk."

"But, the woman on the stage? The slinky black dress?"

He laughed. "Ah, yes. Sylvia Aasgard. You remember her? The president-in-training of the Ladies' Decency League? She gave up that decency business and has been trying to create a scandal for years. I keep my distance."

"I'm stunned." Her mind whirled. Why hadn't Simon married? With his looks, his personality—

"So you wanna dance?"

That would be wonderful. And terrifying. "I wouldn't want to start gossip."

"Then let's dance up here. Seeing you again, I'm already four stories high."

Her mind jumbled. All these years, she'd stuffed her feelings about Simon into a drawer next to his ring. If she danced with him, those pent-up emotions might escape. The only way to risk this was to make it light-hearted. "You ever find the *wacipi*?"

"What?"

"I kidded you at prom that you weren't letting the dance flow through you."

A lopsided grin filled his face. "Fast dancing? I'm the laughing stock at weddings. And slow dancing? I haven't *slow* danced since prom. We'll see what these Lutheran legs do."

He held out his palm, as he did in high school when they acted the scene of Romeo and Juliet's first touch. And their first touch.

She couldn't resist. She extended her palm and brushed his.

Electricity.

He took a step toward her and laced his fingers with hers. His other hand touched her bare back.

A lightning bolt.

She lifted her hand to Simon's shoulder and closed her eyes. Lyrics reached them about dancing in the moonlight. Hugging through the night. She lost herself in the flow and moved her hand above his clerical collar and found his neck. She inhaled the woodsy scent of his cologne. Her body melted into his.

They said nothing. They didn't need to.

The song ended, but their dance didn't.

"We had something special," Simon whispered.

Had something special. Her head spun. "I'm a little dizzy."

"I'll take you down."

They rode the elevator, its whirring engine the only sound. The back of their hands brushed once.

"Let's walk along The Falls," Simon said.

Where Simon had proposed. "I don't know."

"We'll ditch our shoes, like then."

She peered down at her two-inch heels. "Gladly. And no pantyhose to shed this time. I gave up those wretched things years ago."

"You *are* a liberated woman."

They kicked off their shoes and hid them behind a peony bush.

Simon grabbed her hand. "Come on."

They skipped across the spring grass, leaving the sounds of the crowd and the band behind.

When they reached the smooth rocks near the base of the cliffs, Simon slowed the pace. "Careful. It's slippery."

"I remember."

They moved their way forward until The Falls towered over them. Cascading water misted their raised faces. They laughed and held their mouths open to capture the drops on their tongues.

A surge of life flowed into Deb. She raised her arms. *"But he that hath the steerage of my course Direct my sail!"* she shouted over the rumbling water.

Simon clutched her arm. His face twisted like he'd been gut-punched. "That's what I said when we were here before. That we'd trust God to lead us. Never let anything come between us. Then your mugshot in the paper. I called and called, but you didn't answer. You left without a goodbye."

She lowered her head, her gaze falling to the hem of her gown and her wet toes. "I was so ashamed. What I did was beneath us."

"I figured Elaine tricked you. I tried to find you for years. But no trace until Wounded Knee. Then you vanished again."

He hunted for her? That thrilled her—and filled her with regret. "What I did was unforgivable. Then after Wounded Knee, I had to hide." She shook her head. "Hiding got so convenient, I lost myself."

He rubbed his forehead. "Not sure I know who I am either."

"But I saved a part of you, like you told me to." Her hands shook, and she struggled to lift the chain holding Simon's ring from over her head. She held it out.

"My class ring?" He rolled it between his thumb and forefinger, stopping at the engraved feather on the side. "We are the Warriors."

"Always will be."

They exchanged smiles.

She had to ask something. "Simon, why didn't you marry?"

His hand skimmed her bare shoulder.

The touch was wonderful. And frightening.

His face held a cavern of sadness. "You're the one who taught this torch to burn. I've never burned for another."

Burned—the same fire that had blazed in her all these years. Flames that consumed her and left her conflicted because she'd never experienced that burning with her husband. It wasn't right to feel this way about Simon. It was an affront to the memory of Glen.

"Deb."

Simon's voice pulled her back.

"I asked you to keep this ring until I replaced it with a—"

Her fingers shot to his lips. She pulled back, embarrassed she'd touched them. "Don't say that."

"Why not?"

She held back tears. How could she explain this? Simon visualized her as the idealistic girl he knew in high school. Anyone less would disappoint him. "Simon, I'm not who I used to be. We were going to change the world, remember? Instead, I let it change me." She faced The Falls. "A lot of water's run over these rocks since high school. Nothing's the same."

"One thing hasn't changed," he whispered. "My feelings—"

She spun around. "No, Simon. It's too late."

She rushed away.

"Deb." His voice came from behind.

She bit her lip and didn't stop.

CHAPTER 53

Tricked Again

Deb reached the observation tower and extracted her stilettos from behind the peony bush. She hopped on a foot to pull on one shoe, then the other.

Why did she always run from conflict?

A question with no answer. But she'd returned his ring. Now to get out of here.

Near the band, she found her old friends circled around Dad. He was the centerpiece in a rapid-paced rendition of the "Chicken Dance."

She broke into the circle and yelled into Dad's ear. "We're leaving. *Now.*"

He continued flapping his wings, his cane flying in the air. "Not me."

"Then I'll wait in the car." She turned away.

Dad grabbed her wrist. His eyes locked on hers with a fierce love. "I want you here."

She pulled her arm away. "No."

"Ladies and gentlemen." The bandleader interrupted them at his microphone. "It's time to dedicate the statue."

Floodlights flicked on, illuminating The Falls and the *David* statue. The crowd cheered and engulfed Deb and Dad, sweeping them toward the chairs.

"Come on," Elaine gushed. She circled arms with Deb, moving her to a front-row seat facing the dais. Haddy and Dad took both sides of her, and Elaine headed to the stage.

Deb crossed her arms. "I *don't* want to be here." But who was she kidding? Despite her fear, she yearned to see Simon once more.

Out of the corner of her eye, she glimpsed his khaki pants climbing the steps up the podium. He combed a hand through his hair, then turned to the mic, his face ashen. "Thanks to the band for taking us back to the past." He glanced at Deb.

Pain seared through her. Why did she tell him it was too late?

Simon turned his attention to the crowd. "As we welcome the *statue* of *David* to its new home, the daughter of Ivar Ruud, who donated it, will address us. Please welcome, from the class of nineteen sixty-eight, Elaine Ruud."

Simon turned toward Elaine and led the assembly in applause.

Haddy leaned over. "I'm so scared for Elaine I could sprout a zit."

"I'm . . . . " Deb's voice drifted off. She was a mash of emotions. Eager to hear her speech. Scared for Elaine. Shattered by being vulnerable with Simon.

Elaine approached the lectern with the smile of a beauty queen.

The crowd hushed.

Elaine slipped on reading glasses and giggled. "Need cheaters these days."

Make eye contact, Elaine.

She didn't. All her ease dissipated. She stiffened like cardboard. "Thirty-two years ago my father brought the statue of *David* to Sioux Falls to a rather mixed reception," she read, her voice wooden.

Pause, girl.

Elaine did, and the throng laughed and exchanged knowing glances.

That was good.

Elaine returned to her pages. "Through the years, we have grown to appreciate this bronze replica of Michelangelo's masterpiece."

Now give it passion.

Elaine removed her reading glasses. She tittered. "I need to say something."

Deb and Haddy exchanged glances. Elaine going off-script? Disastrous. She'd never produced a clear thought on her own.

Elaine folded and unfolded the edge of the paper. "I'm the one."

Deb leaned forward. What did she say?

Elaine twisted a strand of hair. "I spray painted the statue."

Deb gasped.

A murmur ran through the crowd.

"I didn't mean for Deb to take the blame, but I got scared. Didn't want to get into trouble." Her voice cracked. "Deb got robbed of giving the graduation speech. She should give this one. So please welcome my friend, Deborah Running Bear." She began clapping with a frenzy.

Numbness clutched Deb.

Dad turned to her, a smile wrapping across his face. "It's your time." He raised himself to assist her to her feet.

Applause rang in her ears. Her feet moved automatically, propelling her forward. When she reached the platform stairs, a hand extended toward her.

Simon's.

She grasped its warmth, and the strength of his arm drew her up the steps, near his beaming face.

Elaine pushed the speech into her hand and indicated where she'd stopped.

"But—"

"It's my way of saying *sorry,* silly," Elaine whispered.

The clapping trailed off.

Deb willed herself to face the town that had shunned her.

She turned.

A field of people stared. Waiting.

Her mouth was as dry as tinder. She caught sight of Arthur.

He gave her a wink.

Haddy wriggled in her seat.

Barry offered a vigorous nod.

Jordy suspended his pen over his notepad.

Dad rested his hands on his staff. Even from this distance, she caught the twinkle in his eyes.

Deb lowered her gaze to the text. Her hands trembled. "History is the record of successes and failures."

She needed to project more. She took a long breath and released it slowly. "Each person's life is composed of a series of decisions. Good ones, and bad."

Her hands shook. "The historic David left us an example of both good and bad choices.

Bad choices. Like her life.

"As a shepherd, a musician, and a warrior, David's performance was outstanding. As a king, his record was mixed. And as a husband and father, he was a disaster. His life is like ours. A mixed bag."

But she wasn't a mixed bag. She was a bag full of holes that carried nothing. She'd lost years by hiding. Now she was telling others how to live?

"From David . . . . "

The shaking in her hands moved to her legs. Her bad knee ached.

Deb looked up at the sea of faces. "I can't do this."

She dropped the speech and tripped down the steps, catching the railing before she fell flat. She weaved through the chairs toward the parking lot and locked herself in Methuselah. She dropped her head and arms on the steering wheel.

After what seemed like an eon, a tapping came from the passenger window.

Dad.

Deb unlocked the door, and he galumphed onto the seat.

She cranked the engine and lurched away as the windshield misted over.

Inside the Holiday Inn, Deb nuzzled Bobby. "No more adventures, buddy. We're going home."

Deb and Dad exited the hotel into a downpour.

Lightning flashed near them, followed by a thunder crack.

Bobby sprang out of Deb's arms and jumped into the street.

"No!" Deb yelled.

She dashed after him into the headlights of an oncoming vehicle.

The car blasted its horn and veered around them.

She scooped up Bobby and bolted to Methuselah where Dad waited. "Let's get out of here."

She turned the vehicle west onto I-90.

Dad brushed the rain off his jacket sleeve. "Splitting town in a storm? *Déjà vu* all over again."

Deb winced at the reminder of their first exodus from Sioux Falls.

The windshield fogged up, and she reached for the defrost button. The knob fell off and rolled by her feet.

"Don't fail me now!" She patted the floor mat, but couldn't find the knob.

Dad picked up the pink feather duster from the seat and skimmed even rows across the glass. "Your old teachers, Mr. Tollefsen and Miss Sherwood, said you and Simon's romance inspired theirs. Been married thirty years now."

Deb stared straight ahead.

"And Elaine and Harley Hart? You should have seen them cut up the dance floor."

She slammed her fist against the wheel. "Don't tell me about happily-ever-afters."

Dad was silent for twenty miles, wiping the windshield automatically. Finally, he turned to her. "Deb—"

"And don't call me that high school nickname."

He waited until her breathing slowed. "Elaine delivered the rest of your speech. What you wrote was good. That David owned up to his errors. That we should forgive ourselves. And that the statue of *David* represents learning from our past. Leaving it behind."

A sob burst from Deborah. "I want to, Dad, but I can't."

"Why not?" His voice carried the same gentleness as when she skinned her knee as a child and crawled onto his lap for comfort.

"I don't know." Her eyes filled, and the road ahead blurred even through the slap of the windshield wipers.

"Whatever happened back there with you and the speech and Simon—

"It's not about Simon. It's about me!"

He placed a hand on her shoulder and waited until her sobbing slowed. "It's about the fear of coming alive, and running away won't fix that."

"Running away is all I know."

"Then it's time you lead your moccasins down a different trail."

He rolled up his jacket, pressed it against the side window, and lay his head against it. "One more thing. Thanks for taking the risk of coming. A great adventure for me. And thanks for telling us in your speech that it's never too late to become who we're meant to be."

That's not what she wrote.

She gripped the wheel so hard her hands ached, then she reached over on the seat and found Bobby napping. She caressed him. "Before sunlight, we'll be home, little fella. No complicated relationships there. Just you and me and my books."

Methuselah's wheels ran over the highway seams with a monotonous *thunk-thunk*, as tedious as her life had been until the last few days. As tedious as it would be again.

The car lights illuminated a wooden billboard at the edge of the prairie grass. She read it through the motion of the windshield wipers:

All Roads Lead to Wall Drug

Not for her.

In a few miles, another sign popped up:

33 Miles to Wall Drug

Deborah's insides tensed. She guessed what the next billboard would highlight. She was right:

Famous Wooden Indian. Wall Drug

She had been that Famous Wooden Indian.

Now, she wasn't.

She was nothing.

At three in the morning, she rolled into the town of Wall and pulled into Trail's End Rest Home. Deborah helped Dad out.

The night nurse met them at the door. "Thought you'd never come back."

He sneered. "Had to. Missed the tapioca."

Deborah hugged him sideways. "I'll call you after I get some sleep."

Now one more stop. She turned onto Main Street and took a right into a vast, empty parking lot. She propped the pink feather duster against the front door of Wall Drug. "Now I owe you nothing, Big Hair."

She navigated Methuselah out of town, turned onto the same dirt road as always, and passed the weathered wood sign that announced *Tumbleweed Trailer Park*. She slung her duffel over her shoulder and carried Bobby up the same chipped concrete blocks leading into her single-wide. A twist of the key, and the aluminum door creaked open as usual. She flicked on the light.

Home.

Down the short hallway lay her single bed, unmade. She fell onto the rumpled sheets, and Bobby curled up beside her.

"We've got each other, buddy."

She turned off the light and couldn't hold back the gush of tears.

CHAPTER 54

Wakantanka

Sunlight permeated Deborah's closed eyes. She forced them open and focused on the digital clock. Ten? Why hadn't Ivar harassed her awake? Her neighbor's rooster never let her sleep after dawn cracked.

She pulled her legs over the edge of the bed and slipped into her moccasins. "Okay, Bobby. Let's get going in this new, unemployed life."

Bobby padded to the kitchen, where Deborah sprinkled kibble into a saucer. "I'll be right back after I get the mail."

She opened the door an inch, anticipating the usual attack from Ivar.

No sign of him. Odd.

She strolled to her rusty mailbox and pushed the lopsided wood post straight. Nothing but bills. She forced the metal door shut. The post sagged back to its forty-five degree slump.

In her neighbor's yard, chickens clucked from the henhouse. She stepped around slick chicken droppings and leaned against the weathered wooden entrance, wriggling her nose from the ammonia stench. Hank bent over a straw nest, his hand under a plump red hen.

"Methuselah survived the trip."

Hank startled, the long braid down his back lurching. He turned, palming a brown egg. His eyes ran over her body. "That's some dress."

Deborah peered at the scarlet gown. She'd forgotten she still wore it. "Borrowed it." She fumbled her hand to her side to cover the slit. "Where's your rooster?"

"Weirdest thing. He was strutting around as usual a couple days ago, then fell over dead."

"Strange," she said more to herself than to him. At least she wouldn't have to fight that fowl anymore.

"By the way, the moccasin telegraph says you're speaking at Crazy Horse Mountain this weekend."

She shook her head. "Idle gossip. I couldn't make that climb."

"Need some eggs? The ladies are producing plenty."

"Thanks." She took six and carried them back to her trailer rolled up in the hem of her skirt.

So the rooster had croaked. Deborah had named him Ivar after her cocky high school principal. Did the rooster's death signify she'd no longer be tormented by his high school ghost?

Her stomach growled. Fry bread was what she needed. She ought to change to sweats, but this fancy dress reminded her of the victories from last night. Elaine had publicly absolved her. And what had been stolen from her had been redeemed—delivering a speech before the city of Sioux Falls.

But she blew it.

A victory and a defeat.

She mixed fry bread ingredients, then phoned her son while the dough rose.

"We're fine here," Bill said. "But you shouldn't have quit your job." His voice held a scold.

"I know, but—"

"I don't have time for excuses. Got work to do. We'll talk later."

Click.

Like she didn't give him time when she raised him on her own? She shot arrows at the phone.

Maybe Dad was in a better mood. She dialed, and he picked up her call on the seventh ring. "Was in the hallway. You should have seen me at breakfast entertaining the canes and wheelchairs with tales of my escape. Now I'm off to deliver my lecture on how an ordinary person can be great. Catch you later."

Click.

Last night's tears threatened to gush again. Everybody had a life, but her.

Forget about waiting for the dough to rise. She fried it and nibbled on a hot piece. Not half as good as what she'd made for Haddy and Elaine. Maybe it tasted better when shared with others.

Outside the dusty trailer window, a single piece of tumbleweed drifted by.

She ought to job hunt. And she had to figure out how to cover Dad's overdue rent. But her mind was too cluttered.

Maybe a book.

Deborah rested in her creaky folding chair and opened the Kublai Khan biography that had arrived right before she left. Bobby curled into a ball on her lap.

She flipped through the pages.

We Khan take the world! The high school cheer ran through her mind.

She slammed the book shut, startling Bobby. "Gotta get out of here."

Deborah shoved the trailer's metal door open, letting it slam behind, and climbed into her wagon. "Make tracks to *Mako Sica*, Methuselah!"

She drove the short distance into the Badlands, passing gray rock spires splitting the sky. Around them lay deep gullies one could get lost in.

She parked Methuselah along the edge of the road and strode through knee-high prairie grass until her lungs rose and fell. Deborah pumped a fist into the heavens. "*Wakantanka*, I confronted enemies. Forgave them. Humiliated myself with that speech. Got my heart ripped open by seeing old friends—by seeing Simon—only to be alone again. What good was all that?"

She waited for a reply.

No drumbeats. Nothing but the disarming noise of silence.

She stood motionless. "Father God." Deborah's voice quivered. "Brother Jesus. Holy Spirit. I've given all I could, and what do I have to show? A dead husband, a dead-end career, and a dead relationship with my son and father."

Not a whiff of wind answered.

She scuffed the ground with a moccasin, then balled her fists. "I give up."

Deborah trudged toward her wagon.

A bird swooped past her face, interrupting her steps. It landed on a tuft of bluestem.

A chickadee. Nothing but a puff of fluff.

She took another step.

The chickadee lifted its black cap and white cheeks and let out a *chick-a-dee-dee-dee.* Then it cocked its head.

Tension inside her began to thaw. Here was this simple bird—nothing elegant like an eagle—singing his usual song. And he was exquisite.

Chick-a-dee-dee-dee.

Her senses heightened. Other sights and sounds joined the bird's sonata. Waxy yellow-green cottonwood leaves clapped their hands against the azure sky. Mottled tree branches swayed in a swish-swish dance. Sunlight shifted across the rock spires, highlighting red bands circling them. Black-tailed prairie dogs stood like sentries, then retreated down their holes when a pronghorn pranced through their village. In the distance, a herd of bison grazed, their shaggy bodies like black cutouts against the sweeping green prairie.

Beauty—in the Badlands.

Deborah lifted her arms, her hands open. All around her, scripture in nature spoke. Everything revealed the glory of the Creator simply by fulfilling its design.

The crescendo of majesty rose within her. She twirled to the music of life, her scarlet dress joining in the dance. "The glory of God is in man fully alive," she whispered.

That's what Dad said years ago. That they were happiest, they radiated, when doing what God fashioned them to do.

Like the animals. The trees. The rocks.

She slowed her pirouette, but her mind still spun. How could she join this holy concerto, not as an occasional sit-in instrument, but as a permanent member?

The chickadee swooped past again and flitted to the top of a cottonwood. He lifted his crown, and his *chick-a-dee-dee-dee* filled the prairie.

"Ah, little fella. You're climbing to a larger stage for your presentation?"

A revelation hit her so hard she struggled to catch her balance.

Climbing.

Larger stage.

Presentation.

Was she supposed to?

Deborah remained still, waiting to see whether the impression rested in her soul.

It settled.

She dipped her head toward the chickadee. "Thanks, little messenger."

Then she raised her face to heaven and lowered her voice. "And thank you."

Deborah strode to Methuselah and steered toward home.

"Fully alive," she whispered.

CHAPTER 55

The Climb

Deborah lifted a hand to shield her eyes from the early morning sun. The fringe trailed from the sleeve of her buckskin dress. She gazed toward the mammoth carving of the Indian chief at the top of the mountain. Ahead lay the path for this annual people's march leading to the image of Crazy Horse. Was *she* the crazy one to attempt this?

No more crazy than the famed Indian. He was crazy only in the sense that he remained unbroken by life's blows. She must prove the same about herself. If she completed this climb, she'd conquer the fear of heights that had gripped her since she'd fallen from the statue of *David*. She'd rise to a larger stage than she'd held as a drugstore wooden Indian. And she'd be the first Native American to address an assembly at the summit of this monument.

She extended her arm, like the chief extended his on the carving. Crazy Horse wasn't the only one whose vision forced him to stretch beyond his reach. Her decision to climb the mountain had stretched her already-strained relationship with her son. "Are you nuts?" Bill said when she told him what she planned. But here he stood at the start of the climb, spreading sunscreen on the face of his fair-skinned wife, Britt. Of course Dad showed up. "Wouldn't miss an adventure," he said, propping himself up with his walking stick.

Even with only a week's notice, her high school friends had arrived. Elaine, in her lavender cropped pants. Haddy, in her oversized, floppy hat. Barry, pushing his wide plastic-framed glasses into place. Jordy, gripping a notepad and camera. Even Mr. Brown, slipping a neon pink baseball cap over his salt-and-pepper Afro.

But no sign of Simon.

Deborah tightened her single braid and glanced through the crowd.

Haddy read the look on her face. "I emailed him when you called," she whispered. "Not a word."

Elaine leaned in. "He took off right after the statue dedication. Hasn't been seen since."

So Simon wasn't coming. Her fault. Because of her fear, she'd closed the door to a future with him.

Her heart hollowed.

Thousands of climbers lingered around Deborah near the starting line. She would lead the pack, but many would reach the summit before her. That didn't matter. It wasn't a race, but a personal achievement to make it to the summit of the world's largest mountain carving in progress. Not even nearby Mount Rushmore could compete with its immensity. Those four white presidents' heads, grand as they were, would fit into Crazy Horse's face. The finished profile and the rough-in of Crazy Horse's outstretched arm already emerged from the granite. Eventually, the warrior would spring from the rock in three dimensions, riding bare-chested on his charging pony.

"Deborah." Dad's voice interrupted her thoughts. "I'll hang out at the visitors' center."

"Wish you could make the climb."

Tears glistened his eyes. "You make it for me. And use this." He offered Deborah his staff with the carving of the head of a Native.

She grasped the stick. "My honor."

Dad reached toward Mr. Brown's arm for support. "Arthur's staying with me. He's Coach's assistant, you know. Now take the first step. It's the hardest. So imagine soaring—"

"On eagle's wings. Even though butterflies are batting around in my stomach."

He patted her hand. "You'll make it. And you'll gain a whole new perspective at the top. So there's the trailhead. Go."

She took a deep breath. Beyond the evergreen grove, she couldn't see what lay ahead. Didn't know whether she'd reach her destination or be left on the side of the path, exhausted and embarrassed.

"Deb." A voice called from behind.

She turned.

Simon weaved his way through the crowd, his boyish grin greeting her.

Her heart leaped.

"Wouldn't miss this." He offered his arm. "Ready?"

If she touched him, would he disappear?

"Ready?" Simon repeated, his placid eyes asking her to trust.

She laced her arm through the crook of his, and he didn't vanish.

"Let's do this," she said.

She took the first step.

Then another, her moccasins padding through the grass. She kept close to Simon, while her other friends and Bill and Britt followed behind.

The path descended into a forest of towering ponderosas. "Why are we going down?" Haddy asked from behind.

Deborah called back. "Sometimes you tread the depths before you reach the heights. Gotta trust the trail."

"If you say so," Elaine said.

"I know so."

Declines were harder on Deborah's knee than inclines, but Simon's arm braced her. "You came," she said, her voice a whisper.

"Had some things to take care of." He pushed a lock of blond hair from his face. His broad shoulders supported his lean neck. His neck?

"No clerical collar?"

He grimaced. "A collar with jeans? Bad taste."

She laughed. "I agree."

She glanced behind. Her son stared with a *who-is-this* look. She'd forgotten about introductions. "This is Simon, an old friend."

"I'm not *that* old," Simon said.

"And this is my son, Bill, and his wife, Britt."

Simon gave Bill a vigorous handshake, while Bill's jet-black eyes narrowed to study him.

A Lakota couple from her church greeted her with *Haw Mushkay.* The tattoo of a bison leaped from the man's brown arm, and his ponytail traveled to the middle of his back.

Deborah offered her hello back and straightened the string of beads around her neck.

This was remarkable. Most of the climbers around her were white, ranging in age from youngsters to oldsters. Crazy Horse's legacy had crossed time. Generations. Race.

She wiped her brow, took another step.

The face of the chief burst through the tips of the evergreens. Deborah studied the pensive warrior. *My lands are where my dead lie buried,* he'd said.

His lands. Her lands. *Paha Sapa,* the Black Hills upon which her feet trod. The center of the universe, the heart of everything material, everything spiritual.

Then whites stole their land.

She trembled. Sometimes history's wrongs were like boulders careening down a mountain, leveling trees, crashing onto the plains. Wrongs that were never made right. But this was mercy's mountain, calling her to climb its heights, to live honorably by planting healing flowers along the path like the *on'glakcapi,* the purple coneflowers, her moccasins nudged around.

The trail began its ascent. The midmorning sun taunted her. "Ten kilometers to the top. More than six miles. How far have we gone?"

Simon's mouth pursed. "Better we don't know."

Deborah's right palm chafed from gripping Dad's walking stick. *Never too late to become who we're meant to be,* Dad had told her. *We're God's kids, made to rest in his love.* Dad's wisdom propelled her forward, one step at a time.

She hit a loose rock. Her leg twisted, and pain seared through her knee. Simon caught her fall, but she collapsed anyway. "What am I doing?" A tear tracked down her cheek. "Even if I make it to the top, I don't know how I'll get down."

"You make it up the mountain. I'll get you down."

Calm filled her. Simon had changed since last weekend. More focused. "You're different," she said.

His lips raised in a slight smile. "Had to find my footing." He helped her to her feet.

They entered a grove of paper birch, their leaves flicking in the breeze like applause. Her head spun. Was it from the heat? Fatigue? She licked her parched lips, and without asking, Simon handed her a water bottle. "Thanks." She quaffed a long drink.

Another step. Keep going.

She did, and her knee loosened. Her mind cleared. She giggled, then laughed out loud. "I am doing this!"

He gave her his killer grin. "This is most certainly true."

Ahead lay a tumble of lichen-flecked granite. Simon held her arm, and they scrambled through it. Deborah reached back, helping Haddy, who gave a hand to Elaine. Together, they made it.

Finally, they reached a steep, gravel road created by blasting crews to reach the mountaintop. Deborah's breaths came in spurts. Would she have air left to deliver her speech?

Simon leaned in close. "You've got this."

"Thanks."

She set her eyes on the uphill route and trudged across stones glinted with mica, sparkling like jewels. The sun beamed down from high now, but at this elevation, the wind whipped, bringing a welcome cooling. She untied her braid, letting her hair dance in the wind.

They rounded a curve, and the profile of Crazy Horse filled her vision. All breath left her as she gazed at his head. Nine stories high, she'd read. His eyes scanned beyond the thousands of hikers climbing to his summit.

"Almost there," she panted.

She plowed forward, her head down, taking long strides with Dad's staff that banged as it hit stone shards.

Simon stopped her. "Deb, look where you are."

Her eyes lifted.

She'd stepped onto Crazy Horse's raised left arm.

CHAPTER 56

Greatness

Crazy Horse's arm extended nearly the length of a football field, like a runway emerging from the mountain. It teemed with hikers.

She laughed and hugged her friends and Bill and Britt. "We made it."

Up ahead, someone gave a wide-sweeping wave. She squinted. Dad? Holding onto Mr. Brown for balance?

Deborah wove through the crowd and reached him. "How'd you get here?"

"Where there's a Will, there is a way," he said. "I told you to soar on eagle's wings." He motioned to a helicopter near them, its engine quiet. "But Arthur and I hitched a ride in that fat bumblebee."

"What?"

Dad waggled an index finger at Simon. "His idea."

Simon grinned. "A basketball center always reaches high for his coach."

"You mean I could have—?"

"You wouldn't have conquered your mountain then, would you?" Simon's eyes twinkled.

He was right. Satisfaction filled her.

An official approached. "Ms. Running Bear, we're ready when you are."

Dad winked. "It's your time. Got your notes?"

"Don't need any."

She squeezed Haddy and Elaine's hands, then wound her way through the crowd toward the carved head of Crazy Horse. As she lifted a foot onto the stairs leading up the platform, she spotted something. Pebbles. She grabbed a handful and buried them in her pocket. Then she climbed the steps.

On the podium, she turned and faced the crowd milling along the statue's outstretched arm. Even though she towered over everyone from this stage, she was like an ant on a matchbox next to Crazy Horse's colossal face. An appropriate place to be—in the shadow of the chief whose story had guided her on her journey of understanding.

She tapped on the microphone. "Hello? I, uh, have a few words to share."

The throng pushed closer and stared up at her. Waiting for her to say something meaningful.

A chill surged through her. Her lips numbed. Then her mind. Her face stiffened as though she were a drugstore wooden Indian again.

Wakantanka, Creator, help!

She cast her eyes on the faces of her friends. She breathed in their smiles. Only days ago, she'd viewed them as enemies, when in fact, fear had bound her, not wrongdoing on their part.

Something seeped into her like oil filling dry cracks in deadwood. A deep healing.

For a moment, she was eighteen again, standing to deliver the commencement address she'd crafted about the value of having a strong foundation. The words sprang into her head so vividly she could deliver them now. But life had smothered all her youthful idealism. A sure foundation still mattered. After that, what counted was weathering life's storms.

She'd done that.

Deborah cleared her throat and found her voice. "Congratulations to all of us for scaling this mountain."

She rested her hands on the top of Dad's staff. "Up here, the sun-drenched air is rarified. It can leave a soul giddy with a sense of greatness. But Chief Crazy Horse didn't dwell in the mountains. He lived on the plains, where life is plain. Ordinary. *Greatness* was not in his vocabulary. Only duty. Serving his people."

She extended an arm in the direction Crazy Horse stretched his. "In reaching toward his obligations, he found purpose.

"If he were here today, Crazy Horse would ask, *What plains do you live on?* We might phrase it, *What plain life do you lead?* In our everyday activities, our purpose isn't always clear. Often, we see only responsibility piling up before us. Duty to family. Duty to jobs. We dream of mountains. But we dwell in the valleys."

She scanned the endless horizon. "On mountains like this we see unobstructed for miles, with the canopy of clouds above, the cut of conifers below. But not in the valleys. Shadows cover our path. We experience no giddiness of greatness, only the angst of whether anything we do matters.

"This is what Crazy Horse's life tells us—our ordinary lives matter.

"Join me in illustrating this. Each of you, pick up a handful of pebbles."

A murmur rippled through the crowd. Then moms and dads, grandparents and children, couples and singles bent down and grabbed small stones.

Deborah pulled her handful from her pocket. "Now let them fall between your fingers."

They opened their fists and let the stones tumble.

She sifted hers, and they dropped with tiny thuds. "Building homes, raising children, paying bills, giving kindness. These are pebbles we drop along our daily paths. When piled together, they create a mountain. A monument. To simple acts of greatness.

"Today as we descend this peak, we'll head back to our plains. There, let us live—truly *live*—realizing that our ordinary lives are extraordinary. Let us grasp the lesson of Crazy Horse, that as we fulfill our duties, we will find purpose and achieve greatness. In this way, even an ordinary person can be great."

She was done. But she needed something to make her words fly. She raised her arm again. "While descending, let us soar like eagles."

"Look!" someone from the crowd yelled and pointed at the face of Crazy Horse.

She turned to the carving.

Anukasan, a bald eagle, swooped across the chief's face and let out a slow, shrill cry.

The crowd burst into a cheer, and Deborah joined them.

After their applause subsided, she took a step down from the stage.

Simon offered his hand, and she clasped it. His grin greeted her. "Well done."

Friends and family surrounded her. "That was great."

A stocky woman in a striped shirt and Wranglers forced her way in. "Let me through." Her staccato voice interrupted the congratulations.

Big Hair. Deborah's ex-boss.

Big Hair smoothed her Dolly-Parton 'do into place and braced her arms on her stout hips. "Nice speech. Now we ought to let bygones be bygones and discuss your comin' back to the store. People keep asking, *Where's the wooden Indian?*"

Deborah held up a palm. "Not now."

Big Hair leaned in. "We gotta talk. My bonus is coming due."

"Not now, I said. But help us get a photo."

Deborah's friends and family piled cameras into Big Hair's hands, then squeezed together in front of the face of Crazy Horse for multiple poses.

"Thanks," Deborah told Big Hair. "I'll be in touch *if* I want to talk." She turned away.

Bill stood before her, his face lowered. "Mom, what you said in your speech? Made me proud of being Native." His eyes flicked up. "And proud of you."

Deborah bit her lip and touched his raven hair. "I feel the same."

Bill's blond wife stepped forward. "Bill's been saying that no one can make fry bread like his mother. Will you teach me?"

"I'd love to, Britt. But only if you show me how to make Norwegian flatbread. What do you call it?"

Britt's face lit. "*Lefsa.*"

"Deb," Elaine said, "I've got a great idea for a picture of Jordy and me. You take it?"

"Sure."

Elaine and Jordy scrunched together in front of Crazy Horse's face, and Elaine lifted her index finger. "Now get down low," Elaine told Deb.

She took a low-angle closeup. From the viewfinder, it appeared Elaine was sticking her finger up Crazy Horse's nose.

Then Deborah caught a shot of Barry bending Haddy back and kissing her in front of the carving's mammoth lips.

"Don't forget the senior beefcakes," Dad said. He and Arthur posed back-to-back, crossing their arms and sucking in their bellies.

Simon lingered around Deborah but said nothing.

"Hate to break up the fun," Barry said, "but clouds are moving in. We better get down this mountain before a storm hits."

Deborah rubbed her knee. "I'll need to coax my way."

"I can make it easier," Simon blurted out. He gestured toward the helicopter.

"With Dad and Arthur?"

Dad shook his head. "We'll catch another bumblebee."

Deborah turned to Simon, her brow furrowing. "Is this a setup?"

"Pretty good one, huh?" He stuffed his hands in his pockets. "I want to fly you over my new pastoral assignment, Spirit of the Hills."

Deborah gasped. "My church?"

A lopsided smile overtook his face.

Her head spun. The only thing she could come up with to say was something lighthearted. "You'll have to learn to *wacipi*."

"Give these Lutheran legs a chance." He leaned in and whispered, "This is a *proposal*. Will you fly with me?"

Her lips opened, then closed. Her natural response—running away—didn't kick in. Instead, calm filled her.

But she needed time to sort out Simon's words. "I accept the helicopter ride." She lowered her voice so only Simon could hear. "And I'll consider the *proposal*."

Simon beamed, then nodded to the copter pilot. "Ready the bird."

Deborah turned to Dad and cocked her head. "It's time for you to get in your usual last words."

He pulled her tight. "Keep pulling out the splinters, Princess. You're resurrected."

She hugged back. "I love you, too."

Then she met Simon's eyes.

He led her to the copter and held out his hand.

Deborah paused, then grasped his hand, absorbing its warmth, palm to palm. She laced her fingers between his.

They ducked into the chopper and strapped on seat belts. The copter's blades whirred overhead, and the bird lifted.

Deborah's mouth fell open with exhilaration. She clutched Simon's arm.

He laughed. "Let the *wacipi* flow."

As they rose, Deborah's family and friends, waving from below, appeared smaller and smaller. The image of Crazy Horse, the trees, the mountains—all shrank.

Everything took on a new perspective.

AFTERWORD

Characters in this novel are fictional. However, much is real:

- **Wall Drug**, where Deborah worked, is a must-see, where the staff are western friendly.
- **Crazy Horse Memorial**, a work-in-progress outside of the town of Custer in the **Black Hills**, provides Volksmarches each year to the arm and face of the carving.
- **Badlands National Park** in western South Dakota showcases desolate beauty.
- **Fort Robinson** in western Nebraska marks the site of Crazy Horse's death with a stone pyramid.
- **Mitchell Corn Palace** displays "a-maize-ing" murals.
- **Washington High School,** home of the Warriors, now meets at a newer site. The original building has been converted into the Washington Pavilion for arts, entertainment, and science.
- The *Argus Leader,* a presence in Sioux Falls since 1881, was an inspiration to me to enter journalism.
- **Sioux Falls Arena** still hosts community events.
- **Egyptian Theater** in Sioux Falls was razed, a paradise paved and turned into a parking lot before the movie *The Graduate* came to town.
- *Gemini 6* band, with its signature song "Two Faced Girls," has been inducted into the South Dakota Rock and Roll Hall of Fame. You'll find the song at https://www.youtube.com/watch?v=x8olzRSYxPY
- The statue of *David* stands along the banks of the **Big Sioux River** in Fawick Park, south of **The Falls**. When the statue first arrived in Sioux Falls in 1971, some feared it would cause moral decline.
- **South Dakota State University** wasn't the state's hub for business courses in 1968 (the University of

South Dakota was), but I wanted my characters to attend my alma mater (*Go Jackrabbits!*).

• **Pine Ridge Indian Reservation** is larger than Delaware and Rhode Island combined. Along with other reservations in the United State, it is one of the poorest areas in America, with low life expectancy, high infant mortality, and malnutrition. University of Wisconsin researchers reported that eight of the ten least healthy counties in the country are home to Native Americans.

Also mentioned are historic events:

• The **1868 Fort Laramie Treaty** in Wyoming that granted 30 million acres of land to Native Americans.

• The **1874 gold rush in the Black Hills** of South Dakota.

• The **1876 Battle of the Little Bighorn** in Montana in which **Chief Crazy Horse** prevailed and cavalry officer **George Armstrong Custer** was killed.

• the **1877 killing of Crazy Horse** at Camp Robinson, Nebraska.

• the **1890 Wounded Knee Massacre** in western South Dakota.

• the **1973 Wounded Knee "Incident"** in western South Dakota.

In 1980, the United States Supreme Court ruled in *United States v. Sioux Nation of Indians* that the federal government confiscated the Black Hills illegally. It awarded compensation plus interest for one hundred years. The Sioux have refused the payment, instead demanding their land back. With interest, the amount now owed is more than one billion dollars.

ACKNOWLEDGEMENTS AND NOTES

I climbed my own mountain in writing this book, with excellent Sherpas along the way. My thanks to Rocky Mountain Fiction Writers, Belmar Writers (the Belmarians), and Littleton Writers for training and encouragement; Michael Arches, Jordan Davis, Lisa French, Michele Stuvel, and Chris Winiecki for eagle-eye beta reading; Chris Devlin for editing extraordinaire; Margie Ghaffari for technical "shredding"; A.L. Cooper (*Hé·y'uxc* - Jackrabbit) from the Nez Perce tribe for Native American sensitivity; Dale and Linda Hart for Washington High School and Washington Pavilion expertise; Karen Holmes, Joan Jacobson, Debra Johnson, Janet Pence, and the staff at St. Mark's Lutheran Church by The Narrows for decoding Lutheranism for this Baptist-raised girl; Stephen Mountjoy and Kevin Wolf for adding basketball bounce; O. Arnold Snyder for chess finesse; Trina Ernest for horse sense; Valorie Snyder for artistic brushstrokes; Anne Thompson of Ebookannie for design excellence; Linda Johnson for South Dakota bird insight; Dick and Diane Sparks for Black Hills plant information; Nancy Barclay, Susan Kiger, and Rochelle Schotzko for Sioux Falls plant knowledge; Eugene H. Peterson for his encouragement, and all others who pointed the way along the path, including my high school journalism advisor, Lorraine Norman.

For the sake of simplicity, I omitted accent and pro-nunciation keys in Lakota terms. *The Pipe and Christ: A Christian-Sioux Dialogue* by William Stolzman is a fasci-nating discussion of the mesh between Native American and Christian beliefs.

Please contact me at Trish Hermanson.com regarding any typos you find. And forgive me for errors of omission or commission. Move beyond them and contemplate that it is never too late to become who *you* are meant to be— even if it means making mistakes along the way.

ABOUT THE AUTHOR

 I write for those whose lives haven't gone exactly as planned, whether in romance, family, or career. Writing is the way I navigate the tension between how the world is and how it ought to be. As an award-winning reporter and editor of an international skating newspaper, my greatest fulfillment was capturing ordinary people's stories of pride and pain.

My heart is divided between my home at the edge of the Colorado Rocky Mountains and the Midwest prairies where I was raised.

If you've enjoyed this book, please leave a brief review on Amazon. And please visit me at Trish Hermanson. com for occasional posts in my quest to uncover hope and humor along life's highway.

SPECIAL THANKS

With special thanks to Nancy Barclay, Jean Freitas, Susan Kiger, Sharon Knowlton, Judy Litsey, Rochelle Schotzko, Diane Sparks, Barbara Suurmeyer, and Sharon Woodruff. This book grew out of our amazing high school reunion at Fort Robinson and then in Sioux Falls.

Don't worry. You're not in the story.

CONNECT WITH THE AUTHOR

If you've enjoyed this book, please leave a brief review at Amazon. Visit the author at trishhermanson.com and Facebook.

Made in the USA
Middletown, DE
23 August 2017